No Stone Unturned

The Petralist

No Stone Unturned

The Petralist

FRANK MORIN

Whipsaw Press

No Stone Unturned
Book 3 of the Petralist

ISBN: 978-0-9970233-7-4

A Whipsaw Press Original

Edited by Joshua Essoe
(http://www.joshuaessoe.com/)

Cover art by Brad Fraunfelter
(http://www.bfillustration.com/)

Illustrations by Jared Blando
(http://www.theredepic.com/)

First Whipsaw printing, November, 2016

Other Works by Frank Morin

The Petralist Series

Set in Stone   -   Book One
A Stone's Throw -   Book Two
No Stone Unturned -   Book Three
                                    (You're reading it!)

The Facetakers Series

Face Lift   -   Prequel short story
Saving Face   -   Prequel
Memory Hunter -   Book One
Rune Warrior   -   Book Two
Aeon Champion -   Book Three
                                    (Release date in 2017)

Short Stories

Odin's Eye   -   Part of the Red Unicorn
                                    Anthology - *A Game of Horns*
Only Logical   -   Part of *Unseen: United! Box Set*
                                    Anthology to raise funds
                                    to fight plagiarism
The Essence   -   Part of the Dragon Writers
                                    Anthology (Release date in Q4 2016)

Acknowledgements

Book three, and the world of the Petralist just keeps growing in scope, complexity, and awesomeness. Development of this novel was challenging on many fronts, and more people assisted than I could possibly name. To you all, I say, "Thanks!"

As always, my family are my greatest fans. Kate and Kyle are the think tank that never fails to churn out great ideas, while Emily and Jacob pour endless enthusiasm into the mix. My wife Jenny is the fount of all the magic in my world.

Several of my core Fast Rollers team have moved on to college, but the team is thriving with enthusiastic new members. Thanks to all of them for their unwavering support, particularly those who eagerly attended feedback sessions over chocolate-waffle-ice-cream-sandwich sundaes. Gabby Ridenour, Eve Ledesma, Emily Pool, Josh Lee, Tammy Willian, and Gavin Johnston. You're all elite Guardians.

Brad Fraunfelter delivered another stunning cover, and Joshua Essoe is in my opinion the most brilliant editor on the planet. His deft touch and brutally honest insights helped me carve away the excess and reveal the shining heart of the story. And Jared Blando delivered more outstanding illustrations for the new stones.

Thanks to all the many fans who have been clamoring for the book. Your patience is about to pay off.

N
W
E
S
GRANADURE
GRANITE MINE
ALASDAIR
QUARTZ-ZINC GOLD MINE
THE WICK
PUMICE MINE
BASALT MINE
MARBLE MINE
MERKLAND
SLATE MINE
OBRION
SAOL RIVER
CRANN
TRODAIRE
DONLEAVY
MACANTACHT RIVER
FREASTAL
GRANITE MINE
BASALT MINE
GRANITE MINE
CASUR
MULRENNAN
CARRAIG
DEIFUR
LIMESTONE MINE
RAINEACH
LAIGE
SANDSTONE MINES
CHOSTALAN
SPEIRMOR
RADHARC
THE DESERT
BLANDO
THE LANDS OF
OBRION

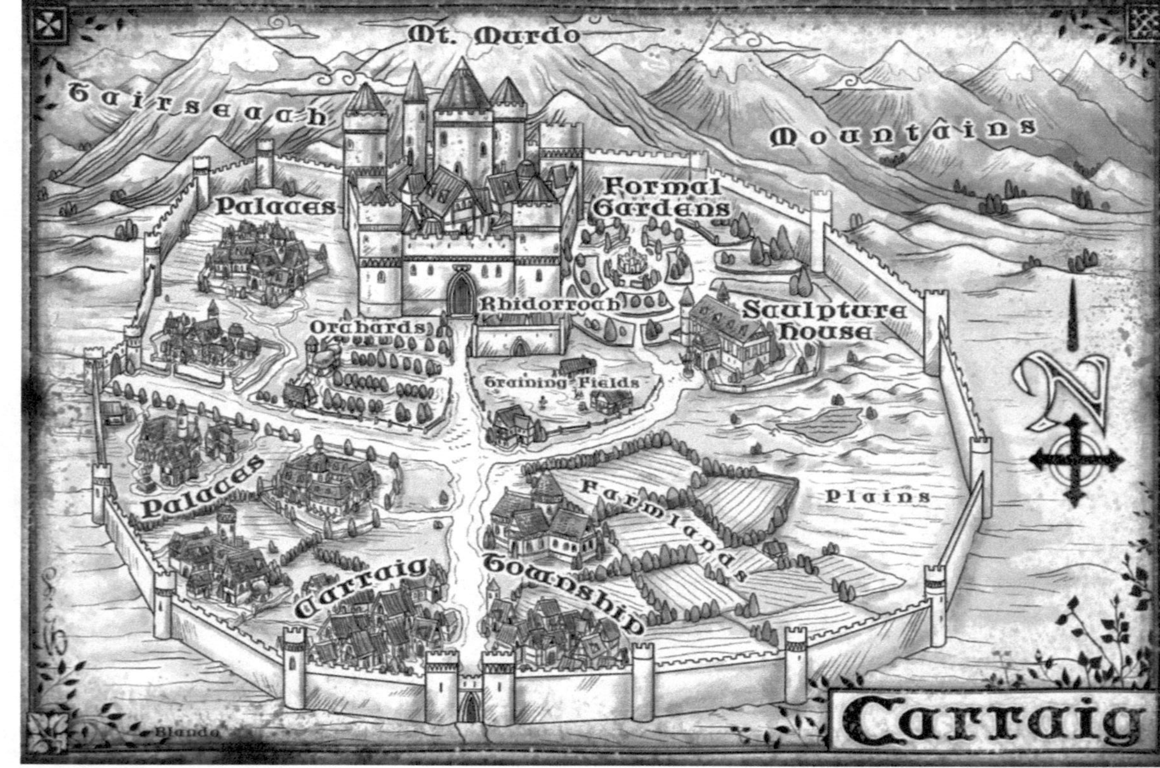

Mt. Murdo
Gairseach
Mountains
Palaces
Formal Gardens
Sculpture House
Rhidorroch
Orchards
Training Fields
Palaces
Farmlands
Plains
Carraig
Township
Blanda
Carraig
N

The Northern Reaches
Varvakis
Orlov
Platov
River Angara
Lake Pyasino
Krashnov
River Olenet
Valeska Rivers
Althing
Jagdish
Granadure
Edduritz
Dagmanson
R. Cnok
Finnlaugur
Ravinder
R. Baol
R. Beergrin
River Sanjit
Prahalad
Obrion
R. Macantacht
Donleavy
The Broken Water
Maninder
The Western Sea
The Eastern Sea
Sea of Olcan
Sehrazad
Ozlem
Hayreddin
Murex
Tabnit
Mahzun
Tabnit
N
The Known World

Chapter 1

onnor stood poised on the balls of his feet, barely restraining himself from joining the fray.

"Stay calm, Kilian," Padraigin urged him. "Ivor's going to start another attack. I can feel it."

It took Connor a second to realize she was speaking to him. He was comfortable in his custom battle leathers and the close-fitting leather mask that concealed his identity, but sometimes the name he had chosen for himself still startled him.

Connor waved away her worry. He and Padraigin had arrayed their shared army in battle formation between two of the rolling hills on the plain east of the Sculpture House. Ivor and Redmund shared another army, made up of the rest of the students and had attacked straight at the center of their lines, as expected. It was about as imaginative as dropping a rock on someone's head, but just as effective.

Connor relished dealing with Ivor's assaults. Commanding an army of Petralists was like controlling a natural disaster, but sometimes it was more fun to get in the thick of things and be the disaster. In this second practice battle of the morning, everyone was eager to perform well. The very next day, permanent army assignments would be made. Then the real group battles would begin.

Captain Rory and his team had been pushing everyone hard over the past week since Connor and the other champions won their nominations. All of the students were involved in the mock battles, from the critical tertiary affinity students to the deep ranks of Boulders already engaged in a heated bash fight in the front lines.

In addition to the students, Tomas and Cameron faced each other in the center, forming the nexus upon which the entire bash fight revolved. They were each supported by eight of their professional Boulders and beat on each other with their usual enthusiasm.

Like they often joked, "No one hits you harder than your best friend."

Although they appeared to be fighting with savage intensity, Connor had spent enough time sparring with them in private training sessions to recognize they were holding back. Like all Boulders, the powdered granite they had absorbed through their skin fueled their superhuman strength. Those two could keep up that pace until they burned through the full measure of their granite.

The Boulder lines had held for almost two minutes, so Connor was expecting Rory to shake things up any second. During the battles of Alasdair, and in his training since, Connor had learned that bash fights never came as often or lasted as long as Boulders wanted.

Striders raced around the flanks in a complex running battle, led by Donald and the other Striders of Rory's company. The groups were turning and closing in sophisticated patterns before breaking apart again, their powder-coated weapons flashing in the late morning sun. Few of the blows struck, but when they did, the Strider would instantly be called out from Pathfinders refereeing the match.

Rory stood with the Sentry teacher atop his tower of earth beside the battlefield. Connor kept an eye on him, trying to anticipate the command that would shake things up. But just as Padraigin had predicted, Ivor attacked, flinging a wave of fire toward the struggling Boulders.

Connor was already sucking on a tiny piece of marble wedged under his tongue and filling his mouth with a steady burning heat. It acted as the gateway through which he could extend his curse and walk with elemental fire. Leveraging that connection, Connor grasped the distant fire and deflected it high and away.

He could have tried wresting control of those flames from Ivor, but he already knew that was harder than snatching a sweetbread away from Hamish. Not only was the big champion more experienced and devilishly clever in managing his elemental forces, but Daly, the single Firetongue in the school, was on Ivor's side.

2

Before the attackers could re-direct their assault, his team's Spitters struck. Using the invisible fingers of their power, they drew water from large buckets placed around the battlefield and pelted shards of ice across the fighting Boulders.

The ice did little real damage. There was a small risk of ice penetrating the Boulders' eyes, one of the few points of relative weakness, but the Spitters were specifically aiming low to minimize the danger. They were more interested in countering Ivor.

Water and fire clashed overhead in a brilliant display of crimson and blue as the elements consumed each other. They bathed the fighting lines in soft hues and seemed to soften the sharp crashing of steel and stone-hard bodies. Padraigin added the finishing touch to the scene by triggering a fanfare of invisible trumpets, one of her unique talents with quartzite.

Who said battle had to be ugly?

It sure smelled ugly. Boulders' muscles weren't their only strength.

Of course, Captain Rory chose that moment to interfere. A piercing whistle cut through the sound of fading trumpets and the professional soldiers seeded into Connor's army took a fall.

Ivor's army got hit last time, but it still didn't seem fair.

As the center of Connor's front line collapsed as if they had absorbed some of the dreaded weakening powder from the Grandurians, Cameron and his men leaped into the gap, driving Connor's forces back. To win the match, all they had to do was capture Connor and Padraigin.

Shona and Jok, the Boulder captains, who had remained stationed near Connor at the rear of the army, started forward to help plug the gap, but Connor called them back.

"We have to go, Kilian," Jok shouted. "They're going to roll our forces back."

"You're not thinking of retreating?" Shona demanded.

"Of course not. What's the best thing to do when you're losing?"

"Figure it out quick," Padraigin snapped. "Because I can't hold them off."

The ground under the battlefield was groaning and slowly buckling, a testament to the underground struggle between Padraigin and Redmund and their Sentries, all walking with earth through the gateway of slate, struggling for control of it. If Padraigin could gain an advantage, she could tumble those Boulders back.

"What's your plan?" Shona cried.

"Unleash The Declan," Connor declared.

"Oh, you've got to be kidding," Shona groaned. "That's never going to work."

Jok asked, "Uh, is there something I should know?"

Connor didn't have time to explain. "Just follow Shona's lead."

"Yeah, Jok," Shona grinned. "Follow my lead. You're good at that."

He glared. He was still locked in second place in the Boulder standings behind Shona, and probably would be forever since the Rhidorroch had not been rebuilt yet and there was no way to post new official times.

As their Boulder line began to roll back, Catriona, of all people, attempted to plug the gap. The pudgy princess shifted into the perfect lines of max-tapped granite and for a second actually looked like royalty.

"For General Kilian!" She shouted and leaped at Cameron.

Laughing, the burly Fast Roller grabbed her by the straps of her battle leathers and threw her over his shoulder. Squawking with the indignity of it, she crashed right into Rory's earthen tower.

She didn't even manage to knock the tower over, but sank up to her neck as the Sentry teacher adjusted to deal with the intrusion. She struggled in vain, screaming to be released, but nobody paid her any attention. Her heroism did rally some of the troops, and they managed to slow the enemy's advance.

Connor turned to Padraigin. "Make sure I reach the center."

"You're cracked," Padraigin exclaimed. "If you get hit, this game's over. We should make a tactical withdrawal."

"If we do that, we've already lost," Connor insisted. "At best, we'd end up tied with Ivor and Redmund for the day. I'm going, and I'm counting on you."

Dipping a finger into a small leather pouch at his belt, Connor absorbed basalt through his skin. The wild freedom of that powdered igneous stone skittered up his arm and filled him with boundless energy. Tapping that fresh power, Connor ran, leaping away faster than a horse.

Shona's voice echoed after him, and even he couldn't outrun sound. Yet.

"You should've used granite. They're going to pound you to dust."

Maybe, but granite wouldn't get him there fast enough. As he closed on the lines of his struggling Boulders he shouted, "Make way!"

To punctuate the order, he again embraced the insanity of fire. Streamers of flame rippled out behind him, swirling in the wind of his passage. At the same time, he reached for the refreshing stability of elemental water. He had downed a mixture of soapstone powder earlier, and its power was already thrumming through his veins. Walking with both elements at once was still as difficult as juggling knives while riding a greased pig bareback.

Practice made for improvement, or regular bruising.

The critical need to turn the tide of the battle boosted his control enough to maintain the connection, even though both elements strained to burst free and turn on each other.

Feeling like he was stuck in the middle of a fierce game of Tug-a-Duck, Connor drew upon soapstone. All the water scattered across the battlefield glowed in his elemental senses and he yanked it all to him. Water leaped into the air, forming little snowballs, which he ringed with fire and threw at Cameron and his Boulders to distract them.

Connor had kept the attack focused enough that it was hard for Ivor or the other tertiary Petralists to turn the elements against him. Luckily they did not launch a concerted elemental attack. It seemed his apparent suicide dash had surprised everyone.

A glorious defeat in front of the entire school did have certain appeal, but he had other plans.

When Connor's forces realized that he was risking himself to come to their aid, they took up a rallying cry and surged forward with renewed enthusiasm. He could tell even they thought he was doomed, but they appreciated him choosing to fall with his men. Nothing motivated like the promise of losing together.

Thirty feet before he reached Cameron, who was beckoning him on, a smile on his brutish face, Connor tapped soapstone and summoned a sphere of water to encase himself.

Then he fracked.

Max-tapping basalt, he reached the critical point where his legs could not go fast enough without altering shape. With a sharp stab of pain that left him gasping, despite being ready for it, his thighs fractured, forming new joints that allowed the top half of his upper leg to rotate in full circles, increasing his speed tenfold.

Connor's speed churned the sphere into a blur of motion. Ivor and his Spitters tried to interfere, but Connor's Spitters waded into the battle of wills, supporting Connor and forming a shield between him and Ivor's team.

The sphere held for three precious seconds, long enough for Connor to plow through the gap in his lines and rush Cameron and the enemy Boulders, who were bracing for impact. At the last second, Connor leaped backward out of the sphere and collapsed it into a sledgehammer of water that struck Cameron in the chest. It staggered the Fast Roller back and knocked several of the nearby Boulders off their feet.

They recovered faster than Connor had hoped, and charged again. Connor met them with whips of fire that he used to knock Boulders flying. He had to extinguish the flames quickly, before Ivor or Daly could snatch them away, but gained another precious couple of seconds.

Connor's Boulders rushed in to help, flanking him and pressing in front of him to shield him from the expected counterattack. Just in time, because Cameron and the hulking, plate-armored Boulders of his professional company tore into them. Connor barely found time to purge the last of his basalt and stick a finger into the other pouch on his belt and absorb a healthy dose of granite.

Connor's lifelong curse, as familiar to him as the debilitating sickness it had caused most of his life, skittered up his arm like a thousand insects. He applied it across his body, and his muscles swelled, shifting into the mighty lines of granite strength. The shifting plates of his custom leather battle suit creaked as they expanded, revealing crimson flames along the left side of his chest and a rippling water symbol on the right.

His forces cheered at the sight, and Catriona's voice echoed across the battlefield from where she was still stuck in the Sentry tower. "Oh, I love it when he does that!"

She honestly had no idea how annoying she was.

Lacking a weapon, Connor struck at the nearest Boulder, who had just trampled one of the students. The Boulder didn't look concerned about getting punched.

He should have thought that one through.

Curse-punching was one of Connor's greatest talents. It was the first thing he had ever done with his curse, and somehow punching with granite unlocked more power than any other way.

Plus, he cheated.

As he unleashed his curse-punch on the foolishly optimistic soldier, Connor summoned eight inches of water in front of his hand, turned it into ice, and used it as a spear which he slammed into the man's chest with the full force of his curse-punch, magnified by a push from soapstone.

The steel plate over the man's chest cracked, and the force of the blow catapulted him backward, right through four ranks of his eager companions. The man tumbled off the field, past the tower where Rory stood, just missing Catriona.

Even in the middle of a bash fight, that was a great hit. Everyone paused for a second to stare, and Connor raised a hand to accept their respect. The men and women of his army bellowed battle cries with renewed vigor, and Cameron's men looked just a bit less confident.

Then the moment passed and more Boulders crushed in all around Connor, beating down his enthusiastic but barely-trained forces. Soon the professional Boulders surrounded him.

He could not beat these men.

Not with granite alone.

So he embraced his elemental powers. Water and fire flickered around him like a dozen extra hands. Tendrils of water caught weapons, wrapped around faces, and knocked soldiers down. Fire flicked at eyes, causing critical distractions.

Connor fought with every ounce of furious intensity he could muster. The elements seemed to like his destructive intent and stopped bucking his control, allowing him to meld them together better than he ever had.

He laughed with the thrill of the moment, riding a wave of elation.

Then Cameron motioned the other Boulders back, and an expectant hush settled over the front lines. Connor used the unexpected reprieve to try catching his breath. His superhuman muscles were quivering with exhaustion. He couldn't last much longer.

"Boy, that was an impressive display of skill," Cameron said with a little nod of respect. "But suicide charges only end one way.

He raised his hammer, and Connor doubted he could stop the next charge.

Good thing he didn't have to.

A bugle sounded across the field and Rory's voice, magnified by one of the Pathfinders, bellowed, "The match is over. Team Kilagain has won!"

"By Tallan's unholy name, how is that possible?" Cameron exclaimed, throwing down his hammer.

"Thanks for pausing for dramatic effect just now," Connor said, clapping Cameron on the shoulder as everyone around them clamored for an explanation. "You might have beaten me if you hadn't."

Rory pointed, and they all looked to see Redmund picking himself off the ground with a blue powder mark on his face. Ivor stood nearby, looking disgusted.

Above Redmund stood little Declan, hefting a battle hammer that looked far too big for him and dancing with glee. He had the presence of mind to reach out a hand and help the far bigger Redmund stand. Then he drove the haft of his hammer into the ground and it rumbled, spraying dirt. A tower of earth lifted Declan off the ground, almost high enough to look Redmund in the eye.

Redmund scowled at the grinning Declan and his tiny tower. Connor laughed and cheered with his army.

Trailed by Jok, Shona pushed through the crowd and threw her arms around Connor.

"You've got to stop doing that," he whispered as he tried to disentangle himself from his lovely patron. "People are going to get the wrong idea."

"Or the right idea," she said, kissing his leather-clad cheek.

Jok pounded him on the shoulder so hard he almost fell over. "You're insane! How did you know that was going to work?"

"The mightiest pedra can fall to a child's knife when distracted by the hunter and his arrow."

Jok blinked, and Shona groaned. "General, please don't do that at a time like this."

"Time most beloved is grasped like water dripping from a cauldron," Connor intoned solemnly.

"Stop," Shona insisted, looking frustrated. "Those weren't even good Sentry-speak anyway."

"They weren't that bad," Connor insisted.

She rolled her eyes. "You're deluded."

It didn't take long for the truth of the victory to spread. Even though Declan had played a critical role in helping Connor win his champion nomination, and even though he had once even managed to raise an earthen tower three entire feet before it collapsed, people still underestimated Declan.

Made it easier to leverage the little guy.

Shona and Jok had thrown the young Sentry right over the battlefield. No one had noticed the kid sail by. They were all so intent on watching Connor's desperate last stand, eager to see the cocky General Kilian finally lose. Even Redmund and Ivor had been so engrossed, they hadn't noticed Declan until he smashed Redmund in the face with his hammer.

Ivor and Redmund pushed through the crowd to confront Connor.

"Team Kilagain accepts your surrender," Connor said.

Ivor rolled his eyes. "That's such a dumb name."

"You're just jealous you still refer to your army as Team Two."

"I'll admit that was some pretty clever work there," Ivor said. "But you should have retreated to fight another day."

"Why? We won."

"There was no way you could know that was going to work."

Connor shrugged. "There's no way to know anything is going to work for sure. But if you trust your people and give them a chance to shine, they might surprise you."

Padraigin pushed through the crowd, grinning. "Kilian, that was such a good idea. Well done."

Redmund decided to do more than scowl. "Padraigin, what did you do the whole time? Hiding in the background, blowing your useless, invisible trumpets while Kilian did all the work?"

"I stomped your feet when you tried walking the earth." For a foreigner, she had almost no accent, and the hulking Redmund didn't intimidate her.

"If not for Kilian, you would've lost almost before the battle started."

She gave him a disgusted look. "Declan hit you harder than I thought. You're not even trying to whine in Sentry-speak."

That elicited a round of laughter, only angering Redmund further. Connor caught several comments from students about how the tiniest person in their army had toppled the mighty champion.

"I speak plainly so that even you can understand," Redmund retorted. "Kilian saved the day, just as he saved you in the nomination. Without him, you wouldn't even be here."

Murmurs of agreement rippled through the crowd, and Padraigin noticed. If she lost the confidence of her army, she wouldn't have a chance to win the upcoming group battles.

"Redmund has a point," Ivor said. "We have yet to see you take a bold stand or win a victory all by yourself. I wonder if maybe you should surrender now and offer to serve as one of Kilian's captains instead."

That generated some laughter, but Padraigin's face reddened.

"They're just trying to goad you into doing something as stupid as they just did," Connor said.

"Be quiet," she snapped. "You keep interrupting and stealing the show. You need to give me a chance to shine."

"It does not work that way," Redmund said. "No one *gives* a champion a chance. They must take it."

"You know what I mean," she growled.

He raised one eyebrow, looking more composed as she grew more flustered. "One cannot force the young pedra to fly and to hunt. It alone must choose to take wing and leap off the cliff."

"Your Sentry speak is getting worse," Connor noted.

"Fine," Padraigin cried. "Right now. You and me, Kilian. I'll show you what I can do."

"Okay, I challenge you to a steak eating contest."

"What?" she exclaimed.

"Well, it's lunch time and we've got that celebration feast to deal with."

"No. We duel."

He shrugged. "All right, let's grab some of those long loaves--"

"Don't," she interrupted. "We duel, or you prove you're a coward."

Hadn't they just won a huge victory together?

"I don't think that's necessary. You did a great job today, Padraigin."

"Are you scared, Kilian?" she taunted.

The students started chanting their names, although most shouted his. Many of the students preferred Ivor or Redmund for ultimate Tir-raon champion, but they would all take Kilian over Padraigin. She was a foreigner competing in the game that defined Obrion and the nobility of the nation, so her very presence was an insult to them.

That's usually why he loved helping her.

The lopsided chanting only made Padraigin more determined. She faced universal hatred on a daily basis with remarkable grace, but even she could be pushed too far.

Captain Rory approached, rubbing his hands. "The feast can wait. Let's set some rules and have a little fun."

Connor suppressed a groan. Captain Rory's idea of fun included storming fortified positions and wrestling with the curvaceous and deadly Grandurian Rumbler, Anika.

Chapter 2

As the rules for the duel were quickly ironed out, Connor wondered how he'd missed seeing that trap coming. The past week of intense training had given him a welcome chance to get to know the other champions. Since armies were not yet defined, Rory had shifted assignments at least twice daily, rotating the pairings of the champions every time, forcing them to meet first as opponents, then as partners over and over again.

It had been a brilliant move. Captain Rory's craggy face, deep, rumbling voice, and no-nonsense demeanor made it easy for students to assume he was little more than a brawny soldier, but he also possessed a crafty mind and a sophisticated mastery over battlefield management. He'd forced them to learn to work together, to understand each other better.

Connor liked the crafty Ivor and deeply respected the elegant Padraigin. He recognized the demands of Redmund's duty, but the burly champion held himself much more aloof than the others. He seemed intent on making sure he considered them all enemies. It was a very limiting world view.

As the masses of cheering students urged the competition to begin, Connor pulled Padraigin aside. "You could have picked a better time."

"I really did enjoy working with you today, but I cannot allow the rumor that I'm unfit to lead to take root."

"Don't worry so much about it," Connor said. "Pretty

soon, Ivor and Redmund will face the same problem. I like you guys, but there can only be one winner."

Padraigin laughed. "That's not helping your cause, you know."

He shrugged. "Reality can be hard sometimes. I'm just trying to prepare you for it."

"The stones are cast, Kilian. None of us can back down, but know it's nothing personal when I destroy you."

He liked her grit. She needed it. The nation of Althing had never fielded a Dawnus before. They had few Petralists, and the fact that she had the audacity to stand as a champion infuriated most of the noble-born Petralists at the school.

He extended a hand. "Good luck. I honestly hope you come in a close second."

She laughed. "Geall on."

As they both thumbed their noses to accept the challenge, Connor considered how best to face her. He could not let her win, but she couldn't afford to lose. Could be defeat her without damaging her standing?

"Prepare," Rory cried, calling them to the starting line to immense cheering.

The contest seemed simple, as simple as racing Hamish to the dinner table, but the duel would challenge their mastery over their various affinities, their creativity, and their tap-rate management.

Padraigin was Agor, one of the rare Petralists who managed to establish affinities with two igneous stones. All of the champions were, which was unusual. In his persona as Kilian, Connor was limited in the same way and had chosen basalt and granite, the same two igneous stones they all used. The duel called for a race across the plain, so granite was out.

As they raced, they'd be challenged to employ their tertiary affinities, but under strict limitations. Few Petralists managed to establish a coveted tertiary affinity with a metamorphic stone, granting them the amazing ability to walk with one of the elements. All of the champions were also Dawnus, able to establish affinity with a second tertiary stone, the polar opposite of their original element. It was considered the rarest of gifts.

Well, almost. As Blood of the Tallan, Connor could theoretically establish affinities with all of the power stones, although as Kilian, he was limited to using only a Dawnus gift.

"Ready!" Rory's voice boomed across the plain, enhanced by his Pathfinder.

Connor crouched, ready to leap into a fracked sprint. Beside him, Padraigin looked determined.

"Begin!" Rory cried.

Connor drew deep from the boundless energy of basalt and flashed across the field, his legs fracking in seconds.

He was ready for the sharp stab of pain. Somehow basalt made the physical transformation possible and allowed him to reach otherwise impossible speeds. Connor grinned with the thrill of basalt. Racing across the plain on fracked legs was a unique wonder. He could outrun the flight of arrows, chase down a hunting pedra, or fly off the tops of low hills.

Padraigin was faster.

Despite his deep affinity for basalt, Connor could not match Padraigin's practiced flair and tap-rate mastery. She fracked a second sooner, accelerated more smoothly, and held a narrow lead as they passed the end of the flat field where the group battle had taken place.

Connor poured on the speed, but barely managed to keep from falling farther behind as they tore between a series of low hills in a gentle arc that would lead them wide around the eastern plain, then back toward the Sculpture House.

The competition was more than just a simple foot race, though. As the two of them sped for the small, round lake nestled in the hills, Padraigin glanced back. She grinned, projecting confidence, but she had to be worried. The second phase of the contest was about to begin.

When they reached the shores of the lake, Padraigin shot out onto the water without slowing, her fracked feet moving so fast she raced across the surface without sinking. Her feet threw up a cascade of spray, aimed at Connor's face.

He blasted through the spray, laughing as he skipped across the water. At the same time, he tapped the gateway of soapstone pulsing inside of him in time with his heartbeat. The lake glowed in his mind, his elemental senses like an invisible third eye. He could have crossed the lake with his eyes closed and never missed a step.

Even Padraigin glowed softly to his soapstone senses. Non-water liquid could be manipulated by Spitters, but it was increasingly difficult to affect the less pure it became. Most Spitters couldn't manipulate blood in the living and students were strictly forbidden from trying. Even if they could, there was something

14

about living flesh that insulated and protected against those ethereal senses.

Soapstone had been his first tertiary affinity, and connecting with it was still far easier than using any other elemental power. It was a sure foundation upon which his most important affinities anchored.

With a tug on his ethereal elemental senses, Connor surrounded Padraigin with a dense spray of water, then opened a sloping hole in the waters just in front of her. With a squawk of surprise, she recognized the trap and tried to call upon air to give her wings. She possessed the strongest affinity to quartzite that Connor had ever seen, but air was a fickle thing, even for her. The water he'd sprayed all around her dissipated her connection, and the air chose not to respond.

Lacking time to stop or swerve, Padraigin skidded down the sloping ramp and crashed into the waters on the far side. The rules of the contest prevented Connor from simply imprisoning her in water, just as she couldn't swallow him in the earth and leave him entombed until she won the race. So Connor snapped his fingers as he banked around the spot where she struggled just under the surface. The water erupted, spitting Padraigin high into the air, back toward the field where they had started.

As Connor reached the far shore and accelerated on dry ground, he glanced back.

"Tallan take it," he muttered.

Padraigin hadn't tumbled nearly as far as he had hoped. She'd tapped quartzite, using the air to turn herself and glide back to the ground on the north shore of the lake. He had gained the lead, but not by enough.

Connor max-tapped basalt and increased speed. He needed to escape the range of her effective earth powers. Maintaining a connection with earth at fracked speed would be as hard for her as stealing a kiss from Verena without getting punched in the throat was for him.

Unfortunately, he was dealing with Padraigin. If anyone could do it, she could. So Connor drew streamers of water out of the lake, letting them flow behind him as he ran, hoping to dampen her connection with the ground beneath him.

He soon entered a deep slot between two slightly higher hills. Most of the students were already positioned atop the hill to his right. The circuitous path of their race granted time for the rest of the school to witness parts of it. When they saw Connor reach the checkpoint first, the students raised a great cheer. He was by far the favorite.

So of course, that's when Padraigin decided to make her move.

The ground bubbled under Connor's feet, but he shot over the softened earth without slowing. The laugh bubbling in his throat died when sinewy fingers of earth shot out of the ground all around, trying to trip him.

Connor drew water into a sphere around himself, similar to the one he'd used earlier in the battle. His fast-spinning legs whipped the sphere into a blur, and the hardened water tore through the grasping tendrils of earth. This time Connor did laugh as he plowed through Padraigin's attempt to slow him. Students on the hills cheered him on, and several of the girls, led by Catriona, shouted, "We love you, Kilian!"

That's when Padraigin raised two heavy pillars of earth just in front of Connor and to either side. That was such a dumb idea. He easily sped between them.

Earth shot out of each pillar, piercing the front of his sphere of water and forming a bar at shoulder height. It only stayed in place for a second before his water severed the ends.

One second was too long.

Connor struck the cross-bar at full speed. The brutal impact knocked him off his feet and rattled him so much that he lost control of the water. The sphere exploded and he tumbled wildly in the midst of a formless wave.

Somehow Padraigin snared Connor's legs out of the waters and yanked him down into the ground, but allowed the frothing waters to continue past, separating him from his precious defense. For a second he was trapped, entombed in the earth, with no air, completely immobile. He felt a flicker of panic. He didn't have any slate, couldn't fight her. He was helpless.

Then the ground spat him out, just as he had thrown her out of the waters. Connor tumbled into the air, spinning so fast his stomach lurched and he wasn't sure he wanted to laugh from the amazing sensation or instead focus on where he wanted to vomit. Invisible trumpets blared around him as Padraigin raced past. He caught glimpses of her waving to the glaring crowds as she again took the lead.

That helped him finally make up his mind. She was too far to throw up on, so he had to beat her.

Limited to his declared Dawnus abilities, Connor couldn't tap quartzite like she had to redirect his flight, and he couldn't afford to wait until he finally crashed back to the earth near the lake. So Connor sucked deep on the piece of marble tucked under his tongue and called upon the crazed intensity of fire.

The first moment of connecting with marble was a beautiful, spicy experience. Then it just started to hurt. There were no flames in the vicinity, but marble allowed him to create fire. He needed to tap more of it, which burned through the little stone in his mouth faster, and intensified the pain. He wasn't a believer in victory at any cost, but he embraced the growing burn and formed an image of what he wanted in his mind.

Fiery wings sprouted from his back, white-hot and dense enough to give him purchase against the air. Connor whooped, a crazed edge creeping into the sound as he embraced the destructive element, which always drove him to cast aside hesitation and restraint.

As soon as the fiery wings appeared, they snapped taught and caught the air. Connor stabilized his flight and banked hard over. The air rushed past, tearing at his face. He squinted, focusing on the tricky act of controlling his flight path.

He was not a very good flier.

He'd attempted flight a couple of times, from his disastrous ride on the out-of-control heatstone oven, to his even more out-of-control attempt to fly on a block of quartzite. He fell better than he flew, so he told himself gliding was just falling sideways. Plus, he had mastered enough control with fire that he could alter the shape of his wings to help keep him stable.

Loving the thrill of it, and not caring that flames were trickling out his nose, Connor swooped low over the hilltop where the students cheered him on. He focused on the fleeing form of Padraigin, who was racing off the plain toward the Sculpture House and the towering mass of the mighty ice dome rearing above the Rhidorroch that Connor had constructed as part of his nomination challenge.

Connor increased the angle of his dive, racing for the ground and picking up speed. He was moving even faster than Padraigin, catching up on the unsuspecting Dawnus.

The air in front of Connor hardened into an invisible wall.

He crashed like a custard-filled tart thrown at a window, and his fiery wings splattered flames everywhere. He fell thirty feet to the ground and barely retained enough presence of mind to draw the flames under him like a hot trampoline.

He bounced back into the air and the rush of wind helped clear his head. As he glared at Padraigin's back, she glanced in his direction and gave him a cocky salute.

Then the air swatted him like a giant hand smacking a fly.

Invisible drums beat a staccato salute as Connor again crashed into the earth, this time hitting so hard he shattered the fires he tried to form into a new cushion.

He should have thought better than to try flying around Padraigin. She was the mistress of the air. Connor, like most of the students, had always considered quartzite the least important battle stone. Most Pathfinders struggled to walk with the fickle element of air and focused almost entirely on directing quartzite inward where it enhanced their senses. Padraigin was proving that there might be a vast, untapped potential in quartzite.

Verena understood. Connor tried to push thoughts of the beguiling Builder from his mind as he struggled to his feet and broke into a run. It took a few seconds to reach full fracked speed, and by that time Padraigin had already rounded the Sculpture House. He needed to focus or she was going to win by enough of a margin that he'd be the one having to worry about damage to his reputation.

As he sprinted toward the Sculpture House, planning ways to delay Padraigin, thoughts of Verena wormed their way into his mind, just as she had so often wormed her way under his arm. Those were precious memories, made all the more valuable by the knowledge that he would never again get the chance to hold her that way.

Instead of rounding the Sculpture House like Padraigin had, Connor threw himself into the air with fire, vaulting the building and gaining a precious second. She didn't try hindering his flight that time. She was so far ahead, she probably figured the match was all but won. All she had to do was round the broken remains of the Rhidorroch and reach the main gate of the Carraig.

The sight of the still-devastated obstacle course made Connor wince. The ice dome was finally being taken down, with pie-shaped sections already gone. The bulk of the construct still remained, rearing high over the grounds of the school in a glittering testament to Connor's success. As soon as the dome came down, the Sentries could remove the earthen banks they had raised around the dark wall of the Rhidorroch. Connor longed to see it standing proud on the field again, rebuilt and ready to test the students.

But first, Connor had to deal with Padraigin.

Sucking again on marble, Connor formed whips of fire around her. The very speed of her legs worked against her, wrapping the flames tight, tripping her, and sending her tumbling.

Connor made sure to keep the flames away from her hair. He'd learned the hard way the dangers of messing with a girl's hair when he'd burned Shona's. The lesson had been beaten home again when he'd been forced to cut off a huge chunk of Princess Catriona's hair.

So leaving the hair, he formed the end of the distant flames into little legs that started running back toward the Sculpture House, dragging the shouting Padraigin in his direction. The earth rose up to block the flames, but Connor kept them running her in circles, distracting her long enough to catch up.

He finally released the flames after sprinting past, again confident that he could win.

She raised a wall of earth right in front of him.

Connor bounced off, spitting mud. It tasted nasty, as if she'd somehow pulled earth from under the distant privy. He turned to the right and tried running around the wall, but it grew, extending to block his path. He increased speed, but the wall kept pace as he closed on the gigantic obstacle of the Rhidorroch.

Connor couldn't let Padraigin take the lead again. They were too close. She wasn't supposed to completely block his path, but what if Rory allowed the wall as a valid delaying tactic? He didn't dare take the time to purge basalt and absorb granite. Superhuman strength could bash through the wall, but that wouldn't win the race. He needed to try something different, something unexpected.

And he needed to do it fast, because he was about to run into the Rhidorroch. He couldn't afford to rush around the far side. That would delay him too long.

He glanced up at the mighty dome rearing hundreds of feet into the air.

And grinned.

Connor max-tapped basalt, sprinting straight toward the looming wall.

This was going to be amazing.

Chapter 3

efeating Padraigin's earth powers would take too long, as would circumventing the vast expanse of the Rhidorroch.

So why not run right over the top?

With a burst of flames to give him lift, Connor soared in a flaming arc over the earthen barrier, reached the base of the ice dome, and *ran*.

With the fire providing a boost, he tapped soapstone again. This time, walking with two elements felt like riding two unruly horses at the same time, and Connor wasn't much of a horseman.

Today he needed those wild horses, so he managed to connect with soapstone and the entire glittering expanse of the dome came alive in his water senses. With a touch of his mind, the surface of the dome in front of him rippled into little ridges that gave better purchase.

That was enough, and he accelerated up the side of the great dome. Even though those streamers of fire must look amazing, setting the bluish-white of the dome flickering with crimson and pink, he no longer needed the boost from behind. So he released marble, strengthening his connection with water, which allowed him to grab the ridged ice along his path up the dome and make it flow upward, nearly doubling his speed.

As he neared the peak, he gained a panoramic view of gawking students streaming past the Sculpture House. The entire landscape of the outer Carraig complex spread around him, from the inner wall ringing the close-packed spires and towers of the palace-city to the huge outer wall running a couple miles away, beyond the plain. He should have maintained his connection with marble. A spray of blue-white fire would add to his reputation.

Padraigin had rounded the earthen wall that had blocked him instead of dropping it. Didn't make sense, but she was a foreigner and a girl, so he'd never pretend to understand her.

At the very top of the dome, a small section of the center was missing. He'd melted it into a mini waterfall during his nomination challenge. Even better than that memory was the moment when the Spitters, led by Ivor, had helped Connor shore up the shaky dome and complete the master work, even though by all rights they should have let him fail.

Trust people, give them a chance to shine, and they just might.

Or not.

The earthen walls holding up the dome shook like a cake taken too early from the oven, and the dome vibrated. Connor slid to a stop right at the edge of the apex hole. Deep cracks sundered through the sides of the dome, booming like thunderclaps and weakening the construct.

What was Padraigin thinking? He glanced toward her, but she had also stopped, and was staring up at him like he was crazy. Well sure, but not crazy with slate. Not so anyone would know anyway.

She didn't look like someone trying to destroy a wonder of the world. The earth rumbled again and the dome shook with it, ice groaning and cracking. Up at the top, the swaying was magnified and the air was filled with a mist of little stinging particles of ice that smelled like impending doom.

Padraigin threw out her hand, and the shaking stopped, but Connor felt a growing chill that had nothing to do with the fact that he was standing atop thousands of tons of ice. Down inside the Rhidorroch, dozens of overall-clad workers had been busy at work repairing the shattered obstacle course. Repairs had progressed more than Connor had realized. The workers were finishing the new false ground, so repairs of the underground levels must have already been completed.

Everyone was looking up at him, and they weren't waving. Connor could feel the cracks and critical flaws spreading through the gigantic structure. Definitely time for an early lunch break.

"Get out of there!" he shouted, wishing he could enhance his voice like the Pathfinders did. His words echoed through the huge space, taken up a second later by Frazier, the maze lord.

"Move!" his shout reached Connor as a distant whisper. "Get out!"

As Connor bent his will to shoring up the cracking dome, Frazier shouted, "Don't you dare break anything, Kilian!"

"It's not my fault!" Connor shouted back.

The earth under the dome shook for a third time, despite Padraigin's apparent efforts to stabilize it. The cracking accelerated, reaching a crescendo. With his mind tightly linked to the dome, Connor felt the thousands of cracks multiplying and reaching a point where not even he could avert disaster.

He didn't have time to worry about who was responsible or why. If the dome collapsed, Frazier and his workers would be splattered.

Connor abandoned thoughts of winning the race. Those lives were in his hands. He scanned the dome again with soapstone senses, feeling the ice breaking into gigantic blocks on the verge of falling.

He couldn't stop them all.

So he pushed one.

The best way to survive an avalanche was to ride it. Frazier and his men would need the proper seats. A block of ice weighing eight tons slipped free of the dome and fell with ponderous inevitability toward the ground below. Some workers screamed, and their flight became a panicked scramble away from the approaching disaster.

"No!" Frazier's voice echoed up from below. "Not again!"

Again? Breaking the dome was completely different.

Connor seized that falling block of ice as it fell and, melding water and fire, he heated it, transforming it in a heartbeat into a cascading waterfall.

"Hold your breath!" he shouted.

The water thundered into the false ground where the obstacle course would rise from the vast cavern beneath. It drove through to the underground levels and Connor scattered the water everywhere, sending it cascading through every level.

He made sure to hit Frazier with a mouthful. Hadn't the man's mother taught him not to swear like that?

As the dome sagged, on the verge of a general collapse, Connor pushed two more blocks out and melted them too, sending waves of water barreling through the Rhidorroch, using them like distant eyes to find every last living soul, then sweeping them off their feet. They'd never get out by running, but the churning waters he controlled could move far faster. He only needed twenty seconds to sweep everyone clear of the impending disaster.

He didn't have that much time.

The northern section of the dome gave way with a roar that reverberated inside and echoed across the entire Carraig complex, the death knell of the giant dome. As the collapse spread across the dome, Connor drove the waters harder, carrying the workers like flotsam on a wild river through the Rhidorroch and piling them up near the western exit.

With a surprisingly musical final sigh, the rest of the dome imploded. Slow at first, but gathering speed, the entire construct collapsed, dragging Connor down with it. His stomach did that fantastic flip-lurch, but he was too busy to enjoy it.

While the sopping-wet workers fled through the exit, Connor seized all the loose water and formed it into a rounded protective barrier to give them precious extra seconds. As ice crashed into the ground of the Rhidorroch, shattering the partially-rebuilt compound, Connor seized more and more water, reinforcing the barrier around Frazier and his workers until it could withstand even the onslaught of the collapsing dome. Then he focused on the tons of ice falling toward them and drained away as much of it as he could, lessening the impact on that area.

Wielding all that water was amazing, and in the moment of the death of the great dome, he became one with the element the same way he had the day he had created the dome. For a split second, as he max-tapped soapstone, he felt a hint of even greater power just out of reach, like the sunrise beyond the next ridge, sensed but not yet accessible. If he could only touch it, he could avert the disaster, but the moment passed, and the ice thundered into the ground and shattered everything.

All that remained was not dying. With a mental tug, he geysered the ice under him, throwing himself into the air. There, he released water and tapped marble, again forming burning wings of fire that caught the air. He got the perfect view of the disaster as thousands of tons of ice blasted the compound into shards.

Breaking the Rhidorroch once had been necessary, but the new disaster was a shameful waste. He loved the Rhidorroch, and had been eager to again see it completed, to run it with the other students and test his abilities against the devious constructs created by the maze lord.

Now it was gone. Again.

The rush of air from the imploding ice blasted Connor another three hundred feet higher. He nearly lost control, but eventually managed to stabilize his flight. As he banked around the shattered Rhidorroch, looking for Padraigin, he swore to find the one responsible for the disaster and make them pay.

He landed with a flourish beside Padraigin, who was white with shock. Before either of them could speak, Frazier rushed out a sagging doorway, with his men spilling out behind.

"You're going to pay for this, Kilian!"

Chapter 4

razier looked angry enough to kill, and he was clearly tapping obsidian. He barely limped, and he moved with the deadly grace that only Blades could manage.

Connor really needed to get his hands on some obsidian and try it for himself. It was the one igneous stone he hadn't yet had a chance to establish affinity with. In the meantime, he purged the last of his basalt and slipped a finger into the pouch of granite at his belt, absorbing a hefty portion. He didn't want to fight Frazier, but he wouldn't allow the angry man to murder him for someone else's crime.

"How are your men?" Connor called, hating that his mask would conceal his genuine concern.

"They would have been better if you hadn't brought that dome crashing down on them," Frazier snapped.

"Come on," Connor said. "You're smarter than that, especially tapping obsidian."

Frazier slowed, and although he looked like he wanted to strike out with the stick he carried like a sword, he hesitated. "Are you claiming you had nothing to do with what just happened?"

"Of course not. I absolutely just saved you and your men from whoever was trying to kill us."

"He's telling the truth," Padraigin offered. "Someone shook the ground. That's Sentry work."

"Who?" Frazier demanded.

"I don't know."

Captain Rory arrived, flanked by his senior men. Students pressed in after, clamoring for details, but Tomas and Cameron organized their Boulders to keep the onlookers back.

"What were you doing up there?" Frazier demanded.

"I had to go over the dome because Padraigin was blocking my path. Besides, since we can't run the maze, running the dome was the next best thing. Did you get my time?"

Rory interrupted. "What happened? Is everyone all right?"

Padraigin spoke up. "I didn't raise that wall blocking Connor. I assumed Redmund or someone else did."

Redmund arrived with Ivor, already shaking his head. "The earth cares not what flight the fox takes."

"So are you the fox, or did you scare it?" Connor asked.

Ivor interrupted Redmund's roundabout, angry retort. "I questioned Mactail about what was going on when we lost sight of the runners behind the Sculpture House. He mentioned that someone shook the Rhidorroch, but they were well shielded."

Rory turned to the teacher of the Sentry class. "Did you feel it too?"

"The smallest rock sends ripples across the face of the waters."

Rory groaned. "Speak plain, man. People could have died."

The Sentry looked pained and spoke slowly, as if normal sentence structure was alien to him. "I felt something. Like Mactail said, obscurity shielded the intent and the identity of the attacker, but the curtain of my will held sway upon the width of the plain and any attempting to walk with the earth from our company would have traveled by my side."

"So you don't know who it was, but you don't think it was Redmund," Rory muttered.

"Thus light reaches even the dimmest corners of the darkened canyon at the rising of the noonday sun," the Sentry said with a nod.

"Someone did it!" Frazier cried, pointing at the shattered Rhidorroch. Ragged piles of ice peeked up over the dark walls.

"Wasn't us," Connor said. "We were having a friendly competition."

"We'll make whoever is responsible pay eleven ways to Dagmanson," Padraigin promised. "They could have killed people, they destroyed the beloved Rhidorroch, and they interrupted my victory."

That wasn't exactly right, but Connor didn't feel like arguing about it. Almost-mass-murder events had a way of sucking the fun right out of everything.

Frazier looked from her to Redmund to the Sentry teacher. "You're all saying none of you had a hand in this." He turned to glare at Connor. "And yet the fact remains that you climbed that dome and brought it down on our heads."

"Next you're going to claim I shook the earth." The fact that he could have didn't matter. They didn't know it, and he couldn't allow them to follow that train of thought. The best way to kill the idea before they could dwell on it was to scorn it publicly.

Frazier faced Padraigin, his stick twitching. "You were the closest Sentry."

"I already told you, it was not my doing."

"And the word of a foreigner should so easily be accepted?" Redmund asked.

"The word of a confirmed champion should be," Padraigin snapped.

Connor said, "You instigated the contest, Redmund. Was it just jealousy that motivated you, or did you want us running this way for other reasons?"

As Redmund sputtered with rage, Ivor said, "Redmund did not suggest the race. That was Captain Rory's doing."

Rory only grunted, and no one dared suggest Rory had anything to do with it. Connor nearly laughed at the suggestion. Ivor loved to find leverage against everyone, but he'd have to work a lot harder to find something on Rory. Unless he met Anika.

"Were there no other Sentries in the area?" Rory asked.

Frazier shrugged. "I have no idea."

"Well, all the Sentry students were accounted for," Connor said. "How many other Sentries are at the Carraig?"

"There are a few," Frazier admitted. "Lord Dail has two in his employ that coordinate the outer watch, and a couple of the high lord representatives have Sentries in their personal guard."

Rory turned to Grahame, his senior Pathfinder, whose eyes perpetually glowed, even when he did not appear to be tapping quartzite. "I want a full accounting of all slate affinities on my desk by dinnertime. Every name, and where they were today during this disaster." Then he asked Frazier, "Are there casualties?"

"I saw some injuries," Frazier admitted, which finally

seemed to diffuse the last of his anger. "But it'll take some time to check everyone."

"Aifric and the other student Healers are already tending to them," Grahame reported.

As the students began to disperse toward the eating halls, Rory pulled Connor, the other champions, and Frazier aside. The captain looked unusually grim.

"I will investigate this crime, and I expect Lord Dail will assign resources to help. Until we discover who was responsible, be on your guard."

"You think whoever did this will strike again?" Ivor asked.

"Then Kilian needs to be careful," Redmund added. "Not the rest of us."

"Think deeper," Frazier said. "Kilian was on top of the dome, and he has strong affinity with water. Chances of him getting killed were slim."

"So why shake the dome?" Redmund asked.

"Perhaps to discredit him," Padraigin suggested. "Kilian has almost as many enemies as I do."

She had a point, but that still didn't seem right. Why risk so much death and destruction on the chance that it might reflect poorly on him?

"Or maybe I wasn't the target."

That got their attention.

"Like you said, I can take care of myself. But if I hadn't protected you and your men, how many would have died?"

No one liked to think they had enemies out to kill them. Frazier was respected for the incredible obstacle courses he developed.

"Perhaps a student who fared poorly in this year's standings has connections to pull off such a stunt," Rory said. "But it seems a stretch."

"Or maybe they just hoped to keep the Rhidorroch from reopening," Padraigin suggested. "Without it, standings are locked in."

"Oh, that's a good one," Ivor said.

"Why not suggest Lord Dail ordered the attack as a way to secure more funding for the school," Connor said. When they all looked at him like he was cracked, he shrugged. "If we're going to start throwing out wild guesses, let's see how far we can go."

"You are so twisted," Padraigin muttered.

"We need more information," he clarified. "Otherwise we're wasting time."

"Like I said," Rory interjected. "Be on your guard. All we know at this point is that someone was willing to risk committing mass murder today. Whoever that is, they're dangerous. Until we catch them, they may decide to strike again."

Connor wondered if Ilse had a hand in the disaster. If she had, that meant she'd abandoned her mission to recruit him and moved to her alternate directive to assassinate him.

If it was Ilse, she would try again, and people were going to die.

Chapter 5

Hamish stood at his worktable in the cavernous room in the Builder compound that used to hold the windrider he and Verena had crashed. He sucked on a piece of soapstone coated with caramel. The custom mixture of sugary coating and refreshing, cool soapstone was close to perfect.

He might add a twist of granite dust so it would taste like cool caramel crackers. He had tried marble, but it didn't mix well with soapstone. Burns were a familiar consequence and he knew how to deal with them. Barely even felt them any more.

In his hands he held two large mugs, one filled with warm water, the other holding a hard biscuit he'd found in his pocket. By prying open just a fraction of the soapstone's embedded power, he concentrated on crafting the stone's connection with nearby water.

Soapstone in its simplest form just grabbed any nearby water and pulled it toward the stone. It was a powerful effect, but was but the tip of the torrent. Soapstone allowed a Builder to connect with water, and as his mastery over his Builder powers had grown, he'd learned that there were more sophisticated ways to manipulate the power stones he unlocked.

It was tricky, because crafting more complex patterns of behavior had to be done by feel. Like trying to weave spaghetti into mittens in the dark.

At the moment, he was directing a slender arc of water from the first mug onto the biscuit in the second. Every time his concentration slipped, he unleashed every ounce of water in the room, soaking everything. Verena could twist water into knots, making the complex process of invisible spaghetti weaving seem simple.

The feel of the water slipping through his mental fingers felt like that time he had dropped a fresh-baked chocolate cake and almost managed to catch it. Manipulating water left a similar invisible tasty trail along his mental fingers, although he hadn't yet figured out how to lick it off.

He was finally mastering the required control. After allowing the water to soak into the biscuit for several seconds to soften it enough for eating, he began drawing the water back to the first cup. The trick was to leave enough to maintain that slightly softened feel.

"Hamish, are you in here?"

At the sound of Verena's voice, his mental fingers slipped. Water sprayed across the room, and Verena sighed.

"That had better not have come from your mouth."

"Of course not. It would've dissolved the caramel too fast." He held up the cup. "Let me see if I can get it all back in here."

"I've got a better idea," she said with that mischievous twinkle in her eye that heralded another new invention.

Verena extended her arms a little. Flames began dancing along her wrists where she wore a new set of matching silver bracelets, set with interlocking, polished marble stones of varying colors. Hamish immediately saw the value of having access to flames on both hands. She could toast bread without having to stand.

Then the flames leaped in slender arcs between her wrists and from there up to a marble necklace she wore. For a second he worried she had lost control, and prepared to douse her with another shot of soapstone.

Verena never lost control, and the flames clung to her necklace like a living ruby pendant. She was smart enough not to let the flames circle her throat and burn her hair, and they remained on the outer layer of the necklace, away from her skin. Hamish had recently learned how bad burning hair stunk. Now he wore his short like a soldier.

The flames thickened as she opened the release rate, dancing between her wrists and neck, continuing to expand until gossamer sheets of flame rippled in front of her. The water he had sprayed her with gently evaporated into mist that seemed to caress her smiling face as it ascended toward the ceiling. The flames began changing colors, from red to orange to white.

"Show off."

The fire disappeared with an audible snap and Verena grinned, "You're not the only one working on special projects."

They were busy producing existing mechanicals as fast as possible to supply the war effort, but that only made the little research time they could still get all the more precious. Verena used it better than most. In the grip of Builder creativity, she was like a tornado of invention. He couldn't tell her that, though.

"I'm sure your new invention will scare off any Petralists we run into."

She shrugged. "If not, I'll speed-crack 'em."

Hamish shuddered to think of her latest battlefield-level tactic. Of course, Kilian absolutely loved it. It was a wallstone combined with basalt. Dropping it formed a standard earthen wall, but riding on basalt, which slid that wall across the ground at tremendous speed for about a hundred yards. Anyone caught in its path would at best only suffer bruises or broken bones.

Hamish was trying to convince one of the local farmers to let him try it in his back pasture with some carefully positioned plows. He was convinced they could revolutionize the entire planting process. Surprisingly, the man didn't seem enthusiastic. Probably because his herd of milk cows had still not recovered from the last experiment he signed up for.

Verena glanced at his worktable. "Is it ready?"

"It is." With a grand gesture, he showed her his masterpiece. His ultimate vision was a full flying suit, packed with deadly mechanicals, but he hadn't combined all the pieces yet. The most important piece, which he lifted to show her, was the armored jacket.

It was beautiful. Starting with a standard leather battle jacket, Hamish had added three interlocking layers of palm-sized hardened granite scales, overlapping to form a dense armor.

"That's it?"

"Of course it is!" he cried. "This is going to change the world."

Verena grimaced. "We'll have to work on your fashion sense then."

"Oh, stop. Help me put it on."

It was a bit bulky, but not as bad as full steel plate. With Verena's help, Hamish fastened the buckles.

"What does it do?" Verena asked, fingering some of the granite leaves.

"A lot, but today I'm just testing the stop-bash property."

"That's not a real word."

"You invent new words all the time."

She shrugged as he led her out of the room. "I'm good at it."

They found Bastien in the practice arena, as usual. It looked like he was packing up his equipment.

"You can't be taking a vacation," Hamish said. "Not with a war brewing."

"What are you doing here?" Bastien asked. "And what is this contraption?"

"I said I'd be back."

"You waited almost too long," Bastien said, examining the armor.

"Are you leaving?" Verena asked.

"I must, lady," he said. "They're shipping me to Badurach Pass where the army's gathered to repel the Obrioners. I'll be training recruits."

"Fighting hasn't started yet, has it?" Verena asked.

"I don't think so, but could be any day."

Hamish wasn't sure how he felt about that. He loved his new home, but he still loved his homeland. He wished Obrion wouldn't invade because a lot of people were going to die on both sides. Politics was a confusing mess that made less sense every day.

He pushed those concerns aside and faced his arms master. "Then it's a good thing you get one more shot at me before you leave."

The swordmaster grunted and switched to Obrioner. "Is you face break."

"No, I need you to punch me in the chest this time." Hamish tapped the center of his new armor. "And don't hold back."

"Maybe you should start out lighter," Verena cautioned.

Why didn't anyone trust him? "No, punch me hard."

"You've opened the strength on those leaves wide, but I don't get the point," Verena said.

"That's because you only think in terms of leveling cities with your stones."

"If you're going to break something. . ."

"Break it big," he finished for her. "This is different. You'll see."

"I'd better go get the Healer then."

"Don't go anywhere." He gestured again. "Come on, hit me."

Bastian still hesitated so Hamish said, "You're losing your touch. Maybe you should get that hair implant I suggested."

That did it.

Bastian's arm swelled with granite power and he slugged Hamish in the chest. The blow threw him from his feet and he sailed five feet before crashing to the ground with a surprisingly musical jingle of the granite scales.

Hamish groaned as Verena helped him sit up. His chest ached where Bastian had punched him, but no ribs felt broken.

"Did you see that?" he exclaimed.

"It was a nice try," Verena said as she hauled him to his feet. Bastian approached, once more normal sized, and actually looking concerned.

"Don't you get it?" Hamish cried. "He punched me with full granite burn, but I only flew a few feet and didn't break anything!"

"I did break something." Bastian pointed out three cracked granite leaves.

Hamish removed the broken pieces and confirmed the second layer was still undamaged. "Wow! They held up pretty well."

"True," Verena said, "but they wouldn't stop a second hit. How does it work?"

"The granite's strong, and overlapping the plates helps disperse the energy."

"How could you possibly know that?"

"I worked in the quarry a lot. One time I helped the carpenters repair the hauling wagon. It used a similar idea in dispersing the weight of those huge granite blocks away from the axle."

"Wow. That's actually a pretty good idea."

Coming from her, that was saying a lot.

"It still needs some work," he said, not letting his guard down. She often punched people right after acting friendly. "But we'll get it. The idea is to diffuse the force of a Rumbler punch."

Bastian shook his head slowly. "It's a good idea, Builder, but there's too much power to stop. You'd need to fight underwater to make enough difference."

Those words blazed through Hamish's mind like a dinner

bell. "That's it! You're brilliant!" He pumped Bastian's hand. "I could kiss that bald head of yours."

He fled before Bastian could hit him again.

"What about the other pieces?" Verena called as she chased him back toward his worktable.

"Later. This is important." He dragged a large wooden crate out from under the table and threw off the lid. Inside, pastries and breadsticks surrounded apples and jerky. Hamish grabbed a handful and stuffed them into his mouth, chewing ferociously.

"What are you doing. . .and where did you get all this?"

"It's for emergencies."

She started asking another question but he waved her to silence. "Didn't your mother ever tell you it's rude to talk when my mouth is full?"

Verena gave him that look so similar to ones Jean used to give him, head cocked to one side, hands on hips. "Then I'd never get to talk."

He shrugged, and Verena stormed out of the room. Good, he needed time to eat, time to think.

Even as he wolfed down a fantastic amount of food, he scribbled like mad on the nearest parchment. Within the hour he had worked out the basic idea, and he wanted to shout. Next time he met Bastian, he'd take the fight to him.

Chapter 6

onnor reached the top of a long set of stone stairs rising from the perpetual gloom of the Carraig's secret, underground levels. He hadn't bothered using a lantern to traverse that spooky expanse of mostly-empty corridors. His quartzite-enhanced vision allowed him to see farther, and his enhanced ears could pick out the muffled footsteps of the few other people nearby.

He had avoided those few travelers of the undercity, despite a powerful curiosity to discover who else knew the secret ways. He had quested through the darkness with enhanced senses, but had caught no hint that Jean was anywhere nearby, and he didn't have time to search more. He needed to make an appearance as Connor.

Shona had assigned Guardians to clear the rubble from the collapsed passage leading up to the Sculpture House. Connor was grateful for direct access, but wished Shona didn't know about it. She was his patron and he was sworn to serve her, but that didn't mean he wanted her knowing everything.

The stair emerged into a little-used storage room in the basement of the Sculpture House. Most of the students didn't even know the room existed, and Ailsa planned to keep it that way.

It wouldn't be hard. Someone had parked a statue of a hideously ugly woman in front of the outer door, blocking most of it. In the shadows of that lower corridor, the menacing statue reminded Connor of Professor Hector in that terrible moment when he'd turned unclaimed and transformed into a rage monster.

Connor had been forced to put down the Hector monster before it could rampage through the school. His hopes of escaping into Granadure with Ilse and her company had died along with it. Witnessing the terrible truth of unclaimed had probably saved the lives of Ilse and her people, as well as Jean, but that truth hung like a shackle around his neck.

He sighed as he brushed past the statue, but then stopped and listened. There were far too many people in the Sculpture House. Footsteps and voices echoed down the stone stairs from above, crisp and clearly military.

Connor tapped quartzite again and applied the liquid warmth to his ears. A flood of sounds rushed in like a flood and he leaned against the ugly statue as he sorted through them. The Sculpture House was full of High Lord Dougal's soldiers.

They were taking the power stones.

Connor rushed down the passage toward the stairs and the vault that held the precious treasure trove of power stones. He only barely remembered to release quartzite and purge its power before reaching the stairs. There a wide-shouldered Boulder in thick plate armor confronted him.

"Who goes there?"

"Ah, I'm Connor," he said, adopting a posture of submission. "I work here for Sculptress Ailsa."

"What are you doing skulking around in the darkness? I was told this level was empty."

Connor nodded toward the steady stream of Boulders stomping past up the stairs, each carrying heavy loads of both unprocessed blocks as well as sacks of powder. "Then what do you call all those guys? Ghosts?"

Like many professional Boulders, the man had tapped granite so long, he'd squeezed his brains into submission. "No."

"Good. I really don't like ghosts. Carry on."

Connor slipped past and trotted up the stairs. The Boulder looked like he wanted to protest, but then he'd have to risk abandoning his post. Connor didn't wait for him to figure it out, starting a mental tally of the stones being taken. At the rate they were going, they'd empty out the entire vault in half an hour.

Usually when he reached the main workroom on the ground floor, Connor liked to pause to breathe deep the comforting scent of broken stone, overlaid with Ailsa's favorite late season flowers. The devastation left after the desperate fight against Hector was mostly gone, the broken columns repaired, and new stones positioned for students to start projects again.

Most of the students were hard at work, but he could barely see them. The maze-like clutter that had choked the room since before Connor arrived with Ailsa had been cleared out with the rest of the rubble, but the room was packed with soldiers, both regulars and Petralists.

The Boulders were working together in a steady rhythm, efficiently pillaging the vault and carrying that precious cargo out the wide outer doors to load into several armored wagons. They looked like reinforced strongboxes on wheels. Four clerks quadruple-checked every load as it passed.

It looked like the other soldiers packing the Sculpture House didn't have anything specific to do, but they didn't look bored. They stood with hands on weapons, scanning everywhere, as if expecting a horde of Grandurians to descend upon them at any minute.

A dozen of them converged on Connor.

"I work for the sculptress," he offered quickly.

One chainmail-clad soldier grabbed him by the scruff of the neck and hauled him toward her office, which was exactly where he had been trying to go before he was intercepted. "We'll see about that."

"What's going on here?" Connor dared ask.

"You're not authorized," the soldier growled.

"What are you going to do with all that stone?"

"You're not authorized," the man growled again.

"Did you have breakfast?"

"What?" The soldier actually paused. No soldier could ignore the idea of food. "Do you have more breakfast?"

"You're not authorized."

Muttering a curse under his breath, the man yanked Connor into the doorway of Ailsa's study. She was sitting behind her huge desk, like a final defensive bulwark against the crowd of officers packing the room. They all wore High Lord Dougal's blue and green uniforms. One hulking man radiated that sense of permanent strength of a Sentry. Another possessed the glowing eyes of a Pathfinder, while a severe woman's blue-tinted blond hair suggested she was a Spitter.

"We caught this one in the workroom," the soldier holding Connor's collar announced. "Says he's authorized."

"He is," Ailsa said, gesturing Connor forward. "This is one of my workers."

The soldier left, but looked disappointed. Connor wasn't sure if it was because he'd wanted an excuse to beat him up, or if he was still wondering about breakfast.

"I hadn't realized we needed such a big round today," Connor said, slipping through the crowd of soldiers to stand in the narrow space beside Ailsa's desk."

"That's none of your concern," the Spitter snapped, her voice as severe as her expression. She wore her hair pulled back against her scalp, and even the braid that hung down past her shoulder was tied so tight, he could almost hear it whimpering. Her uniform was so sharply creased, she could have used her pant legs as weapons.

"Actually, it is." Ailsa looked remarkably calm in the face of the military invasion of her office. "Connor manages the daily rounds and is responsible for maintaining accurate records of our store."

The woman considered him more closely. "You trust such weighty matters to a linn?"

"Connor has never failed."

"And I can count past ten without even taking off my boots most days," Connor added.

"Well, counting will be easier in the future," the woman said.

"You're not taking everything, are you?" Connor asked. He couldn't imagine why Ailsa was allowing them to take any. The daily rounds were a strictly-managed distribution of portions of power stone to students and teachers, but the vault was generally off limits to anyone but Connor or Ailsa.

"There will be sufficient for the remainder of term," the woman said.

"Barely," Ailsa replied, lifting a parchment containing lists of numbers from her desk. "At our current rate of consumption, what you're planning to leave us will be insufficient, especially in granite and slate."

"I suggest rationing then," the woman said. Then she gestured the others out of the room. "If there is no further assistance I can offer, I will leave you."

"Please do." Ailsa gestured the woman out. "My vault cannot handle any more of your assistance."

The woman paused to straighten her uniform. "We all

make sacrifices for the war effort." Then she turned and swept from the room.

Ailsa sighed and dropped the parchment, rubbing at her temples. "It's easy to talk of sacrifice when it's someone else making it."

"What's this all about?" Connor asked, watching the line of Boulders still marching past with their treasure of stone.

"Just what she said. The war."

"Has the war started?" Connor hadn't heard anything official, although the last time he checked the geall boards, betting leaned heavily in favor of open fighting any day.

"Not that I've heard," Ailsa said. "But this company has been sent by High Lord Dougal to requisition extra power stores for delivery to the army on the front."

"We had enough stones in the vault to last the Carraig for years," Connor said. "How much do they need?"

"War consumes all resources at exponential rates. Food, armaments, weapons, power stones, and lives. Both nations will pay dearly for the upcoming conflict."

Connor thought about that as he settled into the single hard-backed chair facing her desk. He'd grown up in Alasdair where they quarried precious Alasdair White granite. The power stone fueled the mighty Boulders, but no one in the village had understood that until armies had descended upon their tiny town.

Even those relatively small clashes had consumed a lot of powdered granite, and managing the powder stores had become a critical issue. Massed armies would need far more. No wonder they were keeping such meticulous records.

"Will we run out?" he asked.

"We can't. Group battles will start soon. I cannot allow the Tir-raon to grind to a halt due to lack of power stones."

"Then what are you going to do?"

"We have no choice. We must institute powder rationing." She glanced at the parchment again. "Probably a twenty percent reduction in the daily portion for students and more like thirty percent for faculty."

Connor grimaced. Complaining about portions was already a favorite pastime. He was going to face a lot of angry Petralists. He had dared hope that his daily rounds would become less dangerous now that Catriona was pacified and Jok owed him a life debt.

The soldiers finished raiding the vault ten minutes later, and Connor watched as they locked the doors on the wagons. Each was pulled by teams of four oxen, and the army that escorted the precious cargo was stronger than the force Rory had first led against Ilse outside of Alasdair.

Connor counted over a hundred regular soldiers, including companies of slingers and even archers. Threescore cavalry with lances set at precise angles and pennants snapping in the breeze made up the vanguard. Two dozen Boulders marched immediately around the wagons, forming the bulk of the Petralist guard, with another dozen Striders ranging around the company. The tertiary affinity officers stood together on a short tower the Sentry raised, which slid across the ground ahead of the lead wagon.

When he and Ailsa returned to her office she said, "We'll deal with the fall-out of the new rations, but oh, Connor, you just couldn't let anyone remove that dome the easy way, could you?"

"It wasn't my fault," he protested. "Someone tried to kill me."

"I heard. Tallan be praised you saved Frazier and his workers."

Connor shuddered at her choice of words. Some days she sounded more Grandurian than Obrioner. He didn't bother to ask how she knew the details. Ailsa was like a spider, with tendrils of influence spreading through the Carraig. Although she rarely left the Sculpture House, she knew more about events throughout the castle complex than almost anyone.

Even with all her resources, she had not predicted what would happen with Hector, had not found a way to help Connor escape the shackles of patronage. Her support was one of the pillars of his life at the Carraig though, and he treasured their daily briefings.

"Any idea who was responsible?" Ailsa asked as she returned to her seat. Connor dropped back into the wooden chair facing her. The previous one had been destroyed, but she'd managed to find another just as uncomfortable.

Connor shrugged. "Everyone swears it wasn't them. Padraigin's still the prime suspect. None of the other Sentries can confirm her claims that she wasn't involved."

"And she's an Althin," Ailsa added. "Many would blame her even had she been on the far side of the castle."

"It's not fair," Connor said. "She's one of the most talented Petralists here. I was the one racing her. I saw how surprised she looked when the ground shook. I don't think it was her."

"It's a good sign that you can draw conclusions that run counter to the prevailing bias," Ailsa told him. "Too few learn to see truths, no matter how clearly they are presented."

"Most of the time, I'm the one people don't trust, so I get it."

Ailsa gave him a reassuring smile. "I'm sure Captain Rory will discover the truth, just as I'm sure you'll be even more vigilant than ever."

"Always." Connor tipped the chair back on two legs, allowing himself to relax. The little office was a safe haven. Everywhere else, he had to stay on his guard, remember which role he was playing, and keep his multiple gealls running. He relished the momentary quiet that had reclaimed the workroom. Most of the students were still outside, watching the departing armored convoy.

"Tell me about the contest," Ailsa urged.

So he did. The process of reporting to Ailsa helped him keep everything straight and see connections he might miss otherwise. Besides, it was a fun story.

"Padraigin will insist on a rematch," Ailsa said when he finished. "She cannot afford any perceived weakness."

"I know," Connor sighed. "I feel bad for her, but I can't let her beat me either. I have to win. My entire village could be enslaved if I don't."

"Not to mention that Shona's other plans depend upon your victory."

Connor usually tried not to think about that. Shona was clearly preparing to marry him. She couldn't afford not to, not when his curse was so important to her. He was trying to generate enthusiasm for that looming event, but wished he had never met Verena. Before that adorably deadly Builder had stormed into his life, Shona's plans for him would have seemed a dream come true.

Ailsa changed topics. "Where is Jean?"

"I was going to ask you. I haven't seen her all week, not since just after she showed me how to use the underground passage."

Ailsa frowned. "I saw her three days ago, but she looked harried and did not stop to speak."

"Shona must be keeping her busy," Connor decided. "Rory must have told Shona about Jean's attempt to run with Ilse."

"She can't dismiss her," Ailsa said. "Jean is too important as leverage to send away, but Shona will want to reduce how much

Jean can do to support you until the final lines are struck and her plan is secure."

Connor frowned. "I'll see what I can do. Shona doesn't have to worry about me anymore."

"And yet, she would be a fool not to," Ailsa said.

"I can't defy her," Connor said, venting his deep frustration. "She's my patron. Unclaimed are real, and I won't risk turning. Plus, she's got Jean, you, and the rest of my family."

"The game is not over," Ailsa said. "Until the final victory is laid at her feet, Shona must worry. Her position is at risk as much as yours."

"I know." He still sometimes forgot that despite her riches and position, Shona was still vulnerable. That's why she needed him so badly.

If only she made it easier for him to want to serve her.

Ailsa rose again and rounded the desk. "Army assignments will occur tomorrow, and you'll finally begin training your own force."

"At least I'll know what I have to deal with." Shona and Lord Nevan had warned him that negotiations were fierce and not trending in his favor. Shona's plan to introduce him as the mystery Dawnus at the last minute had thrown all the carefully-crafted treaties and arrangements between the various high lord representatives into shambles. Months of work had to be redone in a single week. Suffering rolled down hill faster than boiling manure in a hurricane, so they'd make sure he felt their suffering threefold.

"Remember what you have learned," Ailsa said, placing a hand on his shoulder. "Remember all the reasons you wear that mask, and you will find a way."

"The stone's been cast," Connor said. "I'll have to."

Gisela knocked on the door, then pushed it open. She looked completely recovered from the injuries she'd suffered from the Hector monster. "Hello, Connor. I watching you break ice dome today. You are having great skill at breaking things."

"It's part of the legend I'm building."

"Lady Shona has sending summons for you to her palace."

"Thanks."

She made a little curtsy to Ailsa, then retreated. Connor had not found time to speak with Gisela since the nomination day. He had enjoyed their chats about her homeland and the nations of the Arishat League. Plus, she had a secret he needed to learn.

"Be careful," Ailsa urged a final time.

"I'll try to get back to help clean up the mess those soldiers left behind."

"Don't worry, dear," Ailsa said with a mischievous glint in her eye. "I'll have Edan help."

"Just the thing to help him feel like himself again," Connor agreed.

The thin-shouldered sculpting student had fallen into a fit of depression after his beautiful sculpture had been used by Rory as a club in the fight with Hector. He'd only just recently begun working on a new project.

Connor headed for Shona's palace. Even though the air held an autumn chill, he tipped his face up to the sun. The mask he wore as Kilian was quite comfortable, but he preferred walking the castle grounds as Connor, the simple linn.

Well, as long as no one was trying to kill him.

He'd been enjoying the fact that no one wanted to squash him daily, but those happy days were probably about to expire. Rationing Petralist portions would probably be even more dangerous than telling Hamish's family they would no longer get lunches.

Not far from Shona's palace, Connor passed a large group of linn workers walking in the opposite direction. The boisterous group, all wearing Lord Dail's awful mustard and orange uniforms, sported scarves or pins with Ivor's colors. They were loudly arguing about the day's contest, about the collapse of the mighty dome, and about how they felt Ivor would turn the tide on the hated Kilian.

"They are enthusiastic, aren't they?"

The group stopped nearby, but continued their arguments. The man who had spoken was dressed like them, but his face was covered by a heavy scarf. When he removed it, Connor couldn't believe he hadn't recognized him sooner.

Ivor.

Chapter 7

his is the second time I've caught you daydreaming," Ivor said. "Not a good habit, especially not for a commoner who walks in circles above his station."

"You have a knack for finding me when I'm distracted."

Connor enjoyed his chats with Ivor. He could be himself with the powerful champion when he was just Connor, and he found Ivor fascinating. His mastery of his tertiary affinities was well documented, and he was the favorite to ultimately lead his army to victory in the Tir-raon. That should have made Connor dislike him, but Ivor was just too interesting.

Ivor was a Guardian, his situation mirroring Connor's in many ways. Winning would secure his future in a high lord family, guarantee power and prestige and station. He was cunning and devious, and he was relentless in discovering weaknesses of his opponents that he could exploit. Connor had learned much from him in the recent group competitions, both as a friend and as a foe.

It interested him to see how Ivor handled the pressures he faced, and he wished they didn't ultimately have to stand as opponents in a contest where only one of them could win.

He expected Ivor to move away from the nearby workers, or at least motion them to continue on, but he did not. And when he spoke, he stood close and pitched his voice low.

"Tell me about the lady," Ivor said, nodding toward Shona's nearby palace.

Ivor seemed to want to speak in roundabout terms, so Connor obliged. "The lady is unchanged. Still enjoying her position at the center of everything."

"Indeed," Ivor smiled. "Any new developments?"

"None that I've seen."

"Keep me posted."

It was unlike Ivor to accept a lack of progress, especially since they hadn't spoken for several days.

"I'll talk to you then," Connor said, moving to leave.

Ivor grabbed his arm. "Did you watch the contest on the field today?"

"Didn't we all?"

Playing both the roles of Connor and Kilian was sometimes like trying to eat and fire his bow at the same time. Difficult, requiring focus and proper timing. Making the daily rounds was particularly tricky. As Connor he must deliver the portions of power stone to all the students and teachers to fuel their Petralist gifts. Kilian was a champion contender, so he received his portions directly from his patron and Connor hadn't needed to figure out how to deliver rounds to himself. He still needed to slip away, change into his Kilian persona, and return without arousing suspicion. He had felt pretty sure no one had noticed.

"I didn't see you," Ivor said. "Usually you like to be in the thick of everything."

"The Rhidorroch was my favorite spot. Out on the field seems too exposed."

Ivor smiled. "It's less structured. More risk, but far more opportunity."

"I heard Kilian found opportunity today."

Ivor's smile actually widened. "He did. That man's a clever son of a pedra. He's daring, but rash."

"He won, didn't he?"

"Aye, he won. But to take such a risk was foolish."

"Foolish if he'd lost," Connor countered.

"Let's discuss this further." Ivor leaned closer. "And I'd prefer to hold that chat with our general friend present."

He might not have used Kilian's name, but his meaning was clear.

"I'll ask him to join us," Connor offered. It was a foolish risk to agree to meet with the clever Ivor in private, but hadn't he just defended foolishness? He liked Ivor, wanted to speak with him openly as Kilian, but worried Ivor would see through the disguise. Could he risk it?

Could he not?

"Good," Ivor said. "Watch yourself, my friend. The information you hold could easily be used against you."

"What information?" Connor asked cautiously.

Ivor leaned closer and spoke so softly, Connor barely heard over the arguing workers. "You know Kilian's identity. Guard that secret with the greatest care."

Ivor had no idea.

"I'm careful." And sometimes more than a little schizophrenic.

Ivor looked around. "You're a quick study. You picked up on what I'm doing here. Have you thought of why?"

Why shield their conversation in a crowd of loud workers while in disguise, speaking so low that Connor could barely hear?

"You're careful."

"We all have to be. Assignments are tomorrow, and everyone is hunting for any advantage by any means. Think about it."

Ivor turned away, and the still-arguing crowd resumed their raucous journey toward the distant Carraig township at the southern sweep of the great outer wall.

Connor continued toward Shona's palace, considering the strange conversation. Ivor hadn't looked worried, just cautious. He never did anything without good reason.

Of course he had a reason. Understanding struck like a poke from a wet finger, always startling and rather unpleasant.

Pathfinders.

Even a beginner Pathfinder could overhear conversations from a great distance. Connor had watched a lesson where the Pathfinder students had been challenged to listen for Strider footsteps out on the plain while they were standing in the center of the Carraig. Had a Pathfinder been focusing, they could have picked out even Ivor's whispers. Then again, a Pathfinder just sweeping the castle, letting conversations filter through their mind, trying to grasp hold of interesting tidbits, would most likely have missed it.

Ivor had been careful to speak in general terms for the most part. Their words would have blended well with the raucous arguments about the generals and events of the day. Only a Pathfinder specifically focused on them would have paid attention, but would have learned little.

Then he remembered Ivor's odd request of Jok a couple weeks prior. He'd requested the services of one of Lord Dail's Pathfinders. Had Ivor been preparing to deal with eavesdropping back then? Or had he been hoping to use the Pathfinder to spy on the competition?

Connor was going to have to be more careful. He doubted anyone was targeting him, but he couldn't risk making a faulty assumption. As Kilian, he was on guard all the time. So many people were trying to spy on him that Tomas and Cameron had started a sign-up schedule to manage the flow of people lurking around his private suite. No doubt it infuriated the watchers that he slipped away so often. If he played that hand too often, someone would think to search the undercity. Few traveled those dim corridors, but more must know about their existence.

Shona would be watched as well. How did Lord Nevan shield his palace? There must be a way.

As he climbed the steps to the colonnaded entrance, he ran through his mind all the things he needed to speak with her about. His thoughts scattered when the aged butler led him into the spacious second-floor study where they usually met. Shona was seated on a couch, speaking with a tawny-haired woman wearing High Lord Dougal's colors.

Beside the women stood Captain Aonghus, the Firetongue from General Carbrey's army. Aonghus wouldn't know he'd survived the flood. Would he greet Connor as a friend, or try to kill him?

Chapter 8

onnor, come in." Shona gestured him closer, but did not rise to greet him as she usually did.

Captain Aonghus laughed, and Connor was relieved to not see any fire glinting in the red-haired man's eyes. He'd introduced Connor to marble and they'd fought the Grandurians together in the battles of Alasdair, but he'd always made Connor nervous. The man embraced the insanity of marble with far too much enthusiasm, and had always seemed rather unhinged.

Aonghus clapped Connor on the shoulder. "So you did survive, eh boy?"

"Good to see you, Captain." He was relieved that Aonghus didn't appear hostile. Rory and his company had accepted Connor again with remarkably little fuss. When Connor blew the mountain, some of General Carbrey's army had been swept away, and some of them had surely died. He still felt guilty about that, but no other course had been open to him.

"You're the one who blew that mountain, aren't you?" Aonghus asked. "Where'd you get the marble for it?"

"From the Grandurians."

That was mostly true. Connor preferred to say as little as possible about the specifics of what he'd done in the icy depths of that loch. He hadn't trusted Shona with the secret of diorite, and he'd never entrust it to Aonghus. The Firetongue would no doubt try to use the dangerous stone too. Although Connor doubted Aonghus could establish another affinity, he couldn't take the risk.

Shona stood, as did the tawny-haired woman beside her. "Connor, I'm pleased to introduce Spit-nail Camonica."

That was the most ridiculous title he'd ever heard, but the woman's presence rivaled Shona's for sheer gracefulness. She was tall and willowy, with firm brown eyes in a smooth, pretty face, and she rose with the deadly grace of a Blade. Her thick hair hung past her shoulder blades in slightly curling waves that she hadn't bothered to bind in any way. She looked to be in her late twenties and when she spoke, her voice sounded somehow like the rippling of gentle waters.

"Hello, Connor. I've heard much about you."

He bowed like Shona had taught him. "Pleased to meet you, Camonica."

She frowned. "You will use my title in formal situations such as this, boy."

Boy, was she going to regret calling him that.

"I'm sorry. I didn't know that spitting nails was a title."

Her expression darkened, but Captain Aonghus chortled. "She'll be spitting mad if you don't shut up."

Shona interceded for him. "I forgot you didn't know the titles for the chain of command, Connor. Some of the high officers in the army hold the title of chornail." She spoke the word as if the 'ch' was petitioning for transition into a 'k', but hadn't quite succeeded.

Connor managed not to grimace. The name sounded like the hideous soups that foul-tempered Cinaed used to try to force on him and his friends in Alasdair.

"But since they must hold tertiary affinities, their titles are adjusted to include reference to their affinity stone."

"Hence I hold the title of spit-nail," Camonica added with abundant formality, as if saying it with such pomp made it sound less stupid. "I expect you will remember that in the future."

"Of course." Whoever invented that title had scored the ultimate joke, getting a fresh laugh every time it was used.

"They just arrived in the Carraig," Shona explained.

"With that armored caravan?" Connor guessed.

"Aye," Aonghus said.

"I don't like leaving them so lightly guarded," Camonica grimaced.

"They'll be fine," Aonghus reassured her.

Connor wondered if Camonica had actually looked at that army of Petralists and support troops she'd traveled with.

"If anything happens to that shipment, it could have dire consequences for the war effort," Camonica said.

"They'll be fine," Shona echoed Aonghus.

"Pray they are," Camonica warned. "Any mishap would reflect poorly upon your father and diminish his influence at a critical time."

"No one's going to mess with that caravan," Connor offered. "Unless Granadure invaded with an entire army."

"Don't underestimate them," Camonica warned. "They must be given no quarter and no room to escape this time."

"That shipment will make it to the front," Aonghus said, looking disgusted.

"Which front?" Connor asked.

"What do you mean?" Camonica asked.

"High Lord Dougal's armies are massing against the Grandurians, but what about the Arishat League armies?"

"How do you know about them?" Shona looked shocked.

Connor shrugged. It was a risk to reveal that he knew anything, but the risk was worth it. He needed to understand what was going on in the world. Seeing all that power stone carted away had driven home just how close the fighting loomed over the nation. A lot of people would die once battle was joined, and he felt an urgent need to know.

"I've been at the Carraig for months and everyone's talking about the war. Students are already betting on which commands they'll be assigned at the end of term."

The betting was fierce on those, but Connor had resisted the urge to participate. He knew nothing about how commissions were handled, so any win would be little more than blind luck.

"Commissions," Camonica muttered. "Spoiled, untrained, useless children. My blind uncle could fight better than most of them."

He really wanted to know about that uncle. But he only said, "I'd have to live under a rock to not hear anything about the Arishat League."

"How much do you know?" Aonghus asked.

"This discussion is none of his concern," Camonica said, but Aonghus shook his head.

"You're wrong. The boy's been given command. He needs to know the stakes or he'll be at a disadvantage."

"I know a little," Connor admitted. "The Arishat League doesn't seem to want either Granadure or Obrion to gain advantage, and they're prepared to attack either side to prevent that from happening."

"That's a good summary," Shona said. "It's good to see you've got good ears in addition to that good tongue of yours."

"Don't worry about the Arishat yet," Aonghus said. "They won't commit any time soon. What do you know of their military?"

"Not much."

"Not much to worry about," Aonghus said. "They've got few Petralists, so they don't really pose much of a threat."

"Who's giving the boy a disadvantage now?" Camonica asked. "Of course they still pose a threat." She began counting off the nations on her fingers.

"Althins are mostly diplomats, but they possess a mighty navy and could pull Tabnit into the fighting from across the Sea of Olcan."

"They see themselves as the ultimate leaders," Aonghus agreed. "They'll be hoping the war will weaken both Obrion and Granadure enough for the league to pull us in to join the herd."

"Tabnit," Camonica continued. "They're another naval power, but they command vast land holdings in the south, but little is known of them. Rumors suggest they can field a diverse army, but logistics of transportation across the sea are daunting."

"Ravinder," she continued.

"Bunch of helpless farmers," Aonghus muttered.

"They have little in the way of an army," Camonica agreed. "But their food supplies might prove critical."

"If the Arishat moves, we'll just sweep through Ravinder and take it all," Aonghus said with a dismissive wave of his hand. "Fields this time of year burn really well."

"The last time anyone tried invading, the Mhortair assassinated the entire leadership corps," Camonica warned. "If that treaty is still in place, they are not to be trifled with lightly."

"Who are the Mhortair?" Connor asked.

"A topic for another day," Shona said. "We're already covering a lot of ground."

Camonica continued with another raised finger. "Sehrazad. They are fierce raiders, but dislike large pitched battles."

"Striders'll do for them," Aonghus said. "And if the war runs into next summer, the sands in that south desert offer lots of heat to work with."

"Varvakis will be the greatest direct threat," Camonica finished, extending her thumb. "They are hardy warriors, and their smiths produce the best steel on the continent."

"But how can they think to fight us?" Connor asked. "You said yourself they don't have many Petralists."

"They don't," Camonica agreed. "That's their great weakness, but they've been working on that problem ever since the end of the Tallan Wars. Mark my words, they've got surprises in store and a lot of Petralists will die before they're beaten back into submission and again swear fealty to Obrion."

That last comment was the key to Camonica's thinking, like many in Obrion. It seemed the entire world had gone mad. Everyone was so intent on going to war, of conquest that no one even talked about the possibility of peace, of reconciliation, or treaties.

"Thank you for the information, Spit-nail Camonica," he said after a moment.

"During our training sessions and informal communication, you may use my given name," she added, looking like granting him such liberty was a great boon.

"Training sessions?"

Aonghus grinned. "Why do you think we're here, boy? We're your trainers." He spread his hands wide. "We're going to teach you to master your tertiary powers!"

"I can't wait," Connor said, wondering if they'd burn down the entire central keep, or only char his suite.

"You didn't think I was going to leave you without teachers, did you?" Shona asked, looking pleased with herself. "You can't train with the regular classes, and Rory has neither a Firetongue nor a Spitter in his company."

"You've chosen the right stones, boy," Aonghus laughed. "Once I teach you how to get a real burn going, not even that blockhead Redmund and his vaunted earth powers will stand a chance."

Camonica sniffed. "You're all hot air, Aonghus. I wager soapstone will be the critical element."

Before they could launch into what looked like a favorite argument, Shona interrupted. "The good news is he can leverage both." She added to Connor. "You will train with both Aonghus and Camonica daily in your private training facility."

"We're starting late," Camonica said. "Most Tir-raon champions have years to master the skills we'll have to impart to you in a matter of weeks."

"We'll have to cut some corners," Aonghus agreed, a wild look in his eye.

More like he planned to incinerate those corners.

So they'd help him succeed as the masked Dawnus, Kilian, and Aonghus knew the truth about the full extent of Connor's curse, but had they shared that with Camonica?

"Army nominations are tomorrow," Shona said, motioning them all to sit. She pulled Connor onto one of the couches beside her, while the others took nearby chairs. "We have a lot to discuss."

"Do you know who I'll get?" Connor asked.

She shook her head. "The final details are a closely guarded secret. Lord Nevan and the others aren't even allowed to leave the negotiation hall until the assembly. And they've got all the customary wards in place against eavesdropping."

"What are those?" Connor asked, thinking back to his recent discussion with Ivor.

"You planning to break in?" Aonghus looked like he'd volunteer to help.

"I don't think that would help at this point," Shona said.

"I've been thinking. People are already spying on me as Kilian, but they might also be listening in on you here, or watching elsewhere. I'd like to know how to counter Pathfinders hearing everything we say."

Aonghus glowered at Connor. "I can't believe you chose that name! Kilian and I have unfinished business."

"Get in line," Camonica hissed. She'd produced a slender dagger and was gripping it so tight her fingers looked white against the handle.

No one appreciated how perfect that name was. Connor had forgotten Captain Aonghus had battled Kilian in the streets of Alasdair. The Grandurian had been the first Dawnus Connor had met, and the fighting hadn't gone well for Aonghus. He wanted to ask Camonica why she hated Kilian so much, but didn't dare. She looked ready to stab anyone who mentioned the name again.

"There are counter measures available," Shona said. "I could send details along with Jean, but I haven't seen her in a week."

"You haven't?" That surprised Connor.

"Don't play dumb, Connor. It weakens the trust we're rebuilding." Shona looked irritated. "She may be your friend, but she's also my handmaid. I know she's helping you adjust to your new position, and I suspect she's worried about how angry I'll be when I see her again, but she's just going to make things worse."

So Shona did know about Jean's attempted flight, but where was Jean?

"Ah, I'll send her over when I see her again."

Connor struggled to pay attention as his new teachers discussed their planned training schedule. He was consumed by worry for Jean. Was she all right? Had Jok cornered her?

Jok owed him, and he'd thought that would be enough to ensure Jok treated Jean with the proper respect. But Jok had been eager to get his hands on Jean since the first day he saw her. If he hurt her, Connor would kill him.

"Then it's settled," Shona said with a smile. "We'll start this afternoon."

Captain Aonghus and Spit-nail Camonica rose and bid farewell. Connor moved to follow them out of the room, but Shona pulled him back.

"I'm not through with you yet."

Connor sank back onto the couch, trying to look at ease, but racking his brain in vain to think what he might have done. The last week had been extremely busy, and he'd avoided Shona as much as he could. He had needed the time to reconcile himself with the reality of his life and the inescapable prison she held him in. She was his patron, the only shield against the horror of turning unclaimed.

He owed her everything. He was grateful. Really. But he hated not having a choice.

Shona sank onto the couch beside him and surprised him by leaning against his chest, her face nuzzled close to his neck. Her warm proximity unsettled him like always. Shona was beautiful, strongly gifted in granite, and the daughter of one of the most powerful men in Obrion. She was also devious and ambitious.

If showering him with affection was necessary, she would do so without hesitation, but he'd always wonder how much of it was genuine.

"Oh, Connor," she sighed, her breath warm on his neck. "We don't get enough time together. I hate it."

"Life's pretty busy," he agreed, forced to awkwardly hold her as she leaned against him. If he could ever trust anything she said, he could learn to enjoy holding her like that.

Until he thought of Verena.

Shona lifted her head to look him in the eye. "The situation got crazy again, Connor. It seems nothing is ever easy for us, and we're constantly getting pulled apart."

When he didn't speak, she stroked his cheek, her finger cool on his skin. Her faint, rose-scented perfume tickled his nose. "Sometimes all we have to deal with can seem confusing, but this is real, Connor. Together we can win, we can accomplish everything."

"I'll win the Tir-raon for you, my lady," he promised. She couldn't still worry he'd try to run again.

"I know," she murmured. "That's not what I'm talking about." She placed a hand over his heart. "Trust is hard to build, my Connor, and we've had more than our share of trials. We need to rebuild it, to know that we can rely on each other, no matter what happens."

"I'm your Guardian. You can trust that."

And he'd trust her to act without hesitation to punish him and everyone he loved if he failed her. She'd already threatened to enslave his entire village if he didn't perform to her satisfaction. Talk about a stake through the heart of that whole trust speech.

Shona leaned closer, her hazel eyes looking deep into his. Her voice fell to a throaty whisper. "I love hearing you say that. We're meant to be partners in this, the great adventure of our lives. You'll win. I have no doubts."

"And you must know," she added intensely. "I'll be there for you. Trust in the purity of my purpose and the rightness of our cause, Connor. Trust in me."

He nodded, but thought that was as likely as Shona starting to suck on rocks like Hamish.

She smiled that radiant smile that still tugged at his heart strings despite everything he knew about her. And she leaned closer and pressed her full lips to his. Shona took her time with the kiss, starting gentle, then pressing harder, letting him feel her passion.

The first time he had kissed Shona, he'd been overwhelmed that such a beautiful, powerful woman would show him such attention. She was a very good kisser, and he'd have to be max-tapping granite to not be affected by it, or by the feel of her body pressed against his.

So he kissed her back, tried to feel as awestruck as he had before he knew her so well. She must have felt some hesitation though, because she withdrew and sighed again.

She sat up and took his hand in hers. "Oh, Connor. We'll figure things out. I promise we'll find a way to make this work."

He didn't see how, but part of him hoped she was right. He had to learn to embrace this life she was thrusting upon him, or he'd never bear it.

"Now," she said, her tone again crisp. "You have work to do. Train hard, Connor."

"Thank you for getting me some teachers." He desperately needed to learn how to master his tertiary affinities if he wanted any chance of winning.

"We look after each other," she said, her gaze intent, as if trying to force him to accept that. She rose. "Send Jean to me."

Maybe he should tell her about Jean's absence, but he didn't dare. What if Jean was meeting with Ilse? He doubted it, but he couldn't trust Shona, couldn't draw upon her resources to help search for Jean until he had exhausted other avenues.

On his way back, a Strider wearing a full-face helmet skidded to a halt beside him on the path and handed him a rolled parchment.

"You're insane, you know that?" Connor asked Dietmar, recognizing Ilse's Wingrunner despite the disguise.

Dietmar threw a cocky salute. "They haven't caught me yet."

He leaped away before Connor could reply. Again Ilse showed incredible boldness sending the man into the Carraig during the daytime. Connor moved to a concealed corner behind a nearby barn before unrolling the parchment. Part of him was relieved to know Ilse was still in the area and that Dietmar had come with a note instead of a dagger. As usual, the message was short.

We need to talk. Tonight at the north sally port.
Come alone this time.

Chapter 9

The evening meeting with Ilse would require careful planning, but Connor couldn't worry about it yet. He needed to find Jean.

In the weeks leading up to nomination day, he'd often not seen Jean for days at a time, but during those times, Ailsa or Shona had been in regular contact with her. This time, no one knew where she was. Why had Jean looked worried the last time Ailsa saw her? She had managed the difficult days leading up to their failed attempt to escape with Ilse with calm composure, so what had rattled her?

As he rushed back to the Sculpture House, worries spawned in Connor's mind like consumed corn cobs around Hamish' plate during the Sogail feast. He stuck his head into Ailsa's office where she was reading a scroll.

"You haven't seen Jean since I left earlier?"

"No, why?"

"Contact me if she shows up. I'm going to search for her."

Ailsa rose, looking worried. "I thought she was with Shona."

"Shona thought she was with one of us."

"So no one knows where she's been?"

"Apparently not. I'm heading for the inner library."

"Good idea," Ailsa said. "I will begin inquiries through other channels."

"Thanks." Connor rushed for the stairs to the lower level while Ailsa called for Gisela, her voice crisp.

Ailsa's concern reinforced Connor's, and he tapped basalt when he reached the long stair, sprinting at a dead run down into the undercity. There, he forced himself to slow to apply quartzite to his ears.

The sparsely traveled undercity offered far fewer sounds for his enhanced ears to snatch up. Occasional footsteps sounded loud in the quiet realm, otherwise broken only by the creaking of doors, spitting of lonely torches, or the soft breath of cool air creeping toward the surface. Connor focused on each set of footsteps in turn, but none of them matched Jean's graceful tread.

The grid-like pattern of the corridors was still confusing to him, so he also applied quartzite to his nose. The scent of old stone wafted through the dim passages, layered with creeping mold, patches of stale water, and the dusty smell of tired doors, closed perhaps for years. As he trotted along, he caught whiffs of rotting furniture and wooden boxes cankered with age.

Behind all that, he identified the dry scent of old leather, ink, and parchment. He followed those scents like a bloodhound down one dark passage after another. Most were square tunnels boring through the undercity's heart, utilitarian and efficient, but still somehow mysterious. It took only a few minutes to track the scents to the inner library.

With eager haste, Connor shoved open the door and rushed inside. The library was empty, and had that lonely feel of a room long abandoned. The tables were bare, the fireplaces cold, and the overstuffed chairs seemed to beg him to pause for a visit.

Connor wasn't sure what to do, so he paced the library, looking into every corner, hoping Jean might be curled up and napping in one of the hidden nooks. He'd been foolish to search there. Jean loved to read, but not even she could ignore the passage of days, lost in a fascinating tome.

That meant he had to face the uglier possibilities. Had Jok finally tracked her down? He shuddered to consider it, but couldn't block the images that formed in his mind. The powerful and proud Jok could have been driven to recklessness by his obsession with her. Jean would have fought back, flinging foul herbs into his face, making a desperate bid for freedom.

She had not escaped, or they would have seen her. What might Jok had done? Had he hurt her or, driven to fury by her resistance, struck her with granite-enhanced strength? He owed Connor a life debt, but that would only mean he'd attempt to conceal the crime.

The more Connor thought about it, the more he worked himself into a vengeful rage. He needed to hunt down Jok and beat a confession out of him.

On the verge of storming out of the inner library, Connor's eyes fell on a leather notebook lying atop one of the shelves, filled with loose sheaves of paper. He flipped it open and recognized Jean's tidy script. The pages were covered with notes from her weeks of research.

She had treated that notebook like a treasure. Would she have left it behind?

Connor scanned the pages and noticed a handwritten map. That's how Jean knew the undercity so well. She'd explored it and, with her usual thoroughness, had taken the time to map out her findings.

The undercity stretched farther than Connor had realized. He noted passages with annotations about where they terminated at various buildings throughout the greater Carraig complex, including the one that led to his Kilian suite. Another led to a residence hall for teachers. Other notes described stairs descending into the darkness of even lower levels, but he saw nothing of any exploration she might have made down there.

A long passage that extended alone to the east drew his gaze. Jean had noted that it appeared to run under the open plain, and had mentioned a great longing to explore that area if they only had time before leaving with Ilse.

They hadn't left. Had she decided to venture into that unknown area under the plain? Had she gotten lost?

Possible disasters sprang to mind faster than Verena could have punched him in the face. What if Jean had dropped her lantern? Or fallen and injured herself?

If anything like that had happened, she might be stranded there in the darkness. The thought horrified him. She would never have found her way back, lost and alone out there, starving or dying of thirst. He and the students had crisscrossed those plains many times in recent days. He shivered to think of Jean terrified and dying alone in the darkness underground while they passed so close by overhead.

As bad as that might be, it was still better than the Jok alternative. So Connor snatched up the map and bolted from the inner library. This time he didn't bother with stealth. If Jean was hurt, she needed to know he was coming, needed to see the welcome relief of light.

So he tapped marble and ringed his shoulders with flames. As he ran, he pulsed jets of flame around himself, lighting long stretches of square, stone corridors, their stones taking on a crimson hue. He tried tapping quartzite at the same time, but the balancing act proved so tricky he nearly collided with a wall as he ran with basalt speed around a tight corner.

He'd been practicing with water and fire together, but hadn't found much time to try including the other tertiary stones. He needed to find time. Earth and air might not be part of his Dawnus arsenal, but when he needed them, he could not afford any hesitation.

Connor didn't need quartzite to find the long passage leading out into the plain, so he fracked and tore along the desolate stretch, with fire blazing in front of him to light the way.

He easily imagined Jean dirty and hungry, perhaps injured, but teary-eyed with relief that someone had finally come. Instead, he discovered one more of the unending mysteries of the Carraig.

The passage terminated in a long, low cave, covered with odd piles of rubble, interspersed with flat, clear sections. He slowed to stare, tapping more marble and extending wisps of fire like floating lanterns in every direction. It took him a moment to understand what he was looking at, and only when he picked out irregular walls rising from the rubble did the scene click into place.

He was looking at a sunken city concealed under the plain. The rubble had been buildings, the flatter areas the streets, once paved, now cracked and buckled. With a growing sense of wonder, Connor explored deeper into the ruin.

Thicker walls ringed the original open space, unbroken walls that thrust up into the low-hanging ceiling, which was paved in stone. He selected one promising street and discovered block after block of ruins in various states of disrepair. Some buildings had collapsed entirely, with little more than irregular mounds remaining. He sifted through one, letting the grainy sand of broken stones slip through his fingers.

The air was thick and musty, as if any currents that reached the ancient city got stuck and never found their way out. There was not as much dust as he would have expected, and when he sniffed with quartzite, he found little else. The only wood remaining had mostly rotted away, and the stones smelled exhausted, as if holding on to their ancient secrets through sheer stubbornness. There was water down there, but he smelled no plants, no living things.

The city was dead, a tomb dating back to an unknown age. Why had it been concealed like that? The rolling plain that had always seemed such an odd part of the outer Carraig was nothing but a thin burial shroud.

How had it been formed? How did Petralists fashion the long walls, heavy columns, and ceiling to hold fast for so long? If Jean had stumbled into there and gotten into trouble, she could wander for years without finding her way out.

Connor drew deeper from marble until it seared his mouth and the intense heat nearly gagged him. Its deadly thrill made him grin, with flames skipping across his teeth. Fire always triggered wild thoughts of inferno, but there was nothing left to burn in that broken relic. Instead, he sent streamers of fire snaking along the darkened roof of packed earth and long, stone pavers.

By the light of that living fire, he explored deeper, shouting Jean's name with a quartzite-enhanced voice. It felt like the ruin grew older, the deeper he traveled, but many of the buildings were in better repair. Fewer were blasted to complete ruin, and he discovered vast caverns, paved streets, and elegant palaces. In places, the ceiling of the plain barely allowed him to stand upright, while at other times it reared more than twenty feet. Even the lake above was part of the deception. Thick walls of jade crystal held the waters in place. He discovered several other small lochs lurking dark and still in the ruins.

Despite worry for Jean driving him on, Connor slowed to drink in the silent beauty of the secret landscape. Creeping fungus spread across some of the ruined walls like a living stain that reflected the light of his fires with dazzling colors.

So he tried burning some of it.

It ignited like it was soaked in oil, and it was easier to manage that burn than generate his own flames.

He sensed that he could spend weeks exploring the underground wonder, but he lacked time. So he allowed himself to penetrate only eight long blocks, until all of the surrounding buildings were mostly intact. At every intersection, he paused to shout Jean's name, then search the area with quartzite senses. Each time, he found no sign of life, no sign that life had passed by in living memory.

Selecting one building at random, he climbed a crumbling stair and entered a long cavern that was mostly clear of rubble. It might have once been a great hall or cathedral. The roof was gone, as were most of the walls. The skeletal remains of the gigantic stone ribs that had held up the huge structure were all that remained, stabbing into the high ceiling.

Connor allowed the fires to spread across the cathedral, and tethered flames in a massive, cracked fountain that still somewhat resembled a stone tree with eighteen spreading branches. He set fires pulsing along its length, lighting the room with flickering shadows, and wondered what the hall might have looked like when it was whole.

His mouth burned from the prolonged use of marble, and he was tempted to return to one of those hidden lakes and dunk his face in. The first time he'd used marble, he hadn't known how to extinguish it, and he'd burned down much of Lord Gavin's manor house. He'd had to dive into Loch Sholto to put the flames out.

The brightly colored burning fungus cast a multitude of shifting colored lights across the ruined hall, but shadows fought for lordship of the corners, overlaying the ancient structure with soft mystery.

He called for Jean again, his voice booming so loud it rattled loose stones and reverberated from the earthen ceiling. If anyone was standing above, they might have heard a distant echo, like a voice calling from the grave.

The thought made him strangely lonely, and he longed for Verena by his side, snuggled under his arm.

As the echoes of his call faded, he applied quartzite to his ears and listened, straining for any sign that Jean might have passed nearby. He listened so hard, he could have heard her heartbeat in the unending silence.

He heard nothing from Jean, but he did hear a single, heavy footstep right behind him.

Chapter 10

erena didn't bother to look up from her project when she heard the door to her workroom open.

"Hamish, get out," she called. "I'm testing something so I don't have time to come see your new suit, and I don't have any sweetbreads you can borrow."

Instead of Hamish, she was startled to hear Kilian speak.

"It's good to see you hard at work, and I really wish you did have some sweetbreads."

Verena rushed to the lanky Water Moccasin and gave him a fierce hug. He looked tired, his face lined, his hair unkempt. He still managed a warm smile, his blue eyes twinkling as bright as ever.

"I actually do have some sweetbreads," she admitted, opening a drawer in a cluttered desk nearby. "I just can't let Hamish know where I keep them."

Kilian held up a mesh bag he had concealed behind his back. Verena squealed with delight and eagerly accepted the five ripe peaches. "Don't tell Hamish about these."

"They're our little secret," Kilian assured her as he selected a long breadstick from her secret stash and took a huge bite.

"How are things at the front?" she asked.

"Worsening." Kilian frowned while he chewed. "But no major skirmishes so far."

"Production is accelerating," she assured him. "We've got stacks of speedslings, but the hardened granite projectiles take more time, and we need so many."

"How many can we have in a week?"

"We've had some issues with supply lines," she admitted. "We're competing with the Rumblers, but they take priority. The quarries are promising increased production, but it'll take a few weeks to get everything straightened out. Dierk is overseeing the manufacturing teams, and we've got every Builder working on filling orders."

"By next week, we could field threescore speedslings. They hold five thousand projectiles each. We're calling those Hornets. That means we need three hundred thousand hornets for a single arming. They can burn through an entire drum in about a minute. Our goal is to provide enough hornets for three full rearmings, so we've set the target for a million projectiles."

Kilian grimaced. "The speedslings worked extremely well in Alasdair, but what a colossal amount of power stone."

"Those were early prototypes. The new models are even deadlier."

She shivered at the memory of the front lines of Carbrey's army disintegrating under the destructive rain of the speedslings. The little projectiles had cut through shields and armor as easily as they had flesh and bone. They just flew so fast. Even the Boulders had struggled to withstand the onslaught.

"When we deploy them," Kilian said. "Make sure there are teams ready to comb the battlefield afterward to recover as many as possible."

"Already planning on that."

"And windriders?"

"Those are actually pretty easy to produce. We've got half a dozen already assigned to Wolfram's army, flying supplies and scouting parties all along the border."

The recently-invented flying wagons had played a critical role in the battles of Alasdair, and they held a special place in Verena's heart. "The truth is, we can build more than we have Builders to fly them. I'm working on a design that might allow non-Builders to operate the controls."

"How is that possible?"

"At the moment, it's only plausible," she admitted. "But I think I'm on to something. We'll still need some Builders to oversee the squadron and initiate the power to each windrider, but if I can get it to work, that will remove the personnel constraint."

"Keep working on it," Kilian urged. "That might prove a critical breakthrough."

"How many soldiers do you expect we'll need to transport?"

Kilian shrugged. "When open warfare erupts, the flexibility of fielding an entire army just about anywhere could be a deciding factor."

They discussed some of the other inventions for a few minutes. All the healthbeds had been shipped to the front already, deployed to assist the Healers in treating wounded. Wallstones were simple to prepare, and Builder support squads were stationed at strategic locations, along with catapult teams. They could throw soapstone to flood areas and disrupt Sentries, or deploy additional projectiles that were being developed in other parts of the Builder compound, including some that burst into clouds of weakening powder to disable Boulder companies.

The newest inventions were pushing the limits, and it scared Verena sometimes to think of the potential for death and destruction. She didn't want to go to war, hated the need to focus so much of her creative efforts on killing.

What choice did she have? If she didn't find ways to stop the Obrioner advance, how many of her countrymen would die when she could have saved them? She always explored less lethal ways to deploy her stones, but those solutions were tricky, and she needed to be present on the battlefield to look for opportunities to deploy them.

"No sign of any more unclaimed," Kilian said before she could ask.

"Thank the Tallan," she whispered. She still awoke sometimes in the night, shaking with fear from the memory of those raging monsters that had nearly killed them in a narrow gulch in the border mountains. Kilian had somehow destroyed them, but he had never explained how he'd managed it. She was biding her time for the right moment to pry into the secret.

Kilian approached her worktable. "What's this?"

The table stood in the center of the large workroom. Against the distant back wall, she'd set up a continuous waterfall feature with a piece of activated soapstone. On the table, she had created a v-shaped open trench of wood, aimed toward that waterfall. Sitting in the trench was a piece of marble she'd carved down to a rough cone.

"I'm trying to figure out how to get accurate burning projectiles."

Verena touched the marble and opened the release rate wide on the rear side. Fire erupted from the back of the little cone and thrust it down the length of the plank. It shot off the end, aiming for the waterfall. It made it almost halfway before veering off course and crashing into the smooth, stone floor. It ricocheted away, completely missed the waterfall, and of course skittered right under a low, wooden cabinet.

Verena sighed and gestured at the now-smoking cabinet. "See?"

Chuckling, Kilian made a grasping gesture with one hand. Her waterfall leaped across the room, snaked under the cabinet, and withdrew the still-burning marble with a great deal of angry hissing steam. Verena grabbed the marble and snapped closed the release rate, shuttering its power and flames.

"Thanks. I still can't get a reliable flight path."

"Why use marble anyway?" Kilian asked. "Quartzite provides as much thrust and it's not so destructive."

"I want it to be destructive."

She led Kilian to her flying chair, resting on the support base she'd constructed to hold it when the thrusters weren't engaged. She'd added to it, and the flying craft was far more developed than the simple seat she'd started with. Although still very compact, she'd enclosed the entire seat and added armored plating to protect herself.

Hamish had taken to calling it the hummingbird. The name wasn't bad, but it didn't convey the proper tone. So Verena had named it the Swift. The little birds were almost as maneuverable as hummingbirds, and far faster. They were hunters, just like Verena, and she had stenciled the name along the back of her craft.

"Good choice," Kilian noted, glancing approvingly at the latest feature. "And now it's a swift with teeth."

Verena patted the long cylinder of one of her custom speedsling drums attached at the base of the craft, along either side. She had attached a rotating nozzle to direct the stream of hornets they fired, and could adjust aim independently using little quartzite thrusters.

"The next time we run into unclaimed, I won't have to drop you into danger to stop them," she promised. "We'll see if they can stand up to ten thousand angry hornets."

"You're convinced we'll see more?"

"Aren't you?"

He nodded. "It was no accident they appeared on the border. I have no doubt we'll see more of them. But if you've got all this armament now, why do you need fiery projectiles?"

Because she didn't feel safe, even with those speedslings on board. Those unclaimed had been terrifyingly hard to kill, and she felt driven to unleash the full might of all her Builder inventions on them. Some things just needed to be eradicated.

"The next time we face the unclaimed, there will likely be more than two of them, won't there?"

"I don't like calling them unclaimed," Kilian said. "If my suspicions are correct, Dougal has harnessed them somehow, which makes them worse than unclaimed."

"So let's call them rampagers," Verena suggested.

"I like it."

"And they're why I need more weapons. I was practicing with rotating flame jets attached to the Swift. Hamish dubbed them the Puking Dooms, but as much as he loved them, they produced too much back-force and interrupted my flight path."

"So you're searching for a smaller variation?"

"Exactly. If I can figure out how to aim them, I could launch a rain of marble projectiles over enemy forces or rampagers."

"It's a good idea," Kilian agreed thoughtfully as he paced around the Swift, studying the other enhancements she had made. Steel plating covered most of the exposed wood. The added weight had required upgraded quartzite blocks to maintain the same level of aerial nimbleness, but would protect better against slingers or archers.

"Why blue?" Kilian asked, touching the paint of the chest support.

"Blends in better with the sky. The steel glittered so bright in the sun, I'd lose all element of surprise."

"Mix in some white or gray," Kilian suggested. "That way you'll blend in better with clouds."

"Good idea."

"I wish we could develop a thousand of these," Kilian said, patting the Swift. "We could rule the skies and change the nature of battle entirely."

Verena grimaced. "A thousand of these would level cities."

"I'd settle for twenty."

"That we might be able to manage, but we don't have enough Builders, and most of them can barely fly the windriders. The Swift is beyond their capacity. So much of what we're doing is still so new. We haven't figured out all the possibilities yet, or how to train people to do everything we've developed."

Hamish had a knack for flight, but his approach was so different, he'd probably end up cutting her nimble craft into pieces before mastering its unique aerial abilities. Flying made sense to her in ways she couldn't explain. It still surprised her that most of the Builders struggled with concepts she had mastered intuitively. She didn't understand the underlying scientific principles clearly enough to teach others, but some day she would figure them out.

"Keep working at it," Kilian said. "Back in the age of discovery, Builders unlocked amazing secrets, and the world was poised on the brink of fundamental change."

Verena knew the history as well as anyone, but that wasn't saying much. For reasons lost to time, the queen of Obrion had decreed death to all Builders during the Great Purge, had destroyed their laboratories and burned their research. That event had been one of the blackest moments in history.

"You speak about those days like you were there." Kilian was far older than he pretended, but there was much about him that remained a mystery.

"Today holds more than enough evil. No need to dwell on the atrocities of ages past." He placed a hand on the Swift. "You have invested a great deal of effort into developing these new armaments."

"Thank you."

"But even though I believe we have not seen the last of the rampagers, chances are relatively slim that you will encounter them again. What are you really worried about?"

Verena paused, taken aback by the depth of the question. Then she said softly. "I can't lose him again. Connor is in so much danger. I need to find a way to help him."

Kilian folded her gently into his arms and she leaned against him, grateful for his reassuring strength. It felt so good to share that awful fear with someone.

After a moment he kissed her forehead and retreated a step, holding her at arms' length. "Dying is not the greatest danger that Connor faces."

"I know." That truth haunted her every day. Verena hated Shona, but was it possible that her patronage really was protecting Connor from becoming one of those terrifying rage monsters? What if Shona's patronage failed? Worse, what if she learned of

Connor's ongoing attempts to escape and withdrew it? What if, as a last resort, her influence could reach across the distance and snatch him away from Verena even after he made it to Granadure?

With a trembling voice, she whispered, "If Connor turns unclaimed after we get him out, what if I am the one who must destroy him?"

She wasn't sure she could do it. She couldn't explain how he had slipped into her heart, but after losing him once, she longed for nothing more than a chance to see him again. She hated to think that despite all her mighty mechanicals, she might still not be able to keep him safe.

Kilian shook his head slowly. "I would prefer having to put down Connor if he turned unclaimed rather than face the real danger that lurks in the shadows around him."

"You've mentioned that before," Verena said. "But what's worse than unclaimed?"

"It's not worth worrying about yet. The chances are slim, and only under very specific circumstances could my greatest fears be realized."

Verena took a deep breath, forcing herself to believe everything would somehow turn out all right. "You didn't come here just to admire the Swift.

"Correct." Kilian extracted from a deep coat pocket a small, wooden box. The ornate carvings covering every surface were worn, as if from decades of handling.

Intrigued, Verena drew closer as Kilian opened the little box and extracted a dark chunk of stone. It held an almost metallic luster, but it was definitely a rock, not a metal. Even though it was nearly black, it somehow managed a brownish reflection.

"What is this?" Verena breathed as she took the small stone from Kilian.

"A secret I alone have guarded for a very long time. This is blind coal."

Chapter 11

erena rubbed her fingers across the smooth, hard surface, but it did not smudge her fingers. "This doesn't feel like coal."

"Geology masters know it as anthracite," Kilian said. "There is only one deposit, and that is known only to a select few."

Just as she did with every stone she handled, Verena felt for the invisible crack found in power stones, the fissure that she and other Builders could pry open to unlock its power.

This stone had one.

Verena gasped. "This is a new power stone!"

"One I hope will offer advantage in our upcoming conflict," Kilian said.

A new stone? Verena had never imagined finding new power stones. The ramifications were staggering. She was holding a piece of unknown potential in her hands.

So of course she had to taste it. Hamish preferred licking rocks, but although she agreed the taste of a stone was an important aspect of understanding it, she preferred not slobbering all over them like he did. She pressed it to her lips. It tasted like a half-melted icicle sliding across her tongue.

"What does it do?"

When he only raised an eyebrow, inviting her to find out, Verena cautiously pried open that crack that kept the stone's power locked inside. She should have waited, questioned Kilian more, and prepared for what might happen. Some power stones could be dangerous, especially if a Builder unlocked their powers without proper precautions.

Kilian didn't offer any caution though, so she assumed that meant the stone was unlikely to harm her. Even so, she only unlocked the release rate a fraction, tensed to snap it closed if something dangerous happened.

She felt only a strange pulsing radiate out from the stone, like slow vibrations against her skin. She looked up at Kilian, a question on her lips.

And she dropped the stone.

Without warning, it slipped through her fingers. She yelped and snatched for it with both hands, but fumbled and it slipped away again. Kilian caught it just above the floor. He held it gingerly as he lifted it carefully.

Verena asked, "I didn't just get clumsy all of a sudden, did I?"

Kilian shook his head, and immediately the stone slipped through his fingers.

Verena snatched for it, but fingers slid around it, unable to gain purchase. Before it fell free, she flickered out a tendril of her Builder sense and snapped the release rate closed.

She caught it without trouble after that.

"This is amazing," Verena said, studying the little stone. "I've never felt anything like it."

"It is a sedimentary stone," Kilian said. "And as you have noted, it possesses unique properties, including exceptional slipperiness."

"By the Tallan's blessed memory, a third sedimentary stone. Is this another of those secrets lost to the world since the Tallan Wars?"

"As always you're a quick study," he said with a smile. "As far as I know, I am the only person now living who has established affinity with it."

"What can you do with it?"

"I have not yet explored its full potential," Kilian said. "But it does perform at least one critical function."

"This is how you destroyed those rampagers," Verena exclaimed, seizing on a sudden thought.

"In part."

"A new power stone," Verena repeated, rubbing the hard, smooth surface of the blind coal. "What other secrets are you keeping from me?"

"There are indeed other stones still to be discovered or rediscovered," he admitted. "But we will excavate the ancient truths with care and with a measured tread."

"But. . ." She wanted to throttle him and force him to tell her everything.

"Let's not repeat the mistakes of the past, shall we?"

That gave her pause, but the thought of discovery always thrilled Verena and she only barely restrained herself from begging for more information.

"This is your new top priority," Kilian said. "You must investigate the properties of this stone and apply that nimble brain of yours. How can we use this to our advantage in the upcoming conflict?"

"What about my work with orders for existing mechanicals? We're already swamped."

"I've already issued orders. Dierk and the other Builders will carry the load as best they can. You and Hamish are relieved of other duties for now."

"You think this stone is that important?"

He nodded again. "So, what can you tell me about it?"

"It's slippery," Verena said, turning her thoughts to the new stone. She returned to her hidden food stash, grabbed one of her new peaches, and took a big bite. As much as she hated admitting Hamish was ever right, she'd found that eating did sometimes help her think.

As she savored the sweet, juicy pulp, she turned back to Kilian. "How extensive is the slippery property?"

"Let's find out."

Verena considered the stone as she devoured the peach. Then she cupped it in both hands and opened the release rate a tiny bit.

The stone fell right through her tightly clasped fingers. She hadn't separated them, and the stone contained no propulsion that drove it through her grip. It just fell slipped through and she couldn't stop it.

Verena poked it before it hit the ground, but her finger only slipped along its length. That was enough contact for her to snap off its power so she could grab it.

"That's very interesting," she said, considering the little stone.

She tucked it into a pocket of her jacket next and opened the release rate the same amount as before. The stone remained in her pocket, but slipped back and forth, as if looking for escape. She reached in with a finger and opened the release rate further.

The stone popped out of her pocket. She tried to catch it and turn off its power, but she couldn't keep in contact long enough. It fell to the floor and slid across the workroom. Verena scrambled after, trying to wedge it against equipment long enough to turn it off, but it kept popping free.

After a moment, she turned a frustrated gaze on Kilian, who was silently chuckling. "Do you mind?"

Without making any visible gesture this time, Kilian stole the waters of her waterfall again, using them to surround the little stone and lift it into the air. It kept bobbing free, forcing him to constantly adjust the flow of water to keep it contained. Verena drove a finger through the water and turned off the stone's power.

"Aggressive slipperiness," she muttered, examining the stone's smooth, almost metallic sides.

Kilian chuckled again. "That's the first time I think I've ever heard that term."

"It fell through my hands, but popped out of my pocket, so it doesn't just pass through things, driven by gravity alone. It's more like it finds the path of least resistance. Is that consistent with your experience?"

"It behaves differently for Builders than for Petralists," he said. "But the basic principles are similar, yes."

"I'll need to do far more extensive testing," she muttered. "This property has tremendous potential, but not if we drop it every time we try to use it."

The basic approach of simply releasing the stone's power without direction as she had done in the previous tests would not work. She could craft more complex patterns, like invisible sculptures, that would contain and direct the force released from the stone in more precis ways.

So holding the stone on two sides, she again opened the release rate a little, but focused only through sides she was not touching. This time it did not jump out of her hands.

"So it is possible to control," she said. "But to what extent? And will the slippery property affect me as well, or only the stone itself?"

"Let's see." Kilian tried to douse her with water.

Verena lifted her hands toward the wave and increased the release rate on the little stone. The water struck her hands, but then split and tumbled past on both sides, leaving her completely dry.

"Did you split those waters?"

He shook his head. "I was completely prepared to soak you for science."

The little stone was pulsing stronger against her fingers, a slight tingling that spread through her arms and skipped over her skin. "I opened the release rate perhaps twenty percent, and it made me slippery too."

Kilian swept his hands together, and the waters created a wall between them. Verena didn't need him to tell her what to do. She plunged into the wall of water, leading with the little stone. Its pulsing increased along her skin, and she stepped right through the water, again without getting wet. She felt the waters sliding across her skin, but not clinging. It couldn't seem to get any hold on her.

"Impressive," Kilian said as she closed the release rate. "I can already think of several applications."

"Me too," Verena said as possibilities flooded her mind, particularly ways to counter the overwhelming danger of tertiary Petralists. Then she noticed the little rock had shrunk noticeably in her hand. With a flicker of her Builder senses, she confirmed that almost half its power had been spent.

"It burns through its power store remarkably fast. How much of this do you have?"

"Not a lot. The vein we can harvest is tiny."

"So we're not looking at a battlefield-level strategy," Verena said.

"No," he agreed. "This stone could provide an important advantage, but only in targeted situations."

"I'll get to work on it right away," she promised. "Get me some more stones to test with."

"A shipment is on the way. You'll have it within the hour."

He placed a hand on her shoulder. "We don't have much time, Verena. Study hard, but keep the secret of this stone from everyone. Not even Hamish is to know."

"Why not? I thought you said he was also getting new orders." She had been planning to rush right over to Hamish's workroom. This new stone might be enough to pull him away from that suit he'd been working on with feverish intensity.

"He is, but his project is not the same as yours, and I don't need him distracted right now."

"What project?"

Kilian smiled. "I don't need you distracted either. Now get to work."

He snagged another breadstick on the way out.

"Don't you tell Hamish where you got that," Verena warned.

"Your secret is safe with me."

After he left, Verena wondered when she'd learn the next secret, and how many more he alone knew.

Then she started testing the new stone's abilities in earnest.

Chapter 12

ello, Hamish."

"Whoa!" Hamish spun away from his workbench. He had been so engrossed in his work, he hadn't heard the distant door open. Instincts honed from months of daily sword practice kicked in and he dropped into a fighting stance.

It was just Kilian.

The two had a running challenge of seeing who could sneak up on the other the most. Kilian was crushing him, so he snapped open the release rate on the piece of chocolate-coated quartzite he'd been sucking on. The little piece of stone erupted out of his mouth with an angry buzzing sound, shedding bits of chocolate as it shot straight at Kilian's face.

Kilian caught it.

As if that wasn't enough, he not only snatched the little stone out of the air, but then rotated it and sent it shooting back at Hamish. He made the tricky move look easy, with that cocky half-smile on his face that could be so annoying.

Not to be outdone, Hamish caught the little stone in his mouth.

Gagging, he stumbled back against the workbench, that little stone trying its hardest to fly down his throat. He shut the release rate and spat the little stone onto the bench.

"When did you get back?" Hamish asked casually between coughs.

Kilian pumped Hamish's hand. "Barely an hour ago. Nice try."

He looked like he'd been traveling. He must have something important to say because adding another point wasn't important enough to take priority over bathing.

"Has the war started?"

"No major skirmishes yet, but it could start any day."

It felt like the war had been going on for weeks. Everyone rushed about, expressions grim, working at a feverish pace to fill ever-growing orders for more mechanicals. Worse, in the last long line of heavily laden wagons trundling away from the mini-city of the Builder complex, they'd shipped out a large amount of foodstuffs.

The cooks had assured him there was plenty of food, but they had refused to allow him into the pantries to inspect. He'd survived Alasdair and seen firsthand how war always brought with it food shortages. It felt like starvation was creeping up on the world, but no one else had noticed yet.

Hamish had tried convincing the cooks that they should actually begin eating double portions at every meal to get ahead of the looming shortages. The head cook might seem like a jolly woman, but she could swing that heavy wooden spoon like a mace.

He'd try again after he finished testing his new battle suit.

Hamish hated to think of open fighting between his homeland and his new adopted nation. He loved his work as a Builder, but still felt guilty that he was helping develop mechanicals that would be used against his country.

He was tempted to sneak a visit to Alasdair. He longed to see his family again. He longed to see Jean more. The constant yearning for her was a weight on his heart, but even if he did slip across the impassable border and risk the dangerous journey to the Carraig, it would be to beg her to come back with him. More than the fact that in Obrion he faced execution for possessing the banned Builder power, only in the Builder compound could he really be himself. Here they explored the limits of creation, celebrating almost every day a new discovery.

Here they were changing the world.

It frustrated Hamish that the world was so ungrateful.

"How are your projects progressing?" Kilian asked, glancing at the workbench where Hamish's greatest invention lay.

"A little better every day." Hamish was proud of how much he'd accomplished in the precious moments he could snatch between his other duties. Verena and Dierk had helped, but the bulk of the invention bore the stamp of his unique creativity and he was excited to talk about it. But with Kilian, he had to be careful.

General Wolfram might be the supreme commander of the Grandurian armies, but Kilian led from the shadows. He allowed Wolfram to make the tactical decisions, but he was the undisputed leader of all things arcane. Everyone at the Builder compound ultimately reported to him.

Kilian was brilliant, but mysterious. He possessed the rare Dawnus gift and wielded his elemental powers with exceptional control. In the battles of Alasdair, he'd shown a strange dichotomy of unmatched battle prowess, but also a surprising depth of charity. He'd saved Connor's younger brother from a falling building, had respected Jean's demands to leave the villagers in peace, and had gifted Hamish his first sword.

Hamish would follow Kilian and obey his commands, but he did not entirely trust him. Not after Kilian had withheld the truth that Connor had somehow survived after blowing up that mountain. He and Verena had grieved for weeks. Trying to withhold that Captain Ilse's mission was to assassinate Connor in the event that her attempt to recruit him failed hadn't helped build trust either.

Hamish didn't care about Kilian's obscure warning that Obrion could turn Connor into a devastating force of destruction. Connor was his best friend, and friends helped each other. They didn't assassinate each other. It was a basic matter of trust.

So Hamish could not yet reveal the deepest secrets of his new suit. Still, there was a lot he could talk about. Hamish lifted the heavy leather jacket, covered with overlapping granite scales. The newest model looked similar to earlier versions, and that was enough for Kilian to know for the moment.

"We've proven the stop-bash properties of the jacket are remarkable," Hamish explained. "It can absorb a full-force punch from a Rumbler with minimal damage."

"Impressive." Kilian fingered a hardened granite leaf. "But that's not all, is it?"

"That's just the beginning." Hamish pointed out other components spread along the table. "I've got thrusters built in everywhere. I'll out-fly Verena's Swift when I'm done, and I'm developing custom weapons to take the fight to Petralists or any more unclaimed we run into."

"We're calling them rampagers now," Kilian said.

"That's a good name." So Kilian had already visited Verena. "When will you be ready to do a full test?" Kilian asked.

"Soon."

"Good. Verena reported on progress made on the other battlefield mechanicals."

She knew far more about that than Hamish. In recent days, he'd helped manufacture those mechanicals, but had barely paid attention. All his focus had been on fine-tuning his new battle suit. He couldn't wait to test it. The next time he and Verena dueled in the skies, he'd trounce her.

Kilian considered the suit. "Once this is operational, do you believe you can duplicate this for others?"

Part of him wanted to punch Kilian for suggesting he share his invention, but Kilian was preparing for war, so the question was valid. A score of Builders wearing Hamish's invention could change the war.

"I'm not sure," Hamish admitted. "Some of the components are highly customized to my fighting style. Verena would hate it."

"She's got the Swift."

"Wait till you see this in action."

"The potential is clearly remarkable, but is it repeatable?"

"I'm not sure any of the other Builders could use it." Most of the Builders were academics. They lacked the fighting training Hamish was taking, lacked the natural flight instincts of Verena, or her ability to think clearly in the middle of a conflict.

"What of the core jacket?" Kilian asked. "Could we outfit Blades or Wingrunners with these?"

"That's a good idea. The protection could give them a huge advantage."

"Think about it," Kilian said. "And consider what other components could be applied to broader application." He gripped Hamish's shoulder. "I'm proud of the work you're doing here, Hamish. You came to us a refugee from a broken village, but you are family now. Good work."

Hamish might not entirely trust Kilian, but the man inspired loyalty like no one else.

Then Kilian extracted from a deep pocket of his coat a small leather pouch, similar to ones used to hold granite or basalt powder. "However, that's not the only reason I came here today. Your other duties are suspended. I have a new project for you."

He dumped a small stone onto the workbench near Hamish's suit.

Diorite.

Hamish instantly recognized the salt-and-pepper stone. He'd grown up in Alasdair where diorite was uniquely treasured. The Cutters used long chisels of the precious stone to cut granite blocks from the mountain. Those chisels cut through the hard Alasdair White many times faster than the sharpest steel ever could. Connor's father, Hendry the Ashlar, used a precious, double-headed diorite hammer to process blocks of granite in the Powder House, beating them to dust a hundred times faster than any other hammer ever could.

Hamish picked up the little piece of diorite and felt for the invisible crack that held its power locked inside. He found it, confirming this was power-grade stone. He licked it, and his tongue tingled with rippling fire. Once he cracked open its power, it would taste more like lightning.

He'd tasted a diorite stone with its power released, and the memory still thrilled him with fearful excitement. Chisels released only a fraction had cut a foot into solid granite with each blow. Hamish had opened the release rate a tiny bit more for Stuart, and the brawny youth had exploded an entire block of granite with a single strike.

He had opened wide the release rate on the Ashlar's hammer. The lightning-like power concentrated in that tool had shaken him to the core. It felt like holding an entire storm bottled up in his hands.

"Wait," Hamish said, eying the little piece of diorite closely. "You didn't take this from Alasdair, did you?"

"We have sources of diorite in Granadure, although like Obrion, few understand that this is indeed a power grade stone with uniquely destructive properties."

"Cutters somehow tap into the sealed power of diorite," Hamish said. "And Builders can unlock its power, but are you saying Petralists can establish affinity with it?"

"Don't ever suggest that to anyone," Kilian warned, his expression grave. "A few have tried, and most end up destroying themselves. It's too dangerous to ingest and control."

But Builders could. Hamish thought back to the tiny bit of powdered diorite that Dierk had activated and used in the bomb that they fired from the thump driver. That little bit of diorite, mixed with kerosene and some other fuel, created a gigantic explosion.

Hamish had dreamed about other things he could do with diorite. It looked like he was about to get a chance to test his theories.

"Be careful with this," Kilian warned, as if reading Hamish's mind. "I want full safeguards on everything. We cannot afford to damage this facility."

"I'll be careful," Hamish promised as he started tossing the stone from one hand to another, considering possibilities.

"The danger is severe," Kilian insisted, holding Hamish's gaze.

"I understand," Hamish assured him. Who else at the Builder compound could better understand the importance of diorite? His village depended on it as a critical tool, and he respected it as a precious heirloom. He'd still blow it up, but he'd do it with the right attitude.

"Dierk has already done some preliminary research into diorite," Kilian reminded him. "But supplies are tight and the danger is high."

"We can build even more amazing bombs with this stuff than what he did in Alasdair."

"Indeed we can. Dierk's already investigating that potential, but I want you to consider other uses for it. The bombs will be effective in helping to manage the battlefield-level strategy, but how can we use it in more subtle ways?"

Hamish considered the little black and white crystals that looked so innocent, like his brothers always pretended to be just before they got Hamish into trouble. He glanced at Kilian. "This is how you defeated those rampagers, wasn't it?"

"In part."

"The other part is the secret, isn't it?" Hamish asked. "That's why you established affinity with this when no one else could. What's the secret?"

"Don't worry about that. You're not trying to establish affinity with it."

"But others could," Hamish said, excited by the idea, imagining a whole company of soldiers blowing up rampagers and crashing through anything that got in their way. Then he remembered most of what would get in their way would be other people, Obrioners, his people. He felt a little sick.

Kilian shook his head. "The danger is still severe, and we

cannot afford to lose the men it would take to produce competent diorite Petralists."

"What are they called?" Hamish interrupted. "Lightning Fists?" He grimaced. That was a terrible name.

"There is no name for them. There have never been enough of them to need a name. And even if I was willing to sacrifice men to produce such Petralists, the supply is so tiny, we could not field an army wielding diorite."

"It's scarce in Obrion too," Hamish said, thinking of the astronomical cost for diorite chisels. Multiple generations of Cutter families spent their lives paying for a single chisel.

"I don't need bigger explosions," Kilian said. "Your mission is to develop ways that we can use diorite on an individual level by opening a small fraction of that explosive power. How can that turn the tide for normal soldiers or give them the advantage if they are set upon by rampagers?"

Rampagers were downright scary. He'd nearly died in that first encounter, and one of the beasts had destroyed his flying plank. The next time he met them, he would bring to bear the full might of his new suit, but what of soldiers without that protection?

"I'll get on it," Hamish promised. "Right after lunch."

Chapter 13

Connor retreated a step from the towering presence of Evander, but didn't bother running. He'd seen enough of Evander's powers to know the giant could easily swallow him in the earth. Even had Connor carried slate, his fledgling earth powers would have availed him little.

"What are you doing down here?" Connor asked instead. He'd only spoken with the giant once, but not long enough to get a true sense of the man.

In the flickering, multi-colored light of the burning fungus spread across the ribs of that long-dead cathedral, Evander's impassive face looked mysterious and threatening. "Echoes of truth may yet enlighten the dim recesses few have discovered."

Connor had to think about that for a moment. The giant seemed content to wait for him. The man was huge, towering over seven feet, with shoulders more than twice as broad as Connor's. They strained the limits of his immense, black, leather jacket. That leather smell was appropriate, but Connor also caught a whiff of ink. That was intriguing and made him think of Jean.

So he said, "I'm looking for my friend Jean. I was worried she was lost down here."

"The fledgling wanders often from the safety of the nest, but cannot learn to fly without leaping from the tall branches."

Connor stifled a groan. He loved coming up with convoluted Sentry-speak to irritate the students, but this creepy underground tomb wasn't the best place to hold such a conversation.

He tried bridling his impatience. It wouldn't help. One had to work through Sentry-speak conversations with care, like picking through the raspberry bushes on Mount Ingram in the autumn. Here, taking a wrong step might hurt a lot more than getting a thorn stuck in his backside.

"I know you've met her," Connor said. "Do you know where Jean is? I'm worried about her."

"The nuall that wanders far afield rarely finds success that could have been obtained closer to home."

"How could I not get distracted by all this?" Connor demanded, pointing at the burning pillars and vast, ruined cavern. "It's amazing, but what if Jean was lost down here?"

"The impetuous youth may, when motivated by a greater cause, bend their will to study of import worthy of greatest efforts."

He had no idea where to go with that, so best to continue the conversation as if Evander had said something that made sense.

"I already checked the inner library. It doesn't look like she's been there for days."

"All fountains of knowledge lie mapped and secure in the vault of memory thus guarded and cataloged?" Evander asked with a hint of a smile.

That gave Connor pause. Jean had shared with him the secret of the inner library. Had she withheld other locations where she was doing additional research?

A throbbing headache began behind his eyes.

"So you do know where she is? Please show me."

Evander stretched a hand that was bigger than Connor's head up to a massive, cracked stone rib and drove a finger into it. Connor blinked. That was amazing. Sentries could bend earth to their wills, but he'd thought they couldn't walk through solid stone.

Either Evander knew deeper truths, or the man was just that strong. Connor wasn't sure which possibility was more impressive. He felt like a child facing the mighty Petralist.

The giant withdrew his hand, and the hole closed. So it was a deeper truth. Evander fascinated Connor, but he wished they could meet in the sunlight and chat over lunch.

Evander said, "The window does not importune the light, but accepts it every day with willing gratitude."

"Just give me a straight answer," Connor pleaded. "Or I'll assume you want me to punch a few windows into the roof there to let some light shine down here."

"A pebble cast upon the mountain may yet unleash the avalanche." Evander's voice rumbled with a hint of danger.

Maybe he should have backed off, but Jean was one of his best friends. Was Evander holding her prisoner? Had she stumbled upon some secret he guarded in the belly of the Carraig?

"Is the window of her prison open to the light, or are there bars blocking her freedom?" Connor demanded.

"The bird may be caged to keep away the ravages of the hunter."

Was Jean the bird, the cage, the hunter, or was he totally misinterpreting that one?

"Or it could be freed to fly away," Connor retorted.

"Children play with glass and cast aside the words of wisdom that lead to treasures of knowledge." He was starting to look annoyed.

Connor scanned for the nearest exits and pleaded, "Just tell me she's all right."

"Fire can purify or destroy. Winds may cool or tear asunder. Truth that enlightens the understanding may overwhelm even the stoutest heart."

"I'll find her," Connor promised. "Don't worry about how much she can survive. She's tougher than you think."

It felt right to bow to Evander, so he did. Then he left.

He only held a slow walk for five steps before tapping marble and pulling the flames from the burning fungus back to his shoulders. He didn't worry about leaving the giant in darkness. Evander's earth senses could map the entire undercity with far better accuracy than even Connor's quartzite vision.

Before he reached the gap between ancient pillars that would allow him to return to a nearby street and head back toward the less threatening undercity, the earth rose to block his path.

Evander had followed, although Connor had not heard a single footstep. Looming close, the giant gestured at the deep shadows surrounding them. "Secrets of ages past are of need guarded with careful tongues."

"Why wouldn't you want anyone else to know about this place?"

"Swine trample and tear without thought or care. Impetuous tongues are silenced by the stern mistress of dire need."

Connor shivered. No way to misunderstand that one. "I'll keep your secret, but only if you tell me where Jean is."

"At the rising of the sun, shadows retreat into darkness and brightness of hope is rekindled."

Connor decided to interpret that one that Jean would return tomorrow. He couldn't beat clarity out of Evander. Alone in the secret ruin where no one would know to search for him, he lacked much leverage.

"Tomorrow then. If I don't speak with her, my silence is no longer guaranteed."

He turned to leave and the earthen wall blocking his path sank into the ground without so much as a rumble. That simple fact reminded him how much he needed to learn.

Without looking back, he returned to the ruined street and silent buildings keeping their eternal vigil. There he tapped basalt and raced back up the long avenue, eager to get as far from Evander as possible. The giant's voice echoed down the street after him, seemingly magnified by each ruined structure he passed.

"The path to victory is fraught with danger not yet imagined. Hold fast to truth most cherished and soon to be discovered, and the fires of your tribulation may yet purify instead of destroy."

With that dire warning echoing from all sides, Connor ran faster.

Chapter 14

hen Connor returned to his Kilian suite in the central keep of the Carraig, he paced the beautifully-decorated living room, running the cryptic conversation with Evander over in his mind. Sentry-speak was even more challenging to decipher than to speak. Good lines carried multiple levels of meaning and he couldn't afford to miss anything Evander might have been trying to convey.

Besides, some of those lines were fantastic. He didn't quite dare quoting any verbatim, but they might inspire his own Sentry-speak to greater heights of inscrutable perfection. The effort left his head pounding enough that he would have welcomed one of old Mhairi's foul tonics.

Had he understood Evander's promise about Jean correctly? If Jean didn't appear some time the next day, he'd need to act. Would he dare defy Evander and reveal the long-standing secret of that sunken city? He really hoped he wouldn't have to, but he was already planning to return and explore further. He'd seen only a fraction of the secrets lying under the plain.

Since thinking wasn't helping much, Connor changed into his custom battle leathers, pulled on his Kilian mask, and headed for his personal training facility attached to his suite. He was just deciding whether to practice with soapstone or marble when his new teachers arrived, trailed by Tomas and Cameron.

Camonica looked irritated and kept shuffling farther away from Cameron. He seemed linked to her by some invisible thread, because he kept pace, following with an awestruck look on his face that bordered on open adoration.

Connor was definitely going to have to ask him about that.

"This will be a lot of fun," Captain Aonghus grinned as he surveyed the cavernous training facility.

All of the Boulder classes could have used the huge space for mock battles. It was remarkable to consider how much of the enormous keep was dedicated to the private suites of the Dawnus. Then again, the game was everything, and the champions made the Tir-raon possible.

The army of linn workers that Lord Nevan had assigned to prepare the area had produced a series of pools of still water, interspersed with giant open tanks of liquid fuel. A paved track that circled the outer edges of the room extended onto the rounded walls, allowing Connor to race around the arena at full fracked speed.

"First, tell us about what you can do so we can determine how much ground we need to cover," Camonica said after shooing the Fast Rollers out.

"With marble, I've been practicing long distance attacks. I've found that snapping a little fiery distraction at someone can give me an advantage."

"Absolutely," Aonghus agreed. "Too many people fear getting burned."

"Daly's got a pretty neat trick," Connor added, gesturing at a heavy plank lying near one of the fuel vats. "He rides up a pillar of fire and leaps off."

Aonghus made a dismissive gesture. "Too much show and not enough substance."

"I think you've just defined your life," Camonica said, actually cracking a smile.

"You've fallen for the ruse just like everyone else. They expect Firetongues to be a bit crazy."

That sounded exactly right. When Connor walked with fire, he felt that way. Only Ivor seemed to handle that wild insanity well.

"Early in the process, that's often true," Aonghus said, appearing far too thoughtful, despite the little man-shaped flames pacing out his ears and up the side of his head to his unruly hair. "However, one eventually learns the secret."

"What secret?" Connor had to ask. Even Camonica leaned closer to hear.

"I can't tell you, or it wouldn't be a secret!" Aonghus chortled.

Camonica groaned and went to examine the nearby pools of water. Aonghus leaned closer and continued in a fierce whisper to Connor. "No one else understands us, boy. Fire is the great purifier. Only those who step through the flame to the far side realize the truth. Have you completed your journey?"

His burning gaze bored into Connor, who felt a bit intimidated by it. "I'm not sure."

"Then you haven't."

The flames winked out of his eyes and the fires nesting in his hair disappeared. "But you have to before the group battles begin, or you won't be prepared. I guarantee from everything I've heard about Ivor, he has."

"Enough," Camonica said. "A Firetongue talking philosophy is even worse than a Fast Roller spouting sonnets.

"Have you ever heard--" Connor began.

"I don't want to talk about it," she said with a shudder. "Tell me what you can do with soapstone, boy."

"It was my first tertiary affinity," Connor admitted.

That pleased her. "I was privileged to witness that incredible monument you raised above the Rhidorroch."

"Just before you destroyed it!" Aonghus laughed.

"That wasn't my fault." He was getting tired of saying that. Maybe he'd inscribe the words on the back of his armor.

"I sensed its collapse," Camonica said, her tone softening, her expression turning thoughtful. "The sheer magnitude of that dome would overwhelm all but the most powerful Spitters. Tell me about it."

"It was too much to control," Connor admitted. "When we raised it, I couldn't have done it alone. If not for Ivor and the other Spitters joining the effort, I would've only killed a bunch of people."

"And yet you drew them into the matrix." Camonica beamed. "You managed an entire matrix on your first attempt, and with such incredible volume. If I hadn't seen it, I would not have believed it."

Connor shrugged. "It needed to be done."

Camonica poked his chest with a finger. "Only those who become one with water can manage such a feat. Did you feel the threshold?" Her eyes lit with an intensity that unnerved him, and the blue-tinted ends of her tawny hair seemed to glow.

"The what?"

Aonghus hissed like steam in a kettle. "This is a topic we do not discuss, Camonica. You forget yourself."

Her normal calm returned like a blanket. "You're right. We must start at the beginning."

Connor wanted to ask what she was talking about, but didn't want Aonghus erupting. What had she almost said?

"You walk as a trusted companion with water," Camonica declared. "It is a good start."

Aonghus spat and mumbled under his breath. "Purification first."

She gestured toward the nearby pool. "Time to begin."

"What do you have in mind?"

"A simple test."

Camonica motioned Connor toward the nearest pool, then jogged over to another, with a tank of liquid fuel between. She stepped onto the waters and skated across the surface with abundant grace, but still not quite matching the effortless slide of Kilian, the Water Moccasin.

Connor stepped onto the other pool, embracing the pulsing flow of soapstone in his bloodstream. The pools all began to glow to his water senses, and a dim halo appeared around Camonica. Walking with elemental water came easy to Connor and he strode out onto the pool as easily as hiking across solid ground.

On the other pool, Camonica smoothly rose twenty feet into the air upon a column of water. Connor followed. It was a simple thing to drive the water into the shape he needed. After creating the giant dome, he barely had to think about forming something so small.

"Good," Camonica called. "Now, the challenge. I will attempt to wrest control over your pool of water and unseat you while you attempt the same against me."

That sounded like a lot of fun. Connor grinned and Camonica said, "Go."

Her will struck at his column of water like a battering ram and it shook wildly from the impact, leaning dangerously over. Connor only barely managed to hold on, forming the waters around his feet like anchors to keep him secure. For a second, he hung over Aonghus, who scurried away from the impending dousing.

With a surge of will, Connor melded his mind to the element like he had while forming the dome. It became a part of him, sealed to his will. Camonica's influence slid off, like vapors of smoke clinging to the exterior of a steel structure.

His column of water solidified and he returned to face her. She looked startled and in that second of hesitation, he snatched for the pool of water supporting her column. He didn't bother trying to wrest control over the entire pool. All he needed was the top fraction of an inch.

He turned it to ice, then pushed.

The entire column slid across the thin skim of ice. All he needed was for Camonica to squawk with surprise and fumble for a critical second or two.

Camonica was no student. Her will slammed down upon his thin crust of ice, and legs of water speared out of her column, driving through the surface. He tried to maintain his hold, but she held the advantage and ejected him.

"Very good," she called. "Ingenuity, assertiveness, and an understanding of the influence dispersal gradient."

Connor was glad he'd impressed her, but what was she talking about?

"Thanks, but I pretty much just thought it would be fun to knock you onto your back side."

"You first," she grinned.

They resumed the contest, snatching at each other's columns, trying to push, pull, twist, and collapse them, but neither gaining advantage long enough to knock the other off. Camonica manipulated water with an elegant finesse that made Connor feel brutish and clumsy.

Brute or not, he didn't fall. Water sprayed across the training facility, dousing Aonghus so many times that he finally ignited the farthest vat of liquid fuel and stepped into its protective flames.

Connor threw himself into the contest against Camonica, merging his thoughts with the waters until they became extensions of his will, like ethereal limbs.

Limbs that kept getting amputated.

He and Camonica held too much control over their individual pools, so they reached farther, yanking upon the waters of the other pools and using them like battering rams and horizontal waterfalls against each other. They were too closely matched to cause much damage though, because whenever their watery arsenal touched their opponent, they snatched control over it.

Eventually, every loose drop of water in the entire vaulted room was swatted back and forth between them, exploding in cresting waves that broke upon each other's wills before churning back the other way.

Connor laughed in the midst of the flood, then coughed from the water he swallowed. The air was filled to bursting with moisture, and breathing became a challenge. There had to be a way to filter the water out of the air, but he didn't know the trick to it yet, and that tiny distraction gave Camonica the opening she needed.

She clapped her hands together and the waters crashed in on him in a mighty wave. As Connor tried to block it, the heart of the wave condensed into a spear of ice that burst through the flood and caught him in the chest.

The impact catapulted him off his tower and interrupted his concentration just long enough for Camonica to deny him the ability to save himself. A mighty wave smacked him down onto the outer track like flotsam dashed upon the rocks. The impact blasted the breath from his lungs and left him momentarily stunned.

By the time he sat up groaning, Camonica had returned all the waters to their pools. She grinned at him, her eyes still flashing with excitement from the contest.

"You've made far more progress than I had feared," she beamed. "You are indeed a Spitter at heart, young Connor."

"Don't damage his potential," Aonghus growled. He'd snuffed out the fires in his defensive inferno. "He needs to be far more than a simple Spitter."

"Every Dawnus has a primary focus," she insisted. "For Connor, it must be water."

"We'll see about that. Time to ignite the burn."

"Are we just going to try to incinerate each other?" Connor asked, feeling a bit nervous as he glanced at the giant vats of liquid fuel. He wasn't sure he was ready to immerse himself to the purification point that Aonghus kept mentioning.

"Not today, boy," Aonghus said. "Destruction is only one aspect of fire. Let's test those creative sparks in your mind."

"Before you burn them all out," Camonica added.

Aonghus ignored her and nodded at the track ringing the chamber. "Try to keep up."

Without explaining, he dashed away, tapping basalt speed. Connor had not used all the basalt from earlier, so he didn't need to absorb any more, but took off after Aonghus. His worries evaporated as he embraced basalt speed and shifted onto the wall to take the first turn, running horizontal, a laugh bubbling in his throat.

As Aonghus approached the second turn, flames erupted out of a nearby vat of fuel and splashed along the wall in front of him, clinging to the corner like a thin crimson carpet. He dove onto them and, as he rode them around the corner, they rippled beneath him, whipping him forward faster than he'd been running. He catapulted off the flames after the turn, actually slowing in the air before touching back down in his fully fracked sprint.

Connor had never tried anything like that, but couldn't wait to. He tapped marble, his mouth already burning with intense heat. With the flick of a thought, he ignited a spark in that same vat of fuel and cast the flames along the wall in front of him.

Then he leaped. He had used fire to cushion falls before, but never as an accelerant to a dive. So he bounced off the flames and tumbled around the corner, bouncing from the wall to the floor and back again several times, shouting as the world spun madly and his stomach flipped with anticipation of spewing his last meal.

When he finally stopped, he lay face down on the blessedly cool floor for a moment. Every muscle ached, and he'd banged his head so many times, despite the cushioning of the flames, that his vision was blurry.

"Why aren't you healing yourself?" Camonica asked, dropping to one knee beside him. He hadn't even noticed her approaching.

"No sandstone."

"Are you daft, boy?" She placed hands on his torso and healing warmth flooded into him. He closed his eyes and blessed the day she established her secondary affinity.

It took only a moment to feel well enough to sit up. She handed him another piece of sandstone. "You finish."

"Thanks."

She grabbed his chin and pulled him close, whispering fiercely, "Don't ever let me find you without sandstone again. It's as much as your life to leave the safety of these quarters without it."

"I won't," he promised, rattled by the depth of her anger.

He'd long bemoaned the loss of his precious sculpted sandstone pendant, gifted to him from Aunt Ailsa and lost to Jok, then to Professor Hector, and finally to Ivor. He should have paid more attention to always carrying something as a replacement.

"Come on!" Aonghus called from the far end of the hall.

"You're as slow as a frozen Boulder in a bash-induced doze. Catch me!"

Connor bit back another groan as he started to run, but as soon as he tapped basalt, his pains faded under the glorious freedom of speed. Aonghus waited for him, standing several feet out from the next corner.

"Fire consumes itself in riotous living," he called. "You must embrace it, cast away hesitation, and celebrate the purification of destruction."

Connor slowed, frowning. "That makes less sense than any Sentry-speak."

"Because you're not listening," Aonghus said, extending a long, crimson finger of fire and poking Connor in the forehead. "Watch again, and this time see."

Aonghus raced for the corner, again coating it with living flames and leaping upon them. Connor watched, tapping marble and reaching for the fires that whisked Aonghus around the corner at incredible speed.

That time he felt it. Aonghus hadn't simply attached the flames to the wall, but had created three concentric spheres of fire, then flattened them against the wall. The smallest, inner layer rotated in a blur that the outer layers built upon, doubling the speed of the spin with each layer. The resulting spin, visible only as a dense flickering of the flames to anyone not tapping marble, pulsed along the wall faster than a fracked Strider.

"That's amazing," Connor breathed, leaning close to the wall and trailing his fingers through the fast-spinning fire. He had never considered combining his affinities to magnify results. What else could he do by applying that same principle?

"I want you to have this mastered by tomorrow," Aonghus said. Then he motioned Camonica to join them. "Let's see what you can do with both together."

"What do you have in mind?"

"Walking with both elements at the same time will be your greatest challenge," said Camonica. "We will help you develop the foundational skills to increase your chances of success."

"And switch from one to the other," Aonghus added. "Hopefully we can narrow the gap between the two until you can bridge it better."

Connor wasn't sure that would work, but he was willing to give it a try. He was looking forward to testing himself against

Camonica, and he was starting to think Aonghus could teach him a lot.

"Get on that pool of water," Camonica ordered.

"And we'll have some fun," Aonghus added.

When Connor rose onto another column of water, Camonica said, "You will circle this hall, from water to flame, as fast as you can."

"That's it?"

"Of course not," Aonghus said, cracking his knuckles. "We get to steal the elements out from under you, and you must relinquish control. This isn't a battle of wills, it's a test of switching speed."

"Begin!" Camonica ordered, and her will snatched at the waters upon which he stood.

Connor barely managed to shatter the column of water, using it to heave himself toward the nearest vat of fuel. He reached for marble even as he released his connection with soapstone. With barely a spicy burn beginning, he flicked a spark into the fuel and seized the rushing flames that ignited.

They lifted him in gentle arms that smelled of burned toast, but almost immediately Aonghus tore at his control. Connor leaped from the flames, which winked out half a heartbeat later. He wouldn't make it to the next pool, but tapped soapstone and seized the waters, forming grasping, liquid hands to catch him and throw him on toward the next vat of fuel.

Already he was panting from the effort, and the contest had barely begun. He tried to settle into a routine, casting himself from pool to vat, and back to another pool, but his trainers increased the intensity of their interference, forcing him to constantly accelerate.

The greatest challenge was switching between the elements. The first few times he had tried connecting with marble, he'd needed to wait for the initial spicy flavor to intensify into searing heat before establishing a strong connection. Aonghus denied him that much time. Water was faster when used alone, but if he didn't completely relinquish marble first, it resisted the connection.

After four jumps, he fell to the ground in front of the next liquid fuel vat, losing contact with the fire before he even managed to ignite the spark.

"Faster," Aonghus chortled.

So Connor returned to the last pool and threw himself thirty feet into the air, arcing across to the oil. If he stayed higher, he'd get precious extra seconds of falling time to switch. He seized the fires of the next vat of oil and crafted five long spidery legs of fire to catch himself and propel himself onward.

"Good improvisation," Camonica called. "Now accelerate the pace."

"I thought I was accelerating!"

He made eight jumps before plunging into a vat of fuel just as it exploded into fire, controlled by Aonghus. For a second he panicked. He wasn't allowed to seize those flames, but how was he going to survive and escape that vat?

He was surprised to see the fire did not extend below the surface. The fuel burned his eyes and he sank fast toward the bottom, but he realized the fuel was still liquid. It didn't become fire until ignited.

So he tapped soapstone.

The liquid fuel was not water, and it slid across his soapstone senses like grease in his mind, slippery and hard to hold. Even when he focused the entire force of his soapstone senses on it, he only barely managed to grasp enough of the liquid to cast himself out of the vat.

He landed on the floor, frustrated that he'd failed to do more, and was completely unprepared when Aonghus rounded the vat, so angry, white-hot flames wreathed his entire head and dripped down his torso.

"How dare you!" he bellowed. Then he doubled over in a fit of violent coughing. His flames disappeared and he groaned in pain.

"You fool," Camonica said, approaching Aonghus. "You've swallowed your marble again, haven't you?"

Aonghus dropped to his knees, clutching his stomach, moaning.

"Marble makes you sick?" Connor asked. Hamish had sucked on every kind of rock, but he'd never gotten that type of reaction.

"Power-grade marble is if swallowed while being tapped." Camonica grabbed Aonghus by his rocking head and yanked him to his feet.

"Can you help him?" Connor cried. Aonghus had turned a sickly shade of orange, and his eyes were rolling back in his head.

"I wouldn't miss it." She punched Aonghus in the stomach so hard, she knocked his feet out from under him.

He crashed to the floor, vomiting all over Camonica's boots.

"Oh, that hurt," Aonghus moaned, rising to his knees.

"You're welcome," she said as the vomit collected and sprayed back into Aonghus' face.

As soon as Aonghus recovered his composure, he popped another piece of marble in his mouth and burned off the vomit sticking to his face. Connor wasn't sure he would have been so quick to embrace marble again after that episode, but Aonghus didn't seem to harbor any fear.

He turned to Connor, his face still burning. "How could you do that?"

"What?"

"Fuel is fire unborn," Aonghus exclaimed. "It's insulting to its very nature to command it is a slave to water."

"It is liquid, cinder-brain," Camonica said. She seemed to be enjoying the moment. "Manipulating such impure liquid demonstrates advanced levels of control."

"No!" Aonghus shouted. "He cannot master the finer points of his powers if he can't grasp such a simple concept."

"I think we've done enough for today," Camonica said.

Connor agreed. Aonghus needed some time to calm down.

"Very well," Aonghus said, but smoke still curled out his ears. "But don't do that again."

"Drop it," Camonica urged.

"It would help if we could bring in a Pathfinder and a Sentry to help recreate challenges he's likely to face from the other champions," Aonghus said, seemingly calm again.

"I'll ask Lady Shona about the Pathfinder," Camonica said. "We might be able to find one with the proper discretion, but I believe we're out of luck with the Sentries."

"There must be one," Aonghus insisted. "He needs to learn to deal with the obstacles of earth."

Connor's thoughts turned to Ilse. Did he dare approach her?

"Most of the Sentries support Redmund," he explained. "They all hate Padraigin, but I'd bet wax to wood chips they'd report everything to Redmund as soon as they left."

"We cannot afford that," Camonica said.

"Unless we purposefully work in some misdirection," Aonghus suggested.

They argued about the merits of that for a while. Finally Connor interrupted. "I might be able to find a Sentry."

"Who?" They both asked together.

"I can't tell you," Connor said, bracing himself for the expected angry replies. Camonica's expression hardened and Connor tensed to run if she came at him with one of those little daggers of hers.

Aonghus just laughed. "You're learning to keep secrets. Good! In your position, sometimes you must." He winked at Camonica. "Don't look so glum. We're here to train him, but he's the champion. You're not in command here, my girl."

"We're finished for today," Camonica snapped, turning away with such fluid grace that she had to be tapping obsidian. "Until tomorrow, then."

She left, her willowy form gliding across the floor. With her obsidian grace and tawny-haired beauty, Connor could see why a lot of men might be foolish enough to fall for her.

He pitied Cameron.

"What's her story?"

Captain Aonghus hopped up onto the edge of the nearby vat of liquid fuel and flames appeared to hold him as he reclined back. He considered Connor for a moment, with points of fire dancing in his eyes.

"Have a care with that one, lad. She's burning with vengeance hotter than any fire I can generate."

"What's she so angry at?"

"You haven't figure it out yet?" Aonghus spat a gob of white-hot flame at Connor, but he tapped marble and flung it back to get absorbed into Aonghus's fiery chair.

"She hates Kilian," Connor said.

Aonghus thumbed his nose in a move similar to the one used to accept a geall. "Aye, lad. He killed her husband, just as he killed High Lady Sileas, Dougal's first wife."

Connor hopped up beside Aonghus and cupped some fire in his hands, considering that. "What battle did they fight in?"

"Weren't no battle," Aonghus said. "In both cases, Kilian crossed the border special to kill them."

"Why?" Kilian was terrifying, but that didn't sound like him.

"From what I heard, they were exploring the deeper magics, accessible only after one ascends. . ." He trailed off and gave Connor an apologetic look. "Sorry, lad. We're getting into that stuff that can't be discussed, even when it's still just theoretical magic for the likes of you and me."

"Can you tell me anything else?" Connor asked, trying to hide his frustration.

Aonghus shrugged. "I'll tell you one thing, lad. This war has as much to do about settling old scores as it does with any political maneuvering."

Connor wondered about that exchange after Aonghus left, but couldn't focus on it too long. He needed to prepare to meet Ilse, but couldn't decide if he'd be walking into an almost-cordial planning meeting, or a pitched battle to the death.

Chapter 15

Once evening extinguished the glittering towers of the Carraig and concealing shadow settled over the land, Connor returned to the Sculpture House via the undercity. The underground ways were even more deserted than usual, and it was easy to imagine he was the only person alive in the world.

Did Evander live down there? What was the man's function at the Carraig? He wasn't involved in the classes, and was seen only on rare occasions. There was a permanence about the man that made Connor doubt he just popped in for a visit, but what else did he do with his time?

As he jogged down the dim, deserted halls, he imagined the giant, leather-clad Sentry stalking the undercity eternally. Did he like to surprise people like he had Connor earlier? No wonder people moved fast with furtive steps. That guy could give someone a heart-stomp.

Connor didn't stop at Ailsa's office in the Sculpture House, but slipped outside and tapped basalt, speeding onto the shadowed eastern plain. He would have loved just running with basalt for a while. That boundless energy, with the wind rushing past and no one else around was a rare taste of freedom.

Ilse wouldn't wait forever. She might already be planning to assassinate him, but he hoped she'd let him talk before trying to kill him. They might not exactly be friends, but he didn't think of her as a true enemy, and she owed him a chance to make things right before killing him. At least he hoped she did.

He slowed as he approached the sally port in the northern section of the great outer wall. Slipping a piece of slate into his boot, he embraced that gateway to the vast elemental earth. The connection came only after he slowed his breathing and released his nervous impatience. With deliberate care, he extended feelers of thought toward the wall, questing for any nearby Sentries.

Despite the danger of getting discovered, he enjoyed the rare opportunity to practice with slate. The strength of the earth radiated up through his slate connection, and he stood taller, feeling more confident. Shadows clung ever-deeper to the land, but he didn't need his eyes to know exactly what was around him. The grasslands of the plain tasted like a hint of fresh salad, while the rich earth underneath was more like a dense loaf of fresh-baked bread. The scents were faint, but helped color the ground and link him to it.

He felt no Sentries anywhere nearby. They patrolled the wall, but there were few on duty at any given time and miles of wall to cover. They might be shielding, but he didn't dare press his earth senses harder into the land for fear they'd discover him. They'd be monitoring the wall, and certainly they would notice if he opened the sally port. Hopefully they weren't watching the surrounding lands as closely.

He'd have to risk it.

Connor released slate and popped a piece of quartzite into his mouth, wedging it into his cheek. Instead of applying the liquid warmth that began pooling in the center of his head toward his senses, Connor directed it outward and grasped for surrounding air.

Padraigin was far better at working with air than any of the other Pathfinders at the school, but even she struggled for consistency. Connor wasn't sure what to expect when he pulled on the air currents slipping past his quartzite senses, like a breeze ruffling a raised flag.

A dust devil rise around him, twirling and tugging at his clothes. It smelled of mountain passes, and he took it as a good sign. Tapping basalt, he rushed the wall. Thirty feet away from it, he yanked hard on the air, hoping to lift himself over the wall.

A howling wind rushed down along the wall and he leaped into it, throwing his hands wide, as if grasping for the reins of a wild horse. The air condensed underneath him and drew him higher. Connor laughed with the thrill of it as wind whistled in his ears and pulled on his skin with icy fingers, drawing him ever higher.

Then it disappeared.

With a final flicker against his face, as if wishing him luck, it slipped away from his quartzite senses and left him soaring unaided through the air.

The wall loomed ahead of him. He'd almost reached it, but he wasn't quite high enough to sail over it without crashing into the crenelated top. So Connor tapped basalt and twisted in the air, striking the stone with already-fracked feet and leaping off the far side in a heart-blink.

He cleared the far side of the wall and accelerated into the landing, transferring his fall into a race away from the wall. A Sentry might have felt that tiny brush against the wall, but he would be long gone before they approached and searched the surrounding countryside.

Feeling a rush of excitement from the near-crash and exulting in the fact that the air had responded to his call, if only for a second, Connor sped away from the Carraig and up one of the shoulders of Mount Murdo.

He slowed after a mile and found a clearing with a jumble of rocks in the middle. Hopping up onto one and settling down to wait, he again tapped quartzite. No doubt, Ilse had noted his approach and knew exactly where he was waiting. She would most likely shield herself from his fledgling earth senses, so he applied quartzite to his ears and listened, hoping to detect something to warn him they were coming.

He didn't think Ilse planned to kill him, but he was alone on the mountain, with no help anywhere nearby. Ilse would be insulted if he didn't feel a bit nervous about the meeting. She was devilishly clever, but would she dare kidnapping him? She was already playing pat-a-pedra with Captain Rory and his forces and couldn't risk escalating the contest. Connor needed to convince her that it made more sense not to kidnap him than risk him turning unclaimed.

As he waited, he second-guessed his decision to stick with basalt instead of switching to granite. If the encounter turned hostile, basalt speed might be his only escape, but if any of the Petralists landed a solid hit, the little piece of sandstone he carried would never save him.

After several minutes of hearing nothing but the gentle sounds of the forest, Connor heard a small branch crack in the distance. It would have been beyond the ears of anyone not tapping quartzite, but he picked up on it and focused on that area, just downhill of his position, screened by a dense stand of evergreen.

Connor listened harder. In the Carraig, sounds crashed in like a great torrent, but in that dark wood, the flow was more like a gentle stream, so he plunged his mind into it and focused on everything he could hear. The creaking of trees and rustling of leaves sounded loud, as did the occasional scurry of small animals. He could almost understand the whispers of the wind as it whistled down from the majestic heights of Mount Murdo, lost in the darkness to even his enhanced vision. He heard tiny pinch-nippers leaping between stalks of grass, while the buzzing of flying insects sounded so loud, he could pinpoint the location of every moth, mosquito, and gnat nearby.

Then he heard the breathing.

They were coming.

Connor spoke loudly into the quiet, but did not enhance his voice. "Took you long enough."

Ilse and Margrit, her Longseer, rounded the stand of evergreen slightly to his right and stepped into the clearing, about forty feet away. Margrit's eyes glowed bright in his Pathfinder vision, and she gave him a tiny nod of acknowledgement.

The rest of the team didn't appear, and he couldn't pinpoint their breathing. The sibling Rumblers had a knack for showing up unexpectedly, but he didn't sense them sneaking up behind his pile of rocks.

Ilse regarded him for a moment. "You lied to me." Her voice was calm, but still chilling.

"You lied to me first," he retorted.

"We've been over that before. I do not lie to you, boy."

"Let's call it creative massaging of the truth, then."

"Tell me about Hector."

Of course she'd know about that. The truth about what happened to Hector was a closely guarded secret. Few at the Carraig even knew he was a Guardian. Fewer still knew anything about his connection with High Lord Dougal, and only a handful knew the truth about his turning unclaimed.

"He tried to kill Ailsa. When we confronted him, Lord Dail pronounced him unclaimed." Connor rose from his seat. "He turned immediately."

She frowned. "I didn't think it worked that way. We've never actually recorded a live witness of anyone turning unclaimed. I was convinced that it was all an elaborate lie."

"Well, I saw it. He transformed into some kind of raging monster. Possessed greater strength than a max-tapped Boulder, and the speed of a running Strider. His jaws changed." Connor raised his hands, trying to show the size of Hector's enormous jaws. "Could have snapped off someone's head. His claws were like daggers. You can't imagine what it was like without seeing it."

In the moment Hector had transformed, Connor had realized their carefully-crafted plan to escape into Granadure had been but a delicious lie.

"Your excuses are getting better," Ilse said with a hint of a smile.

Connor groaned. "I couldn't risk leaving. Even with Captain Rory's help, I just barely defeated that monster."

"The capitain is strong hands." The shapely Anika rounded the opposite side of the concealing trees, which placed her a little closer to Connor. Erich followed, looking disgusted that she'd given away their position.

At least they were across the clearing and not somehow sneaking up behind him, preparing to knock him on the head with stone-hard fists. Connor focused on Ilse. She needed to understand. "I had to stop him or he would have killed Ailsa and rampaged through the school."

Ilse actually looked troubled at the thought of so much death. That was one of the things that Connor liked about her and her team. They were enemies of Obrion, but they did not harbor the intense hatred that he had witnessed on both sides of conflict around Alasdair. He might not exactly get along with Ilse, but somehow they managed to find common ground.

"I had no way to find you," Connor said. "And I have to be more careful than ever. If Shona suspects I still want to leave with you, she's vowed to cancel my patronage and to enslave my entire village. If I lose patronage, I'll turn unclaimed before we escape the mountains. I'd kill you all."

Erich leaned forward, grinning. "Someone die if try rage kill. Maybe bring you head to home."

"You have no idea how dangerous that thing was," Connor insisted.

"Then tell me," Ilse said. "I must pass this information on to Kilian."

That was exactly what he wanted. As terrifying as Kilian could be, he seemed to know more about the deeper truths of Petralist powers than just about anyone. So Connor told them what happened, how it happened, and what he and Rory had to do to defeat Hector.

"The number of people who know your secret is growing," Ilse said when he finished.

"That's all you have to say?" he exclaimed. He was confirming the unclaimed were real, and that he had battled to the death with it. She didn't even look impressed.

Anika looked impressed, probably just because she was thinking about Rory. It was more than a little sickening to see how infatuated she had become with the captain. The fact that they were sworn to kill each other pretty much guaranteed that budding romance was going to end painfully, but they didn't seem to care.

"I point out that fact because that is the truth that will most likely affect your destiny and your freedom."

"I'm aware of it," Connor said. "Ailsa won't talk, and neither will Gisela. And Jok owes me a life debt."

"When more than one person knows a secret, it is no longer a secret."

"Well, the truth about me hasn't been a secret for months," Connor retorted.

"Be that as it may, we need a new plan."

"I'm open to suggestions, but I can't see how to make it work. Maybe you should get out of here before Rory finds you."

He hated to suggest it, but needed to. Ilse was his last link to Granadure, and to Verena. When she left, she would take with her the last slim chance he could escape the life Shona was planning for him.

Of course, before she left, her mission required her to kill him.

He wasn't looking forward to that part.

Ilse actually considered the suggestion, and Connor prepared to flee if she decided the time had come to embrace her secondary objective. Anika looked thrilled with the idea of getting her hands on Rory again. Erich looked more than eager for a bash fight with Rory's Fast Rollers.

They were both insane.

"Leaving is not yet an option," Ilse said. "I will report to Kilian and see what he suggests."

That gave him a little time before the final death battle. Until Ilse was a sworn enemy, he needed to leverage her position as a cautious ally.

"Before you go, I need some help."

"What kind of help?" she asked.

"I'm one of the champion contenders for the Tir-raon now."

Ilse frowned, "Why by the Tallan's glory did you choose the name you did?"

He had hoped she hadn't heard about that.

"I figured you would appreciate it."

"It does have certain poetic appeal," she admitted. "However it only increases the chance that you are going to generate additional enemies."

Connor shrugged. "I have plenty of enemies."

"What do you need from me then?"

"I need you to teach me slate."

Ilse smiled. "You have a lot of nerve, boy."

"I've been saving up. Besides, if you get orders to assassinate me, wouldn't you prefer it be a bit of a challenge?"

Eric laughed and clapped his hands together. "Many like talk. Will make many good fight."

Ilse smiled, a genuine smile. "All right. I will train you so that you can stand against those pampered Petralists."

He breathed a sigh of relief. She was his only possible teacher.

"Know this," she said, her tone turning hard. "When I come to kill you, I will do it quickly so you don't suffer."

The strange thing was, she looked like she meant it as a gesture of kindness, and he felt the honesty of the offer. "Ah, thanks, but I don't plan to go down that easy."

"Then we shall see if that day comes, but I still hold to hope that somehow we will find a way."

"So how do we begin?" Connor asked, wanting to change the topic from his looming assassination.

"Like this."

The earth beside Connor burst upward like a cresting wave and tumbled him and the pile of rocks he'd been sitting on away like flotsam in a raging tide.

Connor spun in the earth, wanting to scream, but not daring to open his mouth. His quartzite senses were useless. There was nothing to see but blackness, nothing to hear but the strangely peaceful hiss of tossed earth, nothing to smell but the dirt shoved up his nose.

He tapped slate and felt for the gateway of earth as the ground stopped tumbling, but did not release him. He was trapped underground, not even sure which way was up. Was Ilse trying to kill him after all?

He couldn't move, couldn't breathe, and didn't have nearly enough breath to survive more than a few seconds. He focused on slate, but the cursed little stone didn't open to his mind.

Connor raged silently, imagining the little stone chiding him for trying to walk with earth while so riled up. If Gregor was nearby, he'd probably say something annoyingly useless like, "The seed of the flower must first be sundered before the flower rises to brighten the world."

Actually, that wasn't half bad. Maybe near-death experiences were good for his Sentry speak.

As he struggled to establish a connection with earth, the ground buckled, tossing him up into blessed air. Connor gasped in a mouthful of dirt that tasted like that moment right after waking from a nightmare. Coughing and snorting out the dirt plugging his nose, he levered himself to a sitting position.

Ilse stood a dozen feet away, frowning at him. "Well?" she asked. "You did think to bring slate for training, didn't you?"

"It's being difficult."

"In a fight, your opponent won't give you time to set yourself," she said.

"I know. I wasn't ready."

She smiled. "You're ready now."

"No wait!"

The ground opened beneath him and he fell back into the pit, which closed over him again. That look in her eye made it clear she wasn't planning to rescue him again. It was up to him to get out.

He almost took a calming breath before remembering that would only kill him faster. Fighting back a growing panic, he focused on the slate again. Allowing the desperate need to fill him, he tried to touch the stone with a calm thought. It was like facing a friend's door at midnight with a charging torc bearing down on him, but needing to knock politely.

This time slate opened to his mind and he drove eager earth senses through. The ground became an extension of his limbs. Ilse was there, touching him with soft, ethereal fingers, but not actively blocking his connection with the earth.

So he seized the ground and lifted himself back to the surface on a wide pedestal, the earth above his head shifting aside to allow him to pass. He rose to the surface and drove the pedestal higher, forming a short tower, feeling a sense of pride at having accomplished the feat.

Ilse knocked him off his tower with a giant fist of earth, and when he struck, the ground swallowed him again.

After that, the training got really hard.

Ilse took the direct approach. As Connor spit dirt for the tenth time, he decided she must be a believer in the mantra that if the training didn't kill him, he might just survive the real thing.

That only left surviving the training, which he wasn't sure he'd manage. She struck over and over, each assault different, from nearly drowning him to dropping him into holes, then clobbering him with spears of earth. Maybe asking her to train him hadn't been such a good idea. She was more deadly as a friend than almost any other enemy.

She did start pausing between attempts to kill him, explaining what she had done and ways he could have blocked it. The fact that she assumed the split second warning before waves of earth overwhelmed him might be enough made him feel pretty good. She didn't need to know that he hadn't felt anything before getting clobbered.

Thankfully, she taught him the basics of shielding.

As he was gasping for breath, exhausted from freeing himself from an underground prison lined with the same stones he'd been sitting on only moments before, she said, "To remain unseen, one must embody what is not there."

"That's the first almost Sentry-worthy sentence I've heard out of you," Connor grinned.

She opened a hole directly under him, plunging him ten feet into the ground. When she let him ascend again she said, "The moth is consumed by the flame, no matter its intent to seek but the comfort of warmth or light."

So Connor threw a fireball at her face.

Apparently that wasn't the lesson she had been trying to teach. She held him underground for nearly a minute before allowing him to rise. Eventually he learned that the trick to a good shield was to pretend to be a hole in the ground, a weight with no weight as Ilse called it. With practice, he started getting a sense for how to create eddies in the earth around himself that would gently divert the senses of probing Sentries without alerting them to the deception.

"Blocking a direct incursion while remaining unseen is more challenging," Ilse warned. "We'll work on that next time."

Connor was surprised to feel a sense of loss that she had switched back to plain speech. It must be a terrible burden for a Sentry to speak normally so often.

By the time the brutal training ended, he was more than exhausted. If not for the replenishing strength of the earth, he would have slept on the mountain. He somehow managed to sneak back over the wall and find the Sculpture House in the darkness and climb to his own little room where he gratefully toppled into bed.

Chapter 16

It seemed only a second later when heavy pounding on the door dragged him awake.

"Leave me alone until morning," he groaned, turning over and burying his head in his pillow.

"Is morning," Gisela said, pushing the door open and poking her head in the room. "Connor, what are doing? Will be late!"

"Late?" His thoughts were as fractured as if his father had been beating them with his hammer all night in the Powder House.

"What is being the matter?" Gisela asked, stepping farther into the room, looking concerned. "Today is assigning armies."

"Oh, that." Connor stumbled out of bed, grateful that he hadn't bothered to undress.

"What have being doing?" she asked, frowning at his dirt-matted hair.

"Secret general training," he said, pushing her out of the room. "I'll be right down."

He gripped sandstone, drawing upon its welcome healing powers as he stripped off his old shirt. Dirt rained out of it, and he took a moment to beat the worst of the dust off his clothes before donning a spare shirt. Then he rushed downstairs where Aunt Ailsa was waiting for him.

"Do you have no concept of time?" She gave him one of those long-suffering looks like his mother often did.

"I've been busy."

"Busyness is more than filling time."

"Time flies on wings of fire while we labor in chains of darkness," he offered.

She gave him a stern look. "I'd tell you to be yourself, but I don't recommend any new disasters today."

Then she pressed a little pouch of rocks and powders into his hand. "You're late. The classes are already gathering. You were supposed to be on the stage by now."

"Arriving fashionably late will add to the legend."

"Hurry," she urged.

He waved and rushed toward the basement to race back to his Kilian suite to change. Gisela gave him a biscuit and a piece of sausage. He thanked her around a mouthful and raced into the undercity. As Connor tore through the now-familiar route to his suite, he thought back to the meeting with Evander the day before. He really hoped Jean appeared, because he didn't want to have to make good his threat.

Connor changed fast and burst out of his bedroom wearing his Kilian outfit just as Tomas began pounding on the door.

"You're late," Tomas said.

"So get me there fast."

They reached the grand assembly hall in record time with Tomas and Cameron leading the way at a pounding run. They weren't Striders, but they could move when they wanted to. Cameron in particular looked disappointed that other pedestrians were smart enough to scatter when they saw the two Fast Rollers charging down the street bellowing, "Make way for General Kilian!"

They finally slowed at the wide entrance, which was crammed with curious onlookers, trying to hear the announcements of the armies. Connor endured the many derogatory shouts and appreciated the few loud supporters that chanted his name.

Just before entering the giant hall, he paused to down a vial of soapstone mixture and to make sure the little piece of slate was in place in his boot. Using slate would risk revealing the truth of his curse, but he couldn't afford to not be prepared. The Tir-raon was about to commence its most important phase, and he was walking into a room full of enemies. The Fast Rollers took him around to the entrance reserved for faculty and champions.

"Try not to make too much of a mess," Tomas said as he pulled the door open for Connor.

"No promises," Connor said, stepping through.

He forced a casual stride as he climbed the four stairs up to a stage at the front of the gigantic room. Every eye was turned his way, so he waved, extending his fingers with streamers of fire.

All of the classes were already standing at attention, with the four Boulder classes at the front, followed by the Striders, then the tertiary affinity students. The long lines of Petralists was an impressive sight, but they barely filled half the hall. Massive stone walls rose over a hundred feet, supporting a vast dome that rose even higher. Tiny windows were set far up the dome, and Connor caught sight of birds flitting between the giant ribs holding up that dome. It was perhaps the biggest space he'd ever seen indoors.

Most of those assembled on the dais at the head of the hall gave him dirty looks, particularly Lord Kane. The hulking representative of High Lord Feichin was Redmund's uncle, and he looked personally insulted that Connor had dared attend.

That wasn't surprising. The man's relentless efforts to uncover Connor's true identity were getting tiresome. Standing beside him was Lord Runda, the representative of High Lord Goban. The man had hinted that he was responsible for the watchers who had been spying on Connor outside of Ailsa's mansion before they came to the Carraig. Runda was a middle-aged man whose outstanding quality was his sheer unremarkabilty. Even though he was a Blade, he could fade into the background and become easily overlooked.

If only Connor had mastered that art, he might have avoided getting dragged into so many gealls when he first arrived at the school. What might he have done with all the free time not spent crawling to Aifric and the other Healers?

Did Runda know the secret of his curse? Connor didn't know how much the watchers had seen. Whatever he knew or suspected, Runda had not run a geall on Connor using that information as leverage. What was he waiting for?

Connor scanned the other high lord representatives. Lady Polglass was elderly, with a stooped stance and silver hair, but her blue eyes were undimmed. Rumor had it that her long, hooked nose could smell out political intrigue better than a Pathfinder. She was managing Ivor's nomination for High Lady Islay, who planned to marry Ivor off to her eldest daughter if he won.

It was strange that she stood beside the fat Lady Una, who managed Padraigin's nomination. The two women were not exactly close, given that their houses were both sponsoring champions. Could they have been the ones, plotting together, to order a secret Sentry to bring down the Rhidorroch and undermine Connor's position as champion?

There was no way to know, so Connor smiled and declared, "Thanks for waiting. I was delayed with all those new fans wanting signatures on their parchments, their foreheads, and some other places I can't really mention in public."

Padraigin almost stifled a giggle, but ended up spitting on Redmund, who glared. Ivor tried to look bored, but the corners of his mouth twitched.

Frazier, the maze lord, shifted into view from behind Lord Nevan. He watched Connor guardedly, as if afraid he would bring down the roof upon all of them. Some people needed to work on their sense of trust.

"How long must we suffer the antics of this fool Kilian?" Lord Kane growled. Most of the other representatives looked displeased, and Lord Nevan made subtle gestures warning Connor to back off.

Too late for that.

"I'll tell you what," Connor said before Lord Dail could take his place at the podium at the front of the stage to begin the assembly. "Lord Kane, your incessant protestations against my name have not fallen upon deaf ears."

That got their attention. Lord Nevan looked decidedly nervous. "And since my name so clearly frightens some of you, I've decided to relent and demonstrate here at this most important occasion, my willingness to work together to make this the greatest Tir-raon this school has ever known."

As he spoke, someone applied quartzite to his voice. He wasn't sure who did it, but he recognized the faint tickle down his throat. His words magnified until they boomed across the hall. Many students began whispering excitedly, and a feeling of anticipation grew.

"So you will reveal the truth and remove that mask?" Lord Kane asked.

"Of course not," Connor said, giving the man an exaggerated look of disgust to make sure the expression showed through the mask. "But you can call me Lian."

"Lian?" Lady Una asked, her jowls jiggling. She represented High Lord Pilib, and Connor had been surprised to learn that she would have been the head of her own house had it not failed during the rule of her grandfather and united with house Pilib. Perhaps if Padraigin won they would win enough prestige to split their houses again.

If Padraigin won, she would be married into house Pilib and swear allegiance to Obrion. Connor still barely believed she was willing to make such a tremendous sacrifice.

"It's a nice, non-threatening name," Connor said. "Just the thing to help settle our poor Lord Kane's nerves." That triggered a round of snickering from the crowd, making Lord Kane all the angrier.

"Enough of this nonsense," he bellowed. "This farce cannot go on."

"Oh, calm down, Kane," Lady Polglass said, rubbing her long, hooked nose, her eyes twinkling. "That flaming wet dawnus is having a bit of fun, and you're making it far too easy for him."

Connor cringed. He really needed to find time to speak with Lady Polglass after the assembly. She might be using a technically correct term, but there had to be a way to describe his powers in more heroic terms.

As Lord Kane started sputtering again, Lord Dail cut him off. "Silence please. I hate being late."

In a loud voice he announced, "It is time."

Even though Lord Kane kept muttering under his breath, Lord Dail proceeded. He greeted the crowd and launched into a long-winded speech about the glorious tradition of the Tir-raon, the grand history and mighty honor that rested upon all those assembled, and the solemn duty that fell to all of them to perform at their very best, particularly at this time of impending warfare.

While he talked, Connor scanned the crowds. Down in the main hall, early morning sun streamed through stained-glass windows set high in the walls under the domed ceiling and cast multi-colored lights over the crowd of students. The air smelled a bit musty and held a lingering chill, despite the number of people packing the hall.

Connor only barely managed not to yawn as Lord Dail's speech dragged on. Most of the assembled students stared straight ahead, faces expressionless, but some began falling to the insistent tug of that monotonous voice. Some heads began to nod, others started to wobble where they stood, although most were nudged by fellow students before they pitched forward or started snoring. A few unlucky ones made the mistake of locking their knees where they stood, then suddenly collapsing. Connor had learned that painful lesson young while standing at attention under the viper-like tongue of Cinaed on those days when she took her turn teaching the children.

To his right, Ivor muttered in a voice loud enough to carry to Connor and to the droning lord of the Carraig, "I want him in my army. He's unstoppable."

Padraigin snickered and even Redmund cracked a smile, but Lord Dail ignored the comment and prattled on. Lord Kane glared at Ivor's lack of decorum, but Lord Nevan and most of the other representatives looked like they secretly agreed.

Even Lord Dail couldn't talk forever, and the excitement of the long-awaited announcement kept the students focused. Each champion contender would lead an army that was supposed to be as closely identical as the make-up of the student body allowed but, as Lord Nevan had warned, the irritated representatives had agreed to dump on Connor the lowest-ranking students, with but few exceptions.

As Lord Dail finally transitioned to the actual army assignments, students perked up, leaning forward, hanging on every word. He seemed to enjoy the effect and took his time reading down the long list of assignments to cheers and clapping. Connor tallied the counts in his mind and forced a smile on his face to rob his opponents of potential gloating over his inferior army.

Although he received a full complement of forty Boulders and twenty-five Striders, they were mostly younger students or those who held lower standings. Then there was Shona. Her appointment to his army came as no surprise, but it did carry with it a number of complications and not a few opportunities.

He wanted to assign her the duty of official latrine cleaner, but she'd just summon him to her palace as Connor and beat him to powder. Maybe he could make her his personal servant and insist she feed him? Still not right, but he'd come up with something.

Of course, he got the team who had helped him win his nomination challenge. Princess Catriona cheered when her name was called. Lorcc waved, but looked concerned at how many low-ranking Striders he'd be leading, and little Declan looked terrified when he realized he would be the army's only Sentry.

The remainder painted a grim picture. Although Connor knew well all the eager Healers assigned to his army, led by Aifric, the remaining affinities were extremely weak. He did win two Blades, two Solas, and three Pathfinders, but one of those girls looked to be twelve years old. He did not receive any Spitters.

The Sentries would prove the biggest hurdle. A single Sentry could wreak havoc over an entire battlefield. After last night's practice, he had felt first-hand the incredible power of a competent Sentry, even when they were more or less showing restraint. With only little Declan on his side, he'd be facing two or three powerful earth movers in each of the opposing armies.

He told himself it could be worse, but couldn't quite figure out how.

At least he already knew most of the assigned students from their runs through the Rhidorroch, and had even helped some of them improve. Although the majority of them still ranked low in the standings, as a group he could transform them into something more.

Before Lord Dail even completed assignments, Connor began plotting ways to leverage his underpowered army to offset their handicaps. One thing was abundantly clear, approaching the upcoming battles in any traditional sense would guarantee defeat.

Come curse or confusion, he had to find a way.

One of the lessons driven home from the battles of Alasdair was that the bigger army didn't necessarily win. He longed for Verena. Not only would he love to hold her one more time, but her Builder powers would have spanked those student armies.

The other three champions all ordered their armies to assemble in their individual training facilities for their first briefing, but Connor chose a different location.

"Lian's army will report to the Rhidorroch."

Chapter 17

As the assembly dispersed into chattering crowds, Ivor clapped Connor on the back. "They grouted you good, Lian. And I had been hoping for a serious challenge."

"The beauty of the weed is the thorn, but the tares may choke the golden wheat."

"Sentry-speak isn't going to save you," Ivor chuckled. "That was a good one, by the way."

"I've been practicing."

"Oh, Lian, you're doomed," Padraigin exclaimed, actually looking sad for him.

"Don't cry when I defeat you," Connor replied. "I hate beating a lady, but sometimes it must be done."

"Even with your clever games, you don't stand a chance."

"See you on the battlefield."

She walked away, head high, with softly beating invisible drums punctuating her graceful stride.

"She's right," Ivor said. "We can't afford to hold back, no matter how unfair the assignments might be."

"And what if I requested this army?"

"You're not insane."

"Are not the victories won despite the odds celebrated the loudest?"

"Fair enough," Ivor said. "You want fame and glory, but just remember, most generals who enter a battle with an inferior position just lose."

"And yet it's the baker who eats the freshest cakes."

Ivor rolled his eyes. "Hey, why don't you stop by later? I'd like to discuss possible joint training together."

There it was, the invitation to meet, phrased in a way that even eavesdropping Pathfinders wouldn't pay much attention.

"Why not?" Connor said. "Could be fun."

Connor waited for most of the others to leave the stage before following. Students were crowding around the stage, eager to speak with their generals, some already calling out reasons why they should be chosen as captains.

Tomas met him at the foot of the stairs. "You're slagged. Even Rory would be hard pressed to leverage the army you've been assigned."

Everyone was as pessimistic as a toothless granny in a prune-chewing competition.

"We'll find a way," Connor promised him. "Where's Cameron?"

"Escorting the young maid, Jean, to your suite."

"Jean? She's here?" Connor exclaimed.

"Showed up just after you entered," Tomas said, pushing through the crowd toward the door. "We figured it safer to send her away. Besides, I knew you were worried about her."

"Is she all right?" Connor asked, so relieved to hear she was back that he wanted to shout with joy.

"Seemed fine, but all worked up over something. On the point of bursting with whatever she needed to tell you."

Many people called to Connor for comments on the army assignments or laughed that he was doomed. He ignored them all and ordered Tomas to get him to his suite double time. Not caring that some might interpret his haste for flight or shame, he and Tomas bolted.

As soon as he entered his private suite, Jean catapulted out of a comfortable chair where she'd been sitting. She crossed the room in a rush, her thick, blond hair streaming behind as she threw her arms around his waist.

Connor hugged her close. Jean was one of his oldest, dearest friends, and for much of his life he had dreamed of nothing more than winning her hand before either Hamish or Stuart could. He and Jean had both grown beyond the possibility of such a union, but he was still overjoyed to see her well.

"Where by the Tallan's hideous teeth have you been?"

"You just made that up," she said, stepping back and giving him one of those looks, hands on hips, head cocked to one side.

"I've been playing Lian too long."

"Who?"

"Me, without the Kil."

"You make less sense than ever." She tried to smile, but couldn't quite make it work. Whatever was on her mind was stealing her good humor.

"I'm glad you're all right," he said, smiling.

"How do you know I'm all right then?"

"You're taking time to criticize. You never do that when you're not all right."

"I'm not all right," she said softly.

"Did anyone hurt you?" His worries and vengeful anger started burning hot again.

"No, nothing like that."

"Then where have you been?"

She led him to one of the fancy couches facing the cold fireplace and they settled onto it together. She pulled a small leather notebook from a satchel she wore over her shoulder. It was full of scribbled notes.

Gripping her notebook, she gave him a grave look. "I've been learning the truth, Connor, and it's crazier than anything we imagined."

He forced himself to wait. He'd never seen Jean so rattled by anything. Her hands shook against the notebook, and there was an unusual wildness around her eyes. She never looked that bad, even when treating badly injured patients.

"Patronage is a lie," she blurted.

Connor blinked. He had to have heard that wrong. "What?"

"It's all a lie," she exclaimed, gesturing with her notebook. "That's what I've been studying. Down in a secret library that no one but Evander knows about. The truth has been buried for so long, but he showed me."

"It's got to be a lie," Connor said, thinking back to his recent strange interview with the hulking Evander.

"That's what I said," Jean repeated. "It's all a lie."

"No, I mean it's a lie that it's a lie," Connor insisted.

"What?"

"He's got to be running a geall on you, but why would he make up something like that?"

"Listen to me." Jean gripped his hand. Her fingers were warm, her face flushed. "I read the original treatise, written by the survivors of the Tallan Wars. They were desperate, and they invented patronage."

"Are you sure it was genuine?" he asked, wanting to believe her, but it was such a leap!

"I'm not inventing it," Jean cried. "I know what you're thinking, Connor, but that's why I haven't been around. I've been studying everything, digging into historical records and learning why they set up this elaborate breeding plan with the noble houses."

"Patronage is real," Connor whispered, but her words were beating into his head like his father's hammer. "I've seen the unclaimed, Jean. I had to kill one."

"I don't know what happened with Hector, but it wasn't what you think."

Connor sat back, hope battling with reality. Jean was the smartest person he had ever known. He had never doubted her before, but how could he believe this? The risk was too great.

"Explain it to me. All of it."

"There's not time for everything. You have to meet with your army."

"Tallan take the army," Connor snapped. "Tell me."

Jean rose and paced away across the rug. "There's too much to cover all at once, but let's start with the Tallan, since you just mentioned him." She drew closer, raising the notebook before her. "Tallan was a man all along. He was the grandson of the king and queen of the Obrion Empire."

He'd heard enough clues that it made sense. "I've never heard more than rumors about those ancient rulers."

"They ruled the entire continent. The land is vast, so much bigger than we ever knew. There's even a southern continent separated by a sea."

"Tabnit," Connor said, thinking back to Gisela's map. "Beyond the Sea of Olcan."

"How could you possibly know that?"

"I know about the Arishat League and a little of the history."

"That makes it easier," Jean said. "I was shocked to learn about those other countries."

Connor had been too. In the sheltered valley of Alasdair, he'd known precious little about their own country, less about Granadure, and nothing about anywhere else.

"They owned it all," Jean said. "King Triath and Queen Dreokt ruled for centuries, but I barely found any direct references about them."

"They must have been powerful Petralists," Connor said. "Gregor's in his eighties, but you'd never know. Only tertiary Petralists could live so long."

Jean nodded. "They were the original Blood of the Tallan. He inherited his powers from them. From what I've read, they could do things that no Petralists today could hope to duplicate."

"Really?"

"Most of the greatest Petralists of the age were killed during the war. Evander wouldn't let me read the list of survivors."

"Why did he show you any of it?"

"I'm not sure. I have some suspicions, and he gave me some strict warnings and conditions that you'll have to agree to."

"And if I don't?" Connor wasn't feeling entirely compliant after Evander hadn't even bothered telling him Jean was all right.

"Don't anger him," Jean hissed, looking terrified. "He'll kill you, Connor. Don't ever doubt that, not for a second."

"Did he hurt you?" Connor asked, his anger building. If Evander had hurt Jean, Connor would find a way to hurt him, no matter how powerful he might be.

"No, but he's such a mystery. I've spent enough time around him that I'm starting to get a sense of him. He's ancient, Connor, and he doesn't do anything without a reason."

"Well he'd better tell me the reasons if he wants me to cooperate."

"Stop it," she snapped. "You can't run a geall on him, Connor. He stands outside of any normal circles we know."

"We need to know more about him," Connor insisted.

"I'll learn," she promised. "But for now, don't cross him."

"It doesn't make sense." Connor frowned. "Why share such a secret, then threaten you? What's his geall?"

"This information is dangerous. People will kill to protect it. Think about the risk to the nation if this truth got out?"

As he considered that, she continued. "I don't know all the details about what triggered the war, but the Great Purge was one of the flash points."

"When they killed all the Builders?" Legends of those dark days at the end of the Age of Discovery abounded, told and retold even in remote villages like Alasdair.

Jean nodded. "The king died around that time too, although I found no specifics about how. Somewhere in there, Tallan rebelled against his grandmother and the war broke out. The fighting killed most of the nobility along with most of the strongest Petralists. The empire shattered, with Granadure and the nations of the Arishat breaking off."

"What happened to Tallan?"

"I found a single reference. I believe he was assassinated."

"I wish we knew more." Connor was starting to understand why Tallan's memory had been demonized so completely if he was somehow to blame for the downfall of the empire.

"I'll keep digging," Jean promised. "There's so much to learn, and I don't have access to it all."

"So how does all that history lead to patronage being a lie?"

"It was those conditions that forced the hand of the few remaining nobles. They were desperate as they scrambled to consolidate their kingdom. They decided that the most important thing they could do was to rebuild their Petralist forces."

"Makes sense."

"But they wanted to consolidate those powers in the noble houses to ensure their rule and to rebuild the powers that were lost. With so many of the noble Petralists killed, they faced the risk that their powers would get diluted. Strong Petralist powers are most often inherited. However, many of the strongest remaining powers belonged to commoners. They couldn't risk common people rising to wrest power from them, but they needed those powers to reinforce and rebuild their own bloodlines."

Connor felt a growing horror as Jean spoke, the harsh reality of those dark days coming alive in his mind.

With her voice dropping to a whisper, Jean continued. "So they invented Patronage. Connor, they invented the whole thing as a way to keep the commoners in check and dependent upon them. This way, any gifted commoner had to come to them. They could pick from the most powerful gifts and adopt those in their bloodlines."

Connor felt sick. "It was all a plan to breed Petralists?"

Jean nodded. "They still run their houses the same way."

Shona and the other nobles discussed their houses and bloodlines like families of horses, but Connor shook his head. "It's compelling, Jean, but I don't believe everyone would fall for such a huge lie."

"No one knows any more," she insisted. "Only the heads of houses are aware of the lie."

"So Shona doesn't even know?"

"I don't think so."

Well that gave him a place to start. "I can try to find out."

"Why?" Jean demanded. "It's a lie. You can leave."

He shook his head. "It's not that simple, Jean. I've seen the unclaimed."

"I'm telling you, that's a lie too."

"How?"

She shrugged. "I don't know."

"We can't act on what you've learned without knowing more. What if somehow patronage started as a lie but has become necessary?"

"How would that be possible?"

"I don't know. Once we understand the unclaimed, we'll know for sure. Until then, we can't assume there's no truth to patronage today. Too many people could die if we make the wrong choice." As she considered that he added, "How can they keep such a secret going? Surely someone must have realized those reports of unclaimed terrorizing villages were all lies."

"That's the thing, they're not." Jean dropped back onto the couch beside him. "I've been studying reports that show there have been well documented instances of attacks for hundreds of years."

"Do they date back to before the Tallan Wars?"

"I haven't seen anything that old. Either Evander hasn't shared that information with me, or the records didn't survive the war."

"So how can patronage be a lie, but unclaimed have been attacking people?" Connor asked. "If it's a lie, then those attacks must be false reports."

"That's what I thought at first, but the attacks really happened. Something did occasionally attack villages and even towns. They're all blamed on the unclaimed, but I don't know enough yet to say for sure."

Connor rose and paced around the room, thoughts tumbling through his head. Jean believed what she was saying, but there had to be more she hadn't learned. Unclaimed were real. If they weren't the result of losing patronage, what were they? How could he find out?

"You have to learn more," he said. "But you can't disappear for days on end. People are noticing."

"There's so much to study," she protested.

"I know, but we need to find a balance. You need to report to Shona. She's getting angry that she hasn't seen you."

Jean grimaced. "I had hoped she was so busy she wouldn't notice."

"For a day, maybe. But you've been gone for a week. She thinks you've been helping me with my new duties, so use that."

"I can make that work," she agreed. "Shona doesn't really care about me serving her every day. She just wants to make sure she stays in control."

"I'll discuss this with Aunt Ailsa," Connor said. "Maybe she'll have some ideas."

"Be careful," Jean insisted. "Evander said we cannot share this information. If the truth gets out, I think he'll kill everyone who knows."

"I'll be careful," Connor said. "Some day, somehow, it has to get out eventually."

"It can't." She looked deeply afraid. "Even if Evander allowed it, the nobility cannot. They'd risk losing control over the Guardians, risk civil war. They're already facing a war with Granadure."

He hated admitting it, but she was right. The political situation was too volatile for such an explosive truth. "But Ailsa has to know. She can keep secrets better than anyone."

"I agree."

"I'll see if I can pry any information out of Shona," Connor added.

"She probably doesn't know," Jean warned. "And revealing that you know is too dangerous."

"I can be careful." When she raised a doubting eyebrow, he insisted, "I can. But even if I just confirm that she knows nothing, that helps verify a little about what you learned."

"I'll get back to studying as soon as I can," Jean insisted. "What are you going to do in the meantime?"

"Think about this some more. There has to be a way to learn the truth about the unclaimed. I'm going to ask Ilse about it when I speak with her next time."

"Be careful," Jean said. "She's not exactly a friend."

"But she can get information from Kilian, and we need as much as we can get."

Jean rose and gave him a hug, leaning against him for a moment.

"I'm glad you're safe." He couldn't have continued playing Lian if she'd been hurt. "Be careful."

"You be careful," she retorted. "You're the one who has to win battles with an army that's too small and too lightly powered."

"They'll get better," he promised. "Time for the first practice."

Chapter 18

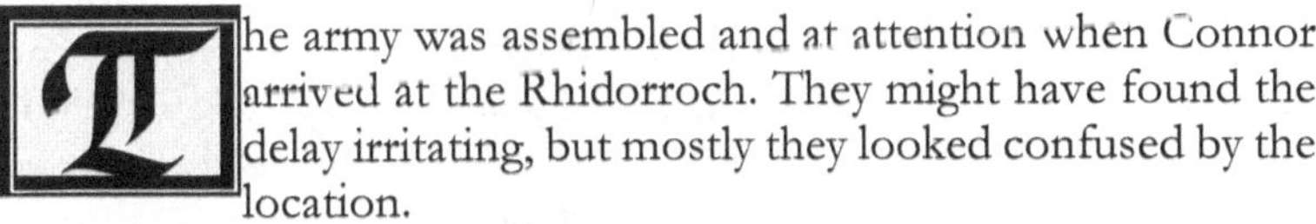

he army was assembled and at attention when Connor arrived at the Rhidorroch. They might have found the delay irritating, but mostly they looked confused by the location.

The broken skeleton of the great ice dome was gone. Frazier must have needed several Spitters to remove it all so quickly. It shouldn't have surprised Connor that he wasn't asked to help. Frazier didn't exactly trust him at the moment. Teams of workers were already busy, starting the rebuilding process all over again.

Connor loved the Rhidorroch, and he felt a lingering rage at its senseless destruction. Even though he'd helped destroy it twice, he had never wanted it broken, and he longed to see it rebuilt. Not only was he excited to run it with the students, but it was an unrivaled training tool that his army desperately needed.

As Connor approached, he forced aside the whirling thoughts triggered by Jean's incredible revelation. They'd solve that mystery, but at the moment, he needed to focus on training his new army for the daunting missions ahead.

Despite the challenges they faced, he loved being a general!

He commanded an army even stronger than the original strike force Captain Rory had led against Ilse and the Grandurian invaders around Alasdair. In the upcoming battles, he'd be playing the outmatched side, and he planned to employ all the lessons he'd learned watching Ilse trounce Rory.

With a confident stride, Connor approached his army. He knew their strengths and shortcomings from their many runnings of the Rhidorroch. Unfortunately, many of them had more shortcomings than strengths, but that wasn't the part that worried him.

The army already looked beaten.

Although they stood at strict attention, they didn't try to hide the fact that they considered their cause hopeless. They weren't fools. They lived with the reality of the standings every day, and their future plans depended on success in the all-important group battles. They would all feel the personal disaster of defeat as much as he did.

Connor needed to solve the lack of tertiary affinity powers, or their negative predictions would prove all too true. These were his forces, and they deserved his best effort. They needed him as much as he needed them.

In the front ranks stood Shona, Princess Catriona, and a tall fellow with broad shoulders, who wore his black hair longer than most. He sported the twin swords of a Blade on his back, and even standing still exuded a sense of danger. Connor knew him by reputation. He was one of the few members of the newly assigned army that held a high position in the standings.

His name was Fearghas, and he came from a city in Dougal's realm, which was probably how he came to be assigned to this army. Fearghas needed to believe, or Connor would never win over the rest of the army.

Behind Fearghas stood a second Blade named Heber, who Connor knew well. Even enhanced by a strong obsidian gift, his fighting skills barely reached average. His natural gifts ran to numbers, statistics, and calculations, and in that realm, he was unmatched. Beside Heber stood Aifric, one of the few students who looked happy to be there.

Fearghas spoke before Connor reached the front of the troop. "General Kilian, request to transfer to another army, sir."

"Denied. And call me Lian."

"Request to ask your real name."

"Denied."

The Blade scowled. "Request to rip off that mask and drive a knife up your nose."

Connor laughed, even though secretly he was testing his connection with soapstone. No one laughed in the face of a Blade's threat, even if it came with such gross insubordination that he should be thrown right out of the army.

"Thanks for breaking the ice for us, soldier," Connor said in a friendly tone that seemed to unsettle Fearghas even more. He raised his voice. "Welcome to day one."

Fearghas tried one more time, "You expect us to follow a general whose face we've never seen?"

"I expect you to follow orders."

"To what end?" Fearghas asked. "We have no chance of winning."

"To be more precise," Heber cut in. "Given the make-up of the armies, we have at best an eleven percent chance of winning."

Fearghas pointed at Heber, "See, even the numbers weirdo agrees. We're doomed."

Heber combed at one side of his head with carefully-trimmed nails, "Actually, my calculations are only rough estimates since I don't know enough about General Lian's battle strategy to factor in the appropriate coefficients and tangential probabilities."

"And that will make all the difference," Connor assured them. He lifted his hands to forestall other arguments. "This army is more than just a bunch of numbers. You're more than your standings. When I learned who was assigned to my army, I wanted to cheer."

At the ripple of doubtful murmurs, he added, "Honestly, I did."

"You wanted a bunch of losers?" Fearghas asked, "Because that's what you got."

"You're no loser."

"That's why I shouldn't be here." His calm pronouncement triggered more muttering, but no one challenged him.

"You're here for a reason, and you'll discover that reason soon enough." Connor filled his voice with confidence. "The reason I felt pleased to have you instead of students with higher standings is because they feel like they already know how to succeed and would blind their minds to what I can teach them. They would limit their own potential."

"Doesn't matter," one Strider called. "At least they *have* potential."

Connor grinned. "You just proved my point. You haven't figured out a winning strategy yet, but you will."

"How is it possible?" the same Strider asked softly, as if barely able to muster enough hope to consider the idea.

"Because we're going to have fun!"

Silence ruled until Fearghas spoke. "You've cracked, haven't you?"

"No, my friend. I just remembered something they've been trying to beat out of us for so long that we've all forgotten." He turned to Shona. "Can't you remember a time when learning about what you could really do with your powers filled you with wonder?"

A soft smile played across Shona's lips and her face softened from the slight frown she'd been wearing.

Connor turned back to Fearghas, "When are you the most deadly?"

"When I'm focused."

He shook his head. "When you really think about it, you'll realize it's when you're enjoying yourself."

"How can we have fun losing?" Heber asked.

Connor tapped his nose and grinned, "That's the secret. When you're having fun, you won't lose."

Heber frowned. "Excuse me, General, but even factoring in the widest possible probabilities, I can't see how you can overcome the lack of Sentries. Statistical analysis of that one factor alone negates any positive fluctuations of the other variables you may propose."

Connor clapped Heber on the shoulder. "You don't have all the information yet, but when you do, you'll see."

"Listen to me," he called to his still-depressed army. "I've seen battles where a tiny force with far fewer resources defeated a much larger opponent. It's possible, but requires hard work and discipline. You must trust me and obey my commands even if they don't make any sense at the time. Above all, you must meet every challenge with the determination to enjoy your incredible powers to the fullest."

"It'll never work," Fearghas muttered.

"If you give up, you've already lost and I can't help you." Connor extended his hand. "Do you have the courage to try?"

After a brief hesitation, the lanky Blade took his proffered hand. "Aye, General. I have the courage, and for now I'll follow you just out of curiosity."

Shona spoke for the first time. "General Lian, I'll follow you for the chance to spit in the eye of everyone who thinks we can't do it."

"Let's crack 'em!" Aifric cried and pumped her fist in the air.

That garnered some more half-hearted support from the army. All things considered, not a bad start. It was a thrill to face an army of mighty Petralists, who were all willing to follow him into battle, knowing their chances of winning were slim to none. He felt a heavy weight of responsibility to find a way to flip the situation in their favor.

Fearghas leaned close and said softly, "If you lead us to failure, General, I'll cut out your heart."

Connor nodded. "I would expect nothing less."

Before he could begin defining their training plan, Frazier appeared atop the nearby wall of the Rhidorroch. The outer stair had been shattered by the collapse of the dome, but a rope ladder hung over the side. Frazier didn't bother with the rungs, but slid down the ropes, hands protected by thick leather gloves.

"What are you doing here, General Lian?" he demanded as the students opened a path for him.

"We're beginning training, or course."

"Where?"

Connor pointed toward the wall of the Rhidorroch.

Frazier scowled. "Don't mock me, Lian. I've got too much work to do, and every time you appear, things get destroyed."

"An occupational hazard," Connor said, vowing to change that record. "But you're going to want to hear what I have in mind."

"I doubt it. The upper level is completely shattered, and half of the tunnels are blocked with debris. That dome set us back two weeks, and I've got every lord in the castle clamoring for a new course so standings can get updated."

"It sounds to me like your workers need a bit of fun to rejuvenate their energy."

"I'm warning you," Frazier growled.

"You doubt me?" Connor asked, feigning shock. "After I just saved your life right here?"

He sighed. "What do you want, Lian? Out with it."

"I propose we help each other," Connor said. "My army needs training, and your tunnels need clearing."

"How do we do both?" Frazier sounded interested, despite himself.

"My army will race through those tunnels," Connor said. "If the tunnels are blocked, their challenge will be to clear them in order to proceed."

Frazier's scowl faded, but he gave Connor a doubtful look. "What's the catch?"

"Just clearing tunnels is kind of boring," Connor said to muttered agreement from the students. "So we need to spice things up a bit."

"How?"

"Do you think your workers would like to throw things at students for a change?"

For the first time in days, Frazier actually smiled.

Chapter 19

"The whole thing is a giant lie," Connor said.

Ailsa did not immediately respond, but leaned back in her overstuffed chair in her office. Connor had rushed back to the Sculpture House as soon as he'd dismissed his army.

"Well?" Connor asked, leaning forward in the uncomfortable chair facing her desk.

"You're absolutely sure?"

"Of course we're not absolutely sure. That's why I'm here. We need to figure out how to be absolutely sure. This could change everything."

Ailsa nodded, then walked around her desk and went to the closed door. Opening it, she stuck her head through. "Gisela, I need you."

She returned to her seat behind the large desk just as Gisela entered the room.

"What can I doing for you?" Gisela asked. Her white-blond hair was pulled back from her face in a ponytail. That was the first time Connor had seen her wear her hair that way, and it highlighted her high cheekbones and made her look even more foreign.

"Close the door," Ailsa said, then added, "Connor, tell her what you just told me."

That was surprising. Connor trusted Gisela, mostly, but she wasn't privy to the full truth. This was the most potentially deadly truth he had ever learned.

"Are you sure that's a good idea?"

Ailsa nodded. "But perhaps it's time for Gisela to share some information with you first so you understand her position."

Now it was Gisela's turn to look surprised. Her always-pale face turned paler still. She shook her head. "I am not thinking this is good idea."

"You owe me some information," Connor said, intrigued by her reaction. "The day we defeated Hector, you said you had a secret, and that you would tell me."

Gisela gave him a disgusted look. "No is fair reminding girl of truth shared in moment of distress."

"That's a ridiculous argument."

"Not if it is working."

Ailsa said, "Gisela, this information is too important. It's time to merge our efforts. We finally might have some actionable intelligence."

"Very well." Gisela straightened to her full height, as if coming to attention. "I am secret embassy from Arishat."

"I thought you were from Althing." Had another friend been lying to him all along?

"Of course I am," Gisela snapped. "But Althing is being leader of Arishat. And Arishat League is wanting information about the situation in Obrion before war is starting."

"Are you telling me you're a spy?" He did love it when friends had such amazing secrets, though.

Ailsa's expression turned pained. "Spy is such an ugly word, don't you think?"

"Are you a spy too?" Connor asked his aunt.

She shook her head. "I am a patriot. I love this country and I want it to be great. More importantly I want it to be free from tyrants who wish to enslave us." She spoke calmly, but her emerald eyes glittered with fervor.

Connor had felt similar feelings during the battles around Alasdair as his loyalties were challenged. If anything, he had begun questioning the status quo more of late. What if Jean's findings could be proven true? He didn't think he could remain loyal to a nation that enslaved its own people and lied about such important truths as patronage. He'd have to doubt the rightness of the looming war and would question everything about what it meant to live in Obrion.

"What does that mean?" he asked.

Ailsa leaned forward. "I have established a network of like-minded individuals across the nation, all dedicated to gathering intelligence to help determine the truth and to establish a plan of action. This nation is on the brink of an historic moment, Connor, a rare opportunity. The Tallan Wars were another such time. Today we are again entering a time when nations will be tested, loyalties will be tried, and the future will be determined, either for good or ill."

"I am in agreeing with you," Gisela said. "That is why I am here."

"Gisela's mother was my first international contact," Ailsa said. "During our time here as students, we recognized that we had to begin making preparations, because change is coming."

Connor could hardly believe it. His aunt was the mastermind of a secret association of international spies. That was one of the most awesome things he had ever heard. "Why didn't you tell me? I could help."

"Our strength lies in the fact that so few know about us," Ailsa said. "You were helping, more than you could ever know. But at the time we thought you were going to leave, so sharing this information with you was not necessary."

She turned to Gisela. "What Connor is going to explain is a Firetongue-level secret."

Gisela looked shocked "I have never hearing such a one."

"What does that mean?"

"It's so dangerous, it could burn anyone who knows it," Ailsa explained.

"And anyone knowing must be crazy," Gisela added.

"As such, it must be guarded by the strictest confidence," Ailsa said. "We're going to share it with you so that you understand the gravity of the situation. But I am ordering you to retain this information private and not share it with anyone, not even your mother.

Gisela looked more shocked than ever. "I am having no secrets from my mother."

"In this you will," Ailsa insisted, her voice as hard as granite. "Or we cannot share it with you. Your mother holds too high a ranking position in the Arishat intelligence community. She would have to pass this on, and it would risk getting picked up by the network of spies run by Dougal or Kilian."

That was even more interesting. "How many spy organizations are there?" Connor asked.

Gisela shrugged. "Is unclear. The Arishat League has a central spy league. But then every nation is having their own too."

"And of course Granadure and Obrion have their official spy agencies," Ailsa said. "But many of the high-noble houses also run individual agents. Dougal is the most notorious. That man has an extensive intelligence organization that may rival that of any of those sponsored at national levels."

Connor had seen enough of that internal bickering, political maneuvering, and attempted assassinations within what the nobles called the Rules of Honorable Sabotage. It made sense to have spies lurking around too.

"I really should have known about this sooner," Connor said.

"You cannot trust anyone, my boy," Ailsa said. "There are more spies per capita at the Carraig than anywhere else in the world. The contracts and negotiations, and the ramifications of the results of the Tir-raon are too important for anyone to ignore."

As Connor considered that, the inclusion of Padraigin in the Tir-raon took on new meaning. Was she a spy? Was Ivor a spy? He must know about the spies, because he was already taking precautions against listeners.

Was everyone Connor knew a spy? The possibilities seemed endless and his head began to hurt. It was like entering a bakery, only to be told some of the mouth-watering pastries on the shelves were stuffed with manure instead of cream. How could he tell the difference?

Why couldn't life be simple? Like facing a charging torc.

"I'm going to have a thousand questions about all of this," Connor said. "But right now we need to deal with the fact that Jean found information that she feels proves that patronage is a lie and that unclaimed are part of the conspiracy."

Gisela rushed forward and gripped his shoulder. "Are you sure?"

"That's why I called you in here," Ailsa said. "We have long suspected the truth about this, but we've never been able to prove it either way."

Gisela nodded. "Patronage is not being necessary anywhere but in Obrion. It is controlling the masses, but I am always wondering how it could be true."

When she released his shoulder, he caught her hand and repeated Ailsa's warning. "Gisela, we cannot share this information with anyone. If word gets out that I shared this information, Evander will kill us all."

Gisela looked terrified. Good.

"You know more about Evander than most of us, don't you?" Connor asked.

Gisela nodded. "Evander is a legend. We are not knowing how old he is, but we are knowing he is older than anyone else, except perhaps one."

"Which one?"

"Stay focused," Ailsa said, "Evander has chosen to act, and chosen to share information that he has withheld for a very long time. Why this, and why now? We cannot risk acting until we better understand his motivations."

Gisela nodded. "What are you wishing from me?"

"I'm thinking we have not gone back far enough in our research," Ailsa said. "I want you to request from Althing that they begin an extensive search of the archives dating back to the Tallan Wars. Have them look for anything that might connect back to patronage, the Carraig, or even Evander."

Gisela nodded again. "Such research will no doubt reaching ears of the various spying organizations."

That made Connor nervous, but Ailsa did not look worried. She added, "By casting such a wide net, we are insulating ourselves. If some of the deep archives are discovered to contain important information, the truth can come from those historical records, not from us."

Connor still felt nervous, but he knew enough to trust Ailsa, and they needed information. "We need to do more than that."

Ailsa nodded. "You're already planning to discuss some of these things with your Grandurian contacts, correct?"

Gisela looked surprised. "You are having contacts in Granadure?"

"Of course. Doesn't everyone?" He spoke casually, and loved how surprised she looked.

"How do you think he was planning to escape?" Ailsa asked.

"I was thinking he was being helped by some of your people."

Ailsa had kept that secret intact, but Gisela knew a lot. "How much have you shared with your mother about me?"

Gisela hesitated and that spoke louder than her words. "Really? You told her about my curse?"

"She is promising to keep your secret," Gisela said. "It is too important not to be sharing."

Connor wanted to argue about that, but Ailsa made a soothing gesture. "The stroke's fallen, Son. I trust Gisela's mother. Let that suffice for now."

They were definitely going to have to talk about that more later, but he didn't argue the point.

"We'll continue our daily briefings here and discuss any new information from our various channels," Ailsa said. "Together we'll discover the truth about this mystery, then we'll know how to attack."

"Geall on," Connor said with a wry grin.

Smiling, the ladies joined him in thumbing their noses to accept what might prove to be their greatest challenge.

"Now," Ailsa said, rising from her seat. "You have to make the rounds."

Connor groaned. He wasn't looking forward to informing everyone the portions were being reduced.

Chapter 20

The assembly and first army training had pushed class periods back to late afternoon. Students were chattering excitedly about their army assignments, showing off their new uniforms, and striving to out-boast each other about how their generals were better. Even the students assigned to Padraigin's army had dropped their resentment and now embraced her with that much more enthusiasm, as if trying to catch up. Their destinies were now linked to hers, and there was nothing like selfish intent to make the strongest supporters.

Connor's army tried hard to maintain their optimism, but they faced universal mocking. Despite how intriguing the masked Dawnus might be, every student possessed enough battlefield management skills to read disaster in the assignments.

He was glad he had already met with his army. For the most part, they withstood the verbal barrage. They weren't yet rabid believers, but they hadn't given up either.

All he had to do was figure out how to deliver on his promises, for their sake as well as his own. Cameron liked to point out that he had a flair for breaking things, but could he break an entire battlefield enough for his little army to win?

The announcement of reduction in daily portions was met with universal grumbling, but not outright hostility as he had feared, at least not in Professor Todhar and Professor Greim's classes. Professor Todhar suggested the reduction was an opportunity to help the students better master their tap rate management, a skill that would be vital in their upcoming group battles. The bearish

Professor Greim only said, "War requires sacrifice at every level. Get used to it."

Professor Nandag wasn't nearly as gracious. The heavyset woman had decided to dislike Connor the very first day he'd arrived at the Carraig, and although her anger had waned in recent weeks, it rebounded instantly. He was used to her verbal assaults though, and weathered the storm long enough to receive her signature accepting the rounds.

If he grew desperate, maybe he'd recruit her into his army. She could browbeat the enemy Sentries until they tongue-tied themselves into knots.

The Striders laughed off the reduction and challenged each other to run just as far with less powder. On his way back into the inner city of the Carraig to deliver the tertiary affinity stones, he ran into Jok, who was lounging just inside the gate.

The burly Boulder pushed off from the wall he'd been leaning against and fell into step beside Connor. "You're an idiot."

"You're in rare good humor this morning," Connor said, glancing to make sure Jok wasn't tapping granite. The fact that Jok owed him a life debt should have made him feel pretty safe walking beside him, but that greeting made him nervous anyway.

"Just trying to decide if saving your life when you don't even know it resolves my debt."

"Deciding not to punch me to death doesn't really count as saving my life."

"How about stopping some of my friends from beating you to a pulp for reducing the rations?"

"I'd take that as a sign of friendship at least," Connor said. "But it wasn't my fault."

Jok shrugged. "You know what they say, beat the bearer of bad news."

"Actually, I thought you were specifically supposed to *not* blame the messenger for the news."

"Depends on which side of the news you stand on."

Connor slowed near the entrance to the grand hospital building and faced Jok. "Thank you for stopping them."

"That wasn't a good enough reason to beat you to death." He looked like he was considering other reasons that might justify it, though.

"You didn't meet me today just to warn me I haven't been beaten up yet, did you?"

"Let's talk inside."

Intrigued, Connor followed Jok into the huge building and halfway down one long, empty hall. Some idiot had decided the best place for the Healers was on the second floor, so the ground floor wasn't heavily used.

"So why am I an idiot today?" Connor asked when Jok stopped.

"You just can't do the smart thing, can you? Even when I set everything up for you, you manage to screw it all up."

"Some people call it a gift," he quipped.

Jok scowled, and with those heavy brows, he could scowl really well. "Do you really want to be Shona's slave?"

"What are you talking about?"

"It's a simple question, Connor. We both know what she wants from you, what her father wants. You can't be stupid enough to feel happy about that."

"Are you planning to be the first psychologist Boulder?"

"Don't pretend you've got pedra droppings for brains."

"What makes you so concerned?" Connor asked. "There's not much I can do about Shona right now, is there?"

"You are such a stupid linn," Jok exclaimed, punching Connor in the shoulder and knocking him sprawling.

"Some day you'll have to teach me punch code," Connor groaned.

"What?"

Connor raised a hand to forestall getting hit again. "Just try explaining your point without using your fists. I can't translate fast enough." Whatever was riling Jok up had overwhelmed his limited self-control.

Jok glared. "You think it was easy to orchestrate that dome collapse?"

"That was you?" Connor exclaimed, climbing back to his feet to face Jok. "You nearly killed a bunch of people."

Jok made a dismissive gesture. "No one died."

"They could have."

"Not if you'd used all your powers!"

The hall was still empty, but how far would that shout echo?

"We had an agreement that you'd keep my secret," Connor said softly. "That includes not shouting so loud everyone in the Carraig can hear it."

"Like I said, I've got your back," Jok said, moderating his voice. "Why didn't you use all your powers, Connor? There couldn't have been a better opportunity to declare yourself."

"Are you cracked?" Connor asked. "I loved the Rhidorroch and that stunt destroyed it all again."

"They'll rebuild it. It was worth the risk."

"And by the time they finish rebuilding, the term will be over, which means you guaranteed you'll never get another chance to beat Shona in the standings."

Jok had been desperate to supplant Shona, but now he surprised Connor by making another dismissive gesture. "That was more important. If you'd been smart and showed your curse, once the truth was known, you could have sought patronage from my father and escaped Shona's trap. I was helping you gain the upper hand."

"And tarnishing Shona's position at the same time," Connor pointed out.

Jok shrugged. "We both win. The best kind of geall."

So Jok had actually pretended to think things through before embarking on such a stupid plan. From one point of view, the attempt actually made a twisted kind of sense.

Connor shook his head. "It wouldn't have worked."

"Of course it would have. It was perfect."

"Except for when Shona enslaved my entire village in retribution."

Jok's enthusiasm faded. "She'd do that?"

"Already promised it. I appreciate the thought, but I've gone over all of this in detail. There's no way for me to break publicly with Shona without causing more damage than benefit."

Jok frowned. "Runda's not going to be happy to hear that."

"Lord Runda? What does he have to do with it?"

"I needed someone to shake the dome. He's the only secret Sentry I know."

"How did you learn he's a Sentry?"

"One of the benefits of my dad being lord of the Carraig is I learn secrets like that."

"You didn't tell him about my curse, did you?"

"Didn't have to. He seemed to know already, and he was happy to help."

So Runda really had been responsible for the watchers around Ailsa's mansion outside of Raineach, and they had seen him training.

"Why is Runda keeping quiet?" Connor wondered.

Jok shrugged. "He's a hard stone to crack, Runda is. I figured he was hoping to gain advantage for his high lord when Shona lost control of you. High Lord Goban is one of Dougal's allies, but everyone's worried about how much power Dougal's acquiring through this war effort. I think everyone would be happy to see him lose for once."

"There has to be more to it than that. I wish you hadn't involved him."

"And I wish you'd used that opportunity. Now you've grouted the whole geall."

"There's more to it than you know," Connor said. "Please promise me you won't try to kill anyone for me again."

"Nobody died," Jok muttered.

"Just promise."

"You can't be planning to submit to Shona."

"I'm working on a plan," Connor assured him.

"Well, you'd better work faster. She's got your nose in a vise, Connor. She can tug you any way she wants."

"You're not actually helping to motivate me," Connor pointed out.

"Watch yourself, Connor," Jok said, turning to leave. "This year's contest will be vicious."

Connor watched him go, not sure how to feel. On one hand, it infuriated him to think about the destruction of the Rhidorroch. But then, if even Jok saw how desperate his situation was, he really needed to figure out a way to flip the geall on Shona.

The problem was, like Jok so eloquently pointed out, Shona held all the strings.

When he entered the healing wing, he was happy to find that Aifric was the senior student on duty. She and the other Healers rushed to greet him, but when they learned he was only delivering the rounds and wasn't actually hurt, several of them looked disappointed.

"I'll try to get hurt soon," he promised. "But it's getting harder to manage. Those Petralists are so distracted by group battles, they lack the drive to beat up a common linn with enough focus to matter."

"We know we can count on you," one of the girls said with a smile. "You're always our most interesting patient."

"I'm happy to see you," Aifric said, shooing the other girls away after they received their portions. "I'm glad you finally stopped by when you were healthy."

"It's not as much fun for you, but I like to try new things."

Aifric drew him to one side, away from the others. "Connor, do you mind if I ask you a personal question?"

"Of course. You've saved my life more times than anyone I know."

"You're from Alasdair, aren't you?"

"How did you know that?" Most people thought he was from Raineach like his Aunt Ailsa.

"I've asked around."

"Why? Is there something uniquely amazing about how my bones heal?"

"No. I've been wanting to meet someone from there."

"It's not really the best vacation location." Even though the valley was truly beautiful, the village was unremarkable, the people ignorant of anything outside of their little world. He missed it.

"Were you there for the Battle of Alasdair?"

Connor hesitated. "Why would you want to know about that?"

"I'm doing research into recent conflicts between Obrion and Granadure."

He hadn't heard about any classes focusing on that. Most of them were gearing students toward participating in the next set of conflicts.

"I was there," he admitted. "It was a crazy time."

Maybe he shouldn't have said anything, but Aifric was one of the few people at the Carraig who seemed to care. He actually trusted her and couldn't bear to hold back a little truth from a friend.

Aifric leaned closer, her expression intent. "Did you see anything unusual?"

He barked a laugh. "I'm a commoner, Aifric. In my village, we barely knew Petralists existed. Everything they did was unusual."

She frowned. "I had hoped you could tell me more."

"About what?"

"I've heard rumors," she said softly. "That the Blood of the Tallan returned and might have been seen there."

How had she heard about that? Very few knew that truth, and they'd worked hard to keep the secret. Connor tried to keep his expression neutral. He liked Aifric, but he couldn't hope to begin speaking about that topic without revealing far too much.

"I'm sorry, but I can't tell you more than what I saw. Petralists are really dangerous." He patted his ribs. "On most days, I've found they're even more dangerous up close."

Aifric squeezed his hand. "Thanks anyway. Let me know if you think of anything that might be useful."

"Sure. Maybe the next time I get beat up, it'll rattle some memories loose. They get stuck sometimes."

As he left to complete the rounds, he wondered how Aifric knew so much.

Then his thoughts shifted yet again to how, by the Tallan's warted nose was he going to win the first group battle with an army that was hopelessly under-powered?

Chapter 21

Dressed in his Lian costume, Connor paused at the entrance to his Dawnus suite in the central keep. The wide atrium was busier than usual, with couriers scurrying to and fro, and newly-assigned captains of the various armies walking in small groups, heads bent in conversation after leaving their generals.

Connor's captains were meeting in Shona's palace. He had chosen her and Princess Catriona to lead his Boulders. With Shona's battlefield experience and top spot in the standings reinforcing her natural leadership talents, she was the best choice. Catriona had made such a big deal about helping him win the nomination challenge, everyone already assumed she'd also be chosen. Besides, it felt good to have royalty reporting to him.

He'd let Shona figure out how to keep her focused and help her become a productive leader. Catriona desperately needed someone competent to take her under their wing.

Lorcc was the single captain of the Striders, He could assign whatever assistants he needed. Aifric was captain of the Healers, and he gave her the Solas' too. He needed the Blade, Fearghas, so he'd assigned him as a personal assistant and bodyguard.

The only appointment that had surprised his army was Declan. Connor had ignored the muttered exclamations and open worry on many faces when he'd announced Declan as the captain of his tiny tertiary force. He needed Declan to build confidence to face the overwhelming challenge of dealing with the enemy Sentries.

It was like asking a flower to stop a charging torc.

"How was your first army training?" Tomas asked. As usual, he and Cameron were assigned guard duty at the entrance.

"I think it went well," Connor said.

Cameron barked a laugh. "We heard you had students digging out blocked tunnels with Frazier and his Guardians throwing broken pieces of the Rhidorroch down on them."

"The best way to learn to work as a team is to face adversity together."

"We've been cleared to hold training sessions with primary affinity groups," Tomas said. "We'll start with your army, if you'd like."

"Absolutely." Despite their casual demeanor, the two Fast Rollers were among the deadliest soldiers Connor had ever met. "Tomorrow morning on the plain."

"We'll be there," Tomas said.

Jean appeared at the far entrance and jogged across the atrium. Her smile seemed a bit forced.

"It's good to see you lass," Tomas said.

Cameron's ugly face twisted into a truly hideous mask of concentration.

> "Fast flies time when we are apart
> life is good only when friends are near
> it is good to see you."

He grinned like he had just won a prize and Tomas looked impressed.

"Am I missing something?" Connor asked.

"I've been practicing my new form of rhyming," Cameron said. "Invented it myself."

"He's getting pretty good," Tomas said. "He's a man appreciated too little by too many and feared too much by not enough."

Jean grimaced. "Ah, you do realize it didn't exactly rhyme."

"He waxes poetic around pretty ladies," Tomas said. "Practicing to impress Camonica."

So Connor had guessed right. "She said something about liking poetry."

"Really?" the two Fast Rollers asked in unison.

He nodded. "She said listening to Captain Aonghus speak philosophy was crazier than hearing Boulders quoting sonnets."

"Poetry and sonnets are two different things," Jean protested.

Cameron didn't seem to care. "I knew there was a reason I invented Flowered Prose."

"Hold on," Jean said. "Prose is the opposite of poetry."

"That's why no one expects it," Tomas said, tapping the side of his nose. "The element of surprise is just as important when speaking as it is on the battlefield."

"Um..." Jean looked to Connor for help.

"You're the experts on battlefield strategy," Connor admitted, trying to keep a straight face. "But Jean might know a little more about poetry."

"She is a girl," Tomas conceded.

Cameron nodded. "Gregor looked disgusted when I tried it out on him, and Aonghus sort of spontanably combusted."

"Stick to ladies for sure," Tomas agreed. "It's just a matter of getting the beats right."

"What do you mean?" Connor asked.

"Flowered Prose is a structured form," Cameron said. "It's in formation, so to speak. It's got to have six beats, then seven, then five."

"Beats?" Jean asked, although she looked like she really wanted to leave. "Do you mean syllables?"

Cameron frowned. "I don't think so."

"Syllables means the vocal breakdown of words," Connor offered.

"Don't break words," Tomas exclaimed, looking horrified. "They don't work when they're broken."

"You guys are hopeless," he groaned through a smile.

"And you got the beat count wrong in those lines earlier," Jean added.

"I couldn't have," Cameron said. "They sounded perfect."

Jean just shook her head and Tomas chortled. "She's gone and busted your formation, Cameron."

"He busted it himself," Jean insisted. "I just counted the words."

"Counting is overrated," Cameron muttered.

"But you're the one that said the word count was important."

"Beat count," he said. "Not the same thing."

"I give up," Jean cried.

"It's all right, lass," Tomas said. "Not everyone is ready for higher forms of entertainment."

"Keep practicing," Connor offered.

"Aye, try the next one out on Camonica," Tomas said.

That sounded like a really bad idea.

Connor asked Jean, "What are you doing here? I thought you'd be busy for a while."

"You won't see me much," she admitted. "Shona was very cross when I showed up, but she's meeting with those other captains." She gave him a warm smile. "Brilliant move assigning Catriona with her. She's going to have to work hard to keep the princess from doing something stupid."

"They're perfect for each other," Connor agreed with a smile.

"I have to get back," Jean said. "Shona wants you to stop by as soon as you can."

"I'll go see her as soon as I finish with Ivor."

That caught their attention.

"Don't start brawling with him," Jean cautioned.

"But if you have to, beat him down fast," Tomas said. "He's a crafty one."

"We're going to talk," Connor said. "I think it's a good opportunity."

"Be careful," Jean cautioned.

"Always." He turned to the Fast Rollers. "Do you think he's alone right now?"

"Aye," Tomas said. "His captains left five minutes ago."

"Good." Connor headed toward the distant entrance to Ivor's suite, guarded by a pair of Lady Polglass's Boulders.

"Just break something if you need help," Cameron called after him.

Chapter 22

The guards at the entrance to Ivor's Dawnus suite were expecting Connor, and one of the huge soldiers escorted him inside. As they passed the huge, private practice room, Connor noted that it looked like it had originally been configured much like his own. However, scores of workers were busy reconfiguring it.

Connor hadn't thought of that. The Rhidorroch might be closed, but as a Dawnus champion, he had access to enormous resources. Just about anything he wanted could be set up, all paid for by Shona. He smiled to himself and decided a new challenge course would be perfect.

He should have thought of it sooner. Ivor already had a strong lead in getting his facilities updated. Connor couldn't afford to dally. He was already at a serious disadvantage.

Ivor was waiting in his sitting room, which was comfortable, but not lavish. Vibrantly colored rugs were positioned under chairs and couches, but the rest of the expansive room was tiled in geometric patterns.

"Lian, I'm glad you came," Ivor said, greeting him with a strong handshake, then gesturing to an overstuffed chair. Servants brought silver trays piled with fruits, sweetbreads, and drinks, which they left on a nearby table.

"Happy to be here," Connor said. "We have a lot to discuss."

A woman entered the room wearing the distinctive orange and yellow colors of Lord Dail. She looked vaguely familiar and a bit older than most of the students, maybe in her early twenties. Her long, brown hair was silky smooth, her pretty face neutral, but she couldn't quite pull off the subservient look. Something in her big, brown eyes that glowed softly with Pathfinder light suggested a strong personality barely held in check.

"Sheigra," Ivor greeted her. "See that we are not disturbed and that our conversation remains private."

"I'll see it done." She retreated from the room and a moment later, wind began rushing down the outer corridor, sounding loud in the otherwise quiet suite.

"What are you doing with a Pathfinder from Lord Dail's entourage working for you?" Connor asked, even though he remembered that strange conversation between Ivor and Jok a few weeks prior.

"An arrangement. Sheigra helps with perimeter security, and I grant Lord Dail's house certain privileges."

That was a nice way to say Jok had needed to buy his captaincy in Ivor's army. Connor was already thinking a lot about spies and Pathfinder eavesdroppers, so Sheigra's purpose was obvious.

"Do you have any idea how well her interference actually prevents other Pathfinders from listening to what you say in here?" They were deep enough inside the vast bulk of the central keep that Connor doubted any Pathfinders on the outside could hear anything, but what about someone in the building?

"It's hard to quantify," Ivor admitted. "But our tests suggest active blocking, especially in a confined space like this, is extremely effective."

The second insight into improving his own suite in as many minutes. Connor should visit Ivor more often. The man was a quarry of information.

Ivor ignored the alcoholic choices on the food tray and took a glass of chilled juices, then gestured to Connor to sample some of the drinks. He declined. With so much energy being expended in security measures, could Connor trust that the drinks had not been tampered with? He had seen enough of Jean's herb mixtures to know some could produce powerful effects, including the loosening of one's tongue.

Ivor saluted with his glass and took a long sip. "To your impending doom."

"You gloat with style," Connor said, leaning back in the comfortable chair, happy his mask concealed his worry.

"There's no other possibility." Ivor spoke with blunt confidence. "Assignments are final, and they've made your army a laughing stock."

Connor selected a ripe pear from the tray. "The prey cannot be consumed before the hunter has loosed the arrow."

"The battle will be a formality," Ivor responded. "The only question is how bad the beating will be, and how low your soldiers can fall in the standings. Most of them are already near the bottom."

"Not for long."

"I appreciate the bravado," Ivor said. "I'm disgusted by the decisions the representatives made. I was actually looking forward to a good contest. Now I can't even enjoy beating you."

"But winning for me will now be far more precious," Connor said, taking a big bite of the pear.

"Redmund won't show any mercy," Ivor continued, ignoring the retort. "Padraigin might, but she can't afford to lose either. By the Tallan's shameful glory, Lian, the stakes have never been higher. This could have been such a mighty contest!"

"It'll still be fun," Connor insisted. "I worry about you sometimes."

Ivor laughed. "Worry about yourself. You're clever, Lian. I like that. You have a good head for battlefield strategy, and you don't get rattled by surprises. You react fast and you seem to understand that these games aren't games."

"They're not," Connor agreed. "They're simulations of reality."

"You pulled out a creative win in that last battle," Ivor said. "But you risked too much."

"Not taking the risk guaranteed defeat. Sometimes we have to risk everything to win."

Ivor grinned. "Sure, but remember it's not just a game. In a real battle, you wouldn't have risked the lives of your men like that, or risked your own life. You would have tried for a strategic withdrawal and lived to fight another day."

"Perhaps," Connor said. "But how many of my men would have died before we escaped?"

Ivor leaned back. "You care, Lian. That can be seen as a weakness."

Connor shook his head. "I've seen what happens to those who don't care. They've already lost."

"You see the best in others," Ivor said thoughtfully. "And

you actually count on others to respond as their best selves. That's a dangerous way to live."

"Better than expecting people to be their worst."

"Perhaps," Ivor said. "But I like to make sure I'm not left exposed and disappointed."

"Then don't give anyone a reason to disappoint you."

"Perhaps not." Ivor looked thoughtful. "The strategy did work to get us to help you build that ice dome on nomination day."

"Better to be part of something amazing than whine about the disaster after the fact," Connor responded.

Ivor laughed and saluted with his drink. "You won the nomination with flair, Lian. Maybe you will make a stronger showing in the battle than I expect. I honestly hope you do."

"A good commander deals with the situation at hand," Connor said. "Not the one he wishes he'd gotten."

"Like when you had to put down Hector," Ivor said.

"Like Hector," Connor admitted, growing serious. Few knew about that, and most of them thought he had fought the monster as Kilian. So many things had gone wrong that day. And yet, if what Jean had discovered was true, there must be another aspect to that moment that he did not yet understand. What had really happened there? What had Hector become if not unclaimed?

He didn't realize he had lapsed into silence until Ivor stood and selected another drink. "I wish I had been there. From what I heard from the boy, Connor, you could have used some help."

Connor appreciated the reminder that he wasn't visiting Ivor as himself. The line was growing blurred as they talked. "It was ugly. I wish you'd been there. Together maybe we could have subdued him, given him a chance to regain his humanity."

"Tell me about the fight," Ivor said eagerly, handing Connor his own drink. Connor accepted it and took a sip. He had to show some trust somewhere, didn't he?

He liked Ivor and wished they had met under different circumstances. Ivor was smart and seemed to understand things better than most Petralists. He would make a fine commander someday, if allowed.

So Connor described how Hector had transformed from the vain teacher into a raging, unclaimed monster. Ivor asked penetrating questions about the strength and speed of the monster, and Connor did his best to explain it.

Perhaps he should have held back, kept some information secret, but he couldn't see what benefit knowing about the unclaimed would grant Ivor. Besides, talking through the memory helped Connor organize his thoughts. As he spoke, he felt there was a truth lingering there in the shadows, but couldn't quite put his finger on it.

"I don't think anyone but a Sentry could have stopped it," Connor said finally. "Except for a Dawnus. Although it was tricky to maintain the focus to work with both water and fire at the same time."

Ivor grunted. "Took me forever to figure it out. Wasn't till I shifted to the Smaladair Technique that I finally got it."

Ivor noticed Connor's quizzical look. "You don't know that one?"

"Not yet."

"You should try it. Reduces interference and I can manage a far stronger burn."

"I will." Connor hesitated for half a heartbeat before continuing. "As soon as you show me how." He tried to keep the statement calm, but he wanted to beg Ivor for the information.

"What technique do you use?" Ivor asked. "The Chan-eil-Greim, or the Floating Burn?"

Connor shrugged. "For me, it's more the Ragsbat Technique." When Ivor shook his head, not recognizing that one, he added, "That's the Riding Angry Galloping Stallions Bareback Together technique."

Ivor laughed, but his mirth trickled away when Connor didn't join him. He leaned forward, looking surprised. "You mean you still bull through, using them as separate elements?"

"Well they are, aren't they?" Despite all the reasons to pretend he knew secrets he didn't, who could teach him if not Ivor? Even if that meant letting Ivor know his limits, he needed to take the risk.

Ivor slapped his leg and barked a laugh. "I can't believe it! You have no idea what you're doing, do you?"

"I'm here, aren't I?"

Ivor leaned back. "It makes sense, finally. That's why they entered you so late, even though they had to know the representatives would give you a weaker army. That's why they had to keep you secret. You just barely manifested Dawnus, didn't you?"

"Pretty recent," Connor admitted, hating that Ivor knew, and hating more what power that knowledge might grant him. Still,

Ivor had twice proven himself willing to step up and help Connor. Would he do it again when no one was watching?

"Amazing," Ivor said. "It's a miracle you survived the nomination."

"I learn fast."

"How in Tallan's name did you ever think you could make that dome when you're so new?" Ivor asked, a little awed.

Connor shrugged. "You never know until you try, right?"

Ivor gaped and Connor added, "Like we discussed earlier, I had you and the other Spitters there to help."

"You couldn't have known," Ivor said, shaking his head in disbelief. "You can't be that naive."

"It's not naive to trust you'd all want to help save people's lives. If you'd let that dome collapse, it would've wrecked your chances as much as mine. There's no Tir-raon if half the school is dead."

"You've got more nerve than a blind torc rider," Ivor said. "I like that, Lian. It's your big advantage."

"I'll take what I can get at this point."

"Everyone's got an advantage," Ivor added. "That's the first thing you need to learn. You've got to study the field. Padraigin is a genius at absorption and tap rate management. Redmund's stronger in earth than anyone I've ever met, except maybe that Evander character."

Ivor was speaking to him as if he was a student. Maybe things would turn out all right after all. Connor hoped he'd keep talking, dared to hope they could find a way to work together.

"And what about you?" Connor asked.

Ivor grinned. "I study harder than anyone."

"Study what?"

"Everything." He took an apple from the tray. "I know my limits, but more importantly I know everyone else's. I win, Lian, because I know exactly how to beat every opponent before I take the field against them."

Connor had beaten him more than once in practice encounters. Now that Connor had revealed so much truth, would Ivor hold the advantage the next time?

"Why are you telling me all this?"

"Because I know enough about you to see the truth."

"What truth?" Connor asked slowly, worried how much the clever Dawnus had figured out.

"You can't hope to win, not with being so new to your tertiary affinities, and especially not with that army they've chained around your neck." When Connor opened his mouth to protest, Ivor cut him off. "You've got to try. We all do, but there can be only one winner."

Ivor leaned forward, completely confident. "I can arrange for you to take second place, and in return, you reinforce my ultimate victory."

Was it arrogance if his confidence was well grounded? Ivor didn't speak with false pride. From where he sat, the offer must have sounded extremely generous, the assumptions he was making solid.

Under any other circumstances, Connor would have agreed. But he couldn't afford to lose. Too many lives hung in the balance.

"You're assuming I'll accept that I can't win."

"You can't," Ivor said, making a dismissive gesture. "But if you agree to work with me, I'll train you, Lian. That Firetongue and Spitter that Shona appointed for you might know their individual elements, but no one but a Dawnus can teach you how to meld those elements into a mightier whole. You don't have time to figure it out on your own."

When Connor still hesitated, Ivor rose and paced away. "You're smart, Lian. If you had the advantages I have, you'd be unstoppable and I'd be the one trying to make a deal for second place. But the stones are cast, and you're smart enough to face reality."

"I can't commit to second place."

"You'll see reason soon enough," Ivor promised. "Think about it, and I'll leave the offer open, but if you wait until after getting trounced in the first group battle, I might not be able to help you."

"Even if I don't agree to helping you come in first," Connor said, trying to rescue something from the conversation. "We can still benefit from working together."

"How?" Ivor asked.

"Like you said, no one can help Dawnus improve better than another Dawnus. Let's train together. You can show me some of what you know, and I guarantee I can show you some tricks you haven't considered yet. That's a win for both of us."

Ivor considered the proposal, looking torn. Connor added, "What do you have to lose?"

The big man grinned. "You know what I like best about your idea?"

"Besides learning from a master of improvisation?"

Ivor snorted. "We're supposed to be enemies, Lian. What better way to prove we're more than our patrons think we are than by teaming up?"

Connor could think of a couple of things, but didn't dare share them with Ivor. "Geall on."

As they both thumbed their noses to accept the challenge and embark on the crazy plan, Connor vowed to never succumb to Ivor's arguments, no matter how persuasive. He would show Ivor there was more to winning than cold logic. Ilse had defeated Rory with nerve, with logic, with creativity, and by changing the board to her advantage. He was going to have to do the same thing.

He grinned. "So how exactly do you manage that Channeling Grime technique?"

"Come on, and I'll show you," Ivor said, rising and gesturing toward the door.

Connor hoped to pry as many secrets as possible from Ivor as they began practicing in his echoing training facility, after shooing out all of the workers.

"The Chan-eil-Greim technique is perhaps the least effective of the advanced dual-tapping techniques," Ivor said, stopping beside one of the huge tanks of water. "But it sheds light on some underlying principles that alone are worth your oath to agree to my plan."

"Show me, and we'll see," Connor said, trying to hide his excitement.

"Fire and water are unrelenting enemies at the most fundamental level." As Ivor spoke, water bubbled out of the tank behind him, and purplish flames erupted out of a nearby vat of liquid fuel. Both elements arced across the open space and met directly over Ivor's head, twirling together with crackling hiss of steam. It was a great demonstration. Ivor didn't seem to struggle to mesh the two elements together, but even that little show would have taxed Connor's control.

"Trying to force them together is like trying to grill a steak in a hurricane," Connor agreed. He had managed by sheer stubborn willpower and desperate need.

"That's because you're making the same mistake we all do at first. You're trying to force them to get along face to face." As he spoke, the elements separated over his head, flowing into the images of men facing each other.

"So what's the secret?"

"Simple," Ivor said with a grin, and the man-shaped elements above his head turned to face away from each other. "You have to convince them to stand back to back, like duelists just prior to the start of their contest."

"That's it?" Connor wasn't sure he believed it.

"The trick is to release them before the duel starts."

Connor considered the idea, forcing down his initial doubt. It had to be more than a clever mind game. He grinned. "I've got to try that."

"Be my guest." Ivor gestured at the nearby tanks.

So he did. Connor established affinity with water first, and drew a man-shaped globe of water out of the tank, tethered by a slender cord. Then he sucked on marble and embraced the burn, drawing flames from the liquid fuel. For a second, it looked like it was going to work, and he exulted as the flames morphed into the shape of a man.

Then the flames turned white-hot and exploded, shredding the water.

Ivor laughed, shaking his head. "Again."

It took a few tries, but Ivor did not ridicule him for the failures. After the fifth explosive failure, Ivor said, "Stop focusing on how the elements are shaped. The trick is maintaining the illusion in your mind."

On the third try after that, Connor finally understood. It was how he envisioned the gateways that mattered. In his mind, he'd been thinking of them as invisible doors facing each other. The trick was to instead imagine them facing away from each other. It was a bit weird, but his mind was not limited to the same constraints as his physical limbs, and he could indeed stretch his thoughts around the gateways to enter from opposite sides.

It might have all been mind games, but positioning himself mentally that way allowed him to establish affinity with both elements without them raging against each other like snarling dogs on chains. As long as he kept both elements focused away from each other, it was like they could pretend the other element didn't exist.

"This is amazing," he laughed when he produced his first intertwined column of fire and water, vague silhouettes of people hugging, but not quite mixing.

"You're a quick study," Ivor said, approving. "Took me a while to get it."

"I'm motivated."

"This is just the beginning, Lian. The other techniques I'll teach you after you agree to my terms help bind the elements even tighter together."

The not-so-subtle reminder of Ivor's intention didn't even dampen Connor's good mood. "Don't push it."

"Ungrateful."

"You haven't seen what I can do for you."

"What can you teach me?" Ivor asked, looking doubtful.

In response, Connor drew liquid fuel around the two of them in a hollow column that reared ten feet into the air, using soapstone to command the liquid. It was slippery, like soap on his thoughts, and he had to focus as hard on that single element as he had trying to meld two opposites, but he managed to get it to obey his command.

Then he lit the column on fire.

As soon as it began to burn, he switched to marble to command the flames. The liquid in the center of the conflagration still obeyed his soapstone will, though.

"Only the outer surface of liquid fuel actually burns," he explained. "The rest of can be treated as liquid, not fire."

Ivor looked disgusted, but he didn't fly into a rage like Aonghus had. He must have established affinity with marble first. He was a fast learner though, and he resisted his initial disgust to consider the idea.

"I never even considered looking at the fuel separate from the flames." Ivor sounded amazed.

"They may be fire unborn," Connor said, quoting Aonghus. "But until the spark ignites them, they are liquid."

"Non-water manipulation of liquid is tough," Ivor said, and Connor felt his will slipping across the edges of the liquid fuel, probing. "And students are discouraged from testing those limits too much."

"I think that does everyone a disservice," Connor said. "You've got to keep an open mind if you hope to have any chance of winning. The fleet-footed eoin is incapable of escaping the nuall when its head is buried in the sands."

Grinning, Ivor seized control over part of the burning column and knocked Connor soaring into a tub of water.

After that, the training session degenerated into a brawl twenty feet in the air as the two of them threw themselves back and forth across the training facility, swatting at each other with fire and water.

When they eventually terminated the private elemental battle, laughing from the thrill of the contest, Ivor clapped Connor on the shoulder. "Don't worry about the damage. The workers were already planning to rip out those sections."

Chapter 23

onnor returned to his rooms in a good humor and allowed himself to believe he and Ivor could keep training together, despite all the reasons they shouldn't. He plopped down onto one of the comfortable chairs in his suite. He still had to find a way to win the first group battle, but hopefully Ivor could finish a close second. That wouldn't damage their growing friendship, would it?

"What has you in such a good mood?"

Connor leaped to his feet and spun to face Ilse. He hadn't noticed the Grandurian captain lounging in the corner, gnawing on a roasted chicken that was supposed to be part of Connor's lunch.

"How exactly did you get in here?" Connor demanded, scanning for Anika and Erich, but not seeing any of the rest of Ilse's team.

"The same way I entered Lady Shona's palace or other areas of the Carraig deemed necessary for my mission," Ilse said, taking another big bite of chicken.

She didn't elaborate and did not look like she intended to share the secret. That ability to move with impunity through the heart of enemy territory was one of the mysteries about Ilse that kept Connor perpetually nervous around her. That and the fact that she might decide to assassinate him at any time.

Since she hadn't tried to kill him yet, he decided he was happy to see her.

"We have to talk." He gestured toward one of the couches.

"I bring word from Kilian," she said, accepting his invitation and settling gracefully onto the sofa. The move would have looked elegant if she had been dressed in a formal gown. In her long, black coat and battle leathers, it only made her seem deadlier.

"That was fast." Connor had figured it would take a few more days to get a response.

"He was motivated. Word of Hector's transformation stirred up a lot of interest. It turns out that Kilian only recently destroyed two unclaimed on the borders of Granadure. They match the description of the transformation you witnessed in Hector."

"I thought no one had seen unclaimed," Connor said, sinking into a nearby chair. "Especially in Granadure."

"We haven't. Hence the interest. Two sightings at almost the exact same time, but hundreds of miles apart." Her expression turned grave. "It appears unclaimed are a reality after all."

"Or maybe not."

Connor told her about what Jean had discovered. Despite Evander's threat, he had to share the information with Ilse so she could get it to Kilian, especially if he had encountered unclaimed on the border.

When he finished, Ilse didn't speak for a moment, mulling over the information. "How sure is the girl?"

"The sources seemed genuine. She's going to search deeper, but you need to know that there's someone here named Evander who has threatened to kill us if we reveal the truth to anyone."

Ilse frowned. "That is a name I've heard, although I know little about him."

"See what you can find out," Connor suggested. "And pass this information on to Kilian. We're going to hunt for more details, but we need some way to confirm what's really going on. Are unclaimed a reality, or are they part of some deeper lie?"

"You should come with me," Ilse said.

"You know I can't," Connor said, feeling for his granite curse. Was this the excuse she needed to try kidnapping him or removing him? He didn't think so, but didn't dare make any assumptions.

Instead of trying to kill him, Ilse sighed. "No, you cannot. Our presence here grows more precarious every day, but we must run this mystery to ground before we act upon it."

She rose. "My time is short, but if you can guarantee we'll remain undisturbed, let's walk with the earth again together."

Even though his muscles began aching just thinking of training with her again, Connor eagerly accepted. With the new insights into working with multiple stones, perhaps he would gain new mastery over earth.

If Ilse didn't beat him to death first.

Connor asked Tomas and Cameron to clear out all the spies and then ensure he remained undisturbed for some private training. Ten minutes later, Tomas reported the facility clear.

"The spies are pretty upset," he commented. "Messed up the entire afternoon's schedule."

"I'll try to make it up to them," Connor promised. "Maybe let a couple of them spy on my dinner tomorrow."

"They'll appreciate it," Tomas said with a nod. "We'll arrange for fish if you promise to bring some marble and put on a show."

"What kind of show?" Connor asked slowly.

Tomas shrugged. "We spread the word that fish makes you gassy."

He really didn't want the Fast Rollers peeking in on his training with Ilse to make more ridiculous requests, so he agreed. Tomas left, whistling a happy, if not quite harmonious tune to himself.

His private training facility lacked a lot of earth, but he and Ilse found some packed around the liquid fuel vats.

"Today we'll focus on fine-tuning applications of earth anyway," Ilse said. "This will do."

Connor slipped some slate into his boot and imagined the gateway to earth more as a sunken pit, lined with slate stones carved with barely-decipherable words of wisdom. He imagined stepping down into the soft earth inside that pit to immerse himself in the element.

It seemed to like him thinking of it like that.

Ilse directed him in forming spears and grasping fingers of earth. The element worked less well than water or fire in creating flexible constructs, but even a slender finger of earth possessed incredible strength.

Connor's control improved rapidly under Ilse's brutal tactics, and he almost held his own against her a couple of times as they sparred with their reduced earthen arsenal. The wily captain always managed an unexpected move though, tripping him or distracting him at a critical moment.

"You will grow stronger than me soon," Ilse admitted while Connor was spitting dirt out of his mouth and healing fresh bruises from getting thrown halfway across the training facility. "But I'll still trounce you every time."

"The hawk, though chased oft by the blackbird, may yet one day turn and conquer," he said solemnly.

"Not on my watch." She thumped him in the forehead with one forefinger. "Brawn alone is not enough."

"Good," he said. "Because my army is lacking in brawn."

"Ponder the lessons you learned in Alasdair. The fog, though barely tangible, envelops entire mountains and holds valleys enthralled by its gentle touch."

"You're using slate too much," Connor said. "It's getting to your tongue."

Chapter 24

onnor enjoyed a sumptuous dinner in his suite, considering the lessons Ilse had taught while he ate. The huge table in his private dining room, piled high with food, was too much for a single person. So he called Tomas and Cameron to join him. They protested until he showed them the food.

Before the meal was over, he began to wish for that blessed silence he'd abandoned. Cameron insisted on practicing flowered prose, claiming Jean's feedback had been the key element he needed to perfect it.

He was wrong. If anything, those awful excuses for poems got steadily worse. Finally Connor couldn't take it any more. "I think you should share what you've learned with Captain Rory."

Cameron growled something that sounded like, "blasted fist full of bony knuckles."

Tomas chuckled. "The captain said if he ever heard Cameron spout such ridiculous nonsense again, he'd be cleaning latrines for a month."

"Maybe you should mention that Anika likes poetry."

"She does?" Cameron exclaimed.

"I'm pretty sure."

He left them arguing about whether or not it was worth the risk. Laughing, he sped through the undercity, back to the Sculpture House. He saw no one on the journey, lit no torch to guide his path. He was like a ghost slipping through the darkened corridors.

Why did he feel like someone was watching?

After changing back into his regular linn clothing, he stopped at Ailsa's office to discuss the events of the day. She had no new information to offer, and Gisela was away on an errand. Ailsa was pleased that he had already spoken with Ilse, and urged him to follow up with Jean.

"I'll see if I can," he promised. "Shona summoned me to her palace, so I'm heading there now anyway."

"Exercise caution," Ailsa warned. "We had to share this truth with those we've already contacted, but guard the secret from Shona."

When he reached Lord Nevan's palace, Shona and Lord Nevan met him in the second floor study where Shona usually held audiences. Lord Nevan wore a dark evening jacket over another of the heavily starched white shirts he favored. His expression was a bit haggard, and he eagerly made room for Connor.

Shona looked angry. She wore a formal gown of crimson and gold. The late afternoon sun streaming through the windows set the bright colors alive and played across her blond hair. She looked like a queen holding court, and gestured for Connor to approach, but did not rise to greet him, or suggest he take a seat like she normally did.

Connor greeted them both formally. "Lord Nevan, you look tired. I imagine negotiations were difficult."

"More like a disaster," Shona snapped, eyes flashing as she turned back to Nevan. "You didn't even get us a single decent Sentry."

"Declan has heart," Connor said. She spoke as if the army was hers, and he needed to nip that idea in its bony heart. "And as his commanding officer, I consider that the most important element for success."

Shona snorted, ruining the elegant effect her beautiful gown was trying to convey. "Don't pretend to greater abilities than you have, Connor. I taught you everything you know about battlefield management."

That was not exactly true, but she was clearly not in a mood for a reasonable argument. Maybe it was better if she also underestimated some of his abilities.

"Speaking of the army though," she rolled on, glaring at him. "What possessed you to make Catriona the other Boulder captain? She's a hopeless incompetent."

"Catriona has made more improvement in recent weeks than any two other students."

"Because she started at zero," Shona shot back. "I demand you replace her with someone else of my choosing."

"No."

That single word seemed to echo through the room, and the air suddenly felt chilly. Lord Nevan coughed into his hand. "If you will excuse me, I must review a number of contracts prior to meetings tomorrow."

Shona didn't even seem to notice him scurry away, her gaze locked onto Connor. For his part, Connor struggled to face her and keep his expression neutral.

"You would deny the order of your patron?" Shona asked in a whisper as hard as steel.

"Of course not," Connor scoffed. "I've sworn an oath to obey your every command, my lady." He paused for a single breath. "But where the army is concerned, I am your commanding officer, and there you are sworn to obey my commands."

Shona leaped to her feet. "How dare you?"

"You're the one who insisted I become a general. You swore an oath to the school to follow the orders of your commander in the Tir-raon."

As she started sputtering with anger, unable to make a coherent comment, Connor said innocently, "It's all part of the game, isn't it?"

She lunged, her beautiful dress flaring dramatically as her muscles hardened and her body shifted into the perfect lines of granite. She raised a fist, and Connor braced himself to take a blow that, as her Guardian, he dare not block.

Maybe he had pushed her a little too far?

It had felt so good, though. He'd take a hit for this.

She leaned forward, her blue eyes flashing with indignant anger, but did not quite unleash the blow. Instead, she spun and marched away, crossing the entire long room before returning. Her pale cheeks were still colored with anger, and the look was quite alluring. Like a lovely pedra deciding whether to rip his head off.

"You try my patience, Connor."

"Sometimes it's hard for me to juggle both halves of my position here. I am your Guardian, Lady Shona, and I am sworn to your service. But you must allow me to act as general, or I cannot win this game for you."

"You must win," she said, sinking back into her chair and motioning him to sit nearby. "Oh, Connor, I'm sorry I let my anger get the best of me. It's just, with the assignments today, and dealing with Catriona all afternoon, I'm ready to snap."

"You should come practice with me in my Dawnus suite," Connor suggested. "Plenty of room to break things."

Her anger faded, replaced by a sly little smile. "Why, Connor, are you suggesting I sneak into your rooms tonight?"

That was not what he meant at all. He had been thinking how fun it would be to drench her in giant tubs of water.

She misinterpreted his smile and reached a tender hand to touch his. "You drive me crazy sometimes, my Guardian. Life is never boring around you."

Or safe around you, he wanted to say. Instead, he decided to try out Cameron's new flowered prose.

"Waves break against rocky shores
Birds wheel through the heavens, free
Truth glows with beauty."

Shona frowned. "Your Sentry-speak is getting worse."

"It actually a new form of poetry I'm learning."

Her frown deepened. "It's awful."

"It's kind of a battlefield tactic gone bad," he admitted.

She grimaced. "I must. . .request that Catriona be reassigned, General Lian." She stressed his name and even tried to look imploring. It was a good look for her. He needed to find ways to make her do that more often.

"I'm sorry, Captain," he replied crisply. "But I must deny your request."

"Why?" She exclaimed, slapping the arm of her chair. Those full lips of hers made for excellent pouts.

"Think about it. Catriona is a princess, and she's made a big deal about helping me win the nomination. Not granting her some kind of position would only create hard feelings, and I cannot afford that. We're already walking a fault line."

When she didn't immediately argue, he added, "Besides, she really is making progress. If anyone can help her learn how to be the leader she's supposed to be by birthright, it's you."

The compliment helped, but she grimaced again. "I don't know if anyone can help her."

"You must," he insisted, taking her hand in his. She seemed to like physical contact, and he needed her on his side. "I need the Boulder corps functioning at top capacity if we're going to have any chance of winning. So I'm relying on you to lead, but help Catriona think she's the one doing it."

Besides, keeping Shona occupied with Catriona and the Boulder squads would hopefully give him some extra time to hunt for the truth of patronage.

Shona sighed, then gave him a little smile. "I love that quick tongue of yours, Connor."

"Thank you, Captain."

"No," she said, leaning closer and drawing him to her. "Right now, I'm speaking to you as Shona."

She kissed him. A short, but deep kiss that left him breathless. Shona sure knew how to use those lips of hers when she wanted to.

Connor was just trying to figure out how to ask her more about patronage when she said, "Before you request more time from my serving girl, I will have you know that she will be busy and unavailable." When he tried to protest she shook her head. "Jean cannot ignore her duties to me, no matter how important your needs may be. She must remember her place."

Which of course was a reminder to him to remember his place, despite that recent kiss.

"Furthermore," Shona said. "I have approved Jok's request for Jean to attend him during a formal event in two days' time."

"What?" Connor exclaimed, but lowered his voice when she raised a single eyebrow in censorship. "I thought you were keeping him at a distance."

"He has promised to treat her with courtesy beyond her station," Shona said, looking unconcerned.

Connor was far from satisfied. He still fumed about Jok's orchestrating the collapse of the dome, and he didn't trust Jok around Jean for very long. He had wanted to get his hands on her since the first day he'd seen her.

"She is my servant," Shona said, her voice again haughty. "And her fate is entirely in my hands."

How much of that decision was based on Shona's desire to put Jean in her place, and how much was a warning to Connor? "It is your right."

"Let's not quarrel," Shona said, once again sounding pleasant. "What are your orders regarding training over the next days?"

Her good humor faded when he explained all of the modifications he planned for his training facility. "I need them as soon as possible. Ivor is doing the same thing, and I suspect the others are too. We're behind schedule and have to catch up."

"Do you have any idea how much all of that will cost?"

"I could take up a collection to raise funds," he suggested, schooling his face to remain neutral. He loved taunting her though.

"Don't you dare," she snapped, looking deeply offended, as expected. "My father is the richest high lord in the realm."

"Then I'm sure he'll agree to help in any way he can so I can train an army to win the Tir-raon for you."

"Of course," she said, looking resigned. Then she leaned against him. "We have to win, my Connor. We must."

That was perhaps the opening he needed. "Would losing affect your ability to maintain patronage for all of your Guardians?"

"What? Oh, of course not. I might be forced to accept agreements that could compromise my future plans, but patronage won't be at risk."

Did she mean she might be forced into an unwanted arranged marriage? He knew the feeling.

"How can you be sure?" Connor prodded. "You said before that you weren't sure of the limits."

Shona sat up and gave him a questioning look. "Why such an interest?"

"After Hector turned unclaimed, it makes me wonder."

"Hector's fate was a terrible tragedy," Shona said, taking his hand and massaging it with hers. The movement was surprisingly distracting. "Don't worry though, you're at no risk."

"It's just, with his patronage intact for so long, I would have thought it would have taken a lot longer for his curse to turn against him."

"Me too," Shona said with a thoughtful frown.

"How long have other Guardians who lost their patronage taken to turn?"

She shrugged. "I have no idea. As far as I know, no one has ever lost patronage after gaining it."

"Really? Even if they committed a crime?"

"Any crime severe enough to lose patronage is severe enough for execution," Shona said. "So they would have been executed."

She had threatened to rescind patronage if he defied her again. Would she do so, or just have Rory assassinate him? He hated having so many people he respected possibly preparing to kill him. It really dampened the possibility for lasting friendship.

Connor tried to ask another question, but Shona pressed her finger to his lips. "Enough of that for tonight. It's depressing."

"But--"

"In fact, I never want to discuss Hector again," she said. "I received word from my father just today that Hector's quarters will be emptied and all record of him will be expunged. So let it go, Connor."

She glanced down, then looked up through her lashes in a teasing way that Jean used to do to Connor and his friends while they were trying to win the first kiss from her. "In fact, I know the perfect way to restore our good humor."

Shona leaned forward to kiss him again, but Connor was not sure he could keep up the act. So as she leaned in, full lips parted slightly, confident in her mastery over him and the influence she wielded through her sensual advances, Connor leaned in to meet her, reaching out to caress her cheek.

And lit his fingers on fire.

Shona shrieked and jumped back, patting her precious hair, the terror in her eyes making it clear she had not forgotten the last time he burned her hair off. It was just growing back into a respectable length too.

"What are you doing?" she cried.

Connor didn't have marble in his mouth, but he had sucked in some of its power before joining Shona, and he was happy he had. He shook his hand vigorously, trying to put out the fire, but only managed to spray sparks into the room.

Shona leaped away shouting, "Turn it off, dolt!"

"I'm sorry," Connor said, snuffing out the fire. "I don't know what happened. I guess I just got too caught up in the moment and lost control."

"You can't afford to lose control," Shona hissed. "Especially not with marble."

"I'll be more careful," he promised, rising. "Was there anything else you needed, Shona?"

"No," she said with abundant disgust. "Go away."

Connor hid his smile as he left. Verena wouldn't have

shrieked and run away if he had threatened her with fire. She would have punched him.

Thinking about those happy memories, Connor exited the building. In recent days, he'd felt depressed every time he thought of Verena, but for the first time he held on to a slender tendril of hope. Maybe there was a way.

Come hammers or high treason, he would find a way if it existed.

As he walked up the lane through the gathering darkness, Connor thought about the planned clearing out of Hector's quarters. That would remove anything that might help him learn the truth.

Connor had to search them first.

Chapter 25

The next day passed in a blur of activity. Connor made the morning rounds, on high alert for an ambush, but the students were too distracted with their new army assignments to do more than grumble. He barely managed to change into his Lian costume in time to train his army, followed by a meeting with the architect about reconfiguring his private practice facility.

He met out on the plain with Aonghus and Camonica for his personal training since workers were already swarming his suite to begin renovations. Tomas and Cameron and a squad of Boulders provided security and kept the session at least marginally private. That gave Cameron several opportunities to stroll past, reciting horrific renditions of flowering prose.

"I think that man's lost all pretense at sanity," Camonica commented after one exceptionally bad poem. "Rory should put him out of his misery."

"I think you're the one who needs to put him out of his misery," Connor said.

"I can't go around breaking the heads of Rory's company," she protested. "That would be bad manners."

"But breaking hearts is not off limits?" Aonghus chortled. He'd been in rare good humor all day, and seemed to take great pleasure in Cameron's odd behavior.

Camonica glanced toward Cameron, who had paused on a nearby hill to look back at her. She groaned. "I don't see how to make it any more clear that the fool is wasting his time."

"You're right, he's completely cracked," Aonghus said, then exploded into the air on a column of fire.

Connor decided to join him and leave the angry Spitter alone for a moment. The two of them practiced intense Firetongue maneuvers high above the plain. That basically meant they tried to immolate each other while falling toward the ground, then blasted themselves back into the air to try again.

It was a lot of fun.

At one point, Connor sprouted fiery wings again and soared in a graceful arc out over the little lake. Of course, Camonica tried to rip his wings off with grasping water hands that erupted from the surface, but Connor was ready.

"Ha!" he shouted as he morphed his wings into spears of fire that severed the watery hands. "You can't get me with that one again!"

"About time," Camonica said when he settled to the ground nearby. "Your head gets so muddled when you're flying."

"He flies well though," Aonghus said. "I never could get the hang of gliding. I always found it too. . .what's the word?"

"Sensible?" Camonica responded.

"Underexciting," Aonghus countered.

"I'm not sure that's a real word," Camonica said.

Aonghus shrugged. "It's not half as bad as some of the stuff Cameron's been making up to fit his rhymes."

"Don't ever mention him again."

Connor did manage to find time to meet briefly with Ailsa and Gisela and ask them to find out where Hector's quarters were located so he could sneak in there after dark. By sunset, they had not yet sent word, so Connor dressed in nondescript clothing and prepared to leave his Dawnus suite. Every passing moment increased the sense of growing urgency he felt to search Hector's quarters. There had to be something there to shed some light on the mystery.

He was surprised when Jean exited the secret door to the undercity just before he opened it from his side.

"Just who I was looking for," she said.

"It's good to see you, but why are you here? Shona said she was going to keep you busy."

"She thinks she is," Jean said with a grin. "But she really has no concept of how long it actually takes to get things done, so I managed to slip away."

"You just barely caught me," Connor said. "I'm on my way to the Sculpture House."

"Don't bother. I came from there. I know how to reach Hector's quarters, but we need to hurry. The cleaners could arrive any time."

"You're coming?"

"Of course," she said. "I know the way. Besides, two sets of eyes can search a lot faster than one."

Connor followed her onto the long stair leading to the undercity. With a flicker of thought, he re-lit her lantern. He had removed the marble from his mouth earlier as part of an experiment to see how long the power he absorbed from the stone lingered. He'd managed to sustain it for over two hours so far.

"I hope this isn't a wild eoin hunt," Connor said. "If there was really something important in his rooms, why wait until now to clear them out? They've had weeks."

"Maybe it was overlooked," Jean said. "High Lord Dougal has to be busy with overseeing the war effort, and Shona doesn't even want to think about Hector."

"Or maybe he was just waiting for Camonica to arrive so someone trusted could deal with it," Connor said.

"I just hope we find something," Jean said.

The narrow beam of her lantern seemed pitiful against the darkness between the far-flung fixed lights, but it didn't feel right to risk a lot more light on this mission. Sneaking needed to be done in the dark.

"I hope we get there in time," she said.

"We have to. We need answers."

"Then let's hurry."

So Connor scooped her into his arms, not needing to tap granite to handle her slender weight. "Hold on," he grinned, then tapped basalt.

Jean managed to not cry out as he sped through the undercity, but she clung to him. With his senses enhanced by quartzite, he could see well enough not to run into a wall. He could feel the pounding of her heart and matched his footsteps to its rapid staccato.

He had to slow a few times at complex intersections for Jean to determine the way, then tore off again. They traveled toward the center of the Carraig, and at one point, they stopped to creep through a creaking wooden gate that led from the dusty, seldom-used passages of the secret undercity to an entirely different world of underground halls.

The wide, well-lit corridors were clearly used daily, and Connor wondered if most of the people who traveled those happier halls even knew about the dark undercity he was learning to traverse so well? With his enhanced ears, he easily identified other travelers of the deep and avoided them, just in case.

In a remarkably short amount of time, he slowed before yet another long stair leading back to the surface.

"This is it," Jean said, gesturing at a tiny placard on the wall that declared the destination of that particular stair. "Hector's apartment is in a residential tower right on the river."

"I thought the teachers all lived in the teacher dormitory."

"Most of them do, but Hector must have amassed some wealth before becoming a teacher. This is a prestigious area."

"Which is why he would need to be here." The man was one of the vainest people Connor had ever met.

Jean seemed relieved when he set her down to lead the way up the stairs. After emerging through a basement, they climbed a central staircase that circled a beautiful atrium in the center of the tower. Wide, stained-glass windows topped that hollow core of the building, and must have bathed the atrium in beautiful colors during the daylight hours. Hector lived on the third floor.

They passed no one as they jogged up the wide, mahogany staircase with its carpeted runner and fancy brass lanterns. The atrium included a well-manicured garden, and the entire central nave of the building smelled faintly of flowers. A little waterfall created a pleasant background noise that helped mask their furtive steps.

When they reached the third landing, they found Hector's quarters at the end of a short hall. A heavy set of wooden doors, covered with engravings of fanciful creatures and scenes of battle led into the suite. Connor prepared to break the lock, but Jean gestured him aside.

"We can't leave any trace that we've been here," she cautioned.

"Then how do you suggest we get in?"

Jean pulled a long pin from her hair and produced what looked like an ice pick from a pocket. She deftly worked them into the lock and jiggled them around.

"Where did you learn to pick locks?"

"My research isn't all theoretical," she said, her brow furrowed in concentration. "Although I haven't practiced as much as I should have."

After twenty long seconds, during which time Connor was convinced someone was going to walk by and discover them, he grew impatient. "I'll melt the lock. No one will be able to tell from the outside."

With a loud click, the lock snapped back. Jean grinned. "Will is the strongest force."

"Will you stop being so smart and open the door?"

She twisted the handle and eased the left-side door open enough for them to slip inside, then carefully closed the doors again. Connor let out a soft whistle as he surveyed the dim expanse of Hector's rooms.

"This is going to take half the night."

They had entered a large, high-ceiling salon, richly decorated in thick rugs and comfortable furniture. A cold fireplace sat in the right-hand wall, with a wide mantel barely large enough to hold all the trophies and memorabilia that Hector had accrued through his years as a teacher.

Two larger-than-life portraits hung on either side of the fireplace, both of Hector, of course. The first depicted him in a set of his favorite tight-fitting leathers, with every muscle clearly defined beneath. The second showed a much younger Hector wearing standard battle leathers, max-tapping granite. He had been intimidating in his youth.

Even though no one had inhabited the rooms for weeks, they didn't smell stale and abandoned. Connor wondered if someone tended the rooms still.

A short hallway led off the entry salon, with doors opening to either side. On the right, the first door opened into a study full of books, a heavy desk, and two reading chairs. The second door led into a huge closet that might have been even larger than the study, packed with Hector's favorite leathers. No less than five mirrors positioned strategically around the room guaranteed he could admire himself from every angle. The only exception in clothing was his bedclothes, which were made of puffy, soft cotton in various pastel colors.

On the left side of the hall, they found an armory and trophy room, filled with glass cases that held plaques and trophies with his name engraved in gold. He had owned an astonishing array of weapons. Most Boulders preferred simple, heavy weapons or just fought with battering-ram fists. Connor wondered if Hector had actually known how to use all the weapons he displayed.

A garderobe, complete with washbasin and an extensive counter of oils and lotions was the last door on the left side of the hall, which terminated in a bedroom as big as the entry salon. Hector's bed was perhaps the biggest sleeping platform Connor had ever seen. His entire family could have slept on it with room to spare. Thick, carved posts rose from every corner, supporting a slender wooden lattice that held silk drapes, drawn aside to reveal the puffy, down blankets.

"That's really too much," Jean muttered.

"It fits his personality," Connor said, scanning the rest of the giant room. It held an assortment of cabinets, trunks, and chests, any of which might conceal something important. One entire corner of the room was dedicated to painting, but he couldn't really judge Hector's talent because the only thing he seemed to like painting was himself.

"If Hector had been the last man alive in the world, would he have loved himself just as much without other people to impress?"

Jean giggled. "Focus, Connor. We don't have enough time as it is."

Long, curtained windows ran the length of the outer wall, overlooking the river. The building was built right against the bank, across from one of the parks that broke up the tight cluster of palaces, towers, and immense buildings of the Carraig. Hector must have paid a fortune to live there.

Connor stepped through a pair of glass doors and out onto a long balcony where several comfortable chairs and a chaise lounge would have allowed Hector to enjoy the view, or the cool evenings. Three stories below, the narrow river meandered directly under the balcony. The soft sound of gently moving water would have been a soothing melody to help him sleep. A gentle breeze blew through the Carraig, generating a soothing melody from the many gargoyle flutes attached to many of the towers.

Hector had lived well. Too bad he had died so badly.

"Let's get to work," Connor said.

They split up and began searching the apartment, looking for anything that might shed some light upon what had driven Hector or turned him unclaimed. The deep shadows made searching a challenge. Jean used her small lantern, shielding most of the light, allowing only a glimmer to illuminate her work.

For Connor, it was a great excuse to practice with quartzite. He popped the little stone into his mouth, tucked it into his cheek, and sucked hard. The liquid warmth of quartzite pooled in his head and he directed it to his eyes. He blinked against a stab of pain and rubbed the now-faceted crystal orbs that his eyes had become.

The dimness of the night no longer bothered him, although the vibrant colors that usually infused his Pathfinder vision were muted. With the benefit of enhanced vision, Connor worked through the apartment, but found nothing helpful.

He wasn't sure what the clue might be, although it would be really nice if one of the golden plaques held the inscription, "This is the secret you're looking for!" or one of the elegant trophies contained a glowing scroll explaining everything.

They didn't. He checked.

He did find many documents in the study and piled them on Hector's desk. A quick scan of their contents suggested they weren't important, but he might still take them with him when they left.

After fifteen minutes, they met in the entrance salon.

"Nothing," Jean said. "You?"

"Me neither. Just need to check this salon."

Jean looked around. "I doubt he'd hide anything under the cushions."

"Maybe he's got a hidden stash somewhere," Connor suggested, trying to maintain his optimism as he tapped quartzite.

Connor slowly crossed the room, scanning for any telltale hints of concealed secrets, hoping for a last minute lucky throw of the stones. He actually found one on the far side of the room twenty seconds later.

He should have known.

Behind the painting.

"You've got to be kidding me," he muttered as he pulled at the painting of Hector in his favorite leathers. "That's about as subtle as a Firetongue farting in a volcano."

Jean giggled and rushed over. "I hope you found something."

Connor pointed at the wall beside the painting. "There are little scratch marks on the wood, like he moves this painting regularly, but it's securely fastened to the wall."

"Try twisting it."

That worked. If he wasn't so eager to find out what was concealed behind the wall-mounted safe hidden behind the painting, he would have been annoyed at how often she was right.

"Can you open it?" Jean asked as they studied the small, steel door. It lacked a handle, and only sported a rotating dial on the front face.

"This I might have to melt."

Before he could reach for a piece of marble, the silence of the suite was broken by a rattling at the door.

The handle began to turn.

Chapter 26

ean snapped the painting back into place, then grabbed Connor's hand and yanked him after as she fled the salon and darted down the short hallway.

"But that's got to be it," Connor protested in a fierce whisper, hating every step they took away from the little safe.

"We can't get caught in here," Jean said, slowing in the deep shadows near the bedroom.

Together they glanced back. The outer door opened and Camonica entered, followed by two men and a woman wearing Lord Dougal's colors. The men carried lanterns, and they moved to light the lamps in the salon.

"Search everything," Camonica told them. "Bring me anything that looks important."

As the group spread out, Connor and Jean slipped into the bedroom and out onto the balcony. They closed the doors after making sure the drapes were down to conceal their presence, and Connor tapped quartzite again.

He applied it to his ears, impatient for the lobes to elongate and for the rush of sounds to pour into his mind. He ignored the night sounds of the Carraig and focused on the soft noises inside Hector's apartment. Jean pulled one of the lounge chairs closer, and the two of them sat together to listen.

"What are they doing?" Jean whispered.

"Searching, just like we did."

"So they're not here just to clean out his things after all," Jean said. "But what are they searching for?"

"Maybe they're trying to figure out how he turned unclaimed so fast," Connor suggested. "Lord Dail had seemed shocked by it."

"Maybe," Jean agreed.

Connor listened as the group moved through the apartment. The woman assistant brought the stack of documents Connor had amassed to Camonica, but she dismissed them after a moment.

He silently hoped they'd find nothing and begin removing furniture. They probably had a wagon waiting. If they all left to take a load of Hector's possessions downstairs, he'd risk sneaking back in for a crack at that safe. It wouldn't take long to melt the hinges. He only hoped he didn't burn whatever might be concealed in there.

His hopes were dashed when he caught the faint scraping sounds that he recognized as the same sounds the painting had made when he'd slid it aside.

Sure enough, Camonica called excitedly to her team. Either they knew the combination, or one of them was skilled in figuring out how to bypass the wheel because only a moment later, he heard a loud click, followed by the shuffling of several papers.

Quartzite hearing was so amazing! He wondered how often the Pathfinder students got distracted by all the little secrets they could learn from people who thought they were alone. Then again, they probably had to get really good at filtering out the sounds of people using the privy. Hamish might love rating farts, but the Pathfinders were all girls, and they would probably find those noises disgusting.

"I have what I need," Camonica declared, and Connor picked up the sounds of papers shuffling. "Burn these, and everything else flammable."

"Oh, no," Connor breathed, gripping Jean's hands. "She found some papers in that safe, but she's ordered someone to burn them."

"We have to do something." Jean looked terrified, but determined. "That's our only clue."

Connor stood, planning to rush into the suite and fight Camonica for the papers. Hopefully Shona's influence would help shield him from the consequences of that rash act. But even as he reached for the door leading back into the suite, he heard a rush of fire and the crackle of burning paper.

"She's got a Firetongue," he grimaced, sagging against the door. "We're too late."

"What are we going to do?" Jean asked.

In the suite, the sound of flames was growing as the Firetongue swept through the apartment, consuming everything flammable. They could prevent the flames from spreading beyond the suite, and would destroy anything that might have clued Connor in on Hector's past.

Dougal had declared that everything to do with Hector be destroyed, and Camonica was proving far too efficient.

"We need to get out of here," he told Jean. Turning away from the balcony doors felt like abandoning his only hope of learning the truth. "We'll have to look elsewhere."

"Where?"

"I don't know yet, but I won't give up."

Connor wanted to beat Camonica for a week. Why hadn't she waited just a few more minutes? He hated failing, but the secret was gone.

Releasing quartzite to embrace soapstone, Connor drew a slender column of water out of the river below the balcony. He and Jean stepped onto it and he lowered them to the bank.

The balcony doors of Hector's rooms were flung open, and Camonica rushed out, followed by a billowing cloud of smoke. The apartment glowed with the light of the flames inside. Connor grabbed Jean's hand and fled into the shadows. He doubted Camonica had seen more than a fleeting glimpse of them, not enough to recognize them, but his heart raced with fear anyway.

"How did she know we were there?" Jean asked.

"She must have been tapping soapstone," Connor said, cursing himself for using that stone. "Perhaps to help douse the smoke. She would have felt me manipulating the waters."

"That was close," Jean said, her cheeks flushed with excitement.

"Close enough for one night," Connor agreed.

They didn't speak much on the long trek back to Lord Nevan's palace. He left her there and continued on to the Sculpture House, lost in thought as he traipsed through the chill darkness.

Hector had been hiding something.

Was it the secret they sought, or something different?

How was he ever going to find out?

Chapter 27

amish entered Verena's workroom without knocking. In recent days, she had barely let him step inside before chasing him away. Whatever she was working on, it had entirely consumed her attention. It was like she'd gotten a secret mission too.

It was time to share what he had learned and snap her out of her solitude. They worked best as a team and time was too short to delay.

Besides, he needed more things to blow up.

Verena's workroom was a cluttered mess. The cavernous space opened to the outside, but the giant double doors were closed. A windrider sat near that outer door. It looked like one of the new models Verena had been working on. She had suggested she could modify them to allow for non-Builder pilots. Hamish wasn't convinced, but was interested in seeing her ideas. Verena was as clever in her way as Jean.

Hamish grimaced as he scanned the room. He had to stop thinking about Jean so much, but her face popped into his mind at the most random moments, and thoughts of her distracted him whenever he wasn't focused on his work. He really needed to sneak across the mountains and visit his family in Alasdair. In fact, he had decided that part of the field-testing of his new suit would be to also risk a visit to her. Connor might not be able to leave the Carraig yet, but maybe Jean could? Even if she couldn't visiting them would boost everyone's spirits.

Tables, benches, and cabinets cluttered much of the workroom. Battle leathers and dozens of pairs of gauntlets, from simple leather gloves to armored battle fists, covered one entire table.

Verena walked around a tall wardrobe, concentrating on a steel-clad gauntlet on her left hand.

"Since when do you use gauntlets?" Hamish asked, walking closer.

Verena frowned at him. "This isn't a good time, Hamish. I'm busy."

"We're all busy, but that's not a good enough excuse any more. We need to talk."

"Tomorrow. I promise. But right now I'm just too busy." Verena gestured at a desk near Hamish. "I've got some sweetbreads in the center drawer. I've been, ah, saving them for you."

He rushed over. They weren't just sweetbreads, they were the good ones. The cooks had started limiting the quantities he could take when he visited the eating hall. Hamish grabbed up several of them and shoved them into his pockets, then popped an entire pastry in his mouth.

He closed his eyes to savor the soft sweetness. It was glazed with a bit of honey, and was still warm. How did she manage that?

"Wis mmm wunful," he muttered around the mouthful of treat.

"You're welcome," Verena said, turning back toward another table. "See you tomorrow, Hamish."

"Before I go, why don't you tell me the big secret you're working on?"

"What are you talking about?" Her voice sounded a bit strained, like when she was deciding whether or not to punch him.

"You wouldn't have admitted you had food in here if you didn't have something even more important you were trying to hide from me."

"I'm not supposed to tell you. That's what secret means."

"Secrets aren't supposed to be kept from friends," Hamish said. "Otherwise they become a security risk."

"That doesn't make any sense."

"Of course it does. If you keep a secret from me, but I know you're keeping secrets, then I won't trust you with my secrets either, so our work can't get done and we'll have to tell someone we trust less. They'd be a security risk, so it's better to tell me instead."

"How much marble have you swallowed today?"

"Not much," he responded carefully. "I've switched to obsidian. Better for the mind."

When Verena hesitated, Hamish added, "Fine, then I won't tell you my secret either."

"You can't keep secrets," Verena said.

"I can if you can."

"I mean, you lack the capacity."

"I do not," Hamish exclaimed. "I haven't told anyone about my research with diorite."

Verena smiled. "Arguing with you is so much fun sometimes, but diorite isn't much of a secret. Dierk has been researching it for months."

"Not my kind of research," Hamish assured her, extracting a throwing dart from a pouch at his belt with a flourish. "Kilian requested something more subtle."

"Diorite isn't subtle," Verena said, but she drifted a bit closer. Verena loved research even more than Hamish, and the promise of something new was a chance she couldn't ignore.

"It's as subtle as I am."

"Again you prove my point."

"I'll give you proof." Hamish took aim and threw the dart.

It struck the closest strut of the distant windrider and exploded. The thunderous sound echoed really well through the huge chamber, and a cloud of dust concealed the wagon for a moment. When it cleared, the strut was gone, the wagon listing badly as it leaned on broken supports.

"See. Subtle."

"Breaking that wagon is not subtle," Verena exclaimed. "I just finished repairing the faulty thrusters on that one."

"If I had used more diorite, I could have destroyed the entire thing," Hamish explained. He didn't explain that he had been aiming for the pitcher of water on the table next to the windrider. He had glued a single grain of diorite to the tip of that dart. "That little bit does targeted damage."

Using the darts had been a brilliant idea. He didn't have a lot of diorite, and it was so dangerous, he didn't dare use an entire piece of stone. So he'd focused on determining the smallest amount possible and what it could do.

He'd gotten his testing down to a single grain, but trying to throw that at things was really inaccurate. Gluing them to the darts gave him a stable platform.

And it looked awesome when those darts obliterated things.

A single grain of diorite, with its release rate opened wide, could blast a hole in standard armor, and even crack the outer layer of hardened granite scales on one of the Strider vests he'd created. Blowing off the strut of the windrider was another great test. He should have thought of that sooner.

He had tried to convince a local farmer to let him try it out on one of his recently-butchered goats to get a sense of how it would perform against flesh and bone, but the man had seemed offended by the idea of losing the meat.

"I don't see why Kilian would entrust you with diorite at all," Verena said. "That's a recipe for--"

"For brilliant results," Hamish finished for her. "So what did Kilian order you to study and keep secret from me?"

She paused. "How. . ."

"Oh, come on. He told me to keep diorite secret just like he told you. Kilian is always saying things that don't make sense. You know I know, which means he knew I'd know you know, you know?"

She sighed. "You're probably right, although don't ever repeat that last sentence again."

"I've been wanting to run some of these ideas by someone anyway," she added, then extracted a piece of dark stone from a drawer. The hard, smooth-sided stone had an almost metallic gleam to it, but was clearly a stone. "This is blind coal."

"I haven't heard of that one."

"It's a new power stone," Verena said, excitedly.

"What does it do?" Hamish slid a finger along the smooth edge of the stone and leaned forward, but Verena pulled it out of reach before he could lick it.

"Don't be mean. How else am I supposed to get a feel for it?"

"You are not licking my stone," Verena said. "I'll give you a little piece later."

"So what does it do?" he asked again, eager to get his hands on it.

"It's aggressively slippery."

Hamish laughed. "You mean it'll help you fall even on flat ground."

"Not exactly."

"So what, exactly?"

"I'll show you." Verena retreated several paces. "Throw one of those darts at me."

"No way," Hamish said. "Didn't you see what it did to that wagon?"

"Do you want to see what this can do, or not?"

"Not if it means hurting you." Hamish liked Verena, but even if he was willing to risk hurting her, everyone in the compound would take turns beating him for a month if he did. They all loved her.

"Do it, Hamish. I won't get hurt."

"Fine, but I warned you." Hamish drew out another dart, but did not open the release rate on the grain of diorite before throwing it.

Verena snapped out a gauntleted fist, and the dart deflected away just before striking the gauntlet. It was almost as if she'd activated a mini shieldstone.

She frowned, then picked up the dart. "I can't prove this thing if you don't open the release rate."

"It's a bad idea," he repeated.

She tossed the dart back to him. "Open it this time, or I'll open it and throw it at you."

Hamish considered the dart. He approved taking necessary risks as part of their research, but she was acting foolish. "Let's set up the gauntlet on a dummy and throw the dart at that."

Verena shook her head. "I've been testing this with all kinds of stuff already. I know what I'm doing."

"If you get hurt, it'll be my funeral."

"Do it." She got that obstinate look in her eye that made him nervous.

Hamish took a deep breath, aimed, and threw the dart.

He held his breath as the dart flicked across the distance between them. Again she punched out with her gauntleted fist. The dart didn't explode, but again deflected past her without quite touching. It struck a tall, steel cabinet behind her, then exploded, knocking the cabinet over and leaving a black dent in its side.

"Told you," Verena laughed.

Hamish couldn't wait to try it himself. "How'd you do that?"

"Like I said, blind coal is slippery. When I open the release rate just a fraction, it creates a slippery barrier. Things just sort of slide off and slip past. I can step right through elemental barriers. I even walked through a closed door the other day."

"Really?" That was amazing. Hamish needed one of those gauntlets. Did she realize they could access the locked pantry any time with that?

"It felt really strange," she said. "I had to open the release rate more than fifty percent for that one, and the stone disintegrated after I walked back through. Only lasted a few seconds opened that much."

"That seems awful fast."

She nodded, showing him the gauntlet. He noted tiny pieces of blind coal worked into the armored glove. He touched one and felt for the invisible crack that held its power in check. Verena had opened the release rate only a bit, perhaps ten percent. The stone felt like a quarter of its power had already been drained.

"Was this a new stone when we started?"

She nodded. "With stones this size, I can usually get up to three uses before they crumble, but it depends on the amount of force it's deflecting. For stronger barriers or greater force, the stone burns out really fast."

"That could be a problem trying to use this in battle."

She nodded. "That's what I've been struggling with. It could be a life saver, but only once or twice before needing to be replenished."

"You could use bigger stones."

She shook her head. "I tried that. The larger stones burn out fast too. It's strange, but I don't get twice as much protection from a stone twice as large. This size seems to be the best protection to duration balance."

"So either we need to use a lot of them and cycle through them," Hamish said. "Or we use them only in very specific situations."

"Like fighting rampagers."

"What else have you discovered?" Hamish took a seat on a nearby stool and popped another of the sweetbreads into his mouth.

"Combining the slippery property with basalt increases the spin rate on speedslings by fifty percent," Verena said, gesturing toward her Swift, which sat on its custom rack.

The little craft looked menacing, as if crouched to leap into the sky. She had painted the armored exterior a mixture of blue and gray, which would help it blend into the sky. The speedslings slung along the sides of the seat were longer and narrower than the standard weapons. By increasing the spin rate, she'd get those little projectiles moving even faster. He shuddered to think what they could do to any soldiers unfortunate enough to get hit.

They might even stop the rampagers.

"Did you add the puking dooms to your Swift?"

"Not facing front. I added them to the base. I can incinerate anything under the Swift, and all it'll do is add more lift. It's a good compromise. What about you?"

"I tried using diorite in a speedsling," he admitted. "But they're too volatile. Even just bouncing around inside of one as they come up to speed, they tend to explode."

"You didn't hurt yourself, did you?"

"Not bad. I poured some sandstone into the bandage and it healed up pretty fast."

"It would be nice to have exploding projectiles," Verena noted.

"Not if I blow myself up. That hurts."

"What if you embedded the grains into something else?" she suggested.

"I'm working on that. Caramel didn't work, but there should be something that could protect them from the little bumping they do in the speedsling, but not enough to keep them from exploding on impact."

"And it can't adversely affect the air-slip-drag ratio," Verena said.

She was always throwing out new terms she invented to explain what they did. Flying was so new, there weren't enough words. She was good at inventing them, and she was smart enough to eventually teach all that formal book learning to new flyers. Meanwhile, Hamish would be soaring over the countryside in his new suit.

"Maybe some kind of tiny arrowhead," Verena added, getting sucked into the creative process. "Or even using the standard hornets from the other speedslings. You could attach those little grains between the projecting edges, which would shield them from accidental damage."

"Better to drill a hole in them and place the diorite inside," Hamish said.

"That would be better, but would take a lot longer. No way we could produce enough for the standard speedslings."

"We don't need to enhance all of them. Those weapons can

already chew through people and armor, and probably even pierce slow Boulders."

Verena nodded slowly. "You're right, but we could make some of the modified hornets in our custom speedslings for when we're facing rampagers."

Hamish nodded in turn. They needed every advantage the next time they faced those monsters, and having the ability to unleash thousands of exploding hornets into their faces would be just the thing.

"I knew coming here was a good idea."

The door behind Verena opened and Kilian stepped through. Hamish shushed Verena before she could speak and pulled her around to face Kilian as he approached.

He gave them a long look, then sighed. "Can neither of you follow orders?"

Chapter 28

At first Verena felt a flash of guilt, but Kilian didn't look angry, or even surprised. More like resigned.

"You knew we'd end up talking about our projects, didn't you?" she asked as she rushed up to give him a hug.

"You waited until you had each gained a foundational understanding of the stones assigned to you and made concrete progress in your research, didn't you?"

"So it was all part of your plan?" Verena asked.

"You don't need to play games about it," Hamish said, approaching more slowly to shake Kilian's hand.

"If you'd started comparing notes immediately, you would have gotten distracted," Kilian said. "We don't have time to waste. I do what I do because it must be done and I don't have time for delays."

"I don't think working together would have delayed us," Verena said. She could see his point, but she didn't agree with it. Hamish might have gotten distracted, but she wouldn't have. Would she?

"Regardless of how we got here, show me the fruits of your labors," Kilian said.

Verena explained about the progress she had made with blind coal, then showed him the gauntlets. "I started with jackets, but they required too much stone to work properly, and they didn't allow the wearer enough flexibility in positioning the stone."

"I like this idea," Kilian said, trying on one of the gauntlets and examining the stones.

"As long as you see the blow coming, you can position your fist to take the hit," she said. "And it'll slide past."

"What about applying it to shields?" Kilian asked.

"Possible," Verena said. "I considered that, but the stones only give us a few defensive blocks. On a shield, they'd be spent blocking hits that the shield might have been able to handle on its own. I needed something more specialized."

"Makes sense," Kilian agreed.

"You know, we could add some blind coal to the scale granite armor I've been working on," Hamish suggested. "That way you'd only need to add your stone to the places most likely to get hit. The stop-bash properties of the scaled granite could do the rest for the less important hits."

They discussed the idea for a minute, and the potential was enormous, but Kilian interrupted before they could get to work trying it out. "That's a good idea, but we don't have time right now. We need to focus on what's already completed."

Verena and Hamish took turns reporting on their research. He looked pleased.

"We need to do some field testing," Verena completed. "But I think it'll all work."

"Test it on the way to the front," Kilian said. "Take everything you can. We get one windrider to pack it all in."

"What's the rush?" Hamish asked, sounding worried. "Has the war started?"

"Tensions are high, but Dougal hasn't dared his first major assault. There is still knowledge he lacks that places him at a disadvantage."

"The weakening powder," Verena realized.

Kilian nodded. "We've been successful in keeping the secret from him, despite the number of spies he's committed to ferreting out the truth."

"You know how many spies he has?" Hamish asked.

"We know many of them," Kilian said. "We track them and make sure they don't acquire anything too important, and monitor them to identify any spies that have slipped through."

"Plus, your spies in Dougal's army are funneling information to you as fast as his are," Verena guessed. She hadn't paid enough attention during the boring spy management class she took in junior academy.

Kilian nodded. "The Arishat League also has people involved. Then there's the official spy agency from Obrion."

"It must be getting crowded on the front lines," Hamish said. "It's a wonder there's any room for soldiers."

"Dougal does not have that one secret he so desperately yearns for."

"How do you know?" Hamish asked.

"Because he hasn't attacked yet," Verena answered before Kilian could. She prayed the Tallan's blessing that the secret would remain secure.

"Is that why we're going to the front?" Hamish asked. "To beat up some spies?"

"No," Kilian said, his smile fading. "We're going to trap some rampagers."

"Have you seen more of them?" Verena asked, shivering to think of those terrifying monsters. The Swift was far better armed than the last time they faced the beasts, but she still wasn't looking forward to the next encounter.

"They've been spotted a couple of times," Kilian said. "But there have been no additional clashes. With the latest report out of the Carraig, I am more convinced than ever that Dougal has somehow learned how to master them."

"Connor?" Hamish asked.

"Is he all right?" Verena asked at the same time.

"Ilse sent word. Connor failed to escape the school because he had to fight an unclaimed monster right there in the Carraig."

"How is that possible?" Verena asked.

"One of the professors, who happens to have secret ties back to Dougal, apparently lost patronage and turned unclaimed," Kilian explained. "Apparently he was trying to murder Connor's aunt. The boy destroyed it, but it was a close thing. What's important for us is that his description of the beast that teacher turned into exactly matches the monsters we fought in that canyon."

Verena's heart raced with fear for Connor, even though the fight was long since won. She imagined him facing one of those raging monsters, and she wondered what he must have had to do to defeat it. "Is he all right?" she asked again.

"He cannot risk leaving the Carraig."

"Of course he can't," Hamish said. "We told you unclaimed were real."

Kilian shook his head. "There is a threat, that much is certain. However, your girl Jean recently uncovered documents that confirm that patronage was instituted as a grand lie to control the commoner class."

"She's the smartest person in the world," Hamish muttered, his cheeks coloring a bit. "But, how could--"

Kilian shushed him. "We don't have time to discuss your girl now. Save your questions for the flight to the front."

"If patronage is a lie, then why doesn't Connor come to us?" Verena asked.

"Because there is some kind of threat," Kilian repeated, pacing away. "I've always doubted patronage, but what if they really have found a way to sabotage the commoners' gifts? We must know the secret before we can act with confidence."

"That's why you want to trap one," Hamish said. "You want to study it."

"We must. Ilse reported that they are following some limited avenues of research and investigation there at the school, but we must follow every possible lead here."

"How are you going to lure them in?" Verena asked. "If Dougal is indeed somehow controlling the rampagers, he's not going to risk them lightly."

"He will when the potential prize outweighs the possible risk," Kilian said with a sly smile.

"The weakening powder. You're going to lure them in with it."

"It won't weaken them," Hamish said. "They're not Boulders."

"It's brilliant," Verena said as she considered the ramifications of the idea. "Dougal must gain that secret for his invasion to succeed, but rampagers won't care about it if they're just mindless monsters. They'll only attack and try to obtain the secret if they're driven by the will of another."

"Exactly," Kilian said.

"Hold on," Hamish interrupted, frowning. "If they're ravaging monsters, how can anyone control them?"

"That's the question," Kilian said. "If someone can somehow gain control over them, then they aren't mindless. There is a way to train them, to perhaps trigger the rampager effect, and perhaps even reverse it."

"How is it possible?" Verena couldn't imagine anyone regaining their humanity after transforming into one of those horrible monsters.

"I don't know yet. The goal is to set a trap that precludes any but the rampagers from any chance of success. If Dougal has no choice but to risk them, then does, it confirms my suspicion that he somehow controls them."

"And if they don't, then they're just monsters?" Hamish asked.

"Perhaps," Kilian said.

"I'm not sure we're ready," Verena said, glancing at the Swift and considering what other weapons she could pack onto the tiny craft. If Dougal decided to use the rampagers, how many would he send? How many could they defeat before being overwhelmed?

"We cannot afford to wait," Kilian said. "We must root out the truth of these monsters before the war commences."

"Connor needs to know too," Hamish said. "I agree. Let's do this."

Verena took a deep breath, calculating all of the gear they were going to need. "I think we should take two windriders."

"Only if you and Hamish fly them," Kilian said. "I can't spare more Builders."

Verena pointed at the windrider Hamish had just damaged. "Even after repairing that strut, that new prototype's not quite ready to fly. I'm training the first non-Builder pilot, but the mechanical's devilishly complex, and it's not quite done."

"I still don't think it'll ever work," Hamish said.

It would. She felt that deep in her heart. There had to be a way to make it work. She just needed a little more time. They were exploring concepts so new they were still little more than half-formed ideas floating in her head.

"So you fly it," Verena suggested. She would rather take less gear than get saddled with the slow-moving windrider. She needed the long flight up to the border pass to test her Swift."

"No way," Hamish said. "I have to test my battle suit."

"Figure it out," Kilian said. "Take turns if you have to. Either way, we leave as soon as possible."

"We can leave after lunch," Verena promised him.

He nodded. "That can work. I've already initiated the plan. Intelligence is being leaked to a couple of Dougal's spies. The weakening powder is being moved to a forward staging area near the front lines. Our forces are on alert for an assault and will be able to stop regular troops. I expect an attempt tomorrow night. Dougal's best chance to make his move will be during the confusion of the battle. That's when he'll unleash the rampagers."

The plan made sense, but Verena worried about so many soldiers exposed to the destruction the rampagers could unleash upon them. She glanced at the pile of gauntlets she'd been experimenting with, wondering how many more she could complete.

Kilian noted her glance. "We will lead the strike team against the rampagers. We cannot risk releasing any of your new inventions to any soldiers outside our team."

"Why not?" Verena exclaimed. "We could save lives."

"These inventions will save lives," Kilian said. "But we cannot reveal the full extent of our mechanicals to Dougal in the first encounter. We will use them, but we must do so with extreme care. For this first skirmish, we limit them to our team."

Verena didn't like it, but she saw the wisdom in Kilian's plan. "All right, we'll use this as our final field test for refined calibration."

"It's a long flight to the border," Hamish said, moving toward the door, looking excited by the prospect of taking on the rampagers again. "I'll talk with the cooks about extra rations."

"That might not be a good idea," Verena said. "Didn't the cooks ban you from the eating hall outside of strict meal times?"

Hamish waved away her concern. "That was because they want to make sure there's enough food ready. The head cook loves me. She even said once that she'd pay to transfer me to the front lines. Getting some extra food should be easy."

Chapter 29

onnor knocked on the door to Jean's small room near Shona's quarters. It was almost the dinner hour at the end of a very hectic day. He'd delivered the rounds, alert for signs the frustration at the reduced rations was growing to the point that students might decide to beat him, despite Jok's intervention. The army training seemed to keep them distracted enough that he didn't have to dodge Boulders yet.

His army training went well, and his soldiers were beginning to function as a cohesive unit. He still had no idea how they were going to win the first battle, but they were making great progress.

He had learned that Camonica's rooms were situated in Lord Nevan's palace, and he hoped to find time to sneak in and search them. But none of that mattered at the moment. Jean was preparing to leave to meet Jok, to attend him at a formal event. Connor hated that Shona had allowed it. He needed to talk with Jean. She was probably terrified.

Jean opened the door and Connor gaped. She looked gorgeous, more like nobility than any of the Petralists he knew. Only Shona could rival Jean's beauty and grace.

Jean wore a spectacular midnight-blue gown she must have borrowed from Shona. The square neckline revealed more of her chest than the modest dresses she normally wore, and a simple ruby pendant drew the eye like a lodestone. Her hair was plaited and wound atop her head, highlighting her perfect features, and she wore powder and lip color. He had never seen her so elegant, and for a moment was at a loss for words.

Jean gave him a radiant smile and a little hug that wouldn't risk rumpling the beautiful gown. She was wearing some kind of perfume, and the delicate scent left him breathless. Was she planning to attend Jok at the event, or single-handedly conquer the Carraig?

"I'm glad you stopped by," she said, pulling Connor into her room and closing the door. She directed him to the single chair beside a desk with a mirror above it. Her powders and beauty supplies were placed there with the same order as her medical kit.

Jean pulled her leather writing pad out of a desk drawer and settled onto her narrow bed, which was perfectly made, and tucked her feet under the voluminous skirt. She made a brushing gesture, as if to push her hair behind her ear, but with her hair done up in that complex tumble atop her head, her graceful neck was exposed and there was no loose hair to tuck.

"What have you found?" he asked, wanting instead to ask her about the looming event with Jok. "Did you speak with Evander?"

She shook her head. "He wasn't there, but I found another book in the secret library. It wasn't there before."

"How do you know?"

"There aren't really that many books in there. I think he has an inner secret library where he keeps the full collection. He only shows me the pieces he wants me to see."

"There are too many levels of secret library in this place," Connor grumbled.

"Isn't it exciting?" Jean's eyes sparkled.

"More like annoying."

"Regardless, this new book had exactly the information I was hoping to find."

"Like he knew what you were looking for?"

She nodded. "I don't know how he does it, but I'm glad he did."

Connor wasn't so sure. Was Evander somehow eavesdropping on them? Or had he hired another Pathfinder to listen to their conversations? He was already feeling paranoid enough.

Jean flipped open her folder and scanned through some of the loose pages filled with her clean, flowing script. "There's so much to share. I took lots of notes, but I wish he'd let me just take the books out to show you."

"Has he forbidden that?"

"In his roundabout way."

"Any idea why he's sharing it with you now?"

"Not yet. But listen, this is important." She leaned forward, gesturing with the notebook. "The volume he left for me tracked all known instances where unexplained attacks have happened across the country ever since the final days of the Tallan Wars."

"They've been tracking the unclaimed?"

"Maybe other things too. All the attacks are blamed on unclaimed, but I think some of them were caused by something else."

"What else is there?" Connor asked with a grimace. "It's pretty clear if someone saw an unclaimed or not. At least, if they survived, they'd know how to describe it."

"One interesting fact is that actual sightings of unclaimed with first-hand witnesses didn't start appearing until just the past twenty years or so."

"But you said the book's been tracking attacks for hundreds of years."

"It has. There were fourteen attacks in all. Four in the three decades immediately following the Tallan Wars, three in the two centuries after that, and seven in the past twenty years."

"That's a strange pattern."

Jean nodded. "I thought so too, but when I dug deeper, I noticed other patterns. All but one of the attacks that occurred before the past quarter century were atrocities where entire villages were destroyed."

"Entire villages?" He easily imagined unclaimed rampaging through Alasdair, slaughtering everyone.

Jean nodded. "There were few survivors. They all spoke of gigantic monsters that seemed immune to damage."

"How did they stop them?" Connor asked, filled with cold dread to think of an unclaimed monster as big as what she was describing.

"Most of the accounts are unclear, but in three of the records, there were witnesses who saw a second giant appear and destroy the marauding monster."

"Two monsters in the same place? Lucky they didn't get along."

"Stranger than that," Jean said. "The accounts are a bit contradictory. One says the other monster was made of living waters that burned, but the other two spoke of fire incarnate that left steaming tracks."

"Were they waxing poetic?"

"They seemed to be speaking literally," Jean said, studying her notes. "They claimed that both monsters were formed from elements that rose to take living form and battled with such fury that they broke mountains and laid waste to entire valleys."

Connor thought of his own recent training with fire and water. Was it possible for the elements to come alive? He was learning to walk with the elements, but did they ever walk alone, get upset, and take it out on anyone unfortunate enough to get in the way?

"I've never heard of elements acting without a Petralist involved," Connor said.

"Apparently it happens sometimes. I found a reference to a name for the monsters, although I'm not sure if it's for a particular one, or a broader label, since descriptions of the monsters vary pretty widely."

"What name?"

"Elfonnel."

"I've never heard the term before," Connor said. "I wonder if Aunt Ailsa has."

"You should ask her. I'm going to study more tomorrow. The elfonnel were sometimes referred to as Tallan's Fury."

"I don't like that," Connor said.

"One account called them Builder's Folly."

"What does that mean?" Connor asked. That definitely didn't sound good.

"I don't know." Jean gave him an apologetic smile. "That's all I found about them. I don't think the giant elemental elfonnel monsters were responsible for the spate of recent attacks. Those all involved smaller numbers of casualties and more witnesses. Those accounts match what you saw of Professor Hector's transformation. Those were unclaimed monsters, raging out of control when they lost patronage."

"So what changed in the past twenty years?"

Jean shrugged. "I don't know yet what makes unclaimed a reality now when there's no record of them ever before, but there is enough evidence that they do exist."

"They exist, but we need to know how, and why."

"I'm studying as fast as I can."

"I know." He rose and paced across the little room. "I spoke with Gisela briefly this morning, prior to my rounds. She hasn't learned anything useful from her Arishat contacts, but told me that their armies are on the move."

"Has the war started?" Jean asked, sounding scared.

"It could any day. A major skirmish is brewing on the border. That'll probably trigger everything else. Obrion and Granadure will be fighting there, but she said the various armies of the Arishat are positioning themselves to react to whichever country gains the upper hand. They could invade before winter."

"I don't see how finding the truth about the unclaimed will make a difference," Jean said.

"Don't you see, once we know, we can find a way to get the word out. With the Guardians no longer fearing the loss of patronage, Obrion would face revolution. They couldn't afford to go to war."

Jean shook her head. "It's not that simple, Connor. Evander won't let us reveal the truth."

"We'll find a way. Once we know it, we'll find a way to share it."

"Be very careful." Jean rose and took his hands in hers. "If we move too soon, we'll die. You can't fight Evander, Connor."

He sighed. "Maybe not, but there has to be a way."

"First we learn," Jean said. "Look deep, see clear like Gran always said."

"Then we act," Connor promised.

Jean grimaced. "But until then, I have to go meet Jok and attend him at this ball celebrating the commencement of group battles."

"It's a ball?" Connor asked. "Do you even know how to dance?"

She glared.

"I mean, the kind of dances they dance."

"Don't worry," she assured him. "I can handle it."

He believed her.

"If he gives you any trouble, remind him that he owes me."

"I'll be fine," she assured him, but she looked nervous. "Even though I might be the only commoner there."

"Don't worry. You're prettier than any three other girls combined."

She glared. "Are you calling me fat?"

"No, really--"

"I know," she interrupted before he started panicking. "Just teasing. Good luck with your training."

They left the room together and Connor got an idea. "Wait for me to change into my Lian costume, and I'll escort you to the ball. How's that?"

"I would love it," she said, looking relieved.

When they arrived at the grand ballroom, a huge hall Connor had never entered before, it was filled to bursting with finely dressed lords and ladies. Many paused to stare at Connor and Jean, and for once, the majority of the comments were not directed at him in his mask. Noblemen stared with open admiration at Jean as she glided along beside Connor, while many of the women watched her with thinly-veiled jealousy.

Jok appeared a moment later, resplendent in a rich doublet that almost made his hideous house colors of orange and yellow seem not completely hideous. When he saw Jean, he dropped his wine glass. He snatched for it, but only managed to knock it flying and spray wine over the gowns of two Petralist girls that Connor recognized from Ivor's army.

They shrieked in dismay, but Jok barely noticed. He approached and took Jean's hand, his expression wondering as he bowed low over it.

"You look lovely tonight, Jean."

"Thank you, my lord Jok," she said, making a deep curtsy.

Jok glanced at Connor. "Are you joining us tonight, General?"

"Unfortunately, I have other business." He had received an invitation, but hadn't realized what it meant. As much as he wanted to keep an eye on Jean, the thought of attending the ball and actually trying to dance terrified him. Besides, if he lingered, he'd probably find an excuse to start a fight, or set all the refreshment tables on fire.

Chapter 30

Connor's army clashed on the eastern plain, behind some low hills that offered some concealment from spies from the other armies. The Boulders pummeled each other with admirable enthusiasm, studied by Connor and his captains from a platform of earth that Declan had raised with great difficulty in about ten minutes.

While they watched the practice, Connor discussing the maneuvers with his captains, along with their plan for the first group battle, which loomed just two days away. Well, he called it a plan, but it was more a loosely-affiliated bunch of ideas that hadn't decided if they liked each other yet.

"Boulder companies look strong," Connor commented as he studied the formations clashing in the center of the flat valley.

"That last training with the Fast Rollers really helped." Shona looked pleased. She had done a great job motivating the Boulder students and helping them unite in an effective fighting unit.

She had convinced Catriona to lead the fighting in the front line as a way to develop her leadership persona. Catriona had eagerly accepted, and that did seem to have a positive impact on the other Boulders, although Connor suspected they just wanted a chance to beat on the pudgy princess.

"I should be out there," Lorcc muttered, bouncing on the balls of his feet, his gaze locked on the running battle whirling around the packed ranks of Boulders.

The two dozen Striders he commanded tore across the plain, forming complex patterns as they closed, then broke apart, barely slowing to strike enemy runners. Inspired by Lorcc's bottomless energy and infectious enthusiasm, their running battles nearly rivaled those of Donald and the professional Striders of Rory's company. The day before, Connor had noticed Donald speaking in private with Lorcc after practice. He suspected Donald was trying to recruit Lorcc into Rory's company.

"You're my captain," Connor reminded him. "So that means stopping once in a while so we can plan."

"The primary affinities are strong," Fearghas commented, arms folded as he surveyed the field. "They'll stand firm against any other army."

"That's not the problem though," Shona said, turning from the battle.

Fearghas nodded toward Declan. "The problem is, how is our little tower of terror here going to stop at least three Sentries at the same time?"

Declan seemed to like the title, despite the sarcasm, although he looked terrified as always when he thought of facing off with the other Sentries.

"Declan, you're making great progress," Connor assured the little Sentry.

"I love your enthusiasm, Declan," Aifric said, giving the terrified little guy a warm smile. "But I worry for you."

Not as much as he was worrying for himself.

"Storm clouds gather over lofty peaks," Declan declared, but then hesitated, his expression turning worried. "Ah, and drench the plain," he finished with a cringe. He was getting better at starting Sentry-speak sentences, but struggled with the closers.

"The imagery was good on that one," Connor encouraged him. "Keep practicing."

Then he turned to Papil, the gangly girl who he'd assigned as his Pathfinder captain. "We need to leverage our other strengths to support him,"

"We're working on it." She had a habit of clasping her hands nervously across her stomach, and not meeting his gaze.

She was barely fifteen and looked more like a girl than a young woman, with her freckled face and blond hair cut just above the shoulders. Her blue eyes looked almost too big for her face, but when she tapped her quartzite affinity, the glowing orbs looked quite alluring. She was quiet spoken, and her voice was usually a bit squeaky until she applied quartzite to it. Then it rang forth with amazing power, rich and sonorous, capturing the attention of everyone who heard it.

Papil possessed a quick mind, and Connor needed her to succeed.

"How far has testing proceeded?" he asked.

"We've managed to throw Boulders, but not consistently enough to enter battle with confidence the plan would work."

They were focusing on the largely-ignored potential of elemental air, but only with limited success so far. He didn't care if they ever figured out how to trigger invisible instruments like Padraigin, but he hoped they could learn to walk with air well enough to leverage it in the first battle. A tornado in the right place could scatter Spitters and maybe distract Sentries long enough for Declan to hold his own. Shona had stolen Carbrey's stone rain idea and suggested they throw Boulders over enemy lines to get at the critical tertiary affinity Petralists.

"Keep working on it," Connor urged her. "We need that air power."

"What if it doesn't work?" Fearghas asked.

"It'll work," Connor insisted.

"We need to be prepared if it doesn't," Fearghas countered.

"He's right," Shona said. "We can't enter a battle with a half-formed plan, relying on unproven tactics."

"We still have two days," Connor said. "We'll figure it out."

"I think I'm still your best choice," Fearghas declared.

"Of course you do," Shona scoffed. "Your head's so full of yourself, you actually think you can take on a Sentry."

His hand drifted to the hilt of one of the swords on his back, and his stance shifted, becoming more graceful somehow as he tapped obsidian. Shona's skin faded as she tapped granite and grinned, as if eager for him to strike so she could punch him off the platform.

"Cut it out," Connor snapped. Even though he'd love to see Fearghas humble Shona, he couldn't risk one of them really getting hurt. "You two fighting doesn't help us."

"So what about it?" Fearghas pressed, releasing his sword.

"Maybe."

Conventional wisdom dictated that Connor focus on defensive measures since they'd be facing armies with far greater elemental powers, but conventional wisdom also guaranteed he'd lose. So he and Fearghas had begun exploring the idea of sending the Blade on a lone incursion against enemy armies, protected by Connor's elemental powers. Fearghas was arguably the deadliest Blade in the school, and if he could close on a Sentry, he could possibly disable them.

It was a high-risk gamble, and it would tie up Connor's tertiary powers, but it was that kind of daring maneuver they needed if they hoped for any chance at winning.

Connor still felt like he was missing something, though.

Like three more Sentries.

Donald raced up to the platform and beckoned to Connor. "General, you're summoned to a meeting with Captain Rory in Command Central."

"Keep practicing," Connor told his captains before hopping down off the platform. "Hopefully Rory's ready to tell us something about the first battle."

Then he tapped basalt and raced after Donald.

Chapter 31

ommand Central was situated in the top room of a massive tower sheathed in white granite that towered over the central keep. It was one of the tallest towers in the entire Carraig inner city, and the view of the closely-packed palaces, towers, and mighty halls took Connor's breath away. Tall windows encircled the entire room, and Connor wanted nothing more than to slowly walk the circumference, staring at the amazing view.

Instead, he approached the huge, circular table that dominated the room. Crystal chandeliers hung from the vaulted ceiling overhead, although the candles had not been lit. The floor was covered with a thick, golden carpet that muffled their footsteps.

Connor had arrived for the meeting first. Captain Rory rose from his seat on the far side of the table, and Connor circled the room to shake his hand.

"How's training going?" Rory asked.

Connor felt like he'd been ordered to produce his mother's famous stewed rabbit recipe, but had been given only a pair of Hamish's stinky socks as ingredients. He was doomed to failure, unless he fundamentally changed the stakes.

So he smiled behind his mask. "Everything is falling into place."

"You actually have a plan?" Rory asked, looking doubtful.

The outer door opened and a servant wearing perhaps the ugliest version of Lord Dail's uniform ushered the other champions into the room. Rory gestured them to take seats. Connor waved to the others. Ivor smiled in greeting, Padraigin waved back, and Redmund only grunted.

"In two days' time, you will meet in the first group battle," Rory said without preamble. "This command meeting is your official notice. You will meet around the lake on the eastern plain."

"Why are you telling us in advance?" Padraigin asked

"Some battles are a surprise, while the location of others is clear long in advance," Rory said.

Connor thought of the impending conflict on the border between Obrion and Granadure. The location of that first clash between the nations had been clear to everyone for weeks.

"I decided to start with the most straightforward and obvious battle you will face this year," Rory said. "The location is known. The starting positions are known. The strength and disposition of your forces are known. Furthermore, there is a ready supply of water. That's not always the case, but we wanted to start this year with equal advantage between the Spitters and the Sentries."

The other commanders looked excited, and were studying the little map Rory unrolled on the table, as if they weren't already intimately familiar with that area. There always had to be a map.

What if he burned all the copies of the map? Would that postpone the battle?

The others looked confident. Why wouldn't they? As Connor looked from Padraigin to Redmund to Ivor, he considered all the wild ideas he'd invented with his captains for defeating those crafty Dawnus and their armies. How could he leverage his forces in a way they wouldn't expect?

Would the key be the Pathfinders, or Fearghas? Could he somehow leverage the Solas? He wasn't sure.

Then, all of a sudden, he was. The various pieces snapped together in a way he hadn't expected, but which he absolutely loved. The answer had been right there all along. He could use the Solas, Fearghas, and the Pathfinders.

About time. He'd begun to worry his brains had melted under all that training with Aonghus.

He banged a hand onto the table, interrupting an indecipherable comment Redmund was making and drawing all their eyes.

"I'm willing to accept anyone's surrender prior to the

commencement of the battle. Once the fighting begins, I won't be able to show any mercy."

Redmund banged the table in turn. "The kindling piled atop the embers of yesterday's ashes does not think to boast itself upon the logs that await their turn to burn."

They all looked at Redmund like he was cracked. Ivor said, "Ah, you tell him, Redmund."

Padraigin frowned at Connor. "Lian, I figured you were hoping to survive only because we'd be too busy fighting each other to pay any attention to your pitiful army, but I think you just killed those chances."

They were getting upset, but he needed to really rile them up. "The pedra rules supreme in the skies until through pride it makes an attempt upon the armed hunter."

Ivor sighed. "It looks to me like the first order of business in this upcoming battle is abundantly clear."

Padraigin nodded. "I really had hoped you could at least come in second place behind me, Lian."

Redmund looked pleased with the idea of crushing Connor first. "Though enemies oppose, a common foe may yet unite them for a time. Until after the destruction of the greatest fools, they may turn to important business."

The meeting trended downward after that.

Rory pulled Connor aside after the other three departed. "Lad, I thought you were a clever boy, but what you just did was tantamount to suicide. You cannot afford to lose this contest."

"Captain, think back to the battles of Alasdair. You and General Carbrey outnumbered Ilse's forces many times, yet she prevailed against you because you became overconfident."

Rory shook his head. "We weren't overconfident, lad. If she hadn't brought to bear those new Builder powers we'd never seen before, we would've been justified." He looked more closely at Connor. "You haven't gotten your hands on any of those infernal mechanicals have you? I cannot allow them on the battlefield."

If only he were so lucky. Connor shook his head. "You know what I have on hand, Captain. We're outnumbered and they possess far greater tertiary affinity abilities."

"Then why goad them like that?" Rory asked.

"I can't win this game by surviving only because no one bothers to take the time to attack me. I need to prove to them and to my own army this battle is far from hopeless, and that it's the other armies that need to fear us."

"That's all fine and well, lad, but you need to deliver on promises like that."

Connor smiled. "Captain, don't you start doubting me too. Just have a little faith, and get ready for a very interesting battle."

"All right, lad." Rory said. "I believe you, I really do. What is your plan?"

Connor shook his head. "There are too many spies and Pathfinders with big ears in the Carraig, Captain. I'm sorry, I can't risk telling this to anyone."

"You can risk it here," he said, gesturing at the room. "All the windows are triple-paned, with dead air in between. That's supposed to block Pathfinders.

"I can't risk it, Captain."

Rory shrugged. "You've taken the pedra by the jaws, lad."

With those happy words ringing in his ears, Connor rushed off to make plans with his captains. He was about to flip the entire geall on everyone.

He shouldn't have been surprised when he explained how he'd provoked all the other generals that they pretty much panicked.

"You're as insane as a marble sucker during a meteor shower," Shona gasped.

Declan was nodding so vigorously it looked like his head might roll off his pudgy shoulders. "We're completely grouted, General."

Connor shook his head. "Have I ever let you down?"

"You haven't really had a chance to yet," Aifric pointed out.

"But it seems you're planning to start big," Fearghas muttered.

"At least listen to the plan!"

"It had better be good," Fearghas said. "Defeating a single army would have been tough. Letting them weaken each other before they turned on us would have been a better survival strategy."

"We need to do more than survive," Connor insisted, leaning forward and banging a fist on the table. "The Tir-raon is not won by just surviving. We need to beat them, and beat them so completely, they'll be left wondering what happened, and will be terrified to face us next time."

"That was a very pretty speech," Shona admitted. "But pretty speeches do not win battles."

"You're right," Connor said. "We win battles."

He glanced to each of them in turn, holding their gaze with his, willing them to believe. "Fearghas, you'll get your chance for a crazy assault. Papil, your team will ride the air, and we will unleash the Solas's like they've never been seen before."

When their angry expressions faded to lingering doubt, he added, "Now help me finalize a plan to beat every other army at the same time."

Chapter 32

onnor stood on the eastern rolling plain at the crest of the same wide, low hill Evander had split during his spectacular entrance on nomination day. All of the trappings of that day were long gone, leaving the hill bare. His army stood in ranks just below him, facing east toward the small lake.

"Think it'll work?" Fearghas asked softly from his position to Connor's right.

"I'll work," Connor assured him. "Their overconfidence will play right into our hands." Then he asked Declan, "You ready for this?"

The Tower of Terror, which had already been adopted as his nickname by the rest of the army, tried to speak, but only a high-pitched squeak came out, so he nodded instead. The move set his chubby features jiggling. Connor cringed.

They would be so grouted if they ever planned to fight fair.

"You'll do fine," Connor assured him. "Stick to the plan and ignore everything else."

"This is going to hurt," Shona muttered from the far side of Declan.

Connor ignored her and turned to Catriona. "Your lines must hold, Princess."

"They will, General," she assured him with a crisp salute before moving downslope to take her place in the center of the front lines.

Despite the daunting challenge they faced, knowing Catriona would willingly suffer for him warmed his heart. If she knew his true identity, she'd probably rip out the rest of her hair.

Directly across the lake from Connor's position stood Ivor's army, with Padraigin to Connor's left on the north side of the lake, and Redmund directly across from her on the right. The arrangement made sense since the Dawnus powers balanced out and assured that no two generals with identical affinities could fight each other immediately.

Rory probably expected the contest to begin as two battles on opposite sides of the lake. That would make it harder for any one force to launch a surprise attack on the rear of another or slip past them and capture their standard, which would spell defeat.

With the lake in the center, the Sentries couldn't just take control over the middle ground like they would wish in most battles, creating an unusual balancing act for tertiary affinities. Connor planned to leverage that fact to the fullest.

He could not allow anything about the contest to be typical. He needed chaos and surprise, and he planned to unleash as much of both as possible.

Four columns of earth, spaced evenly around the lake, rose high into the air, lifting Rory and his observers above the battlefield. The trumpet would sound any second, triggering the match.

Declan licked his lips and said in a hoarse whisper, "General, did you ever notice the ground beneath the plain is solid bedrock?"

"That's what I've heard." Somehow the false ceiling over the hidden city included a unique kind of shielding that prevented Sentries from delving into the secrets concealed in what should have been their realm. Making the ground feel like bedrock would turn the Sentries' interest without piquing their curiosity.

Declan and the others might not know the truth, but Connor did, and that concealed secret would play a crucial role in his plan. Some day he needed to learn the trick to that shielding. Not even Evander could shield the plain every hour of every day.

The blast of the starting bugle rang across the plain.

"Stand fast and we will win the day!" Connor bellowed. His army settled into battle-ready stances, with many of the front-line Boulders hefting heavy shields.

It wouldn't do them any good.

As Connor expected, both Padraigin's and Redmund's armies wheeled toward his and began advancing, even though the moves left them defenseless against Ivor. But Ivor was not one to miss out on a party. He had made such a point of trying to convince

Connor to secretly support him, that he couldn't allow the others to defeat Connor without him.

What Connor hadn't expected was the sudden geysers of water on the lake, and the shaking of the ground on that side.

"Are the Sentries attacking already?" he asked, worried they had already broken the timing he'd planned on.

Declan shook his head. "It's something around the lake."

"Raise the wall anyway."

The little Sentry closed his eyes and his face twisted into an expression of utmost concentration. Sweat popped out on his brow, and with a slow moaning rumble, the earth several feet in front of Catriona began hesitantly climbing upward. It stopped at eight feet, then began expanding to the north.

Connor resisted the urge to tell Declan to hurry. The Boulders could almost build a wall by hand faster. Instead, he tapped soapstone and thrust out fingers of thought toward the lake where he was surprised to sense only one other presence.

Ivor.

The Dawnus pulled the waters in the center of the lake aside as his Sentries extended a land bridge right across the lake. Ivor drove the waters up and over that bridge with a rushing roar of crashing waves, and hardened them into a glittering ice arch that reflected rainbow light across the new construct. It was an amazing feat of water mastery. It seemed Ivor was trying to prove he could make his own wonders any time he chose.

Too bad this one was going to help Connor defeat him.

"They're coming too fast," Shona cried.

"Makes it easier to trap them all together," Connor said.

Declan suddenly gasped and dropped to one knee. The wall he had been painstakingly erecting began shaking, and chunks of it sank back into the earth. "Sentries."

"Make a show of resisting," Connor directed. "Don't make it too easy for them."

"Yes, sir."

Almost before he spoke, the entire wall crashed down with a resounding boom, nearly landing on Catriona and the front ranks, who stumbled back from the danger. They didn't make it far because the ground under their legs rippled and softened and they began to sink, their very stone-hard weight driving them down faster.

"My turn," Connor said.

He grabbed for the waters of the lake. Ivor held sway there, but he was distracted with his new ice bridge and Connor grabbed enough water around the fringes of Ivor's control for his purposes. He threw sheets of hail in wide arcs out toward Padraigin's and Redmund's armies. He didn't bother trying to crack Ivor's ice arch through which his army was already pouring. He needed Ivor's army close, but he needed the water elsewhere.

The Spitters in the other two armies were ready for him, and they blocked his unfocused hail attack. He fought them for control, and water rippled back and forth across the open ground between the armies, leaving random sheets of ice clinging to the ground.

Within moments of the opening trumpet, both armies had closed to a hundred yards and their Boulders broke into a charge, clearly planning to beat down Connor's disabled front ranks. Scores of Striders flanked them, ready to take out stragglers. All in all, it was a solid, coordinated strategy that appeared guaranteed to route Connor's army in record time.

Fearghas said, "Excuse me, General, but we're just about out of time."

Connor grinned. "They're making it almost too easy, aren't they?" He looked to Declan. "Keep them back from the inner circle. I'm almost ready."

Declan saluted, and Connor returned to the fight for the waters. He decided it would work best if all three armies advanced in unison, but Ivor's was a little too far behind, despite their excellent land bridge. So he tapped more soapstone and surprised the Spitters with a far more focused attack.

Water boiled out of the lake, spitting huge boulders of ice that rained down over the advancing armies. Disconnected from the main water source, and with Connor actively fighting against them, the Spitters struggled to connect with the airborne ice and deflect it. The unexpected barrage crashed into the charging Boulders and toppled them like pins in a game of Tumble-Tosser.

His army cheered as the charge faltered on both sides, but the victory was short-lived. As Ivor's army began pouring onto the western shores of the lake, Connor withdrew his influence and the Spitters regained control. They showed excellent mastery over the water, and had they trained in working together instead of only focusing on individual tactics, he never could have gained even that temporary advantage.

Connor studied the battlefield, the advancing armies, the patchwork sheets of ice on the ground, and his own bogged-down Boulders.

Everything was set up perfectly.

As the armies all resumed their charges Shona cried, "Con--come on, General. They're about to overrun us."

"Remember the plan!" He turned to Declan, who was panting, one hand driven into the ground to enhance his connection to the earth. "Now, Declan."

As the Sentry bent to his task, Connor turned to the two Solas hovering nearby. "As soon as they rise, light 'em up."

"Yes, sir," they said in unison, eager anticipation on their faces. Solas almost never got to play important roles in battle tactics other than lighting a nighttime engagement, so Connor's plan thrilled them.

Out on the plain, just below the front ranks of Connor's lines and in front of each of the advancing armies, the ground began cascading upward to reveal the trump cards Connor had procured the night before, then concealed with Declan's assistance. The enemy Sentries could have stopped them, but they were expecting a different tactic and the move caught them by surprise.

Into the air rose three of Frazier's ingenious prism lanterns from the original Rhidorroch. Those three had been the only ones salvaged from the devastated area and had been stored for safekeeping in a warehouse where Connor found them the night before.

Frazier was going to kill Connor after the battle, and Connor counted on the fear of the maze lord for the tactic to work. No one dared strike down the rising lanterns, and that gave Connor all the advantage.

Fearghas bellowed, "Eyes!"

As the army clapped hands in unison over their lowered eyes, the Solas blazed into battle. Lights erupted like miniature suns between the lanterns, and those incredible magnifying prisms transformed the lanterns into starbursts so bright Connor had to turn partially away, despite already shielding closed eyes.

For the advancing armies, most of whom were already staring at the prism lanterns with wide-eyed surprise, the unmatched brilliance proved disastrous. Rank after rank of soldiers cried out, clutching at their blinded eyes. Striders at full sprint fell to the ground and tumbled like dice across a rough board.

Ivor's army, many still caught on the land bridge under the brilliant arch of ice, suffered the most. That very arch, Ivor's monument to his dominance of the waters, reflected the brilliant light back down upon his army, magnifying it.

In that one instant, the Solas disabled three entire armies.

"Shutter!" Connor shouted.

As the intense light faded away, Connor grinned.

Time to win a battle.

Chapter 33

aving his arms mightily, Connor shouted, "Go, go, go!"

Declan immediately began launching missiles of hardened earth at all three armies. The Sentries might have felt the initial pulsing of the ground, but once those boulder-like projectiles broke into the air, the Sentries lacked the ability of the Spitters to sense their approach. The blinded armies stood helpless before the barrage, which proved to be far more substantial than Connor expected. Maybe Declan had some talent buried somewhere in that pudgy frame after all.

Even blind, the Sentries reacted to the cries of alarm and screams of pain. They erected walls around their forces, which helped shield against some of the barrage while the blinded armies slowly regained their sight, but also served to hem them in and prevent them from blocking Connor's special strike forces.

"Papil," Connor shouted. "Make it rain!"

In unison, Papil and the other Pathfinders bent their will to walking with air. The three girls, looking vulnerable and small, despite their glowing eyes, flung hands out and unleashed the fury of the air.

Wind howled across the plain, ripping water from the lake and toppling student soldiers. Catriona led a dozen boulders who, thrown by companions, snapped open wings of canvas that caught the air and drove them across the battlefield like sparrows before a storm.

The wind was blowing out of the north, so the flying Boulders rained down over Redmund's still-blinded army and attacked with overwhelming fury. Connor had warned them to not speak so as to not make it easy for the Sentries to pinpoint them, so they smashed opponents to the ground in freakish silence.

Connor grinned. Redmund's army was in tatters. Time to spread the joy.

At his next signal, twelve pairs of Striders launched down the hill, pulling Boulders on wide planks attached to long ropes. Max-tapping basalt, with legs already fracked, the Striders sped across the muddy ground on both sides of Connor without slowing. Fearghas leaped astride one fast-moving sled to take his place leading one strike force, making the tricky maneuver look easy.

Connor reached out with soapstone to the seemingly random patches of ice scattered across the battlefield and shifted them around into long, slender pathways pointing north and south around the stalled armies. The Striders split into groups that straddled those ice paths so the planks slid along the ice, reducing the drag and allowing each trio to move at almost full speed.

To disguise their movements, Connor shouted, "Charge!"

Squads of Boulders broke free of the clinging mud and raced for the disabled armies, while Striders sprinted out to net or disable the enemy runners. Although heavily outnumbered, his enthusiastic troops suddenly posed a very real threat.

The blinded Sentries would be drawn to the thunderous advance of the main assault rather than the less-imminent threat of the special strike teams, but Connor could not leave anything to chance. He gripped Declan by the shoulder. "Disguise the strike teams!"

"I can't," an exhausted Declan cried. "Not even Gregor could shield so many running."

"I didn't say shield them, I said disguise them."

At Declan's uncomprehending look he added in a reasonable tone, "When you're walking with the earth, you sense movement like flickers against your skin, right?"

"How did you know?"

"Doesn't matter. Shielding blocks any touch on the Sentry's senses, but we can't do that."

"That's what I said."

"They can't see, so they're focused on their earth senses." He gestured at their Boulders charging the enemy lines. "We're already distracting them, but you need to overwhelm them with so much contact they can't focus on those Striders."

Declan grinned with understanding and drove his hand into the ground in a move so similar to Gregor's, that Connor felt a surge of pride. Declan really was standing against every other Sentry. The ground began to rumble and little waves radiated out in every direction.

Connor wished he could use quartzite and scan the faces of the other generals. They had to be furious, and frantic as their guaranteed victory slipped away and their dominant forces were reduced to frightened masses of confused soldiers.

With Declan committed, Connor joined the fray.

Through his soapstone senses, he could tell the blinded Spitters were seizing control of the waters of the lake and struggling over it as they all tried to fashion it into protective barriers around their armies or prepare to unleash their powers on the charging Boulders.

They could have the lake.

He had a source they knew nothing about. Focusing on the base poles of the still-blazing prism lanterns, Connor connected to channels of ice he had fastened to those bases that extended down below the range of the shielding over the plain. Once below the false roof, he could sense another underground pond, a hidden one that no one else knew about.

He seized those waters and unleashed them.

Just as the ground in front of his charging army began to ripple and shake with imminent Sentry attacks, geysers of frothing water exploded out of the ground in the center of all three opposing armies. The Spitters, focused entirely on their struggle for control of the lake, were caught completely by surprise as Connor blasted water through the center of their forces, tumbling Boulders and Striders alike in every direction.

He drove those waters through the armies, flooding the command positions. Padraigin, Redmund, and the other Sentries all formed towers of earth to rise above the flood.

That just made them easier targets.

Connor hardened some of the water into fast-spinning spheres and smashed them into those towers, tumbling the masters of the earth into water that temporarily blocked their powers.

The Spitters, along with Ivor, reacted with remarkable speed. They were probably getting their sight back, and they could feel all of the moving waters with their soapstone senses. They fought for control, but ended up struggling against each other as much as against him. This time he did not let them have the waters, but kept slapping down as many enemy forces as he could with it, driving holes through the defensive walls ringing their armies.

Through those delaying tactics, he granted his Boulders enough time to close with the enemy armies and begin a very one sided bash fight.

Tomas would be proud.

As the battle raged in all three armies, Connor called Papil to him. "Speak to me, and use your quartzite voice."

She began to report in that lovely, rich voice, and his smile grew wider and wider.

The three strike forces had already skirted the confused armies and closed on the standards left behind and protected by small forces made up primarily of the three or four Blades in each army. All of the generals had made the same mistake in their single-minded focus on crushing Connor's army. They assumed their coordinated assault would end the battle quickly. He supposed they had made an alliance and agreed to return to their starting positions before re-engaging.

Their plan almost worked, so they were almost justified.

Almost never won anything but games of Much-A-Duck.

Shona led the strike force tasked with Ivor's distant base on the far side of the lake. Before they arrived, Fearghas and his assault team attacked Padraigin's army, while Lorcc led the third strike team against Redmund's.

Fearghas led his strike force with the grace and speed of a fully trained Blade and faced down three opponents simultaneously in a blur of steel until his Striders could net them and his Boulders beat them into submission. Lorcc launched himself at a Blade and punched the man with arms fracked and blurring with unstoppable speed, raining dozens of blows on the unfortunate Blade before he could manage to fall unconscious to the ground.

Shona faced the greatest challenge. Positioned so far from the battlefield, Ivor's Blades were not affected by the blinding prism lanterns and saw her team coming. They fought with desperate strength, but those three Blades could not stop a determined Shona backed by eight Striders and three Boulders. She took half a dozen nasty blows before the short, ugly fight ended.

According to the pre-arranged plan, Shona ripped the flag from Ivor's standard first, and only then did the other two teams take theirs. The three embattled armies never even noticed danger, and were completely surprised when Rory's voice boomed over the battlefield.

"General Lian's army wins."

The look of dismay on the faces of the other generals filled Connor with a sense of relief. He'd actually pulled off the surprise win! He made a point to wave at them as their stunned armies clustered together, trying to understand what happened. Redmund was too busy shouting at Rory that Connor won by cheating, and the entire contest needed to be rescheduled. Padraigin looked stunned and threw out her hands as if to ask what happened.

Ivor shook his head and saluted, a wry grin on his lips.

Connor didn't get a chance to speak with the other generals before his cheering army swept him away to the victory celebration in the castle, where they feasted on mountains of food and regaled each other with their exploits. Declan glowed with pride at the constant barrage of compliments. At one point, an impromptu chant started, with the army shouting loud enough to shake the windows.

"Tower of Terror!"

The two Solas nearly floated off the ground with how big their heads swelled. "No one will ever doubt the battle powers of a Solas again!" they cried so many times Connor was amazed no one threw them out one of those still-quivering windows.

He enjoyed the party, and the newly won loyalty of his army helped him feel at home in the castle like he never had before. It might be a false home, but he would take what he could get.

Shona saluted him at one point, but she wore a smile of victory as if the entire plan had been her idea. She was his patron, no matter that he was general in the field. His victories were her victories, and he'd have to be dumber than a duck roasting in a cook pot not to realize he'd only managed to seal himself tighter than ever to her ultimate plans for him.

The army began chanting Connor's name, so he rose from his seat at the center of the head table and raised his glass high. "To victory!"

As the chanting continued, he decided he didn't really like the name Lian. It lacked the class of Kilian, but then again, any name he chose was just part of the mask he wore, all part of the geall he was running on the school with Shona. So he made a decision and raised his hands for silence.

"In honor of our great victory, you are now ready to receive another of my names."

That elicited a round of laughter and cheers.

"You may all now call me General Anxiety, because every time anyone in any other army meets any of you, that's exactly what they're going to feel!"

The cheering shook the room as his army stomped feet and pounded tables so hard one of them collapsed, spilling food and drink in every direction. That just triggered yet another round of cheering.

Connor seated himself, pleased with the day.

Then Frazier marched into the room, already yelling about the theft of the prism lanterns.

Chapter 34

The only bad thing about flying was the cold.

But flying, well, flying was the most amazing thing Hamish had ever experienced, especially in his new, custom battle suit.

Verena flitted past, like a bat in the still, predawn darkness, with Kilian perched on the supply box attached to the back. Heavy clouds obscured the moon and most of the stars, disguising them from watching eyes. She looked at ease in the air, strapped into her deadly Swift, with its many thrusters able to pivot, roll, and turn with the nimble grace of a hummingbird.

She couldn't lie back and take a nap while flying, though. Hamish hadn't gotten a chance to actually try dozing off, but when hovering, he loved rolling over, hands behind his head, staring up at the clouds. With a flicker of directional thrusters, he could roll again to watch the distant ground below.

He was one with the air, his suit working better than he'd hoped. His main thrusters were built into his boots and along his legs, but he'd adopted the same trick as Verena and added quartzite blocks everywhere he could squeeze them in. The suit granted him as much mobility as her Swift, but did not lock him into a rigid seat like hers.

"Come on," Verena called to him as she ascended. They were too high up, with too much wind noise to communicate normally. Plus, their helmets, goggles, and face masks, required to protect them from the fierce wind and cold of the heights, made speaking to each other impossible. So they'd installed speakstones.

Hamish laughed as he soared high over the Grandurian army, camped in the single pass leading through the Maclachlan Mountains to Obrion. His voice sounded a bit thin, partially because of the mask he wore, but mostly because the air so high up was thin, like dough stretched to the breaking point.

The dark plateau upon which the army camped was already almost ten thousand feet above the distant lowland plains of central Granadure. Hamish was flying at least three thousand feet above them and still climbing.

Verena had explained the strange phenomenon of the air thinning the higher they flew. To Hamish it made perfect sense. It was like his mother's best soups. The chunky bits always fell to the bottom, leaving the top layers thin and watery.

Dawn would soon creep upon the world, and they needed to complete their reconnaissance while they could remain unseen in the shadow of the mighty Mount Osterwald. When holding a hover, the little Swift was almost as quiet as his battle suit, barely louder than a distant wind. Only when Verena threw wide the release rate on the main quartzite blocks to ascend quickly did the Swift roar like a hungry pedra.

Hamish hated that he didn't know the Obrioner name of the towering peak that formed the pass which would soon become a battlefield. He'd been shocked to learn the Grandurians had different names for everything. He'd always known the Maclachlans as the impassable mountain range protecting their northern border. To the Grandurians, those mountains were their southern defense. They called them the Abwehr Mountains.

"That's weird," Hamish had said when he found out. "Saying the Drumwhindle Pass is in the Abwehr Mountains is wrong."

"You think our names are weird," Verena had said with a smirk. "Who came up with the name Drumwhindle anyway? A drunk bagpiper?"

"Hey, don't give bagpipers a hard time," Hamish had retorted. "You try making those pipes sing. It's not as easy as they make it look."

"I've heard the noise they make. If that's singing, you must think howling cats sound beautiful."

"What do you call the pass then?" he'd asked.

"It's the Badurach Pass."

Whatever they chose to call it, the area was breathtaking, with sweeping vistas to the north, east, and west. Hamish rotated slowly, drinking in the view, even though most of the land lay in deep shadow. The army filled the high plateau that narrowed as it rose toward the pass. Mount Osterwald reared at least two thousand feet above the pass in twin towers of sheer, snowcapped stone, split down the middle by Badurach Pass, as if a giant ax stroke had sundered the top of the mountain. The peak was impassable on either side, and there were no other good passes anywhere through the range. It was simply the most daunting natural barrier Hamish could imagine.

Impassable to everyone who couldn't fly.

Verena swooped in close on the Swift. She and Kilian were both bundled against the cold, and Kilian looked relaxed, despite the long drop back to solid ground.

"Are you falling asleep in that suit?" Verena called.

The armored jacket was a bit bulky, with its layers of overlapping granite scales on the outside, an inner leather jacket on the inside, and a unique bladder full of water under that. That bladder was the ultimate key to its effectiveness. The thin layer of water, moving in a constant gentle current by a touch of soapstone, would help absorb and dissipate the force of direct strikes. Plus, after adding a tiny bit of activated marble into the mix, he kept it warm enough to offset the bitter cold of the high altitude.

His limbs were not as heavily armored, but retained the flexibility he needed for aerial maneuvering and combat. They were packed with weapons and inventions and Builded stones, an arsenal he could activate by a flicker of thought and in which he felt confident facing even another pair of rampagers.

"Lead the way," Hamish said, gesturing at the looming peak and the dark split of Badurach pass.

Verena shot off in that direction, with Kilian clinging tight. Hamish gave chase, adjusting the force of the many quartzite thrusters built into his suit. He was still experimenting with the best position for flight. When hovering, he preferred lounging, although upright felt natural too. For fast flying, he found that horizontal was by far the most efficient, with hands down by his side. For an added burst of speed, he could add the force of his hand thrusters.

Hamish glanced back at the army. Sappers on high earthen towers formed a picket at the front and along the flanks of the army. Longseers shared their towers, and Wingrunners zipped back and forth in a constant stream of messages, like the lifeblood of the army.

Hamish wondered why they bothered. When he and Verena had arrived in the camp the evening prior, they had delivered another hundred pair of speakstones. The marvelous devices made communication a breeze. Each officer was given one, and all he had to do was speak into it. All of the paired stones were kept in a central listening tent, adjacent to the main command tent, so all information was gathered for the commanders, who then issued new orders.

On the Grandurian side of the pass, the plateau grew very narrow, rising through a steep-sided canyon the last few hundred yards. A thick wall of builded granite with a single, heavy gate blocked the entrance to the slot of the pass. To the north of the gate, that deep canyon was blocked by no less than four high walls, topped with crenellations and manned by many soldiers.

The path zigged and zagged between those walls, with the only openings set at the very ends, right up against the canyon walls, forcing any Obrioner intruders to pass down the length of each wall to reach the next opening. To make it even more difficult, angled barriers of spiked steel blocked the way at regular intervals.

The sight of the fortifications and armed men drove home the reality of the looming war. The armies were prepared. They had all known for a long time that the fight would come there, and they were ready. When the fighting started, a lot of people were going to die.

Hamish shivered. He'd seen enough battle to know it was better avoided. There had to be a way to prevent all that useless death. Was the work he was doing with the Builders going to save lives, destroy them, or both? Were his inventions going to save more than they claimed?

Plagued by those dark thoughts, Hamish swooped into the pass behind Verena, a thousand feet above the wall. The Badurach Pass ran in a straight line for nearly a quarter of a mile, little more than a deep cut through solid rock. Sentries would be unable to bring to bear the might of their earth powers there. The pass was as dark as pitch, and Hamish slowed, drawing close to the others.

Verena activated a single, faint beam of light from a piece of limestone. Set in a focus prism, it cast a beam of light that Verena played across the walls that were barely a hundred feet apart. The beam would be difficult to detect even by Pathfinders far below, but Hamish still wished they could have avoided it.

He was sneaking across the border, back into his homeland, but as an enemy to the nation. The fact that he would be executed if he landed on the Obrioner side reinforced his conflicted worry. He loved his nation and did not want to see her citizens get killed, but Granadure was his home and he cared for them too.

The narrow confines of the pass magnified the sounds of their thrusters, turning the steady wind of their passage into an echoing roar. Again, Hamish doubted anyone could hear them, and he saw nothing threatening. It was blacker than the inside of a cast-iron kettle.

They slowed as they reached the southern boundary of the pass, and Verena cut off the light. The gray, pre-dawn sky looked bright against the dark walls of the pass and made it easier to navigate.

Another wall with a heavy gate, manned by a large company of soldiers, blocked the Obrioner side of the pass. Hamish and Verena settled into a nearly-silent hover and floated high above the unsuspecting men, slowly emerging from the pass to study the defenses.

Instead of a deep canyon leading from the pass, the Obrioner side was more like a narrow causeway. The mountain just stopped, and cliffs fell away on both sides of the passage, forming another daunting barrier. Three walls with offset gates blocked the causeway. If the Grandurians attempted the first frontal assault, they'd lose a lot of men. Would such mutually-guaranteed heavy losses hold the armies back?

He doubted it.

The Grandurians held a unique advantage. They could launch an invasion into Obrion almost anywhere along the border by flying their army over the mountains in the windriders. Did General Carbrey understand that risk? Was he ready for it?

The Obrioner camp was massed close to the top of the plateau on the far side of the causeway, as if barely restraining themselves from shoving through the gap to get at the enemy. Even from such a height, Hamish felt the tension of that camp, as if soldiers there were prepped and ready to throw themselves into battle. He shivered to think how soon such an assault might commence.

Hamish activated another new invention as the three of them hovered in the throat of the pass. Opening the release rate on a set of thin, quartzite blocks attached to the outer edge of his goggles, a clear image of the breathtaking view rippled across his goggles.

Despite the popularity of the speakstones, Builders had found only limited success trying to unlock quartzite abilities to enhance other senses. Instead, they had focused on the air power of quartzite, exploring its potential as the catalyst of flight.

For Petralists, applying quartzite internally to enhance the senses was far easier, and the benefits of that use for military purposes was widely accepted. Few of them bothered trying to tap quartzite externally because for them, walking with the air was so unstable and unpredictable.

Hamish had made a major breakthrough only a week prior as they studied the potential for quartzite to enhance vision. While holding a piece of quartzite in either hand, he'd taken a break from peering through each of them in turn to lean forward and take a bite out of a pastry sitting on his work bench. When he'd drawn the two activated stones apart and thrust his head between his hands, his vision had blurred, then sharpened dramatically.

It had been a wonderful experience. He'd never seen any pastry look so beautiful. He could count the individual grains of sugar coating the golden-brown surface, see the fluffy dough stretched to the breaking point.

Once they understood the concept, they'd quickly developed the custom goggles they both wore while flying. Verena had dubbed them Long View Goggles. Activating them above the pass, it took Hamish only a few seconds to fine-tune the release rate on the various stones until the image projecting onto the surface of his goggles exactly matched what he had seen with his natural vision.

Then by carefully increasing the release rate, he zoomed in. It was like swooping down upon the camp, but without moving. His focus narrowed, but grew far more detailed and he was able to scan the camp with astonishing detail from thousands of feet overhead.

Sentries on their earthen towers were easy to spot. He picked out Boulders, Striders, and even a number of Spitters near huge, wooden reservoirs. Thousands of soldiers and cavalry made up the bulk of the camp. He spotted the central command tower, but did not see General Carbrey. He almost missed the gigantic piles of earth rearing along the flanks of the army. They were so big, he at first mistook them for natural hills.

After silently studying the camp for another ten minutes, the three eased back into the pass and slipped down its length to the Grandurian side. Dawn was fast approaching, and the sky was already far lighter. The sun would appear on the eastern horizon eventually, but the army was already easily visible without the long view goggles.

"Did you see those huge mounds of earth?" Verena asked as Hamish drew close and flew beside them, lying on his side as if on a couch.

"Must have taken every Sentry in that camp a week to move that much earth," Hamish said.

"With that much material on hand," Kilian added. "They might be planning to lead with earth after all."

"I didn't see any sign of rampagers," Verena said.

Kilian shook his head. "I would have been surprised. If we're right, they're Dougal's secret weapon. It did look like the army was massing for some kind of movement, though."

"Do you think they'll take the bait and try a raid on the weakening powder?" Hamish asked.

Kilian nodded. "It appears so."

"When?" Verena asked as they swooped across the plateau and waved at the Longseers stationed in a pair of hovering windriders positioned high above the pass.

"They will come tonight."

Chapter 35

The screaming was louder than Verena expected.

The cold air carried the sounds up to her with a crisp clarity that made her shiver in her seat on the Swift. She couldn't explain why the thin air high above the plateau facing the Badurach Pass could both make breathing difficult and sharpen the sounds that reached her. Perhaps those sounds had to be far more determined to claw so high above the fighting.

The sun had just set, leaving a bright orange stain across the distant western peaks that colored the fires raging in the pass a more sinister red. As Kilian had predicted, the Obrioner army had attacked into the pass through that waning light.

"If the assault is only a diversion, as I expect it will be," Kilian had explained during their briefing with General Wolfram, Anton, and the other army leaders, "they will attack late in the day, but they will keep their inventory of earth so painstakingly prepared in reserve for the real assault."

Facing south into the darkening gap of the pass, Verena saw no sign of Sentry activity as she hovered high above the Grandurian fortifications. A little below her position, four windriders hovered, bearing Longseers equipped with speakstones to relay their reports back to Wolfram. Dierk also rode in the lead wagon, as did one of his mighty diorite bombs. Only four of the huge bombs had been produced. Hamish had dubbed them The Last Word.

Dierk could unleash the weapon if the incursion turned out to be a full assault and managed to break through the first and second layer of defenses. Verena hoped he didn't need to. They had not actually tested that bomb. Projections of its explosive power suggested it could lay waste to the pass and wreak terrible destruction upon both armies.

Verena was supposed to be stationed to the north, closer to compound where the weakening powder was supposed to be stored, but when the pass began to burn, she couldn't help but draw closer.

Now she utilized her long vision goggles and scanned the pass. It was all deep shadow and stark, crimson fire as the Obrioner army pushed forward. They were using Spitters to form shields of ice in front of their army and to cover any traps on the ground. Their soldiers crept forward inch by inch, pushing tall, steel barricades on wheels.

Firetongues sent sheeting flames whipping down the pass where the Grandurian Flameweavers wrested control and sent them back. It made for an impressive display of raw elements, but seemed to accomplish little. At the pace of the advance, it would take the army another hour or two to approach close to the Grandurian gate.

"Verena, we've got movement," Hamish's voice startled her, speaking into her ear through the tiny speakstone fitted inside her helmet. "Where are you?"

"Just completing reconnaissance of the main battle," she replied, banking the Swift in a tight turn and accelerating north down the plateau, over the massed army, back toward her station.

"I can't believe you got distracted," Hamish replied. "And you said eating six helpings of that stew was going to make me sluggish."

"It will," she snapped. "It's amazing you even squeezed into that suit of yours."

"All suits shrink a little in the evenings," he retorted. "Now get back here. Something's scaling the western cliff. Has to be rampagers."

Verena drove the Swift harder, the wind whistling in her ears, despite the protection of her helmet. Flying so fast was exhilarating, but she felt too nervous at the thought of facing the rampagers again to really enjoy it.

This time would be different. This time they held the advantage.

Why did she still worry, then?

Moving fast, Verena swooped over the plateau toward the northwest corner where a two-story wooden compound stood apart from everything else, built right against the edge of a thousand-foot cliff. The large structure was surrounded by a hardened earthen wall with towers at every corner. It was dark, with only a handful of guards visible even to her long vision goggles.

That was the spot Kilian had leaked to Dougal's spies as the location where they stored the precious secret powder that weakened Boulders. That was where they would spring their trap.

She slowed beside Hamish, who was hovering several hundred feet above the compound, out over the long drop beyond the cliff. He had painted the hardened granite of his armored torso a mottled gray color that blended extremely well with the gathering shadows.

When Verena slowed to hover nearby, Hamish pointed down toward the cliff. She took a moment to study his suit. She had helped design some of the elements, but had not entirely believed the concept was going to work. Hamish possessed a brilliant, if somewhat distracted, mind. Some of his ideas were nothing short of revolutionary.

He credited the sweetbreads.

Whatever inspired him to create that flying suit, she hoped it continued to send him ideas. The suit was a marvel. He was almost as nimble in the air as she on her Swift, and he possessed better armor. They hadn't tested their various weapons yet, but that streamlined suit packed an incredible punch. Tonight they'd get to see if they could punch hard enough to stop the rampagers.

Verena scanned the cliff, increasing the release rate on her long vision goggles. The darkness was already deep, but the western-facing cliff enjoyed the last of the fading light, so she could pierce the shadows a little.

There! Movement drew her attention and she sucked in a soft gasp.

"They're so fast," she whispered.

"Definitely rampagers," Hamish agreed, his voice calmer than she would have expected.

The monsters were racing up the sheer face of the cliff in fantastic leaps and bounds, moving faster than a running human could on flat ground. They could rival Wingrunners for speed on the flats, but watching the insanely muscled creatures throwing themselves twenty feet straight up was a stark reminder not to underestimate them.

Verena activated the other speakstone she had attached to the front of her helmet, just under the edge of her facemask. "Kilian, we have visual. Rampagers are closing on the compound."

"How many?" He responded immediately.

"I see seven," Hamish said. "Wait. Eight."

Verena's pulse quickened with fear. Eight rampagers. Two of them had destroyed an entire squad and very nearly killed Hamish and Kilian. She passed on the report.

Kilian did not sound surprised. "Very well. Allow them to enter the compound. All teams, prepare for operation Reclaiming the Lost."

Hamish glanced at Verena. "That's such a good name."

"It's a gift." He had been frustrated initially when Kilian had chosen Verena's operational name over his suggestion. He didn't seem to understand that Operation Chopped Monster didn't exactly fit the mission objective of capturing at least one of the creatures. She was happy he'd gotten over it.

In silence, they watched the squad of rampagers close on the compound. They had to be some kind of military unit. Monsters raging out of control would never work in tandem like that. With the sheer brute force they could bring to bear, the thought of the beasts also possessing some kind of rational control was terrifying.

When they reached the edge of the cliff, they leaped right over the high barrier wall. Two of the monsters split off and attacked the sentries in their watchtowers. Those men managed to leap off the wall and avoid getting ripped apart. One of the rampagers ignored the fleeing sentries and jumped into the compound after his companions.

The other leaped after a running soldier, clearly intending to remove any witnesses. The man max-tapped granite and faced the monster.

Kilian had shared reports with Verena about the Rumblers whose arms had gotten ripped off by the first pair of rampagers. In any other situation, that brave soldier would have died an ugly death.

Not tonight.

As the rampager leaped toward him, the man punched out a gauntleted fist. Verena smiled to see the anthracite blocks worked into his glove work as planned. The beast's raking claws somehow slid across the man's arms and torso without gaining purchase, and it stumbled past, its terrible maw opening. It didn't roar in frustrated anger as Verena expected. It really could control itself.

Before the beast could attack again, the ground liquefied under its feet, and fingers of earth shot up to snag it and drag it down. This time it did howl, a sound that sent a new shiver of fear rippling down Verena's spine.

The other rampagers, who had already burst through the main door and were ripping their way through the compound responded with amazing speed, leaping out windows and doors and bounding toward the outer wall.

They could actually communicate.

"They know!" Verena cried. "That was a warning shout."

"Too late," Kilian said. "All teams, go!"

His voice echoed through Verena's helmet with the intensity it carried only when he was embracing marble.

Kilian appeared from inside the wall surrounding the compound where he had crouched concealed during the rampagers' initial assault. With hands burning with both fire and water, he leaped down into the court at the front of the compound and faced the seven rampagers alone.

They swarmed toward him and Verena couldn't bear to hold back like she had been ordered. She dove with the desperate speed of a pedra, driving the Swift with every thruster thrown wide open. Hamish had reacted at the same time, and together they tore through the sky to help, knowing they would arrive too late.

Kilian laughed in the face of the rampagers and fire exploded from him and whipped the monsters. They barely flinched as they leaped through the flames.

He jumped back, and a wall of ice materialized in the air where he'd been. The monsters crashed into it, cracking it, but not breaking through. They bounced back, tumbling to the ground.

Anton was waiting.

The huge Sapper, along with two other earth walkers, stood atop the compound's outer wall, hands embedded in the surface. When the rampagers struck the ground, they all sank into liquefied earth that hardened around their thrashing limbs.

Howling with rage, the monsters ripped and tore at the restraining earth that formed into grasping fingers to drag them down again. Water Moccasins drew upon concealed tubs of water, and snaking tendrils of liquid encircled the monsters, wrapping them in powerful cords.

Three of the monsters ripped free of the restraints and disappeared into the battered compound while Kilian and two other Flameweavers snapped whips of fire into the remaining rampagers' faces, blinding them and keeping them distracted. Within seconds, four of the mighty rampagers were bound by multiple elements, despite their powerful struggles. Rumblers bearing heavy lengths of chain and wearing anthracite-enhanced gloves moved in to bind the creatures tight enough to secure a hurricane.

Verena slowed her descent, remembering Kilian's command to stay back and observe. Then she spotted one of the monsters who had fled into the compound. It leaped back into the fray with a howling vengeance, vaulting twenty feet and landing in the middle of a squad of Rumblers who had been closing on the trapped rampagers. The beast scattered them and ripped down the back of one of the men. Despite his max-tapped granite strength, the claws ripped chunks of flesh free and the man fell screaming to the ground.

The other two rampagers who had fled into the building burst up through the ceiling in an explosion of debris. They leaped together onto the outer wall, then charged one of the Sappers. They burst through grasping fingers of earth, their red-glowing eyes focused on their prey.

The other tertiary Petralists were all committed in restraining the already-captive monsters, who redoubled their efforts to break free. They couldn't deal with the new threat fast enough.

"Our turn," Hamish said, echoing Verena's thoughts.

As one, they resumed their dive. Hamish headed for the monster attacking the Rumblers, and Verena shot forward to intercept the two closing on the Sapper. As she dove, the rushing air seemed to cleanse her of all fear, replacing it with a fixed resolve.

She would stop them, or die trying.

Chapter 36

The rampagers were closing too fast on the Sapper, who raised a solid wall of earth to block the way.

They smashed through it, shedding the grasping tendrils of earth he tried to restrain them with.

Verena tore out of the night sky, triggering the twin speedslings along both sides of her seat. She'd enhanced them so she could start their spinning by activating a bit of anthracite on either end. That slippery property engaged immediately and enhanced the already-blurring capacity of the drums, bringing them to full speed in a matter of seconds.

Now she opened the restraining ports and pointed the flexible nozzles toward the leaping rampagers and screamed a battle cry.

They turned toward the sound just as hundreds of hornets ripped through the air, buzzing like deadly insects. She adjusted her aim, using tiny quartzite thrusters built into the nozzles, and caught both of the rampagers in the face.

She had also activated her long view goggles, and the first monster loomed large in her vision, a terrifying sight that left her cold with terror. It felt like she was standing right in front of them, rather than diving at them from high in the air.

The red-furred monster stood as tall as a man, with bulging muscles that strained the limits of its thick hide. Its unnaturally long arms were capped with deadly, clawed paws, identical to those on its feet. Its bald, leathery head was elongated, with a maw like a giant wolf's. But Verena's gaze focused on those inhuman, glittering, crimson eyes that burned with bloodlust.

That's where she aimed.

Hornets tore into that hideous face, and even the monsters' extremely tough hides were not immune to the tiny projectiles. They spun away from the barrage, their bodies shuddering under scores of impacts that drove them right off the perimeter wall.

Verena shot over them, pivoting the Swift in the air to fire on the monsters again.

She had forgotten how high they could jump.

In her intense dive, she'd descended to just over fifty feet. It had seemed a safe distance until the monsters leaped out of the dark shadows outside the wall, their many little wounds not seeming to affect their strength, but only compounding their rage. Both monsters rose into the air, terrible claws extended toward her.

Verena unleashed the Puking Doom.

A solid wall of fire erupted from under the Swift, engulfing the rampagers. The force of the flames drove Verena into the air, the pressure like a vast weight on her shoulders.

Laughing from the thrill of the abrupt rise as much as from the thrill of surviving the rampager attack, she snapped closed the marble. The abrupt return to cool darkness was a welcome relief, but it took her a few seconds to regain some night vision. She was high enough that the rampagers couldn't reach her, but the soldiers on the ground were not so lucky.

Blinking rapidly, she glanced around and caught sight of Hamish.

And blinked again.

Hamish had tackled the lone remaining rampager, which had been attacking the Rumblers. The beast was bloodied from half a hundred wounds and lay on its back, slashing at Hamish, who was straddling it, driving his fists into its face.

Verena activated her long vision goggles. She hadn't even known about those enhancements. Hamish had embedded granite into the sleeves of his suit, and they were now stiff, as if all of those pieces had fused together, forming a battering ram that extended just past his knuckles. With each punch, Hamish was opening wide some quartzite thrusters in his elbows, driving those hardened battering ram arms into the face of the rampager with at least as much force as a max-tapped Rumbler.

He was brilliant, but insane.

Those hammer blows were hurting it, but not disabling it. Its slashing claws were tearing out granite leaves and leaving long gashes in his suit. None of the strikes appeared to have cut through yet, but it wouldn't take long.

The rampager kicked out with all four limbs, sending Hamish tumbling into the air. With a burst of quartzite, he caught himself and hovered above the monster as it crouched to spring upon him.

Kilian struck first.

The ancient Dawnus leaped upon the monster's back and drove fists into its ears. One hand was burning with white hot fire, the other rippling with living waters.

The rampager stiffened, rising to its full height, head thrown back in a silent scream as Kilian drove his elements into its head. The monster seemed to swell and it flung its deadly arms out wide.

Then its head exploded in a gush of mingled fire and steam.

Kilian jumped off as it toppled. The dead beast began shifting back into the form of the man it had once been.

Kilian brushed off his hands and turned to look up at Verena, his eyes filled with white-hot flames. "Pick me up. We need to track those two you let get away."

Verena hesitated. In the grip of his powers, Kilian was even scarier than the rampagers. She scanned the ground outside of the compound. Sure enough, there was no sign of the two rampagers she had knocked over the wall.

Chiding herself for losing focus, Verena swooped down toward Kilian. A gout of fire under his feet threw him into the air and he caught the handles at the back of her seat twenty feet above the ground.

"Nice addition," he said when he noticed the stirrups she had fashioned for him back there. His eyes no longer burned, and he seemed remarkably calm after that death battle.

"With how often you hitch a ride, I figured that would make it easier," she replied as she banked away and flew out over the cliff. Behind them, the Rumblers had resumed their work, chaining the rampagers, whose belligerence finally seemed broken after Kilian had killed the last free one.

"I should probably design a two-seater," Verena added as she scanned the cliff for the escaped rampagers."

"Not a bad idea," Kilian said. "Carrying a partner on your missions will probably be a common requirement."

"We'll work on it," she promised.

Hamish joined them, and his panting rang through the activated speakstone. Then he laughed. "That was amazing."

"You took unnecessary risks," Kilian said, but his tone was not quite reproving.

"You jumped right on that one's back," Hamish protested. "And faced all seven of them alone."

"I know what I'm doing."

"There." Verena pointed toward the cliff. It had taken a moment to spot the rampagers because they were not descending the cliff, but racing across its face in mighty leaps. Despite their wounds, they moved with undiminished power and grace.

"They're so strong," she breathed.

"I can't believe you let them get away," Hamish said.

"All part of the plan," Kilian said.

Verena bit her lip, saying nothing. She had forgotten they needed live monsters, and in that moment of battle, she would have killed the rampagers if she could have. She wasn't sure how she felt about the fact that, despite all of her preparation, she hadn't managed to kill a single one.

"What part?" Hamish asked as they took up a hovering position high above the monsters to remain invisible in the darkness.

"Our trap was twofold," Kilian explained. Even though he was not wearing the insulated flight clothing Verena had on, nor a helmet to protect his face from the bitter cold, he looked comfortable. His eyes were flickering with tiny flames again, so he was probably regulating his temperature from within. "The primary objective was to lure Dougal into unleashing the rampagers to prove he does in fact control them somehow."

"Done," Hamish said.

"And that diversionary assault is already retreating," Verena pointed out, gesturing toward the distant pass. She didn't have a clear view down its darkened length, but they had drawn close enough to see that the fighting appeared to have stopped.

"I'm sure Dougal had ordered Carbrey to resume the assault as soon as he commanded the secret of the weakening powder," Kilian said with a satisfied smile. "Perhaps this setback will delay open war for a time."

"Was that the second part of the plan?" Hamish asked.

"No, that's a bonus," Kilian said. "The second aspect of tonight's trap was to track surviving rampagers to their lair."

Verena shivered. "Can there really be more?"

"That's what we need to find out."

In silence, they trailed the rampagers, who eventually descended the cliff to a lower peak, then worked around that one, leaping wide chasms and scaling obstructing cliffs without slowing. Their endurance was remarkable.

"How long can they keep it up?" Verena asked as the monsters leaped a thirty-foot gap and raced up another steep slope.

"Hopefully until they return home," Kilian said.

Over the next hour, the monsters crossed the border, traveling over mountains that would have been impassable to anyone not flying. Once they entered the Obrion side of the mountain range, Verena expected them to circle back toward the main army, but instead they headed farther west into empty wilderness.

The clouds thinned, allowing the sliver of moon to rise. The stars were brilliant, with few clouds. Flying through that remote wilderness was unexpectedly beautiful, but so cold that even in her insulated clothing, Verena soon began to shiver.

Kilian noticed and placed a hand on her shoulder. Gentle warmth radiated out from his fingers and the cold seemed to flee his touch.

The rampagers moved deeper into the uncharted mountains, remaining above the tree line most of the time, and eventually climbed to a barren plateau. There they descended a steep canyon that at first looked like a dead end.

"I think they're getting close," Hamish said as they descended slowly, barely able to make out anything in the deep canyon, despite their long vision goggles.

"They just entered a cave," Verena said, feeling her tension returning at the thought of entering that dark hole and confronting the monsters.

They drifted closer, and only when they were less than a hundred feet above the walls of the canyon did they see the truth.

"It's a slot canyon," Hamish breathed.

"Follow it," Kilian ordered softly. "Stay as high as you can without losing them."

As they floated over the tiny crack in the ground, Verena caught glimpses of movement. The rampagers were indeed following the slot canyon deeper into the mountain. A gigantic knob of stone protruded from the shoulder of the unnamed peak that loomed above the canyon. The slot canyon passed close by that misshapen shoulder of rock, nearly lost in its leaning shadow.

On the far side of the rocky shoulder, they spotted the rampagers' destination. Hamish whistled low and Verena drew in a long breath as she stared at the secret valley. It was little more than a sunken bowl of grass and stunted trees, barely three hundred yards across, accessible only through that slot canyon.

"They're home," Kilian whispered.

In the center of the lush little valley was a permanent military camp, complete with wooden bunkhouses and several larger structures that could have housed a hundred men.

The two rampagers limped into camp, looking exhausted. Lanterns illuminated the parade ground in front of the largest structure, a two-story, wooden building.

The rampagers stopped as five men exited the building. Without warning, they transformed back into men.

"Whoa! They changed back," Hamish whispered, his voice soft in her ear, slightly distorted by the speakstone."

"They actually control the transformation," Verena breathed. She had always assumed that if someone turned unclaimed, they lost their humanity permanently, embarking on a mindless killing spree until they were in turn killed.

The fight at the compound proved they weren't mindless, but seeing them transform back to men was a shocking revelation. They looked haggard, but showed no sign of the wounds they had suffered in their monster form. Did that mean they possessed healing properties, or was the physical transformation responsible for restoring their forms?

"Either that or exhaustion allows them to return to their humanity," Kilian said

"We need to know how it's done," Verena said. There was far more going on than what the stories of the raging unclaimed suggested.

Another man exited the main building, and he walked with the bearing of a military leader. His clothing was almost a uniform, but included no insignia or rank. He was taller than the others, with broad shoulders and flaming red hair.

"We need a speakstone down there," Hamish muttered. They remained distant, high above the camp, hovering in the shadow of the mountain's huge, bony shoulder.

"Hush," Kilian said, leaning forward to peer down toward camp. "And tell me everything you see."

"Looks like they're reporting," Verena spoke softly, relating things as they unfolded.

"That's not going to go well," Hamish said.

"It's not," she agreed. "The leader looks pretty upset."

"Broke their fingers trying to steal cookies." Hamish sounded satisfied, and Verena wondered if he'd ever experienced that particular failure.

"The leader's shouting at them," Verena said.

"I can see that much," Kilian said. "Not very professional."

"How would you feel if your secret squad of rampagers got nabbed?" Hamish asked.

After another minute, the leader wheeled and led the recently returned rampagers inside the main building.

Hamish leaned forward and ghosted down toward camp.

"What are you doing?" Verena hissed.

"This is our chance to get some information," Hamish said. "Now be quiet or they'll notice me coming."

She expected Kilian to object, but he did not, so she watched as Hamish floated over the camp. A moment later he returned.

"What was that all about?" she asked.

He held up a piece of quartzite. "You didn't see me drop the speakstone at the edge of the parade ground?"

"No."

"Good. I doubt anyone else did either."

The three of them flew to the top of the rocky shoulder and settled onto the mountain to gather around the speakstone. After a few minutes, they heard voices, just distant snatches of soft conversation.

"They're too far away," Verena said.

"Hush," Hamish retorted. He had removed his mask and was munching on a biscuit. Where he had gotten that, she didn't want to know.

". . .Dougal. . ." Came a voice from the speakstone.

They leaned closer, and someone moved within range of the distant stone.

"I knew it was a bad idea just to send one squad," a man's voice said. He must have been standing almost right over the stone. "If we're going to strike, let's strike with the entire company. We could have destroyed that army, not taken a beating. Why unleash the Claws of Legend but still keep us chained?"

"Ooh, that's a good name," Hamish whispered.

"Why don't you try telling Dougal you think he's getting it wrong," another voice responded with a harsh, barking laugh.

"After tonight, I won't need to," the first voice said. "I wager the order to destroy will come soon enough."

"It'll be about time."

The voices faded away as the men moved farther from the stone.

Kilian sat back and glanced from Verena to Hamish, his eyes glowing with his suppressed powers, shifting from icy blue to flickering crimson. "This confirms my suspicion. Somehow Dougal is controlling those so-called unclaimed."

"How is it possible?" Hamish asked. "Unclaimed are supposed to happen specifically because they lose patronage and a high lord's control."

"The truth lies in that compound," Kilian said.

"The biggest threat to Granadure does too," Verena added. The thought of more of those rampagers descending upon the unprotected villages of her homeland, or even tearing into the army left her horrified."

"Those men were right," Kilian said. "Dougal cannot accept this defeat. We know he controls the rampagers. He's lost the element of surprise with them. He must unleash his rampagers as soon as possible before we're prepared to meet them."

"Shouldn't we call them claws of legend?" Hamish asked.

"I don't plan to let them make any legends."

"We were ready for them tonight," Verena protested. "There could be dozens in that camp. If he sends them all, hundreds of soldiers could die."

"We need to warn Wolfram," Hamish said.

Suddenly all the mechanicals they had developed seemed pitiful. Verena wished they'd brought one of the big diorite bombs Dierk had designed.

Kilian shook his head. "No. You're right, Verena. The army cannot stop these monsters and dare not face them without risking terrible loss of life."

"You're not suggesting we retreat?" Verena asked.

Kilian grinned, and the expression made Verena suddenly very nervous. "We're going to destroy them all."

"You want me to go get the Last Word?" Hamish asked, echoing Verena's thoughts. The valley was remote enough that they wouldn't risk killing innocents.

"No," Kilian said after a moment's thought. "We only have four of the big ones, and they are key to holding the pass. Besides, if we lay waste to the entire valley, the very evidence we hope to procure will be lost to us."

"We're strong," Verena said. "But the three of us can't take on an entire camp full of rampagers."

Kilian looked from her to Hamish, and the points of fire dancing in his eyes grew to fill his orbs, bathing his face in soft, flickering light that made him look ferocious.

"There is a way. The path I plan to tread holds its own dangers, but it offers our best chance."

"How?" Hamish asked. He looked a little nervous, just like Verena felt.

"Have you ever heard the term Machtig Riesen?"

"No," they answered in unison.

"In Obrion, the term is Elfonnel."

Verena shook her head. Hamish only shrugged. "Stuart had a growth under his arm once. Old Mhairi had to lance it and smear on some nasty ointment. I don't remember exactly what she called it, but it sounded something like that."

Kilian chuckled. "What I am about to explain to you is definitely not an ointment." He settled to the stone and gestured for them to sit nearby. "This is a secret of the deep magic, so I trust you will hold this confidential.

"Petralists walk with the elements and borrow of their strength. However, when one has reached certain thresholds of power, it is possible to do more. A Petralist can allow the elements to rise through them and become the living embodiment of their core power."

"That sounds dangerous," Verena said.

"It is," Kilian nodded. "Extremely. Most who attempt such a union with the elements are consumed in the process, and few can escape with their humanity intact."

"But you can?" Hamish guessed.

Kilian nodded again.

"That giant you summoned at Alasdair," Verena guessed. "I heard a lot about it. I never understood how you managed such a vast summoning."

"That was a special case. Summoning only gives life to a fraction of an element, wrapping it in granite flesh. It would be impossible to summon an elfonnel. They are too vast and far too powerful. To raise one, the Petralist must be willing to commit their entire being, to becoming at least temporarily consumed."

"Why don't you do it more often?" Hamish asked. "I mean, why worry about the Obrion army when you can unleash a giant elemental monster to stop them?"

"There are a multitude of reasons, the chief of them being the danger inherent for myself and everyone else in the vicinity. The elements do not rise to take living form lightly, and they lack the humanity we take for granted. An elfonnel rising in the midst of a battlefield might just as easily destroy both armies."

"Oh. Maybe not then."

"It sounds like the risk might outweigh the benefit," Verena cautioned, her fears mounting with every word Kilian spoke. He looked confident, but more concerned than she had ever seen him.

"It is the only way to eradicate the threat this camp presents," Kilian said. "This location is remote enough that the risk of collateral damage is minor." He fixed them with another grave look. "You must promise to stay back. If I lose control, even for a moment, you must flee."

"We can't leave you behind," Verena exclaimed.

"You must. I will return in time. Probably. But you cannot risk yourselves in the meantime."

"How will we know if you lose control?" Hamish asked.

"I'll try to kill you."

"I don't like it," Hamish said, echoing Verena's fears.

"Good." Kilian gave them his normal roguish smile. "That means you're not completely dense."

"We strike at dawn," he added. "Which will give us enough time to prepare the battlefield."

"What do you want us to do?" Verena asked.

"You're returning to the army." Kilian raised his hands to forestall her protest.

"You're going to get the bombs anyway?" Hamish asked.

"No. Verena will fetch Anton."

So in a way, he was sending her to bring an army of reinforcements after all.

Chapter 37

onnor returned to his Dawnus suite late and dropped into one of the plush couches in the sitting room. While he enjoyed the brief moment of silence, he extracted a small piece of limestone from his belt pouch.

He considered the little, greenish stone, rubbing its smooth sides with his fingers. He still needed to establish affinity with the sedimentary stone. The one time he had tried hadn't gone well. The fact that Ilse had been threatening to kill him at the time might have had something to do with it.

Unlike the igneous stones that he absorbed or the tertiary stones that he connected with in their various ways, sedimentary stones were supposed to be pretty straight-forward. Connor focused on the stone, trying to feel its power like he did with sandstone.

It took a moment, willing something to happen, before he felt a faint flicker, like a flash of lightning beyond the next set of hills, more a hint of light than anything real. He grinned. Any second, and he'd make it work.

Cameron barged into the room, breaking his concentration. "Ivor sent a message. I think you spooked him today. Have a care with him."

"Wow, that was perfect flowered prose," Connor said as he tucked the limestone away.

Cameron frowned. "Course it couldn't be. I wasn't even thinking about it." His brutish face took on the pained expression he'd worn so often over the past week practicing with flowered prose. The concentration usually only seemed to make things worse.

"Well, you did it. Best one ever."

Cameron's expression lifted. "I guess all the practicing is paying off."

"I hope so."

"Ivor requested a meeting," Cameron added. "Might be a good time to strike while his defenses are down."

"I thought you said I should have a care with him."

"You should. Don't mean you don't take advantage of him panicking about you winning when they all thought you were as doomed as a fish three days boiling in a stew."

"I'll go talk with him." Connor said as he pulled his mask on and rose.

They returned to the central atrium where Tomas was lounging at guard. "Ivor's in a right pickle since you took his flag first. Going from favorite to last place hurts, so watch yourself, lad."

"I know what I'm doing," Connor promised.

"Don't break his suite," Cameron called as he headed across the atrium.

"I can do more than just break things," Connor insisted.

"But you don't do nothing half so well," came the quick reply.

Ivor met Connor in his sitting room after sending Sheigra out to shield their conversation. The big champion looked flustered. His sleeves were rolled up, his shirt wrinkled, and his hands were covered in what looked like green paint.

"What have you been doing?" Connor asked as Ivor summoned water out of a nearby bucket to wash his hands, then sent it all cascading back with a flick of a wrist.

"I paint when I get upset," Ivor said, dropping into an overstuffed chair, then motioning Connor to do the same.

"Really? What do you paint?"

Ivor grimaced. "Nothing well enough to show anyone."

"Thanks for leading everyone into my trap," Connor said, selecting an apple from a nearby fruit tray. "Wouldn't have worked if you hadn't all been so intent on punishing me for being arrogant."

Ivor shook his head and chuckled. "After warning you to be careful on the battlefield, you sucked me in like a first year."

"You all saw what you wanted to see," Connor said around a mouthful of sweet fruit.

"And you flipped the geall on us. Best move I've seen in years."

"You all deserve nothing but the best." He felt relieved that Ivor was taking the beating so well. He wasn't sure he would have handled losing with so much grace.

"But why order Shona to take my flag first?" Ivor demanded. "I'm not far behind, but fourth place puts me in a difficult spot."

"I'm sorry about that, but today I had to make a statement."

"No one's going to underestimate General Anxiety ever again, I wager," Ivor said, then grimaced. "That is a ridiculous name, you know."

Connor shrugged. "It's a ridiculous thing they make us do. I lack everyone else's ability to take such things seriously."

"And yet, you devised a cunning plan to stay in the game. A game you pretend to mock, but cannot afford to lose."

"None of us can."

"Exactly why I invited you over." Ivor rose and paced away. "General. . ." He shook his head. "I just can't call you that."

"Then call me friend."

Ivor smiled. "That I can do."

Connor relaxed, but tried not to show it. He had worried Ivor would reject the offer. They had been positioned as enemies, were obligated to lead armies against each other with every bit of cunning and craft they could muster, but did that mean they had to hate each other?

"So, my friend," Ivor continued. "Now we must look forward to the second battle."

"I haven't heard a specific date yet."

"Nor have I, but that's not important. We will face each other again, and I cannot afford to lose."

"We've covered that."

"The men and women who command our destiny require that we fight," Ivor agreed, pacing again. "Each battle requires a winner, but there is one flaw to the plan."

"What flaw?"

"Most years, one general takes the lead and keeps it. Your victory today would usually grant you tremendous momentum to continue winning. Eighty-five percent of all generals who won their first two battles end up ultimately winning the Tir-raon."

When Connor didn't speak, Ivor continued. "But when they've lost the second battle, the results get very inconsistent."

"The tricks I used today were a one-time geall." Not only had Frazier confiscated the prism lanterns, but none of the other champions would blunder into battle with him again. They would bring to bear their greatest strengths. No doubt Rory would keep secret the location of the next battle till the last moment, negating any battlefield prep work Connor might otherwise employ.

"Indeed," Ivor said. "We both know the next battle will be very different. We must destroy you, but no one will underestimate you again." He stopped and fixed Connor with a serious look. "You need an ally."

"And you need a victory," Connor finished for him.

Ivor nodded. "Yes, I do."

"What do you propose?" Connor absolutely needed to win for Shona, but if there was any possible way to work out a plan with Ivor, he would consider it.

Ivor tugged a silver chain from under his collar and lifted it to reveal the sandstone pendant he had worn concealed inside his shirt. The sight of it triggered all the frustration and worry Connor had felt since Jok had stolen it so many weeks ago. Ivor understood the pendant's power, recognized the terrible consequences that would befall Ailsa should the world learn of her unsanctioned sculpting.

Would Ivor use the threat of exposing Ailsa as a way to coerce Connor into cooperating? He said he prided himself on knowing his opponents' weaknesses, but would he really do something so cold a moment after calling Connor friend?

"I believe it's time for a show of trust." Ivor lifted the pendant's silver chain over his head, then tossed it to Connor.

Connor clutched the fist-shaped sculpture, barely daring to believe he held it again. Ivor was in for a pitched battle if he thought Connor would ever give it back. "I thought you were waiting until after the Tir-raon to return this to me."

Ivor dropped into a nearby chair and reached for a glass of wine on a nearby table. "The possible advantage that sculpture offers pales next to the current opportunity."

"What are you suggesting?" Connor asked as he slipped the silver chain over his head and worked the pendant under his mask. With it nestled against his skin, he reached for its healing power, which came like an invisible wave. The rush of health and wellbeing washed through him and he relaxed more completely than he had in weeks.

More than its extreme value, more than access to its incredible healing powers, its return spelled safety for Aunt Ailsa. Even though Ivor was searching for an accord regarding the next battle, returning the pendant was the act of a friend.

Ivor leaned forward. "I have to win, my friend. It's as simple as that. Not only will we two lead the standings, but we'll throw a wrench into the calculations of all of our handlers. That will give us time to figure out a way to derail the entire system."

The daring suggestion appealed to Connor, but before he could respond, a new voice spoke from the doorway.

"The best way to wreck the standings is for me to win the third battle."

Smiling at their surprise, Padraigin sauntered into the room and plucked an apple from the fruit tray. She took a big bite and spoke around a mouthful of fruit.

"I love conspiracies."

Chapter 38

his is a private conspiracy," Connor said, secretly applauding Padraigin's surprise entrance.

Ivor was frowning. "Where is Sheigra?"

Padraigin made a dismissive gesture. "She and your guards will be fine. No permanent damage."

"You launched an assault on Ivor's quarters?" Connor exclaimed. Tomas and Cameron were going to be disappointed that he hadn't done it first.

Losing that first battle had made her desperate. He was impressed that she'd accomplished it without alerting either of them. Ivor could not sense the use of slate or quartzite, but Connor could have, if he had thought to bring either one along.

He had sucked on a bit of marble before entering Ivor's suite, and had downed a fresh draught of soapstone, just in case. None of that helped against Padraigin.

She settled gracefully onto a nearby couch. "I apologize for my lack of manners, gentlemen, but when I was informed of General Anxiety's visit again to your quarters, my good General Ivor, I could not pass up the opportunity to join your discussions."

She grimaced at Connor. "That really is a terrible name."

"Thanks. Glad to know it's working. You knew I visited before?"

"You two are fairly subtle," she said. "But did you really think no one would see? There are more spies per square inch in this building than anywhere in the Carraig."

"They're like roaches," Ivor agreed. He had regained his composure quickly and now offered Padraigin a glass of wine, which she accepted. "We take precautions."

"Now the spies have seen you also join us," Connor said. "How long before Redmund comes storming in here?"

"We probably have a few minutes. So tell me, how exactly are we going to flip the ultimate geall back on the lords of the Tir-raon?"

"I thought you'd be pleased with settling for third place," Ivor said. "That way you could avoid marrying into House Pilib."

"On the contrary, that marriage is part of my plan," she responded. "Third place will not be any more acceptable for me than it would be for either of you."

"That's the problem, isn't it?" Connor said, studying the two champions. Had Ivor planned for Padraigin to join them as a way to twist the conversation to some ultimate end?

There were so many games within games at the Carraig, it was hard to know what to believe. Ivor and Padraigin were two of the most skilled players of the great game in the entire school. Connor couldn't think of anyone better suited to help him break the Tir-raon.

He just needed to decide if that was the best course. On the one hand, if they could fundamentally derail the game, perhaps they could all leverage the situation to win together. If they failed and the geall blew up in their faces, they could lose everything.

"I like your boldness, Padraigin," Ivor said, saluting with his glass. "And your presence does offer certain advantages. As we were just agreeing, my victory of the second battle could set the stage for an eventual unprecedented upset of the games."

Connor hadn't actually agreed, but that was indeed the direction the conversation had been going. With the return of the pendant, Ivor clearly assumed a deal had been struck. Had accepting the pendant solved one of Connor's most pressing issues, or had it played into Ivor's hands?

"And yet, you cannot derail the games while either of you wins the third contest," Padraigin replied. You need me."

Sheigra burst into the room, fists clenched, expression furious, interrupting Ivor's reply.

"Ah, there you are," he said. "This meeting is under control. Return to your post and please make sure we are not disturbed again."

Sheigra hesitated, her pretty face torn between the need to obey and her desire to challenge Padraigin, who ignored her and sipped her wine. No doubt that only enraged Sheigra further, but she was wise enough to realize she could not defeat the powerful foreign Dawnus.

She gave the briefest curtsy, then withdrew.

"Sheigra is a competent Pathfinder," Ivor said. "I'd be interested in hearing what you did to silence her."

Padraigin shrugged. "Competent, yes. But we are not where we are by being only competent."

"Indeed," Ivor said, his gaze lingering on the door where Sheigra left. Connor wondered if he was considering whether or not Sheigra would eavesdrop on their conversation while blocking others. Knowledge of their plot could be extremely valuable.

How loyal was Sheigra to Ivor?

"Assuming your suggestion has merit," he said. "It would suffice to accomplish our aim."

"If our pact proves successful, how to leverage the results to our mutual benefit?" Padraigin asked.

"I think it requires some further consideration," Connor said. No doubt they would plot long and hard. Perhaps they already had. He didn't understand the deeper ramifications of the behind-the-scenes negotiations well enough to make his own conclusions.

He needed to learn. Otherwise, he'd be like a blindfolded Cutter running the rim of the Alasdair quarry. One misstep could run him into a wall, tumble him down to a lower level, or even plunge him over the edge of the cliff to the blocking yard far below.

As much as part of him wanted to ride his army's dedication and his own cleverness to ultimate victory, he loved the idea of breaking the Tir-raon. Like Cameron and Tomas liked to say, breaking things was one of his greatest talents.

Chapter 39

Despite the late hour, Lord Nevan's aged steward still answered the door. He informed Connor that Lady Shona was indeed still awake, but hesitated when Connor asked to see her.

"This may not be the best time, young sir." The old man looked nervous. "The Lady Shona is perhaps not in the best of spirits."

"But she just won a great victory today, didn't she?"

"Indeed, but--"

Connor waved away his concern. "Don't pretend to understand Shona. I know I never do. She'll see me, I promise."

The steward reluctantly escorted Connor to the rooftop garden, with trees and shrubbery lining the paths. Despite the chill of evening and a light breeze, Shona wore only a blue silk blouse and a long, green skirt as she stood looking into the darkness, arms wrapped around herself.

She didn't turn at the sound of his footsteps. "This is not really a good time, Connor."

"I thought victory parties were supposed to make you happy." Connor absorbed a little granite, and the skittering itch of his curse helped center him. He needed information, and he was tired of her deflecting his questions. "Did you drink too much or something?"

One time during a Sogail summer festival when Connor was eight, he and Hamish had goaded Stuart into drinking half a keg of the old timers' fresh mead. Connor had never seen such spectacular vomiting. He hoped she wasn't suffering the same way, but stopped far enough away to dodge just in case.

"Don't act a fool," Shona snapped, turning toward him. Her voice was angry, but her eyes looked troubled.

"How else can I act when you don't tell me anything?"

"You know enough to do your job. Don't assume you need to know any more of my affairs. You may withdraw."

Prudence suggested he back off, but when did her suggestions ever really help? Besides, he'd always gotten more information out of Shona when she was angry than when she controlled the conversation. Time to break through her barriers.

"Fine, I withdraw from everything. You try winning the Tir-raon on your own."

He spun away, but barely took two steps before she caught him by the back of his shirt and lifted him off the patio with granite strength. She pulled him close, her face livid, and hissed, "Don't ever forget I am your patron, Connor. You owe me everything!"

Her rage was fearsome, but he retorted, "And you've got nothing without me."

With an angry shriek, Shona threw him across the patio.

He tapped granite a second before crashing through a stand of saplings ringing the garden. The impact uprooted them and would have broken bones had he not been protected by his curse. He tumbled to the low rail overlooking the rear of the palace, and banged into the stone rampart. It took a moment for the world to stop spinning.

Shona reached him a couple seconds later, leaping through the gap he'd made in the copse of trees, her expression concerned. "Oh, Connor. Are you all right?"

"Just a little overwhelmed by your kindness."

She dropped to her knees beside him. "I'm sorry. It's just, you should know better than to anger me like that."

"No need to apologize, Lady Shona," he said as she helped him sit up. "You're my patron. You can do whatever you want."

She sighed, actually looking apologetic. "I'm sorry for saying that too. You caught me in a pretty bad mood."

"Usually beating me up helps you feel better."

She laughed gently, her expression softening. "You're right. It shouldn't, but it does."

"You're not alone. Look at Catriona. For weeks, she didn't feel right unless she sent me to the hospital."

"Well, I don't want to do that." Then Shona sighed again and her expression darkened.

"What's bothering you?" he prodded.

When she hesitated, he dared reach up to touch her cheek. The move surprised her, but then she leaned against his hand and closed her eyes. "Thank you for being my friend, Connor. I don't have anyone else to confide in here."

"You can tell me anything." Really, he wished she would try it.

Shona stood and pulled him up beside her. Slipping her arm through his, she drew him into a stroll around the perimeter of the patio. For a time she didn't speak, just leaned against him as they walked. She smelled faintly of lilacs, and her skin was cool against his.

"You know our standings become important negotiating elements in some complex contracts between noble families," she said, without looking at him.

"Like marriages?"

She nodded. "Many marriages are finalized during the Tir-raon. The two great responsibilities for noble families are managing their quarries and their bloodlines. The Tir-raon is part of the great game that the houses play. We may oppose each other at times, but ultimately we must work together toward the purification and strengthening of our bloodlines."

"There's more, isn't there?" He gently turned her to face him and was surprised when she didn't protest. She met his gaze and her hazel eyes looked large in the dim light. She shivered.

"There is more," she admitted softly and her gaze fell.

"What were you so worried about when I arrived?"

"Have you ever heard the term First Breed Rights?"

"No." He wasn't sure he wanted to know

Shona actually blushed. She paced away and Connor let her. She wrapped herself with her own arms and he could tell she struggled with whatever truth he was trying to get into the open. If it was that bad, it was probably something he should have known about a lot sooner.

"Connor, you need to understand that the high families are under oath to do whatever it takes to restore the full extent of the lost Petralist powers."

"The Blood of the Tallan?"

"Yes."

"Why?"

"I don't know!" Pent-up frustration burned in her eyes.

"It doesn't make sense to seek the powers of the one who destroyed our country." Connor dared voice his greatest concern about his curse and all the interest shown in it. Why would they want powers that shattered everything Obrion had once been?

"There's much I don't know," Shona said, "but the duty was placed on our families after the Tallan Wars and by royal decree, we must obey."

"So what are you saying?"

Shona took a deep breath and spoke in a rush. "The champion of the Tir-raon proves their bloodline is strongest, so they have an additional duty placed upon them, one that all high families are honor-bound to acknowledge and accept."

"What duty?" She had set him up to be champion. What hadn't she explained?

"First breed rights. It means that a champion can choose any partner to. . .share bloodlines with."

"You mean?" The words failed him as the horrible truth became clear.

Shona nodded. "The bloodlines matter above all else. Usually the choosing of first breed rights is the result of extensive negotiations, but the ultimate choice is up to the champion. They can choose anyone they want and they have the right of intimacy with that person until a child is produced."

"That's disgusting."

"It's our duty," she said softly, but the fire in her eyes made it clear she despised it. Maybe she did understand how he felt about the looming union she planned between the two of them.

"The child becomes the property of the champion's family," she continued. "And the person they chose can then marry whoever the families have arranged."

"I had no idea." No wonder she was so driven. The revelation left him feeling sick. "So if I win," he asked, his voice hoarse as he considered the ramifications of the newly revealed truths, "I need to choose someone to. . .to breed with?"

"You can choose me," she said, gripping his hands. "Then there's only ever the two of us. That's why what we're doing is so important. We save and protect each other."

She had never actually spoken aloud her ultimate plan. He needed to hear her say it. "You would want me that way?"

Shona nodded, standing close, her hazel eyes wide in the soft moonlight. "Have I ever given you a reason to think I don't want you?"

"Not really. Your plan hasn't been entirely clear before now."

"Let me make it clear."

She leaned forward to kiss him, but he pressed a finger to her lips and gently shook his head.

"You're a very good kisser, Shona, but that's not what I was asking."

"What do you mean?" For once she sounded a bit unsure of herself. She had always tried to influence him with her beauty.

"You plan for us to be together, to breed, to marry, and for me to become your partner in your world. To what end? What do you think we'll accomplish together?"

"Anything we want," she laughed. "Connor, don't you see? We can build upon the wealth and prestige my father has acquired." She gripped his hands, her eyes bright with excitement. "With me by your side, you'll take your place at the head of our armies. You'll lead us to victory, in uniting all the lands once ruled by Obrion."

"What if I'm not sure those lands would be better united again?" he dared ask.

"Don't ever suggest that," she hissed, looking around nervously. They were alone on the rooftop, but out in the open, they were perhaps not shielded from any listening Pathfinders. They should have considered that before discussing such weighty matters.

"It's a valid question," he whispered, leading her toward the stairs. "Obrion has been broken for centuries. Wouldn't it be better to find ways to get along with the other nations? Wouldn't that save a lot of lives?"

Shona shook her head. "There's so much you don't understand yet, Connor. The only way for Obrion and the entire continent to reach our greatest glory is for everyone to unite under one ruler."

"I don't think they'll serve King Turriff."

Shona leaned close, and for a second, Connor wondered if she was just going to revert to trying to kiss him into submission again. With her face nearly touching his, she spoke so softly he could barely hear, even though her lips were close enough that he felt the air of their movement like whisper-kisses on his skin. "They won't follow the king, Connor. They will follow you."

The implications of that statement struck like a hammer stroke to a fault line. Shona grabbed his mouth before he could speak, shaking her head vigorously and leading the way into the protection of the palace.

"Don't ever mention that again, not even to me. Not yet." Her tone was deadly serious, but her eyes glittered with that deadly secret.

"You're not planning a simple life in the country, I guess," Connor said as they continued strolling slowly together, arm in arm.

Shona's rich laugh caressed his ears. "We will live life to the fullest, my Connor. We will make history and we will reshape the world."

He'd wanted her to confide in him, but he'd never imagined she'd share so much. He glanced at her, walking in step with him, her head held high, every inch the conniving, ambitious daughter of perhaps the most powerful high lord in the kingdom. What she had shared with him could get them both executed.

Well, he'd probably get chained in a dungeon and bred like a captive stud horse until he produced an heir with his powers. Then they'd execute him.

Shona was guiding him into a life of warfare, conquest, and eventual reign.

He'd prefer taking up his father's hammer in Alasdair.

Shona drew him to a halt in the parlor where they normally met, leaned against his chest, and sighed, "Oh, Connor, how did the world become so crazy?"

Because she and people like her ruled it.

She thought it was crazy now? His future was finally becoming clear, as clear as a falling off a cliff, strapped to a pair of hungry nualls. The only alternative was learning the truth about patronage and the unclaimed.

"Good night, my lady," he said after accepting another kiss from her.

"Good night, my champion," she breathed, her eyes bright with emotion.

Shona looked exceptionally lovely standing in that darkened doorway, but he'd rather take his chances with the nualls.

Chapter 40

erena swooped down toward the rampager camp from under the early morning shadow of the mountain. Her heart beat faster than the rush of wind against her mask. She glanced to her left where Hamish soared, Kilian clinging easily to his back. Anton had supplanted him on the Swift, but Verena had gotten plenty of practice compensating for the huge Sapper's bulk during the long flight back from the army headquarters. Unlike Kilian, Anton did not like flying.

As the tiny assault team descended on the tiny valley, like wraiths materializing from the night, Verena struggled to find that same bubble of insulating calm she usually wrapped around herself during a battle. All of her worries clamored for attention, seemed intent on convincing her the plan was fatally flawed.

Forty men had gathered at dawn in the parade ground in the center of camp, assembling with a noted lack of military precision, looking more like a gang than an army. Their leader alone carried himself with military bearing. He was that wide-shouldered, hard-faced man with flaming red hair. The speakstone Hamish had dropped the night before had caught a hint of what he was saying, but he possessed a strong hillman accent that Verena barely understood.

After berating the troops for the previous day's failure, he had proclaimed the day had come when they were being unleashed upon the world. The men had cheered and clustered around, eagerly snatching something he began handing out to them.

"We should have brought the Last Word," Hamish had muttered.

"We won't need it," Kilian had replied, his eyes glittering with points of living flame. More flames had jumped merrily across the blue-tinted tips of his dark hair. "Stick to the plan and trust in that new battle suit."

The closer to the start of the assault, the more nervous Verena had felt. She knew nothing about elfonnel, but Anton had looked grave when he heard the plan, and anything that made the indomitable Sapper nervous terrified her. Kilian, on the other hand, seemed more energized every second.

As they dove toward the parade ground, still unseen in the shadowed sky, Kilian leaped off of Hamish's back. The abrupt weight shift sent Hamish spinning. Anton stepped back off of the Swift at the same time, plummeting toward the ground a hundred feet below. Verena recovered from the weight shift quicker than Hamish, and they hovered near each other, watching the opening assault play out.

As he fell, Kilian ignited the fires of his Flameweaver gift. Twin jets of white hot flame exploded out of his feet, slowing his descent and announcing him in spectacular fashion. The roaring of the flames echoed across the valley in a growing crescendo that drew every eye.

"Today is a day of choices," Kilian bellowed as the gathered men turned to face him.

Anton drove into the ground like a falling meteor, but landed with a gentle thud, sinking to his chest in the earth. He bounced right back up, lifted a dozen feet into the air atop a wide earthen tower and frowned down upon the gathered men.

Kilian threw out his arms as he landed about thirty paces away from the rampagers. "Choose your fate. Surrender now and live." His expression hardened and fires danced in his eyes. "Or not. What say you?"

The leader of the rampagers shouted, "Claw and fang, boys! We are unleashed!"

As one, the rampagers howled, a sound of unrestrained bloodlust from throats already shifting from human to monster. The shout was part animal rage and part tortured humanity, and it echoed louder than Kilian's flames had, sending shivers of dread rippling up Verena's limbs.

"They control when they transform," she cried. Hamish at least would hear via the speakstone in his helmet. How was it possible?

"So be it." Kilian spoke calmly, but his voice cut through the din.

He threw his hands out wide and the front of the command building exploded outward under a horizontal waterfall. The waters spread into a narrow sheet that flowed around the rampagers' feet as they changed into thick-clawed paws. The earth along the fringes of the parade ground erupted upward in solid waves that reared high above the transforming monsters as Anton prepared his part of the assault.

Verena watched in awed amazement at the speed of the rampager transformation. It took only half a dozen heartbeats for the men to change into monsters that howled for blood as they tore across the narrow gap separating them from Kilian.

He met them with sheets of flame and whipping ropes of water, swatting them out of the air and tumbling them back. His wild laughter echoed from the nearby cliffs, and his hair ignited, but didn't burn.

Anton sent waves of earth crashing over the rampagers, sweeping them away and burying them from view, transforming the parade ground into a frothing maelstrom of wild earth. For a moment, Verena dared hope that the mighty Sapper had defeated them all and Kilian would not need to tempt the dangers of the wilder elements.

Then the rampagers began bursting from the ground, tearing the restraining earth with steel-hard claws and fighting free of Anton's influence. They vaulted fingers of earth that snatched at them, or tore through restraining walls, the delays only seeming to drive them to greater heights of fury.

That level of ferocity would have wreaked terrible damage on even Petralist-enhanced armies standing in their path. They burst through Kilian's defenses and swarmed over him, first three, then seven, then dozens.

The ground around Kilian whipped into the air, although Verena saw no wind. Heavy dust churned around him and struck the onrushing monsters like a mini sandstorm. They clawed through the winds, which obscured Verena's view, and closed on Kilian.

Verena gasped to see Kilian leap to meet them. He moved with Wingrunner speed, like a blurring shadow in the sandstorm. He collided with the first rampager, and an explosion ripped through the storm, a burst of brilliant light and white-hot fire that catapulted the rampager away.

More monsters swarmed around Kilian, but he met them all with explosive power, tumbling them away. So many rampagers raged around him, slashing and biting, they should have torn him apart in seconds, but he struck down every single one.

"How is he doing that?" Hamish exclaimed. He was leaning forward, straining to see through the raging sandstorm, same as Verena.

She didn't understand either. He was using diorite again, just as he had against the first two rampagers, but the explosions were smaller and faster. He was faster. No Wingrunner she knew could have moved that fast, fought so many at the same time. What other secrets did Kilian conceal behind that roguish smile?

When the last rampager tumbled away, the sandstorm subsided and Kilian stood, arms thrown wide, head back in exultant victory.

Verena tapped her long vision goggles to get a better look. His clothing wasn't even torn, and his eyes blazed with lightning-like fire. His laughter, laced with marble madness, again rang across the battlefield.

One of his hands was encased in fire so intensely white, Verena couldn't look at it. The other was surrounded by pulsing water that looked black and turbulent, as if the waters of a flood had been somehow condensed into that little space.

"Come on!" Kilian shouted, beckoning at the already-stirring monsters. "Come meet your doom!"

Kilian in the grip of battle fury was a terrifying sight. He didn't need granite to look imposing. He radiated power, his entire frame glowing with the might of his tertiary affinities. She had never seen anything like it.

It wouldn't be enough.

The monsters recovered quickly, shaking off the effects of the explosions. Despite bloodied flanks and broken teeth, they leaped for Kilian again. Anton formed a protective sphere around Kilian, but the beasts tore at it, trying to dig through to murder him.

Verena settled into a hover about eighty feet above Kilian's dome and opened fire with her custom speedslings. Hornets ripped the air, buzzing angrily as they tore into the rampagers, toppling them from the dome, gashing their tough hide, but only seeming to anger them more than ever.

Rampagers leaped high, snatching in vain for her. Hamish intercepted them, shouting curses in both Obrioner and

Grandurian as he dove around them like an angry sparrow, blasting their faces with fire and water from his suit. His agility was amazing, and his bravery ridiculously foolhardy.

He passed within inches of the snatching claws of the rampagers as they fell back toward the earth. If any of them caught hold of him, they'd rip him out of the air and tear him to pieces.

Momentarily distracted from the concealed Kilian, the rampagers proved they could still think rationally, at least some of the time. Pairs of them began throwing companions, casting them high enough that they could almost reach Verena.

She and Hamish shot them out of the air, but couldn't seem to damage them enough to make a difference. She would run out of hornets first.

They should have brought a diorite explosive after all.

Hamish threw his diorite darts in several of their faces, the explosive blasts strong enough to rip the heads off normal men and severely damage even max-tapped Rumblers. He managed to crack a couple of those terrifying jaws, but the Rampagers didn't seem disabled and still howled with rage as they fell back to the earth.

Then the rampager captain, who Hamish had dubbed Carrot Face, rose into the air on a column of fire and sprayed flames at Verena and Hamish. Some of the fire enveloped Hamish for a moment, but he activated soapstone in his suit and burst free in a cloud of steam.

Verena rolled a complete somersault, barely avoiding the flames, and dove, slipping between a pair of grasping rampagers, trading altitude for speed. She sped away, soaring back up into the sky a couple hundred yards away, turning vertical and shooting up along one of the cliffs, so close she could have touched the stone.

Spinning back, she hunted for the Firetongue. He was not immune to her weapons.

The rampagers had already resumed tearing at the earthen dome, but in that moment, it erupted in a geyser of crimson flames that tumbled the rampagers back again. The flames grew, forming a man-shaped giant that reared sixty feet over the valley floor.

Verena blinked, trying to accept the reality of the elfonnel. Kilian had described it as living elements, but she hadn't imagined it could be so huge. Kilian's elfonnel solidified, the flames forming into glittering armor across its torso, shifting in beautiful patterns from crimson to white. The giant glanced at Verena and gave her a roguish salute. It vaguely resembled the man who had given it life, with waving tongues of fire for hair and pools of boiling water for eyes.

The heat struck like a wave, then bounced back from the cliffs. Within seconds, the entire little valley was hotter than the inside of an oven, the air filled with shimmering heat waves. Verena caught sight of Hamish soaring away from the giant's back, tossed around by the same bucking air currents that made the Swift shake and tremble under her control.

Verena ascended to find more stable air above the surrounding cliffs. She wished Kilian hadn't chosen fire for the elfonnel. She felt the murderous rage of the living element like the heat on her face, and shivered with dread. How could Kilian control such a monster?

The elfonnel turned upon the rampagers and tore into their ranks, beating them down with arms that extended into whiplike flames. It snapped rampagers out of the air and ripped their limbs off as easily as they had dismembered their human prey.

The howling monsters had seemed unaffected by Verena's weapons, but they writhed in the grip of elemental fire. Their limbs blackened, their howls of bloodlust changing to screams of animal terror as white-hot blades of fire tore through their joints and poured down their wide open maws, immolating them and casting their charred ashes into the superheated wind.

Verena felt sick. Hamish's voice came softly over the speakstone in her helmet. "By the Tallan's bad breath, do you see this?"

She glanced at him hovering on the far side of the monstrous elfonnel. His helmet concealed his face, but his voice sounded awestruck. He was shifting back and forth in the air, as if torn between drawing closer to the inferno and retreating. He held a giant malve puff in his hand, half-raised toward the flames.

She couldn't imagine how he had transported the delicate confection. He'd discovered the puffy treat, made from the marsh malve flowers, was delicious when lightly toasted, then mashed between two of his favorite breadsticks. Roasting a malve puff on the back of a fire elfonnel was dumb, even for Hamish.

Howling like rabid wolves, the rampagers swarmed the fiery elfonnel. Verena watched in disbelief as the monsters tried to destroy the living element with tooth and claw. In the throes of their fury, they had lost their earlier reason, and Verena shuddered to watch them leap upon Kilian's elfonnel, trying to rip and tear and climb to its face.

They were already dead, and just needed a few seconds for their bodies to realize it. Their brazen optimism was terrifying, though, and would have challenged even Petralist-enhanced armies.

All they managed against the elfonnel was to enrage it. The air thrummed with energy as the elfonnel stomped and beat on the smaller monsters, consuming them with its blistering flames. They didn't burn quickly or die easily, thrashing within the restricting fire, their resistance to burning only prolonging the inevitable.

Then a pair of rampagers threw a companion high into the air. It actually bounded off the back of one of the giant's arms and leaped for the giant's face.

The elfonnel swallowed it.

Verena gasped as the rampager disappeared into that fiery maw. She caught glimpses of it tumbling down through the elfonnel's body, blackening, burning, shrinking back into a man. It was as if. . .

"No, Kilian!" she shouted, but the words were whisked away by the constant hot wind.

She lost sight of the rampager, but she'd seen enough.

"Flee!" Anton's voice rose like distant thunder, echoing across the valley, confirming her worst fears.

The flames forming the body of the giant took on a purplish hue, and the boiling waters of its eyes shrank to angry amethyst points. The elfonnel dropped to all fours, its arms transforming to legs, its head lengthening until it resembled a gigantic fiery wolf. It threw wide its white-hot maw and a sound bellowed forth like stones shattering under impossible heat.

That sound held an edge of madness that filled Verena with terror. By swallowing the rampager, the elfonnel had somehow absorbed the monster's power, been infected by its madness. It seemed to be losing the little humanity Kilian had imbued it with.

Not good.

Every instinct screamed at Verena to ascend far beyond the raging elfonnel's reach. If Kilian was losing control, they had to flee before getting caught in its mindless rage.

So Verena pivoted the Swift and threw wide the release rate on her thrusters.

And swooped down toward Anton, who stood atop his earthen tower two hundred yards behind the elfonnel. The Swift rocked wildly through the unstable air, and Anton tried signaling her away. She ignored him and settled into a hover near the top of his tower. The heat blistered her, despite the protection of her mask and goggles. She couldn't imagine how Anton had withstood it for so long.

The Kilian elfonnel was leaping about, snatching up rampagers, and gobbling them like a starving child at the Sogail. With each rampager, the purple hue of the giant's flames deepened.

"This is bad." Anton's voice sounded calm, but his expression was deeply concerned, and he didn't seem to notice his Sentry speak had failed him.

"We need to get out of here!" Verena shouted, hovering right up against the earthen rail beside him, gesturing toward the back of the Swift.

Anton shook his head. "The raft upon the waters can but steer within the torrent, but the dam athwart the chasm may subdue the raging flood."

"You can't be serious," Verena exclaimed.

The remaining rampagers, finally recognizing they were doomed, scattered from the elfonnel, fleeing in every direction. Tongues of white-hot fire churned across the ground after them without mercy. One rampager passed right beneath Verena, its feral eyes wide with terror, but the flames snatched it up and dragged it howling and thrashing back toward the maw of the giant.

The sight sickened her, adding to the nausea she felt from the heat and the stench of burning hair and cooked meat. Then she just felt terrified as a tendril of white-hot fire whipped up toward her. Earth exploded out of the front of the tower, forming a living wall that deflected the flames.

Three racing heartbeats later, the fires coiled above the defensive bulwark like giant snakes.

"We have to go now!" Verena exclaimed. "Get on. Kilian ordered you not to interfere. You cannot stop this."

"Victory is weighed on scales of success, not solely upon the heartstrings of the martyr."

Anton's defensive move seemed to have drawn the attention of the fiery giant. It turned toward them and growled, the sound like a thousand pine trees exploding, boiled from within by their own burning pitch.

"What do you have in mind?" she asked, panting in the stifling hot air. Sweat was stinging her eyes, and heat was sucking her strength. She could barely breathe, and activated a jet of fresh air from one of the quartzite stones in her helmet. They had to leave, or they'd be consumed in seconds.

Anton threw out his hands toward the giant, his expression tightening in concentration. The ground rose into a cresting wave, flowing across the valley as if it had turned to liquid. The wave crashed into the elfonnel, spraying its fire backward in an explosive blast that vaporized nearby buildings. The giant took a single step back under the onslaught, and the fires forming its head pulsed and darkened.

Verena caught sight of the rampager leader soaring through the air on pillars of fire, heading for the command building, with Hamish close on his heels. He was taking an awful risk trapping himself inside an enclosed space, but if Hamish could complete his part of the mission and gather information from the leader, they might be able to salvage something form the disaster the raid had turned into.

As the giant gathered itself for another attack, Anton glanced at Verena, then gestured toward the immense rocky shoulder of the mountain looming over the hidden valley. "Reason at times may be found in the depths of shocking distress."

"You're planning to sucker punch an elfonnel?" Verena exclaimed. "With a mountain?"

"Go!" Anton shouted, sweeping an arm into the air and deflecting a dozen lances of flame that Verena hadn't even seen the elfonnel create. "To you it falls to witness the resolution and bear record to Kilian when he returns."

"Don't you dare die on me," Verena urged, tears mingling with the sweat stinging her eyes.

A falling mountain didn't represent much danger to Anton, but if his plan failed, she didn't doubt he would embrace the elements himself and try to bring forth his own elfonnel to face Kilian's giant.

He had suggested the possibility in their final conference prior to launching their assault. Kilian had been adamant that he not do so, confident that he could survive the ordeal and return to humanity, but equally confident that the mighty Anton would not. The powerful Sapper had not looked convinced. If the mountain did not shake Kilian out of the madness, Anton would sacrifice all in a final attempt.

She would have done the same thing. Kilian was too important to allow him to descend into madness and rampage across the countryside, even if he would probably wreck more in Obrion than in Granadure.

Hating that she couldn't do more, Verena shot into the sky, thrusters opened wide, blinking her eyes clear as she surveyed the monster that had consumed Kilian. She soared high above the giant through the turbulent air, not sure how far it could reach with those deadly flames, but suspecting the only safe place would be somewhere on a different continent. The giant was stalking after Anton, whose earthen tower was retreating, flowing over the ground and moving deeper under the shadow of the mountain's shoulder.

Terrified by what was about to happen, but powerless to do anything about it, Verena hovered and watched as Anton positioned himself close to one of the steep sides of the hidden valley. The giant closed on him, picking up speed now that it looked like he was trapped. Whatever Anton was going to do, he needed to do it quick.

The mountain above shook, its entire flank rumbling, dust and debris boiling into the air and sheets of earth sloughing free and avalanching down. The giant paused to look up.

Anton's tower dropped into the earth, sucking him out of sight just before the dust cloud obscured him.

Verena soared higher to get a better view. The mountain shook again, then the sound of thousands of tons of stone shattering rent the air, violently shaking the Swift. The sound intensified until it seemed the entire mountain was coming down.

Verena hoped Kilian survived, but couldn't imagine how even that giant could withstand the might of a falling mountain.

Then she remembered Hamish.

Chapter 41

erena shouted as billowing clouds of dust descended upon the valley. "Hamish, get out of there!"

"Don't come down here. It's ugly." Hamish's usually cheery voice sounded subdued.

"Haven't you heard what's going on?" she exclaimed, happy he wasn't lying dead in the bowels of that building.

"No. I was kind of busy, and there was some kind of interference."

"Kilian's been infected by the rampager madness," she cried, swooping toward the gaping hole in the front of the building. "And Anton's bringing down the mountain to stop him. The valley's going to get stomped."

"Seriously?"

"Get out of there!" Verena shrieked, swooping right into the building. The aroma of fresh-baked bread and fried bacon assaulted her nose, washing away the gritty scent of broken stone and clouds of earth she'd just flown through.

Hamish rose through a hole in the kitchen floor, carrying a small, charred sack in his hands. He paused to stare at the extensive breakfast strewn all around the kitchen, but only muttered, "What a waste. Let's get out of here."

She pivoted the Swift and shot out of the front wall, the blast wave of her thrusters tumbling tables and chairs back and whipping bacon into the air.

"Hey, be careful," he cried. "Didn't your mother teach you that ruining food was bad?"

"She taught me that dying in an avalanche is worse!"

The two of them rose into a murky twilight of churning dust. The sound of the mountain breaking apart echoed from all sides. It was hard to know which way to go in the turbulent clouds, so Verena reached for a piece of quartzite. "Hamish, stay very close!"

"What?" His voice sounded distant, choppy, as if all the debris was interfering with the speakstones.

She couldn't see him through the gloom, so she lit every piece of marble on the Swift, creating beacons of foot-long jets of flame he could orient on. "To me!"

He appeared out of the murk, his suit covered in grime, nearly invisible until he clutched the back rail of the Swift. He still held the tiny sack to his chest. "I can't see anything."

The rumbling was growing closer, and Verena prayed they would emerge from the dust cloud to see how to avoid the disaster. Fighting back primal terror, she activated the quartzite block in her hand. Instead of releasing its power in a concentrated burst like the thrusters, Verena carefully fashioned its release into a domed shield.

The shieldstones were a particular specialty. Air didn't exactly harden into impassable barriers, and earlier Builders had discounted the idea of using air as a shield. Verena had persisted and figured out the secret.

Unlike water, air could be compressed. A lot. At its heart, the shieldstone was a dome of air, compressed so tightly at its outer limit that its internal pressure was greater than that of objects striking from the outside.

As soon as the shieldstone formed, the air near the top of their little protected space calmed, but dust continued to swirl up into it from below. She was tempted to encase them entirely, but had never tested how long the air in such a bubble would last.

Then a huge rock, the size of a cabin, tumbled out of the obscuring darkness and struck the shield a glancing blow. It rotated away on impact, but still shook the humming shield.

"That was close," Hamish breathed, still flying beside her with one hand on the back rail.

That rock would have knocked them right out of the air. If it had struck a more direct blow, it could have killed them, even with the protection of the shieldstone.

Verena slipped on one of her special gloves, lined with blind coal, and angled their flight to the left. If one stone had fallen so far, more would. They really had gotten turned around in the murky air.

More boulders rained down around them, passing like wraiths in the gloom. Some glanced off the shield, and each time, Verena angled their flight path farther, hoping to avoid the path of destruction.

The rain of debris slowed, and for a second she allowed herself to hope they had cleared the worst of the danger.

Then a mighty boulder loomed above them, the massive stone far too large to dodge. It struck with incredible force, flattening the shield dome and knocking the quartzite block right out of Verena's hand.

"Hold tight!" Verena cried, raising her gauntleted fist and screaming defiance as she threw wide the release rate on the blind coal stones lining her glove.

They struck the boulder and plunged into darkness. The unique slippery feel of blind coal slithered down her skin and coated her with its protective embrace as the boulder slid by. On both sides.

It didn't shatter. They didn't die. Somehow they slipped right through its heart. The hard stone particles that formed it just parted and slid around Verena, Hamish, and the Swift. For a second, they were encased within the giant stone, surrounded by absolute silence. All sound ended, severed. Darkness slid past, so deep it felt like all the light in the world had been snuffed out. She smelled nothing, didn't dare even try to breathe.

The only link to reality was that pulsing, slippery feel of blind coal. What if it ran out before they emerged? Would they be trapped inside the huge boulder, like fossils turned to stone?

She barely had time to feel truly terrified before they erupted out of the boulder and returned to reality with a shocking abruptness. Verena laughed, inhaling the turbulent, dust-coated air with desperate joy, grinning at the sight of murky gloom boiling around them, and savoring every bucking, gut-wrenching lurch of the Swift in the turbulent air.

Hamish gripped the rail behind her back so hard it creaked. "What just happened?"

"We survived."

Verena activated her last piece of quartzite, forming a much smaller shieldstone as she banked farther away from the sounds of destruction. She prayed they wouldn't collide with another giant boulder. The blind coal lining her gloves had disintegrated a second after they emerged from the last one. Even if it hadn't, she didn't think she'd dare attempt flying through another stone.

The sound of the avalanche shook the darkness. Hamish leaned close and shouted something, but she couldn't hear. The gloom boiled with vast amounts of moving earth, and the sound of the mountain coming down was far too close. They had escaped the valley floor before the avalanche had really begun, but it sounded like Anton was bringing down more than that one bony shoulder of the peak.

The air churned, making flight difficult, tossing them to and fro like a tiny raft on an angry sea. She opened every thruster as well as all of the puking dooms along the bottom of the Swift for extra lift. They bounced wildly in the turbulence, sometimes falling for stomach-wrenching seconds when they hit empty pockets of exhausted air.

If Verena hadn't been strapped in so tight, she would have been unseated twenty times. Hamish couldn't fall out of his suit, but he was shouting through the speakstone, challenging the storm in a final act of defiance. He still clutched that little sack tight, though. It must impede his flight effectiveness, but he seemed determined to carry it to the bitter end.

Then they burst out of the cloud of dust and soared into the clear morning sky.

Verena gaped. Anton had outdone himself. The rocky shoulder had toppled into the valley, followed by the peak that had reared above it. The dust cloud continued to boil outward from the catastrophe, chasing Verena and Hamish higher and higher into the air until they reached heights where they had to supplement their breathing with air from quartzite.

"I can't believe it," Verena whispered.

Hamish placed the charred sack into the supply box at the back of the Swift, then hovered next to her, half-reclined in the air. He peeled back his goggles, and his eyes were red-rimmed and haunted.

"He wouldn't stop," Hamish muttered looking down at his gauntleted hands. "I had to kill him."

"Carrot Face?"

He nodded. "He barely even tried defending himself. He was so intent on destroying that sack. I couldn't let him do it. I. . ."

Verena shifted the Swift close enough to grip his hand, drawing his gaze to hers. Hamish had thrown himself into his military training with such enthusiasm, she sometimes forgot how new he was to battle and the hard realities of war. Having been born closely related to the royal family, she had been taught and prepared her entire life.

"You did what you had to," she said, squeezing his hand. "You can feel proud of that."

"It's just as ugly as when I didn't know how to fight," Hamish said. "But now I'm the one doing the ugly things."

"The necessary things." She pointed down at the boiling dust cloud so far below. "If we hadn't destroyed that camp, they would have murdered thousands."

"I know," Hamish said, regaining a bit of his stubbornness. It was a good sign. "It's just such a waste. I couldn't even save any of the bacon."

Verena laughed. Hamish was going to be all right. "An entire mountain nearly fell on top of us. Kilian is lost to some kind of madness while the elements walk through him. That giant could level cities and kill tens of thousands. But you're worried about the bacon?"

"You don't have to state the obvious. I'm not even hungry right now, but that's the emotion talking. We need to maintain our strength, Verena, so when we can do something to help Kilian we're ready. You have to think in broader terms sometimes."

"Hamish, you're the only person I know who can justify your obsession with eating in a way that makes it sound like it's vital to the war effort."

Hamish shrugged and gave her a reassuring smile as he pulled a squashed and dirty malve puff from a pouch at his belt. "That's because I'm one of the few people who understand cause and effect. Enjoy the little things in life whenever you can. They become the big things."

He stared at the pastry for a moment, then sighed and offered it to her. "You're stronger than me. You eat it."

How could she refuse? As she munched on the sweet, she ignored the grit she tasted with every other bite. In that moment, she understood Hamish just a bit better. He was a friend worth having.

"What's in the sack?" she asked.

"I think it's the secret that will explain the entire rampager camp."

"Really?"

"Either that, or it's a sack of half-burned flour and Carrot Face is the craziest food critic I've ever heard about."

Chapter 42

'm surprised you're both still awake," Connor said as he entered Ailsa's office and closed the door behind him.

"Gisela and I were comparing notes."

"Have you learned anything new? I could use some good news."

"So could we," Ailsa said.

Gisela added, "We are learning just today that ancient archives are having been suffered small fire in the past."

"Let me guess," Connor said. "Information about Evander was all burned."

"Along with tomes that might have shed light on the early days of the Carraig and the days right after the Tallan Wars," Ailsa added. "Someone's gone through a lot of effort to protect these secrets, but I had hoped their influence did not extend to the Arishat archives."

"Is great troubling," Gisela said.

Connor sighed. Of course things would not be easy. He was surrounded by half-truths, intrigue, and layers of corruption. He struggled to maintain the confidence he'd felt earlier that they'd find a way to sort things out and define their own destiny.

"What about you?" Ailsa asked.

"Nothing but more lies. Have either of you heard the term 'threshold' as applied to Petralist powers before?"

Gisela shook her head. Ailsa hesitated. "I'll have to give that some more thought."

"What about first breed rights?"

They both nodded.

"You both knew, and neither of you thought to tell me?"

"I thought you are knowing this duty always," Gisela said.

"And I had hoped you would be gone prior to the end of the Tir-raon," Ailsa said.

Connor really wanted to burn Shona's hair again. Every time he felt he understood what he needed to know, he learned there were even worse things waiting for him that everyone but he seemed to take for granted.

"I can't keep doing this," he muttered. "This is insane."

"You can't give up now," Ailsa said. "The only way out is through."

"Is it? Every day, Shona wraps more chains around me and ties me tighter to her plans."

"Her hold is not as tight as she assumes," Ailsa said. "That's why she's trying so hard to secure you."

"Maybe we're going about this the wrong way," Connor said. "What if I just remove the mask and reveal to the world what I am?" Even though he had discounted the idea, he felt desperate enough to explore it again. "Maybe I could gain the upper hand in negotiating my future."

"I am thinking this is a bad idea," Gisela said.

"Why?" he challenged, even though he knew she was right.

"I suggest caution," Ailsa said. "I've considered this question at length."

"What did you decide?"

"That it's a last, desperate option. Don't forget that Shona has promised to enslave your entire village if you break with her again."

"But would she dare if I have other offers that undermine her position?"

"Perhaps, but even if some other family offered you a better deal, they have no direct influence in Dougal's realm and could not help save your family from Shona's vengeance."

That threat was still the greatest danger, like a shackle around his neck, and thinking about it enraged him. "So what if I gained patronage somewhere else, then left with Ilse and grabbed my family on the way to Granadure?"

Ailsa considered the idea. "Could you take the entire village? Or would you leave them to suffer Shona's wrath for you?"

Could he take the village? Would Ilse agree to try? Would the villagers agree to leave, to join the hated Grandurians?

"While you consider that," Ailsa continued. "Remember that Dougal is a very dangerous man. Shona's plan surely ties in with plans he has in the making. Defying Shona is dangerous enough, but defying Dougal is a deadly mistake and must be done only with great care."

"Aren't you supposed to be the encouraging one?" he grumbled.

"I'm supposed to help you stay alive and find the path to freedom," she responded with a smile. "The final point to consider is that once everyone knows the full extent of your powers, you will be swarmed by the other high families. You might gain patronage on more favorable terms, but there's no possible way you could ever slip away to Granadure after that."

He hadn't expected to win that argument, but losing didn't help him feel better either. "I'll maintain the act for now, until the gealls run their course."

So he changed topics. "Have you heard the term elfonnel?"

Gisela gave him a blank look, but Ailsa leaned forward, her gaze intent. "Where did you hear that?"

"It popped up as part of Jean's research. Elfonnel may be the name used for when the elements sometimes rage out of control and take living form, rising as gigantic monsters that attack remote villages and towns."

"This happens?" Gisela asked, eyes wide.

Ailsa nodded. "Such events are rare, but I have heard the term."

"What do you know?" Connor asked.

"Not much more than you just described, and it's been many years since I heard that much." She leaned back in her chair, her gaze drifting toward the ceiling as she considered it. "I don't know why they form, but elfonnel do rise on very rare occasions, the elements incarnate, raging with a fury that cannot be quenched. They wreak terrible destruction before disappearing again."

"Jean read reports of a second elfonnel sometimes rising to fight."

"I've never heard that," Ailsa said. "But I'm not surprised."

"Why not?"

"Think of the disruption such an elemental manifestation would generate. Such a concentration of one element would trigger ripple effects across the nation. It's not surprising that other elements might be stirred up. Always they balance and counterbalance each other."

"Let us hoping the elements are much happy," Gisela said.

"I haven't heard of any elfonnel in a long time," Ailsa said. "But I worry that when the war breaks out and so many Petralists unleash the might of the elements against each other that they might trigger a backlash that could give rise to such a monster."

War was terrifying enough on its own without the thought of the elements rising in anger for being misused.

"Perhaps this is one of the reasons the Arishat League is opposing the war," Gisela suggested.

"Is there any way to find out what the Arishat knows about the elfonnel?" Connor asked.

"Perhaps, but I am thinking it might be a secret hard to learning."

Connor sighed. "I'm tired of secrets."

"I know no other secrets about the Tir-raon," Gisela offered.

"And you've already learned the full measure of the duty that will be laid upon your shoulders," Ailsa said. "Those truths are not the things we should be focusing on, though."

"I know," he said, feeling frustrated. "But I feel like I'm getting blocked at every turn. I don't know where to look next for information about what happened to Hector and what unclaimed really are."

"How about in Hector's other set of quarters?" Ailsa asked, her eyes twinkling.

"His what?" Connor exclaimed, his gloomy thoughts burning away under a dash of new hope.

"Is true," Gisela said excitedly. "We are learning just tonight. The professor kept more rooms. Was very great secret."

"How did you learn about it?" Connor asked.

"One of the many clerks employed by Lord Dail owes me a favor," Ailsa said. "I had spread the word that I was interested in anything related to the late Professor Hector. She made a note of the rooms while processing a rent payment."

"Who paid the rent if Hector's dead?"

"I asked the same question. My contact is hunting for that information."

"How did you recruit Lord Dail's clerks?" Connor asked, intrigued with the whole secret spy network side of his aunt's life.

"There are many ways," she said. "One must be open to opportunities. This clerk owes me a debt for interceding on her behalf after her son made the mistake of interfering with an Assassin."

Gisela shivered. "Assassins are most dangerous. It is making bad day to interfere."

"For one's extended family as well," Ailsa said. "If they get upset, they'll usually remove all your relatives too."

"You speak of them like they're different from other killers," Connor said.

"They are," Ailsa said. "Others may kill, but they are not known as Assassins, who call themselves the Mhortair. They are a very secretive group. Although they are not officially affiliated with any political body, they have alliances with the Arishat League."

"Even we know less than very little about them," Gisela said.

"They just go around killing people?" Connor asked, thinking back to the first conversation with Camonica and Aonghus. They'd mentioned the Mhortair as allies of Ravinder.

"It's more complicated than that," Ailsa said. "They are semi-independent. Their primary mission is preventing the return of the Blood of the Tallan and keeping Obrion from expanding."

"So they'd want to assassinate me?" Connor asked. Why did so many conversations go there?

Gisela nodded. "If they are learning about your true powers, they would have sending an Assassin already."

Great. One more thing to worry about.

"And you told your contacts in the Arishat League about my powers, didn't you?" Connor asked.

Gisela hesitated. "We are not being enemies, Connor. In fact, if you are wanting to flee from duty of champion, and if Granadure is not being the best choice for asylum, perhaps you will come and visiting my country."

"We'll consider those options later," Ailsa said.

"So they know," Connor groaned. "And Assassins might be hunting me already."

"I am very sorry," Gisela said, looking like she meant it. "But my mother has promising not to reveal the truth to others until I am knowing more about you."

"Which means she probably already told everyone," Connor grumbled. "And they promised not to tell anyone else, which pretty much means the Assassins know where I am."

At least most of the people planning to kill him were friends. It felt strangely unsettling to know that a complete stranger was planning to murder him. How did they live with themselves?

Connor wondered what unspoken conditions Gisela's offer of asylum included. Would they look to him to fight against Obrion during the upcoming war? He doubted they would leave him alone, but could their plans for him be any worse than breeding him like a racehorse?

"Anyway," Ailsa said a little more loudly. "No one else appears to know Hector's other rooms even exist."

"Where are they? Connor asked.

"I will take you," Gisela said, and he wondered if she made the offer as a way to make up for having revealed his secret to a band of murdering assassins. She was going to have to work a little harder to cover that debt, especially if he got assassinated.

"You stay outside," he warned. "I'll go in alone."

They agreed to meet after dark to make the attempt. As Connor headed back to his Dawnus suite for some power stones and a change of clothes, he allowed a sliver of hope. What better thing to keep in secret rooms than the secret Connor hunted?

He dared to believe he was due for a bit of good luck.

Chapter 43

"There it is," Gisela said softly, pointing at a blocky stone building that looked drab and uninviting compared to most other buildings in the Carraig. Even the warehouse they crouched beside looked grander.

Midnight had come and gone, and a sleepy hush had settled over the area. No lantern poles illuminated the dim street. Connor had only passed a couple of times through that area on the east side of the Carraig, not far from the inner wall, and it hadn't stood out in his memory.

"Are you sure?" Connor asked. It was unlike Hector to associate with anything not of the finest quality.

Gisela nodded. She wore a black wool cap to cover her light hair, but her face still seemed to glow in the darkness. "From what we are learning, important servants are living there when nobles wish to having them closer than the town. The first three floors are having people. The top two floors are being under construction, with never so many people. Hector's rooms are on the fourth floor."

"About to get rebuilt?" Connor asked. Why didn't that surprise him?

"Have care," Gisela warned. "The center hall is blocked with building supplies. Will having to take side hallway to Hector's rooms."

"I've got it," Connor assured her. "Keep an eye out here and watch for anything unusual."

"And if I am seeing anything unusual?"

He grinned. "Use your imagination."

Connor trotted across the street, his nervous excitement growing. He had absorbed granite earlier and downed a little vial of soapstone mixture. Slate wouldn't accomplish much up on the fourth floor, but it offered an easier route to bypass any nosy neighbors.

So Connor slipped around to the rear of the building and connected with the earth through the slate in his boot. Then he silently rose up the side of the building on a slender, carefully-shielded column of earth. He bled away most of the earth before severing his connection. The tiny remaining thread of earth collapsed when he released it, but the resulting pile was small and he doubted anyone would stumble upon it in the darkness.

Tucking a tiny piece of quartzite into his cheek, he applied it to his eyes to improve his vision as he entered the building. Since the top floor was under construction, the door leading into the central stair was not locked and he ghosted down.

He considered preparing marble in case he ran into trouble, but that old building looked eager to burn. He wanted information, not a repeat of the destruction Camonica had wreaked in Hector's main apartment.

No one else walked the stair that circled all the way down to the ground floor. The fourth floor was a mixture of demolition and new construction.

The floor was stripped down to bare wood, and the air smelled of sawdust and broken, old walls. The main hall that ran through the center of the building was indeed blocked with building materials, but he easily found the side corridor that led him back to the hall where Hector's rooms were situated.

The silence of the area weighed heavy on him. No sounds crept out of any of the rooms he passed. Even that late at night, most large buildings full of people would generate sounds.

The few sounds he did hear were not pleasant. The building creaked like an old man struggling to find a comfortable position to rest. When he reached Hector's hall, it smelled of old sweat, and he wondered if they really had the right place. Of course, if Hector really had wanted to hide something important, such a place would be ideal, as long as none of the neighbors decided to steal whatever he had secreted there.

The hall ended just beyond Hector's room, so the only exit was back the way he came. The wooden door looked solid, set in a steel frame, and Connor slowly approached, considering the lock.

The floor creaked loudly under his last step. So much for entering the rooms like a shadow.

The door closest to Hector's opened and a burly man with unruly black hair and a sour expression stepped into the hall. "What are you doing out here, boy?"

"Room service," Connor said.

The man grunted. "No one's home. Beat it."

"I would, but the man who owns these rooms hired me to fetch something for him."

The man approached, swelling with granite strength, his expression hardening. "Wrong lie, kid. It's gonna cost you."

"Not as much as smelling you already has."

The big man lunged, one granite-hardened fist punching for Connor's face. He probably thought he looked intimidating, but Connor had been training with the deadliest Fast Rollers in Rory's army. Compared to them, the man moved with glacial slowness.

Connor shifted to let the blow slide past his head and tapped just a bit of granite, applying it to his fist and arm. The skittering itch of his curse felt so right that it scattered all of Connor's nervousness.

As the man stumbled forward, off balance, Connor curse-punched him in the jaw. He had always possessed an exceptional curse punch, but under his tutors' instruction, he had improved it tenfold.

His hardened fist catapulted the man off his feet and right through Hector's door.

So much for the lock.

Connor followed him into the darkened room, and applied quartzite to his eyes again. There was almost no light, but that meant he had plenty.

He paused and looked around, wondering if he had made a mistake after all. The room was packed with junk. Piles of furniture, stacked haphazardly to the ceiling vied for space with towers of old books and heaps of linens. It looked worse than Lady Isobel's cluttered storage rooms in Alasdair, with only a narrow aisle down the middle leading to a half-open door that led into a second room.

The Boulder groaned and tried to sit up. Connor applied granite to his entire body and grabbed him, lifting him off the floor. "Who hired you to guard this room?"

"Tallan take you," the man cursed and tried punching Connor again.

So he threw the man across the room. He smashed the door into the suite's only other room off its hinges. That room was just as cluttered as the first. The man came to his feet and rushed back up the aisle at Connor, shouting with anger.

Connor set himself and max-tapped granite. The two of them came together like a pair of living statues. The crack of their stone-hard bodies sounded like thunder in the enclosed space. The impact rattled Connor and knocked the other man right off his feet. The guard groaned, spitting curses and threatening to rip Connor's head off.

So Connor punched him a few more times. A proper beating demanded a certain rhythm, growing in tempo to a final crescendo that left the enemy incapacitated. Connor had been beat up enough times to have developed an appreciation for the subtle nuance of a good beating.

The guard didn't seem to understand. He thrashed and kicked and rolled, trying to escape or set himself to throw punches of his own. Connor didn't want a bash fight in the tiny room, worried they'd destroy the very secret he needed to search for, but the guard proved completely uncooperative.

With all the noise they were making, any pretense at stealth was gone, so Connor grew exasperated and threw the guard through the boarded-up window at the far end of the inner room. A four story fall wouldn't injure a Boulder, but it would grant Connor some peace and quiet for a few minutes to search. The soft breeze that filtered in through the broken window felt cool on his skin and helped dispel the stale air.

Connor eyed the piles of junk crammed into the apartment, wondering how many days or weeks he'd need to sort through it all. Whoever that angry Boulder was, he'd be sure to return soon, probably with help.

Why would Hector bother to rent a set of secret rooms, only to turn them into a pigsty? It did make great camouflage for any secrets Hector might have wanted to hide. Then again, Hector would have hated visiting. His pride and vanity would have made it distasteful even to enter the room. He'd never stoop to crawling through piles of nasty debris.

That camouflaging clutter would have hemmed Hector in even worse than they did Connor. The man wouldn't have recognized the problem because he'd assume no one could ever see past the clutter. Connor didn't need to search the entire mess, only the parts Hector might have deigned to touch.

So Connor scanned the room, looking for easy ways into the clutter, or hiding places in plain sight. Even with quartzite-enhanced vision, it was difficult. So he extracted the little piece of limestone he'd practiced with earlier in the evening.

Concentrating on the little stone, he whispered, "Help me out here. Just a new affinity. No big deal."

He felt the same flicker against his mind, but the stone didn't light. Trying to maintain his calm, he said, "Remember, in that last battle, I brought more glory to the Solas than anyone's probably ever done at the Carraig."

Connor didn't believe light was vain, but whatever the reason, the little stone suddenly grew chill against his hand, like a little icicle, and a soft glow began emanating from it.

He should celebrate a new affinity, but that dump of a room was not the place. Deprived of the softening shadows, the rooms looked worse than ever. Not seeing anything useful, he slowly paced the length of both rooms, but saw only unbroken walls of junk to either side.

He needed more time. The seconds seemed to rush past, and he kept starting at imagined distant cries of alarm. He took a deep breath, vowing not to leave until he found what he came for.

So he'd better get finding.

Connor applied quartzite to his nose, then wished he hadn't. Scents of mold and dust and dry rot assault his nostrils, along with the smells of wood, leather, and old cloth.

Then there was the liquid fuel.

He focused on that unexpected smell, trying to isolate it, but it was everywhere. In half a minute, Connor identified eighteen concealed caches of liquid fuel. It was a perfect trap. Any flame, triggered by a clumsy intruder and fueled by all that dry clutter, would consume the room in moments.

Connor took that as a good sign.

No one would risk such a fire unless they had something important to hide. Chances were slim that a Firetongue or Spitter would enter the room. Anyone else would be consumed, along with whatever secrets Hector was trying to conceal.

As Connor returned to the entrance, he wedged a piece of marble under his tongue. Sucking on it, he enjoyed the initial spicy burn. Time was fast slipping away, but his knowledge of Hector was the key, and he would not be denied again.

Standing on the shattered door in the entryway, he scanned the room again with enhanced vision, forcing himself to study the mind-numbing clutter. Old couches and chairs were piled in jumbles with tables and wardrobes bereft of drawers. Old books filled in the gaps, forming walls. Dust covered everything, looking undisturbed except where the fighting had knocked things over.

He looked farther, and was focusing so intently on seeing everything, that he almost missed the clue. Hector probably never even noticed the clutter. He would focus on his target from the first moment he entered.

Grateful that Hector's pride was such a constant, Connor crossed the room and slipped between a pair of tall wardrobes that formed an almost unbroken wall. Behind them, he entered a tiny, clear space, flanked by a jumble of chairs on one side and a pile of drab window covers on the other. The little space, near the center of the apartment, had been invisible from anywhere but the doorway.

At eye level, resting atop that pile of window blankets, he reached up and removed a dark green leather jacket, exactly the style Hector preferred to show off his granite-enhanced muscles. A small, wooden box lay concealed underneath. Unlike the clutter everywhere else, this box was lacquered and polished to a perfect shine.

He was about to pop the latch when he realized the placement of all those secret stashes of liquid fuel radiated outward from this spot. That tantalizing box was the bait and key to the entire trap.

The secret had to be close, but it wasn't in the box. The pile of linens under the box were useless, so he turned to study the wardrobes. They were covered in the dust that lay thick on everything, except for a single point of clean wood halfway down the rear panel of the left-hand one. Fingers trembling with anticipation, Connor pressed the spot, just as Hector must have done.

A secret door popped open and Connor peered inside. The compartment was small, containing nothing but a single leather pouch, about the size of a teacher portion from the daily rounds. Had he gone through so much trouble just to find Hector's stash of granite?

Connor extracted the little pouch and pulled open the drawstring. It did contain powder, but it wasn't familiar granite. By the pure, soft light of limestone, the powdered grains of sand looked purplish red and somehow sinister.

This had to be the secret.

Powdered stone.

Connor returned the dust to the bag and thought back to that crazy day when Hector had turned unclaimed. Just prior to changing into that rage monster, Hector had driven a hand into a pouch of powder. Connor had assumed he was absorbing his last portion of granite, but that wasn't right at all.

Jean was correct. Unclaimed were a lie, a lie fueled by a secret power stone. The magnitude of that revelation left Connor breathless. There were only nine power stones. That was a universally accepted truth.

It was just another part of the lie.

Were there other power stones? He thought back to diorite. Using his father's hammer, he'd triggered the vast explosion that had broken the mountain above Alasdair and released that flood. If diorite was also a power stone, why did no one know about it? Why not this purple powder? Why not others?

Connor tucked the pouch into his shirt and left Hector's rooms the way he came. As he was jogging up the central stair, he heard a commotion down below. Peering carefully over the edge, he glimpsed the Boulder he'd thrown out the window rushing upstairs at the head of a crowd of tough looking men.

Suppressing the urge to whistle a happy tune to himself, Connor returned to the roof and jumped off. Protected by granite, he rolled with the brutal impact and suffered no damage.

"Did you find somethings?" Gisela asked when he met up with her.

"I did," he grinned as they slipped away toward the inner gate. "I'll tell you and Ailsa about it in the morning."

Gisela frowned. "Why waiting?"

"I need some time to think. The night's already half over and I have to put in an appearance with my army early tomorrow."

"You shouldn't waiting," Gisela cautioned.

"Trust me."

After seeing her onto the road to the Sculpture House, he turned back into the inner city. He traversed half the Carraig with a spring in his step and was approaching the central keep when he was surprised to see Aifric walking in his direction.

The Healer didn't look surprised to see him.

"Connor, we need to talk."

Chapter 44

"Aifric, what are you doing out here so late?" Connor asked.

"I might ask you the same thing, but we both know the answer."

"We do?" Connor liked Aifric. She was one of the nicest people he knew, but he couldn't trust her with the incredible secret he'd just discovered. What did she think she knew?

"You're in league with General Kilian-Lian-Anxiety," Aifric said. "You're how Shona passes secret instructions to him."

"How did you know?" He'd never been so happy to hear someone so wrong.

"I pay attention. You're more than a simple linn, and you've been granted access to circles of influence beyond your station. That's why you got beat up so much."

"Why are you telling me this?" Connor asked.

She gave him a sad smile. "I like you, Connor, and I don't like what they're doing to you."

If she only knew.

"It's all right," he assured her. "Things are getting better."

She shook her head. "It's only the quiet before the storm."

"What do you mean?"

"The game is getting crazy," she said. "We won a great victory, but that's only going to raise the stakes. It's going to get ugly, I promise you. Very powerful people are growing desperate and they will not accept defeat without doing desperate things."

"I'm glad the general has you to help."

"I try, but Connor, you must find a way to extract yourself from involvement. I don't think I can protect you from what's coming."

"You have other sources, don't you?" Connor asked.

"Like I said, I pay attention."

"You should share what you know with the general."

She hesitated. "I'm not convinced the general is who he claims to be."

That was an understatement big enough to choke a torc.

"You should tell him anyway."

Aifric shook her head. "I'll deal with the general, Connor. I just want you to be safe."

"Thanks." He took her hand and gently squeezed it. "It's good to know I have friends here."

After she left, he wondered at the exchange. Had she been waiting for him? How could she know where he'd pass or that he'd be out so late? He rarely traveled that road, usually preferring the undercity.

Aifric was more than she pretended to be. He needed to find a way to pry that truth out of her, but should he do it as Connor or as the general?

As he walked toward the central keep, mulling over the questions, someone rose silently out of the earth right in front of him.

"Whoa!" Connor shouted, stumbling back from Evander, trying to control a sudden spike of fear. Could Evander have discovered that he'd shared the forbidden secrets? Was he there to exact revenge?

Evander glanced after Aifric, who was no longer in sight, then turned toward Connor. "Darkness veils the face of purpose, but many walk the shadows."

Had he known she was there, waited for her to leave?

Connor fought down his fear and said, "Don't do that. You could give someone a heart stomp, popping up out of the ground like that."

"Shades of the past walk shadows and whisper truths that few have ears to hear," Evander said, his deep voice pitched low like the grinding of stones in a strong current.

Connor stifled a groan. He was really too tired to decipher Evander's cryptic speech. "My ears are pretty much not working right now, so I haven't heard anything."

He tried to walk around Evander, but the big man slid to the side without even taking a step. That was such an impressive move, Connor vowed to practice it, but doubted he could ever manage it on a cobbled street without breaking everything within twenty feet.

"Storm crows gather to feast upon the battlefield, but the strong heart must endure."

"I have no idea how to respond to that." Connor threw his hands out in surrender.

Evander gripped his shoulder, and the power of the earth flowed into him from the huge man, refreshing his mind and invigorating his soul. He gaped.

"How did you do that?"

"The slow drip of water from hanging stone will eventually fill even the deepest bucket."

"I don't have time to learn by bits and pieces," Connor protested. "Like you just said, the storm crows are gathering."

"And you must finish the race."

"Did you just speak plainly?" That was as scary as anything the big man had ever said.

"The mountain may withstand the assault of ages, but crumble in a single moment."

"You think time's short," Connor retorted. "I've got multiple armies planning to stomp mine flat, intrigue and spies everywhere, and random people trying to commit murder in the Carraig. Not to mention. . ."

He bit off the words he was about to speak. He'd almost talked about the unclaimed, but he didn't dare share that with anyone, especially not Evander.

The giant Sentry pressed a sausage-sized finger to Connor's shirt where the mystery powder was concealed. "The fortified stronghold falls not to a single assault, but relents under the combined might of attacks on all sides."

So much for keeping secrets.

"You've been seeking this too?" Connor withdrew the pouch from his shirt. He couldn't fight Evander, but would not give the whole thing to him.

"The craftsman builds a masterpiece with tools provided by others."

"I know you have your reasons," Connor said. "But don't pretend spoon feeding tidbits to Jean is enough."

Evander settled to one knee, bringing his face even with Connor's. He sighed, his black eyes boring into Connor's. "Know this, young one. Your hunt for truth is but part of a greater conflict that has crept through the shadows of ages."

Two plain sentences in as many minutes? Connor shivered under Evander's stare. They really were standing on the brink of open conflict.

Evander produced a tiny pouch and offered it. That, he could do. Connor carefully transferred a handful of the purplish powder to Evander's pouch, but retained the bulk for himself.

As he rose and tucked the pouch into a pocket of his immense black leather jacket, Evander said, "Duty is the shackle of honest hearts, but victory lies only at the end of the course set before the determined tread."

"And if I decide not to complete the Tir-raon?" Connor asked. "If I choose a different course based on the truth I've learned?"

"The fool celebrates ascending the foothills when the ultimate peak is still in sight."

Connor sighed. "Sometimes it's really exhausting talking like this."

Evander actually smiled. "The rope woven from many tiny strands holds fast against even the mightiest tempest."

"But the sweetbread that falls off the tray and gets kicked under the oven is eaten only after the rest are consumed," Connor retorted.

Evander paused and a frown flickered across his face. That was the most glorious expression Connor had ever seen. He'd actually stumped the big man for a second.

"That doesn't make any sense at all," Evander said.

"Think about how the rest of us feel all the time."

"Good Sentry speak does more than that." Evander shook his head. "Sunlight filtering through a cloudy sky is fractured into many bands, but is all the same light."

"I'll finish what I've started," Connor assured him. "But before I accept the ultimate victory, you and I need to have a long talk. I won't accept the life I'm getting forced into, not without a fight."

"Dross is cast off of the gleaming silver only through the touch of the refiner's fire," Evander said, clapping Connor on the shoulder with a hand as big as his mother's frying pan.

"And what happens when you get what you want?" Connor asked. "Will you kill me for knowing the truth about patronage and unclaimed?"

"The tree knows not to fear the avalanche, but claims the mountainside as its domain."

Was Evander threatening to be the avalanche, or was he planning for Connor to break another mountain? He glanced toward the peak of nearby Mount Murdo, lost in the late night darkness. He'd need a lot more than a diorite hammer for that one.

"Do you know what that powder does?" Connor asked.

"Suspicion, like the invisible canker, rots the foundation before bedrock can be made secure."

"I don't either," Connor admitted. "But if you figure it out, let me know. And stop delaying Jean's research. If we're part of some deeper geall you're running, you have to help us help you."

Without replying, Evander sank silently into the ground without even a rumble of moving earth. The cobbled street settled perfectly back into place behind him.

"I really need to learn how to do that," Connor muttered, resuming his march toward the keep.

He felt exhausted, but his mind was churning. He had to make sense out of it all, had to study Evander's words for hidden meanings that were surely embedded in them, but all he wanted was sleep.

First, he had to find a way to contact Ilse.

Chapter 45

It's definitely a stone," Verena reported to Kilian when he entered the small workroom she and Hamish had spent the past couple of days working in. The little room was located in the wooden compound the rampagers had assaulted, and Kilian kept it under heavy guard, despite the fact that they had destroyed the entire rampager camp.

"You're certain?" he pressed.

Kilian still looked exhausted. Anton had somehow located him and carried his unconscious form to the top of the broken peak where Verena and Hamish had found them. Kilian hadn't awakened until they reached the army camp and the Healers had worked over him for an hour.

He had insisted he was fine, but they hadn't let him join them on the previous night's patrol. Alone, Verena had spied on the Obrioner camp. Hamish had spent the night swooping over the nearby passes, scouting for signs of additional rampagers. The risk was low, but they couldn't take any chances there might be other nests of monsters out there.

Kilian had said little about his ordeal or how he'd survived the raging elfonnel, but his eyes looked haunted. Verena hoped one day to hear the story. She felt a powerful urge to understand more about the elfonnel and the deeper magic that Kilian had used to give the elements life. If he could do so, who else knew the secret or possessed that power?

The entire valley that had once held the secret rampager camp was gone, replaced by a medium-sized mountain. The only thing they had salvaged was the sack of powder that was definitely not flour. They had been tasked with discovering exactly what it was and why Carrot Face had been so intent on destroying it.

"We're sure," Hamish said, standing and rubbing his back. "It passed the teeth grit test and everything."

"You didn't eat any?" Kilian exclaimed.

"Of course not," Hamish said. "I spit it all out."

"I made him rinse his mouth seven times," Verena added.

Kilian still didn't look happy. "It was reckless to try tasting it anyway."

"I didn't try opening its power," Hamish said. "With most powder, it's difficult, so I couldn't even accidentally do it." He looked disappointed.

"Don't stick it in your mouth again," Kilian ordered, holding Hamish's gaze until he nodded. "We must exercise extreme caution."

"I'll be careful," Hamish promised. "Besides, a single grain isn't going to do anything dangerous."

"We don't know that yet," Kilian snapped. "You saw how much the little I absorbed within the elfonnel affected me, even though I should have been insulated by the living flames. Please tell me your proof amounts to more than chewing on the powder."

"Of course it does," Verena said. She decided not to mention that she'd licked one tiny piece of powdered sand too. It was too small to get a sense of it, and it had tasted like charred dirt, so the test hadn't been useful.

She gestured to a custom set of goggles on the table. She'd spent the bulk of the previous day with Hamish designing them. Using similar principles to the long view goggles, this one focused on enhancing a close-up image to previously impossible levels. So she had dubbed them Close-View goggles. Of course, Hamish had wanted to first test it by shining a tight beam of limestone light up Verena's nose so he could get a glimpse of what nostrils really looked like on the inside.

She had refused. So they had tested it by looking inside each other's ears. Hamish had more earwax than she'd expected and, up close, it had looked even more disgusting, like the landscape of an alien planet. At least she hadn't seen tiny bugs or anything.

With great enthusiasm, he'd pronounced her ears equally disgusting.

When focused on the little purplish grains of charred powder, with the release rate of the quartzite blocks powering the goggles thrown wide open, they'd learned the truth. The sands were rock.

The experience of swooping her vision down and ever down onto the sand had been amazing. It had seemed as big as the boulder they'd slipped through. She'd sent for Kilian immediately.

"I still don't see anything special," Hamish said, dropping back into his chair and studying the powder through the goggles again. "It's just a jumbled mess."

"That's the key," Verena explained as Hamish moved over and handed the goggles to Kilian. "Notice how there's no regular crystalline pattern."

"What does that prove?" Kilian asked.

Verena pointed at a little tray nearby. It held samples of several minerals, including salt and quartz. "Take a look at those."

Kilian examined them each in turn. "This is amazing. These goggles reveal the underlying structure in ways no one has ever seen before."

"From my study, it seems clear that minerals have a structured, crystalline form," Verena explained.

"I still don't see what that proves," Hamish said. "The burned sand isn't crystal. Maybe the heat melted the crystals away."

"It doesn't work that way." Verena pulled over another tray she'd just finished examining. It held samples of most of the different power stones, plus samples that had been burned over intense heat. "Burning the stones didn't alter the mini-tiny-view structure."

Hamish had already looked at them. He pointed at the quartzite sample. "But that one has crystals."

She shook her head. "Individual grains are structured because they're made up of the different minerals in the rock, but the rock itself is a mishmash of those different structure types."

"What are your conclusions then?" Kilian asked, still studying the various samples.

"Rocks are made up of various minerals, but they are not themselves a mineral," Verena explained. "Their mini-tiny structures prove that. They're inconsistent. Every mineral I've studied, on the other hand, has a well-defined structure that remains consistent, even when burned."

Kilian straightened and smiled. "Good work. I believe you're right. We're looking at powdered stone here. Without these new tools, we might never have known for sure."

"Rock or no rock, it's not important until we prove it's a power stone," Hamish pointed out. He'd helped develop the close view goggles, but didn't seem to appreciate that important secrets could be revealed through such tiny samples.

"It's hard to activate most powdered stone," Verena agreed. Sedimentary stones worked best, like the healing sand she sometimes applied to bandages, but igneous stones were notoriously hard to activate when powdered. She suspected it had to do with the distribution of the power.

"But we came up with another idea," Hamish announced, pointing to a steel construct standing nearby. He had dubbed it the Smash Packer and was extremely proud of it and eager to test it on the powder.

He showed Kilian how it worked. Its thick, steel sides tapered down to a small box. Hamish retracted the heavy, steel plug to hang by its chain above the opening. They had lined the inner surfaces of the smasher box with soapstone. When activated, it would form a barrier of water around whatever they wanted to smashpack.

"Since it's hard to activate a powder," Hamish explained. "We're going to try to pack some so tight it thinks it's a whole stone again. Kind of like a forced family reunion."

"I don't think you can make a stone by packing the powder," Kilian said.

"Of course you can," Hamish said. "How do you think metamorphic stones are formed? Rocks get smashpacked underground by so much pressure they change into other rocks."

"We're denying this powder the heat needed to transform," Verena said. The explanation had sounded so much more convincing before Kilian arrived. She hoped they hadn't wasted hours for nothing.

Hamish pulled a pastry out of his pocket and mashed it into the tiny smasher box, then activated the soapstone edges, coating the doomed confection in a pulsing layer of water. "Time to test it."

He touched the quartzite blocks mounted on top of the heavy plug suspended over the smasher box, then released the restraining lever. Air blasted the plug down the smash packer and into the smasher box with a loud crack, rocking the entire smash packer.

Verena extracted the plug, and Hamish reached into the smasher box to retrieve what was left of the pastry. It had been crushed flat, like a wafer-thin piece of bread.

He bit slowly through it and grinned. "Tastes great, and it's super dense."

"The pressure is the key," Verena told Kilian. "Water cannot be compressed, so it transfers all the force into whatever's being smashpacked, but maintains a perimeter that prevents it from shattering."

"Let's give it a try," he said after refusing a bite of Hamish's smashpacked bread.

Verena poured a handful of the charred powder into the smasher box and they repeated the process. The plug smashed down with unrestrained glee into the box of water-coated powder.

Hamish worked the crank with excited haste, eager to see their success. The smasher hadn't worked as well on the powdered stone as it had on the pastry. Verena extracted two tiny wafers and a handful of muddy powder.

"This should give us enough to test," Verena said, handing one of the little wafers to Hamish.

"Together then," he said.

Verena counted to three, then focused on the little wafer. When she flickered her Builder senses across it, she at first felt nothing. Then she sensed a faint flicker and cried, "I feel something!"

"Me too." Hamish had of course placed his on his tongue.

"Get that out of your mouth," Kilian ordered.

Frowning, he pulled it out and gestured with it. "This is how I work."

Verena ignored the argument. They needed to know. Besides, with how tenuous the connection felt, she doubted they'd get much effect. Anything would be a victory, though, and they had to know. So fighting down a tremor of worry, Verena snapped open the release rate of that ethereal crack in the sort-of stone.

"Nothing," Hamish grumbled, holding his stone close to his eye and peering at it intently.

"What about you?" Kilian asked her.

"Maybe we didn't smashpack it hard enough," she suggested.

Then it turned warm against her hand, and that heat rippled up her arm, setting her hair standing on end.

"Wait, I've got something!" The warmth flared into searing heat a second later, and the muscles of her hand convulsed around the tiny stone.

Verena shrieked, shaking her hand to try to dislodge the burning stone, but unable to open her hand. Hamish started hopping around, shouting. He'd stuck his little wafer back in his mouth, and it sizzled against his tongue.

Verena gasped under a rush of fear so intense, it was like a physical weight. Tears sprang to her eyes, a purplish haze descended over her vision, and her limbs trembled with terror. She wanted to find a corner to hide in, to weep from fear and the agony of her burning hand.

Hamish bumped into her, sparking an overpowering rage. She punched him and he staggered, eyes wild, and he laughed in her face.

"You can't take it!" he snarled, hands lifting into a fighting stance.

It was his fault she was afraid. Destroying him would make the pain go away. She leaped at him, fingernails lashing out to dig at his eyes and to crush his windpipe. She'd show him what it meant to scare her.

He attacked at the same time, powerful hands balled into fists.

Inches away from each other, they were both swept off their feet by a wave of water she never saw coming. It separated her from Hamish and held her, even as she fought savagely to free herself. She had to destroy him, had to stop the terror and quench the pain.

Then the searing heat evaporated and her hand opened, releasing a whiff of noxious fumes. The intense rage and fear vanished, leaving her sagging with exhaustion in the grip of the watery bonds. A choking cough replaced Hamish's crazed laughter when he sucked in a mouthful of water.

"What happened?" Verena asked. Her voice sounded hoarse, as if she'd been screaming and hadn't realized it.

Kilian approached and studied them both. "Are you all right?"

"I'm not sure," she admitted. "But I'm in control."

"Me too," Hamish said, sneezing a blast of water.

"Are you ever?" Kilian asked with a wry grin. He made a sweeping gesture with one hand and the waters receded, leaving Verena and Hamish both dry and on their feet.

"What happened?" Verena asked again.

"It appears you were successful in activating the power stone," Kilian said.

Verena inspected her hand where a pair of fang-shaped burns had seared into her palm, as if she'd been clutching burning teeth instead of a tiny stone. Hamish stuck his tongue out to reveal a similar scar.

"The effects didn't last long," Verena said.

"Who knows how long it would have lasted with a real stone," Kilian said, touching her palm. She flinched, but a second later, healing warmth flowed into her hand and eased the burn. The scar faded to a pair of thin, white lines.

"What about me?" Hamish asked.

"I'm not sticking my hand in that mouth of yours," Kilian said. "I told you not to suck on it."

"It's how I work."

"Be more flexible." Kilian handed Hamish a small piece of sandstone. "Suck on this for a minute."

While Hamish treated his tongue, Kilian said, "Those stones triggered dramatic reactions from both of you. What happened?"

"At first, it just hurt," Verena explained. "Then I was overwhelmed with fear, mixed with rage."

"I felt the rage," Hamish said. "But not the fear. It was more a feeling of victory, like the best celebration in the world."

"It appears the rage is the linking factor," Kilian said. "That same rage overwhelmed the elfonnel. I couldn't control it, didn't want to for a while. Only getting a mountain dropped on my head knocked me out of the frenzy."

Verena was about to sink into a chair, but gestured Kilian to take it instead. He didn't object. "So the stone triggers uncontrollable aggression?"

"It also seems to magnify other emotions," Hamish pointed out. "It affected your fear and my joy, turning them crazy-intense."

"Imagine the chaos such stones could wreak in an army if dropped into a group of soldiers," Kilian said, his expression grave.

"Don't you dare," Verena exclaimed. "They'd rip themselves apart. They wouldn't be able to stop."

"Don't worry," Kilian said. "I would never condone such a tactic. It would be barbarous."

"Are you thinking that Dougal would do it?" Hamish asked.

"I have no doubt he would if he knew the possibility existed," Kilian said.

"But he has no Builders," Verena objected.

"None that we know about," Kilian said.

She shuddered to think of the destruction Builded rampager stones could cause. "By the Tallan's blessed memory, let's pray they don't ever discover it."

"We need to know what they do know," Hamish said.

Kilian nodded. "Agreed. It's time I interrogate the prisoners."

Chapter 46

As they waited for a prisoner, Hamish looked up from where he'd been pacing the workroom, sucking on a caramel-coated piece of soapstone and wondering how to tap the euphoria of porphyry without triggering that crazy rage.

"Just thinking about rage," he said. "Dougal's going to be furious when he finds out his rampagers are destroyed."

"I'm planning on that," Kilian said. "If he has more rampagers, I hope to goad him into using them recklessly so we can destroy them."

"As long as they're sent against us instead of getting unleashed on defenseless villages," Verena said.

"He'll know it was me," Kilian said. "That makes the contest more personal than it has ever been. Now that I know the secret, he'll know I'll be coming for him. He'll either send rampagers to assassinate us, or keep them close as his final guard."

"If he thinks you're coming after him, he'll keep them for defense." Hamish liked to test himself against Kilian, but if he knew the Dawnus was planning to kill him, he'd already be running. "So when do we leave to get him?"

"All in good time," Kilian said, his eyes flashing with pinpoints of fire. "But on our timetable, not his."

A pair of hulking Rumblers entered the workroom, leading one of the captured rampagers. The woman was heavily chained, barely able to walk. She looked miserable, her eyes wild, her hands shaking.

Kilian displayed the pinch of rampager powder he held in his palm. Her eyes fastened upon it with a terrible hunger and she lunged against the restraints, dragging the surprised Rumblers forward a step. She started to pant, drool dripping from her mouth.

"You want some of this?" Kilian asked.

"Give it to me!" Her voice held an edge of desperation, as if she hadn't eaten for a week.

Verena took a step closer to the wild woman. "You can't bear not to have it, can you?"

The woman tore her eyes off the powder long enough to glance at her. "It hurts," she whimpered. "Every day it must feast on my soul, or it eats away my heart."

Hamish decided maybe he didn't want to suck on porphyry after all.

Verena said, "It's even worse than the addiction that some of the chew leaf sniffers develop."

"People sniff leaves?" Hamish asked. "That's insane."

"You're one to talk, rock licker," Verena retorted.

Hamish grunted. "There's a vast difference between tasting power stones and sniffing a useless leaf. Even you taste them."

"Enough," Kilian chided. "Licking or sniffing, addictions are dangerous. We must exercise additional caution when working with the stone."

"Give me some," the woman begged again, straining against the Rumblers.

"You must give me something first," Kilian said, unmoved by the pitiful act. "First, tell me what stone this is."

"If I do, you'll give me some?"

He nodded.

"Porphyry." She barely got the word out before screaming for him to give her powder.

Kilian took a pinch of the powdered stone and placed it against her throat. She shuddered, then relaxed, a look of ecstasy on her face. For a second her skin turned purplish, then the color receded.

"What have you done to it?" she exclaimed. "It feels all but spent."

"Blame Carrot Face," Hamish said. "He set it on fire."

She moaned. "I need more."

"What else can you tell me about the stone?" Kilian asked.

"Anything," she shrieked. "It's a primary affinity stone. We were tested as children."

"How?" Hamish asked.

"The birthing houses," she whimpered. "Some children from promising families are secretly tested with porphyry first."

"That's horrible," Hamish exclaimed, imagining babies in thrall to the rage of porphyry, their little bodies mutating.

"What is she talking about?" Verena asked.

"In Obrion, all children are tested at birth," Hamish explained. "Commoners with strong curses can be detected that way. They're taken by the high lords and raised in their service."

Verena's face paled, then her expression turned angry. "I'm going to kill Dougal."

"Me first," Hamish said, stoking a similar rage. "It's my people he's using."

"Give me more," the woman begged, and Kilian again pressed a tiny bit to her throat, which only seemed to add to her desperation for more.

"How do you stay in control when transformed?" Kilian asked.

The woman giggled hysterically. "Not firm like reining a horse, but on the cusp of disaster. More like rafting a torrent. The best you can hope for is aiming in the general direction you want and pray for the best."

That sounded pretty incredible if not for the murderous addiction aspect.

They questioned her further, and Verena took notes, but Hamish didn't care so much for details about quantity to duration burn charting and things like that. He had heard enough. Porphyry was the first evil power stone he'd heard of, and it enraged him to think about High Lord Dougal using his own subjects as unclaimed monsters.

When they completed the interrogation, Kilian granted the woman a little more powder. Not enough to allow a change, but perhaps enough to take the edge off her withdrawal.

"We must interview each of the others the same way," he said. "The addiction may explain why they've been acting so wild. They will be sick with the need for it. With the promise of a little powder, they'll talk."

Verena nodded. "We'll see if the others corroborate her description."

"I suspect they will," Kilian said, pacing over to the sack of charred powder and considering the purplish dust. "We must tread cautiously, my friends. This stone destroys even those who establish affinity with it."

"I hope Connor is careful," Verena said.

"If he finds any of this, he'll try it." That truth was abundantly obvious.

"That would be extremely bad," Kilian said. "Even if he established rudimentary control, there may be dangers we don't yet know about."

"You need to send Ilse another letter before it's too late," Verena urged.

"I will, but the risks of porphyry are not his greatest danger."

"What could be worse?" Verena asked. "He could lose control and kill a lot of people."

"He could kill more if we don't get him out of that school soon."

Hamish didn't like the turn in the conversation. "Are you talking about that Evander character Ilse mentioned in that last report?"

"No," Kilian said. "Most of the time, that boy's more a plotter than a killer. If Connor's careful, he won't drive Evander to murder."

Hamish shared an astonished look with Verena. From what he'd heard, Evander was perhaps the oldest person in Obrion. How could Kilian call him a boy?

"You're talking about Connor raising an elfonnel," Verena exclaimed. "You hinted at it before. You're honestly afraid it might happen."

"The possibility worries me," Kilian admitted. "Connor might indeed one day ascend through the requisite thresholds of power that would allow him to raise an elfonnel. However, my fear is that Dougal may have uncovered one of the secrets buried after the Tallan Wars. There is a way for one with the proper set of affinities to push another's mind and wrest control over their will, forcing them to raise an elfonnel."

"That would've been good to know sooner," Hamish exclaimed.

"It is one of the deep secrets," Kilian said. "I wouldn't have shared my fear with you now if you hadn't already witnessed an elfonnel losing control. You understand the consequences."

"How is it possible?" Verena asked.

"I will not share the details," Kilian said. "Not even with you. I had hoped the knowledge died with Tallan. Given the way Dougal is maneuvering your Connor, the fear is growing in me that he may have learned the secret."

"Tell us something," Verena implored. "How do you know all of this?"

"Many secrets were buried since the Tallan Wars, some for better reasons than others. It seems that history is turning full circle, and with the rebirth of the Blood of the Tallan, many of those ancient secrets can no longer remain contained."

For a moment, his eyes looked haunted. "This is the real conflict, my friends. The war is but the excuse to set the board. When the stones are cast, it is Connor's powers, and whether or not he or another controls them that will define the fate of nations."

His expression turned resolute. "You both must prepare yourselves. If we lose the struggle to free him, you cannot hesitate. If Dougal indeed succeeds in controlling that boy, the monster that he could become would make what you saw happen at the rampager camp seem laughable."

"What are you saying?" Hamish asked, hating that he was even listening.

"If we cannot save Connor, one of you may have to kill him to save us all."

Chapter 47

onnor yearned for sleep, but turned away from his Dawnus suite and the promise of his huge, soft bed. Instead, he tapped basalt and raced out of the Carraig, passing no one on the deserted streets.

When he sensed no Sentries near the north sally port in the outer wall beyond the plain, he climbed over and sped onto the mountain. He had no idea where Ilse was camped, but needed her to contact him. So he ran three miles up the first ridge and found a hidden clearing.

Switching to granite, he yanked several trees out of the ground and lay them together, forming a giant arrow pointing toward the Carraig. Then, tapping marble, he blackened them, hoping that Margrit, Ilse's Longseer would smell the smoke, even if Ilse didn't notice the shape on the ground.

Then he tapped slate and stomped the ground, sending out a pulsing soundwave three times. Sentries in the castle might pick up on the signal too, but even if they sent someone to investigate, chances were slimmer than Hamish missing a meal that they'd stumble upon Ilse.

As he returned to his suite, he hoped Ilse would decipher the message and contact him. Despite everything he had to think about, he fell asleep almost before he finished climbing into bed.

The next morning, he tried to follow his regular routine, but found it hard to focus. He nearly triggered a mob in Professor Nandag's class when he almost walked away without actually leaving their portions.

Thankfully, his captains took care of most of the instruction during army group practice. He was scheduled to attend a leadership class on battlefield management, but made up a lame excuse and skipped it.

The secret gnawed at him, even though he'd concealed the powder in his Dawnus suite in a lockbox even a Boulder wouldn't be able to open. How could life go on with a secret like that begging to be confirmed? He studied the purplish powder several times, but didn't dare do more than that yet.

So he brought a little bit of it with him to the Sculpture House to meet with Ailsa and Gisela.

"There is power here," Ailsa confirmed after studying it for a few minutes.

"A new power stone," Gisela breathed, crouching low over the desk to study the purplish grains. "There are being no new stones discovered since the Age of Legends."

"Can you tell what it does?" Connor asked.

Ailsa shook her head. "If I had a solid piece, perhaps. With powder, I can sense if it's power grade or not, but the vortexes and currents within a stone are missing once it's powdered." She prodded the little grains with a finger. "Every stone, even powdered, creates a certain feel against the skin. Granite has a sense of enduring strength, like sunlight on the peak of a mountain. Basalt is more like the rushing of a mountain stream. This." She paused and poked it again. "This is chaotic. I cannot get a solid read. It's like a panicked horse in the midst of a stampede."

"It has to be tied to Hector turning unclaimed," Connor said. "But does it actually somehow trigger that transformation?"

"Or does it only drive him beyond the bounds of patronage?" Ailsa asked. "There is no way to know for sure."

"Actually, there is," Connor said, inching closer.

"Don't you dare try to establish affinity with this powder," Ailsa warned, her voice as sharp as one of her chisels.

"Why not?" He felt a desperate need to confirm it was a power stone, and that it was indeed responsible for the unclaimed.

"Think of what you're suggesting." She fixed a disapproving look upon him. "If indeed this powder triggers the unclaimed, then you would be casting yourself beyond humanity and embracing the raging monster that Hector became."

"I am thinking it would be bad," Gisela agreed. "Many could die."

"But what if it's not responsible for that?" Connor asked. "Hector was declared unclaimed by Lord Dail. He was a Boulder."

"He must have been Agor if this was indeed the power stone he embraced to turn unclaimed," Ailsa said.

Connor considered that. Agor were the rare Petralists who managed to establish two primary affinities, but where did Hector get porphyry, and why wouldn't he have already tried either obsidian or basalt? Would Dougal have supplied it to him, or did he find it on his own?

"But does it work the same way for others?"

"Think about it," Ailsa said. "If patronage really is a lie, as we suspect, then no matter whether Hector was considered in good standing or unclaimed, the powder wouldn't care. It drove him beyond humanity. This is too dangerous to use."

"We have to know," Connor argued. "If it's responsible, then that's the proof we need."

"You should just leave," Ailsa said. "Run to Granadure. This is proof enough."

He wanted to so badly, but shook his head. "I can't. I ran into Evander last night. He warned me that this is part of a broader geall. Even if I dared leave now, he might not let me."

"I wish we knew his purpose," Ailsa muttered.

"What if he's trying to change things," Connor said. "What if this is all part of a plan to avert the war, break the high lords' hold over the commoners?"

"He hasn't interfered in the past," Ailsa said.

"But unclaimed weren't being used against helpless villages in the past either," Connor retorted. "I need to know his geall before leaving."

"No," Gisela said. "Come to Althing. We could studying this powder together."

That was tempting, but Connor didn't want to replace Shona with another set of lords trying to control him and his curse. "Perhaps, but not yet."

"Don't attempt this stone," Ailsa cautioned. "It's not worth it."

"I don't even know what it is."

"It has the appearance of porphyry," Ailsa said, again studying the powder.

"What's that?"

"It is a very hard stone. It is very rare. I'm not familiar with any large deposits."

"That would make sense," Connor said. "If it's a secret power stone, they'd want to keep anyone else from knowing about it."

"Who?" Gisela asked. "Who is knowing this secret?"

"Dougal," Ailsa said. "Hector was his man, and he's devious enough to keep such a powerful secret." She fixed Connor with a grave look. "Yet another reason to tread with extreme caution. Dougal is not one to trifle with. He is perhaps the most dangerous man in the world."

What did that make Kilian?

He left them, torn about what to do next. His steps turned to Lord Nevan's palace. Thankfully, Shona was out, so he went to Jean's room. He shared what they'd learned about the secret powder, hoping she'd encourage him to test it, but she chose the restrictive, logical route.

"Are you daft? What if you accidentally established affinity with it? Connor, it would destroy you."

"You don't accidentally establish affinities," Connor said, but slid the powder back into the bag. If only Verena was there, she could test it with her Builder powers. That would prove something. Maybe.

"You can't risk it," Jean said. "Connor, this is the key we've been searching for, but this means that Dougal's been controlling unclaimed for decades. He's responsible for those attacks I've been studying."

"Unless someone else has been involved too. The other noble houses might know about this too. When you see Evander again, ask him if he's learned anything more."

"I'll go as soon as I can, but I can't today because. . ." Her voice trailed off and she actually blushed.

"Because why?"

"Because I have a date with Jok," she said quickly. "I have no choice, Connor. He insisted, and Shona approved."

Connor grimaced. He'd forgotten she had Jok to deal with. "Don't you have any herbs you can slip into his drink to make him sick?"

"I couldn't do that."

"Why not? It's not like you want to go out with him."

When she hesitated, he exclaimed, "You do want to go out with him?"

"No," she said quickly. "Well, not really. But Connor, he's only acted the gentleman. He's been very nice, and he gave me some jewelry to wear. It's beautiful."

"Don't trust him," Connor cautioned. He couldn't believe Jok was swaying her with pretty things. Jean was supposed to be smarter than other girls.

"I don't." She sighed. "I know it's a bad idea, but it's so nice to spend time with someone who appreciates me. Can't I enjoy myself just a little?"

How could he argue with that? They were neck deep in deadly intrigue all the time.

"Just be careful."

She kissed his cheek. "And you don't touch that powder."

Over the next two days, he struggled with that decision, considering it from every angle. The ultimate truth of the unclaimed was right there in his suite, but did he dare test it? He tried to focus on training his army, learning advanced leadership tactics from the Fast Rollers, and his personal training with Aonghus and Camonica.

His distraction and poor performance in training angered Camonica so much, she forgot to get annoyed with Cameron.

"The poetry's working," Cameron grinned after the instructors left on the third day. "Didn't you see that far-off look in her eye?"

"You've melted her brains," Tomas retorted. "I think I saw them leaking into that vat she fell into at the end."

That was all the excuse they needed to start bashing on each other. Connor laughed until they pulled him into the fight. He enjoyed the unrestrained bash fight that resulted, despite the fresh bruises. Sometimes pummeling a friend was the best way to settle one's nerves.

Ilse finally contacted him that evening and he eagerly met her beyond the northern outer wall, in a little box canyon half a mile into the mountains.

"I have news," Ilse said as she stepped into view from behind a huge piece of stone that had fallen from the cliffs years prior.

"Me too," Connor said. "I found Hector's secret stash of rage monster powder."

Ilse blinked. "You found powder?"

He nodded and revealed the pouch. Of course he'd left half of the powder back in his suite. He was eager to discuss his find with Ilse, but that didn't mean he trusted her. He dumped a little into his palm and showed it to Ilse and her team as they crowded close.

"What is it?" she asked.

"Ailsa thinks it may be porphyry. It definitely is some kind of power stone."

"Burn some of it," Ilse said.

"What? No. I only have a little."

"Trust me. Burn just a bit of it."

Frowning, Connor poured all but a thimble full of the powder back in the pouch, then tapped the marble already under his tongue. Flames erupted out of his palm and consumed the purplish grains. They burned readily, with an eerie reddish hue.

Ilse leaned over his hand and sniffed.

"What are you doing?" Connor asked. The powder smelled like charred flour.

"That's sufficient," Ilse said. "Turn off the fire. This confirms a report I just received from Kilian. A company of unclaimed, which they are now calling rampagers, attacked during a raid from Obrion."

"The war has started?" Connor felt sick. He had hoped to divert the war with the knowledge that patronage was a lie.

Ilse shook her head. "The nations are hovering on the brink, but the assault was only a diversion for the rampagers to strike."

That was a great name. Verena must be involved.

"That's not the action of an out-of-control rage monster," Connor pointed out.

"Indeed. Kilian set the trap to prove that point. Several of the monsters were captured and when they returned to human form, they were again coherent, if uncooperative."

She gave him a fierce grin. "With the help of your friend Hamish and your girl Verena, Kilian tracked the monsters that escaped. They fled deep into the mountains to a secret camp."

Connor smiled to hear that Hamish was well and working with Kilian. His heart sang to hear Ilse refer to Verena as his girl. If only that could ever be possible.

"Are you saying there were more of them?"

Ilse nodded. "Many more. Kilian's team destroyed the camp."

"Was have to be many good fight," Erich said with approval.

"How did they manage it?"

"I don't know the specifics, however Hamish recovered a charred sack of powder. The report stated that it smelled like burned flour. They haven't determined its true nature yet."

"This smelled like burned flour too," Connor noted.

"Indeed. It appears to confirm Kilian's report."

"I think this is another igneous stone," Connor said, extracting the pouch again and peering inside. "I believe it creates the rampagers and that High Lord Dougal and perhaps other high lords have used them to continue the lie of patronage and unclaimed."

"Evidence points in that direction."

He took a deep breath. "Then we need to prove our theory."

"How?"

"I need to test it."

Ilse considered that, then nodded. "I don't see any other way."

Connor grinned. He had expected Ilse to recognize the need. Of course, he usually considered her company certifiably insane.

It was a little scary to think about how often insanity offered the only chance of success.

Chapter 48

onnor's hand shook as he poured a tiny portion of porphyry into his palm. He removed his shirt and placed the pouch of powder on top. He was really going to do it. All his life, the threat of unclaimed had been like a weight around his neck, the chain of evil that made his curse a power to be feared. He had shackled his life to Shona and risked it in her service, all to avoid the dreaded loss of patronage.

Now he was planning to embrace his powers and prove they were no curse at all.

As he concentrated on the purplish grains in his hand, he thought back to that terrible day when Hector turned unclaimed. Other stones triggered marvelous powers, and he loved that feeling of wonder every time he embraced them. Could porphyry really be so different? Would it really transform him into a raging monster? Was it possible to retain his humanity?

Connor glanced at Ilse, who had retreated several paces, her expression grave. The rest of her team had also retreated, although Erich and Anika flanked him about a dozen paces to either side.

Anika winked and blew him a kiss. "Be many strong, Connor boy."

He tried to smile, but it came out more as a grimace. On the other side, Erich raised a clenched fist in salute. "Is good die bravery. If lose mind, I remove you head with many salute."

"Ah, thanks."

"Focus," Ilse urged. "You're a strong one, Connor. I do not believe any powder can consume your ability to control yourself."

"If this doesn't go well, tell Verena. . ."

"I will," Ilse said when he couldn't finish.

Connor focused again on the powder. He couldn't wait any longer. It was like leaping off the cliff above Loch Sholto. Waiting only made it harder to make the leap.

Of course, now with the loch broken and drained, that cliff hung over the edge of a much longer drop that was guaranteed to kill anyone leaping from it.

Not helping.

Connor willed the powder to open to him, drew it toward him like he did granite and basalt. It was hard to focus because the image of Hector's howling fangs kept popping into his mind. Trying to banish the terrifying image, he squeezed the powder into a fist and raised it high.

"Come on," he growled. "Show me what you can do."

Then he felt it.

The powder dug into his skin. Unlike the other igneous stones, it did not absorb and creep up his arm. Porphyry clawed its way under the skin like a hundred little teeth gnawing at his hand. He tried to release it, but his fist locked closed in a spasm of pain.

"This wasn't a good idea," he cried, shaking his hand, but unable to open it.

Ilse rushed forward. "Let it go, boy!"

His reply became a gasp. The porphyry reached his bloodstream and shot up his arm like liquid fire. It struck his heart, and his vision turned purple. Every muscle convulsed, and he threw his head back and howled.

The sound that came out should not have been possible.

His throat burned and he howled again with pain and fear, the sound reminding him of that cry of glorious horror he'd heard Hector make. That meant it was working, didn't it?

Connor's thoughts turned fuzzy and he heard his own voice as if from a great distance, the tortured cry turning more animal with each passing second. If it didn't hurt so much, he'd be really impressed.

His limbs burned, but he barely felt them. The world spun around him, and his pulse pounded loud in his ears. He tasted his own blood, and he smelled fear more clearly than ever before, a sharp, rank stench. Every inch of him ached, and he wasn't even sure he still stood. The world felt wrong. The air felt too cold, the grass underfoot too clear, the sounds of nearby voices too loud. It was terrifying.

Then the pain evaporated like steam from a flash fire, replaced by a rush of strength greater than anything he'd ever felt. He surged upright from the little ball he'd crumpled into, and euphoria roared through him. He felt more alive than he had ever dreamed possible. He threw back his head and howled, exulting in the terrifying sound that echoed back and forth from the mountains, as if the earth itself celebrated his glory.

Nearby voices drew his attention, as did renewed scents of fear. He hadn't been alone, had he? His thoughts were muddy, his vision tinted purple, and when he focused on the form of a hulking man standing nearby, he saw more than the outer shell. He saw the blood pumping through the man's rock-hard form, calling to him.

He wanted to drink it.

The impulse overwhelmed a strange sense of hesitation and he leaped upon the man, beating his puny arms aside, and lifting him high with claws like steel bands. He opened his mouth that had become a maw, and somehow he knew he could crunch right through the stone hard skin to the hot blood beneath.

Then his mouth filled with earth and the ground buckled under his feet, sending him tumbling and breaking his hold. He landed in soft earth that clung to his limbs, trying to restrain him.

Connor laughed, a wicked gurgling growl and tore the earth with claws and fangs, leaping out of the trap. A woman stood nearby, her heartbeat surprisingly calm.

"You are more than this," she stated, but the words barely registered. They were clear, but did not make sense. All that mattered was that she stood between him and the feast.

He'd eat her first.

With a cry of animal fury, he leaped the distance between them, but a wall of earth rose to block him. As he tore at it with frenzied hunger, arms of hardened earth grasped at his limbs.

Then the big man he had almost eaten rounded the earthen wall, carrying a large tree trunk.

"Finally we have fighting!" the man laughed as he wound up a mighty swing and clubbed Connor over the head. The blow drove him into the softened earth like a chisel struck by a mighty hammer, then the ground hardened around him. Even his incredible strength failed to free him.

Connor howled with rage and snapped at the hated humans. The big man hit him with the tree again, so hard two teeth shattered.

"Enough," the woman said. "You're enjoying yourself a bit more than is appropriate, Erich."

"Is respect for enemy," he protested. "Spank with tree for much glory."

"Just stop," she said, then peered at Connor. "You can understand me, can't you?"

Connor snapped at her, but she remained out of reach. He wanted to rage at them, tear them to pieces, but the momentary lack of mobility finally gave that whisper-soft voice in his mind a chance to speak.

He stopped growling and the woman leaned closer. "Show me you understand."

Thinking was hard. Biting was easier, so he bit at her.

Then pain spiked through him and he threw his head back, screaming with it. The sound changed abruptly into a human cry and he felt his jaw retracting. Changing bones hurt. A lot.

His hands and feet shrank back to normal and his body convulsed. It felt like he was getting pounded by his father's hammer everywhere at once, and he clenched his eyes against the pain.

Then it disappeared and he lay gasping in the earthen prison, exhausted beyond reason. He felt empty, like a skeleton wrapped in skin, but lacking anything in between.

"Are you all right?" Ilse asked, dropping to a knee beside him. He knew her voice now.

"Ow," he groaned.

Erich lifted him to his feet. The big Rumbler peered closely at him. "Is Connor boy again?"

"Next time I hit you with the tree."

Erich laughed and clapped him on the shoulder, sending him sprawling. Anika lifted him again and gave him a hug. She kissed his cheek. "Was many brave. Good boy come back."

"Thanks." He tensed, waiting for her to hit him or something. It was so unlike Anika to act like a woman instead of a force of destruction.

When she released him, Ilse said, "So you were conscious the whole time?"

"Sort of. It was like a nightmare." He tried to explain how it felt, how hard it had been to think.

"You need practice," Ilse said. "If rampagers could assault a specific target, they must have developed control over the raw animal emotions that overwhelmed you."

"Makes sense."

"Good." She gave him an encouraging nod. "Then what are you waiting for? Try again."

"Now?"

"If you hadn't noticed, we don't have a lot of time," she said. "The howling might draw attention, although I don't sense anyone approaching yet. That little bit of powder kept you transformed for about four minutes. Try the same amount again."

It took a moment to gather his courage for the second attempt. He realized his teeth had re-formed when he returned to human form. That was encouraging enough that he took another handful of powder.

The second attempt went no better than the first. Ilse was ready for him, and he didn't even get a chance to try eating anyone. Erich was gracious enough to let Anika take turns beating him in the head with the tree trunk. They explained later that they were doing research into exactly how much effort it would take to defeat a real rampager, but they seemed far too eager to get him to transform again.

Dietmar offered them the use of his meteor hammer, but Anika urged him to join the beating instead. Margrit refused the offer to throw rocks, insisting she needed to keep watch.

Ilse kept speaking to him, urging control, reminding him who he was. It was really annoying when he was in the grip of the rampager madness. On his fourth attempt, she changed tactics.

"Think of Verena, boy. Remember her. Be strong or you could hurt her."

That name drove through the purple haze of madness and Connor quieted his wild thrashings in the earthen prison. Erich took the opportunity to hit him again with a tree, and his head rang so hard from the blow, he forgot where he was for a moment.

"Don't kill him," Ilse's voice floated into his rattled ears from a great distance. "I think he's finally getting the hang of it."

"Then I need turn," Anika exclaimed. "Before monster no monster."

Connor forced open one eye in time to see Anika swing the tree with far too much eagerness, grinning as she clobbered him into oblivion.

When he woke up, Connor had returned to human form and the group was gathered around him, looking worried.

"See," Anika laughed when Connor blinked open his eyes and groaned against a splitting headache. "Research many success. And boy is no die."

After a couple of minutes under the gentle warmth of his sandstone pendant, Connor almost felt human again. The transformation restored his bones and teeth, but why hadn't it purged his headache?

"I reached you last time, didn't I?" Ilse asked.

"I'm not sure. I got clobbered so much, the memory is all busted to pieces."

"One more try," Ilse urged, then glanced at the sibling Petralists. "No more hitting."

Anika looked crestfallen. Erich held up a single thick finger. "Hit only two times?"

"No," Ilse said. "You've done enough research. I need to know he can maintain control."

That fifth try was different. Despite the purple haze that descended over him, Connor maintained a shred of sanity by chanting Verena's name in his mind. The image of the deadly cute Builder was like a shield against the storm of rage.

Ilse did not imprison him, but the siblings flanked him, trees poised to strike.

"Are you in control?" Ilse asked.

Speaking was difficult. Connor tried to say, "What do you think?" The words got corrupted in his throat and came out as a long growl with mushed together syllables.

Ilse frowned. "I take it whabba-zoobing means yes in rampager."

He tried again, but Erich burst into laughter. "What is meaning monkey bottom soup? Is many funny."

Seeing the big man laughing at him triggered a burning rage that overwhelmed Connor's fledgling control. He shot across the distance and punched Erich so hard, the huge warrior tumbled through a stand of nearby trees. One of them slowly topped after and landed on him as he stood up, driving him off his feet again. Erich's shouted curses echoed around the clearing.

Connor turned back to the others, and the rush of satisfaction from pounding Erich helped him regain control. He silently laughed, long tongue lolling.

"It did sound like that," Ilse said.

His powder ran out then, but he managed to remain standing as his body shifted back to human. It still hurt worse than pulling out all his teeth with a frozen fish, but he was learning to handle it.

"What happened?" Ilse asked.

"I had it," he said. "Emotions are raw and far more powerful. Erich's laughter triggered a violent rage. The vocals don't really work."

"We noticed," Anika smiled.

"Work on control," Ilse said. "But not unless we're nearby. You can't afford to rampage through the school."

"It hurt too much to try again soon." It was a thrilling sort of terror riding that ultimate edge of control.

"This secret must be shared, and we must be able to prove you can control it."

Connor had consumed much of his powder store. He'd have to manage the rest carefully.

"Patronage really is a lie," he said.

"I'd say we've proven it," Ilse said, crouching next to him. "There's nothing keeping you here at the school."

"There is," Connor said as a single thought became clear. "I'm not done here yet."

"You can leave," Ilse urged. "Study this with Kilian and the Builders. Our work is done here."

He shook his head. "Even if we could slip away from Evander, which I'm not convinced we can, he's running another geall that I need to see to the end."

"What's his plan?" Ilse asked.

"It's tied to deeper secrets and a broader conspiracy, I think. It was a bit cryptic."

"Tell me."

"Later," he said, not wanting to share everything with Ilse. He felt sure that the messages embedded in that Sentry speak had been intended for his ears alone. He glanced at the small team. "We can't just run. Don't you see? This lie has been imprisoning my people for decades. I need to find out who's in league with Dougal and figure out how to flip this geall back on them."

"You can't do that alone," Ilse said.

"No, I can't." He rose and gripped her shoulder. "I'm going to need your help."

"Well, let's not dawdle," Ilse said. "You should know, I've sensed the elements stirring on the mountain. We may not have much time."

Connor glanced around nervously. "You're speaking of elfonnel, aren't you?"

"I felt something I've never sensed before," she said, looking grave. "I don't want to be anywhere near here if the elements rise in anger."

"That makes it even more important to finish this."

"What are you planning?" Ilse asked, for once not arguing.

"Let's meet again after you report to Kilian."

"You need a better way to contact me," Ilse said. "I believe it's time I teach you to summon."

"Like that stone pedra?" That monster had nearly kidnapped Shona, and had been inspiring and terrifying at the same time.

She smiled. "Kilian did the bulk of the work on that one. No, we will start small, with squirrels or pigeons. I will teach you to form them, then you can send them to find me."

"Where? The mountain is a big place."

When she hesitated, he raised an eyebrow. "Really? I'm out here testing secret rampager powder. If I was going to betray you, I would've done it by now."

"Very well." Pointing east she said, "Follow that ridge away from the school. It'll empty onto a wide plateau that extends over a long canyon. In the center is a ruined fort. Send your summoned creature there."

"Okay. So how do I do it?"

"Granite gives them form, the elements provide the life blood, your will grants them life."

"That's why the pedra bled water?"

"Exactly. You can use any element, although some work better with certain animals. For example, the best birds are usually conjured using quartzite, whereas the best squirrels use earth."

Connor wanted to sleep for a year, but he was eager to learn the secret. "I'm not sure I can focus enough to make it work. Turning unclaimed isn't as easy as I make it look."

Ilse barked a laugh. "If that was easy, I'm glad I can't do it." Then she turned serious. "Focus, boy. Time is short. Enemies are closing around us, and the very elements of this mountain are stirring. Trust me, we don't have time to waste."

She needed to work on her motivational speeches.

Chapter 49

onnor's sleep was filled with dreams of turning unclaimed, of embracing that terrifying and exhilarating experience and rampaging through the school, eating screaming Petralists. He woke up feeling strangely satisfied.

Patronage really was a lie. That should have changed everything, but although that shackle was broken, Shona still maintained the threat against Jean, Ailsa, and his entire village. Somehow, he had to work out his escape and reveal to the world the truth about the unclaimed.

It would be easier to tame a pedra and teach it to herd sheep.

Tomas entered his suite as he was attempting to eat a mountainous breakfast. He wished, as he did at every meal, for Hamish's enthusiastic appetite to help with the feasts.

"Best take care to stay masked up, boy," Tomas said. "Too many spies around to keep them all out today."

"I thought you had a working schedule."

He shrugged. "Nobles are growing frantic, and they hate calling you General Anxiety."

"All part of the plan," Connor said, saluting with a thick slab of bacon.

Tomas clapped him on the shoulder, "Not to worry, lad. You're not the only one who can put on a good show." At Connor's questioning look he added, "We've been regaling the spies with some of your peculiarities."

Connor's heart sank. "Which ones?"

"Oh, nothing too wild." Tomas tapped the side of his nose and winked. "There's an art to a proper yarn. You've got to work them up to the really good stuff. Start too fast and they'll realize it's all made up."

"You really don't have to do that. . ." Connor began.

Tomas laughed. "Course we do. Helps explain needing to wear a mask too. We told them the condition's not contagious, but they probably don't want to see what it does to a man's face." He turned to leave, but paused in the doorway. "Any way you can limp a little on the left when you meet your army today?"

"Why?"

"It'd help everyone believe that leg is shorter."

"Why would my leg. . .?" He sighed. "I'll see what I can do."

"Knew I could count on you, lad."

When he opened the door, a woman was standing there, one hand raised to knock. She was quite a sight, with battle leathers highlighting a shapely figure, her face concealed by a white, leather mask. Her hair was an unnaturally bright red color, tied in a complex braid hanging over the front of her shoulder.

"Beg your pardon, ma'am," Tomas said with a little bow, "But no unauthorized visitors allowed."

The woman in the doorway didn't speak, but glanced past Tomas to Connor. As soon as he looked into those bright blue eyes he knew. How could Ilse take such a risk? Someone would surely recognize Anika, even with the dyed hair.

"Uh, she's with me," Connor said quickly.

Tomas glanced back at him, incredulous. "I think I'd remember seeing her."

"She's, uh, a new part of Shona's plan. Just arrived from Merkland." He blurted out the first idea that might explain her presence. "She's a mute daor."

"Imagine that," Tomas muttered, studying her again.

For her part, Anika did a remarkable job not entering the room and clobbering Connor senseless, but she didn't look happy. Tomas must have noticed the slight shifting in her stance or how her body flowed for a terrifying heartbeat into the perfect lines of granite. She recovered quickly and made a curt bow she probably considered humble.

"Why would you need a mute daor, and a masked one at that?" Tomas asked.

Connor shrugged. "When you figure out Lady Shona, explain her to me some time."

"Don't go there, lad," Tomas said with a grimace. "Any man who pretends to understand women is a lying fool. Look at Cameron."

"I'll call if I need anything," Connor said.

Tomas looked from him to Anika. "You sure?"

"I'll send her out shortly."

Tomas shrugged. "As you wish." He waved Anika into the room and as he left, his voice carried back to Connor, "Brilliant. Why didn't we think of adding mutes?"

Anika closed the door and rounded on Connor. "I break you tiny head if you think make me slave."

"I'm sorry. It was the only idea I could think of."

"Bad think idea." She motioned him to one of the overstuffed chairs in the sitting room. "Come, we talk many fast. Make plan."

"What are you doing here?" he blurted as he cautiously settled into the chair close to her. He was amazed Tomas hadn't recognized her striking figure. The white mask and bright red hair lent her a mysterious air but at the same time added a new overtone of recklessness.

"You can't have heard from Kilian already," he said.

She shook her head. That color really was ghastly on her. "Need monster powder."

"I don't have a lot left."

"Will send some Kilian. Clever Builders make study."

That was a good idea. He should have thought of that. Verena could ferret out more about that powder in a week than he could in a year. He retrieved the little pouch of porphyry from the secret safe in his bedchamber and poured a small handful into another pouch.

"Would be many better you came too," she said as she accepted the pouch.

"I can't. There are things here that need sorting. I can't do that hiding in Granadure."

"Time is much short," she insisted. "Best defeat rampagers as team."

Working in tandem with Kilian and the Builders might accelerate their progress. Plus, he yearned to see Verena again and would love to catch up with Hamish.

"I'll think about it."

Could he trust Kilian? The man knew the deeper mysteries, but Connor had learned not to trust anyone's motives at face value. Then there was Camonica's story that he'd learned from Aonghus.

"Together, can make raid," Anika insisted, her eyes glowing with eagerness. "Make Dougal pay for evil and stop war."

"When you send your note to Kilian, ask him a question for me."

"What?"

"Ask him if he really killed Dougal's wife and Spit-nail Camonica's husband."

"How know this?" Anika asked.

"I hear things. Is it true?"

She shrugged. "Many die in battle."

"They weren't in battle. I heard they were studying the deep magic, and he killed them."

"Why care? No is important."

"It could be. I need to know."

"No is important," Anika repeated. "If stay, if win, cannot escape evil plan. Breed for blood gift."

"I'll leave before that," he promised.

"Is dangerous game."

"Tell me about it." Who was she to talk? She was standing in the heart of enemy territory and would be tortured or killed if caught.

"No good thing take woman without even wrestle."

"We do things a little different here."

She frowned. "Yes, you bad ways."

"Our country isn't all bad," he insisted.

"Kill head of snake, can eat body."

"I prefer to think I'm trying to start a change."

"Revolution many good," she agreed, clenching her fist. "When decide come, we help. You die. Shona no your family hurt if you dead."

Connor tensed. Hadn't she gotten enough fun beating him with that tree?

Anika noted his response and flashed a white-toothed smile. "No we wrestle. I no kill. Not yet. You die on battle."

"Dying on the battlefield won't help me escape."

She gave him a mischievous wink. "Die but no die. Is fake. You leave. No you family hurt."

That was probably the best plan for escape. He'd managed to die once before, and for a time it had allowed him precious freedom. It would take a lot to convince Shona he was really gone, but since the lie of patronage no longer held him to her will, it might be time to try escape by death.

He'd have to die spectacularly to make it work.

"I'll work on it," he promised. "Let me know if you have ideas."

A knock on door interrupted her response. Connor rose to answer it, but Anika motioned him back down. "I pretend servant."

"Don't hurt anyone."

She made no promises as she moved to the door. If nothing else, her masked figure would definitely surprise any self-important high lord representative who might have talked their way past Tomas and Cameron.

Anika opened the door and Connor's good mood vanished. No high lord stood there.

It was Captain Rory.

Chapter 50

Anika's disguise didn't fool Rory for more than a single surprised heartbeat.

She punched him in the face.

Even as he rocked back under the blow, both of their bodies shifted with granite power. Rory's muscles swelled and the creaking of the leather plates of his battle armor sounded like the opening of Tallan's own fury to Connor. While the captain's skin faded to gray, Anika's faded to more like pearl. Her body shifted into the perfect lines of the granite goddess that had terrified Connor since the first time he subdued her in the dark wood beside the Lower Wick.

Rory lunged, and Anika slipped inside his fist and tried to throw him. He was ready for the move and wrapped his arms around her waist. The two of them staggered into the room, grappling close together, straining to gain advantage.

Connor absorbed granite, but as his curse skittered through his torso like a thousand itching insects, he hesitated. He didn't dare interfere. Either of the two could tear him apart in a head-on bash fight. What really gave him pause though was their expressions.

Rory was openly grinning as he wrestled with Anika, and she started to laugh. Not an evil or triumphant laugh, but just a laugh of simple joy as she pitted her strength against his and they staggered together into the center of the sitting room.

Rory grunted. "Give up, lass. No one to save you this time."

Anika head-butted him.

The impact tore off her mask and let her bright red hair spill down over her shoulders in an unrestrained wave. The sound of their rock-hard faces smacking together was like the sharp crack of a granite block splitting under the chisels of workers in the blocking yard. Although Rory looked unharmed by the blow, it must have shifted his grip a little because Anika twisted and, with a roll of her hips, tossed Rory over one shoulder.

He sprang back to his feet, but she picked up a couch and clobbered him with it. Rory fell back over a padded chair, which splintered under his weight, and came up spitting couch padding.

Anika blew him a kiss. "Come now, mine capitain, no fight so gentle. Prove me strong hands."

"You asked for it," he said with a grin as he picked up an intricately carved cast-iron lamp and threw it like a javelin.

She batted it aside, but the distraction cost her just enough for Rory to tackle her right through the mortared stone wall and into Connor's bedroom. Anika stumbled to the floor and Rory ripped off one of the thick oak bedposts and beat her with it until it splintered.

Then he tossed her into the air like a child. In a move similar to one Tomas had once used on Ivor, he yanked her around by one arm like a weight on the end of a rope and drove her head-first into the stone floor so hard she shattered it, face sinking several inches.

She lay quiet, and Connor approached, fearing Rory had actually injured her. Rory must have thought the same thing because he gently lifted her by the back of her leathers and brushed back her hair.

Anika grabbed his face and pulled him into a fierce kiss.

Rory's body stiffened with surprise and his grip loosened. She dropped to the floor and punched him in the mouth with every ounce of strength. The blow toppled him over backward and Anika grabbed his feet, spun, and launched him into the outer wall. He slammed into the solid stone with a resounding crash and slid down, head first.

Anika stood in the center of the wrecked bedroom, grinning like a maid during the Sogail. "You good wrestle."

Rory climbed back to his feet, wiping dust from his face. "You're a pretty good challenge too, but what did you do to your hair?"

She frowned and lifted a lock to inspect. "We try brown but Erich no make good soup."

He grimaced. "I hope it washes out."

"Yes, wash soon but first break you heart."

The two launched themselves at each other again, but Connor was ready. Their unique form of flirting might be great for them, but they were wrecking his rooms. While they talked, he had downed a vial of soapstone and drew upon the pulsing current of its elemental power to pull a thick stream of water right out of one of the giant tubs in his nearby training hall.

Just as the two collided and began grappling in moves that Connor swore looked more like awkward embraces, he wrapped them both with the water and hardened it to ice. They ended up locked together, faces scant inches apart, unable to move. Neither of them looked too upset.

"Connor, let us go," Rory ordered, eyes locked on Anika's.

"I'm sorry sir, but you need to let her leave."

"I can't do that."

"You good wrestle," Anika said softly, then bit the end of his nose. "But I kill you before you make prison."

Rory tried to bite her back, but couldn't quite reach. "Let me go, Connor," he snapped.

Connor softened the ice around Anika until she could slip out, but didn't let Rory go. The captain started staining against the ice and it began to crack. Connor reinforced it with the extra water that had been holding Anika.

Anika leaned close to Rory and kissed his cheek. "Erich must make duty of brother to defend mine honor. Will try kill you."

"He's welcome to try," Rory said.

She nodded. "I tell him. Try no kill and we wrestle again."

"Go," Connor told her. Rory looked calm, but within the ice he began redoubling his efforts. When determined, he was a force to be reckoned with, and not even all that ice would hold him much longer.

"Good bye, Connor boy," she said, then blew Rory a final kiss. "Goodbye, mine capitain."

"I will catch you," he promised.

She flashed him a happy smile and trotted out of the suite.

Only after another full minute did Connor release Rory. The captain rubbed his numbed arms as he returned to normal size.

"I'm sorry, sir but they'll be leaving soon and--"

"Enough, lad," Rory said. "We both know they won't leave without taking you with them, or killing you. When she returns, I must stop her."

"I think she wants you to try."

Rory grinned and slapped Connor on the back. "Aye, lad. No doubt."

His smile faded into a scowl. "Makes my job downright complicated."

Chapter 51

he next week passed in a blur for Connor, filled with personal training, army training, and meeting with his captains. Winning in the next battle would generate enormous momentum, but should he attempt to do that, or pursue Ivor's plan to upset the Tir-raon instead?

He, Ivor, and Padraigin had tried to meet again to discuss more details, but Redmund had burst in on their conference almost immediately. His spies were getting better.

Connor had downplayed their secret meeting, telling Redmund, "We were testing the effectiveness of your spy channels. Not bad, except Padraigin beat your time by almost two minutes."

Redmund hadn't seemed convinced, but Ivor and Connor launched into a Sentry-speak contest that Redmund couldn't resist entering. He did end up winning, but Connor came in a close second when he declared, "The full measure of the wind is tested only when the mountain tempts the heights, but the treasure of a whisper is most precious over the scent of a fresh-baked cookie."

Connor kept the thoughts of intentionally finishing in second place secret. He trained his army to win, and they made him proud with their progress. Could he really consider letting them down?

He discussed the conundrum with Ailsa, but she only helped him see more of the potential benefits and the risks of both possible choices. Finally, she shrugged and said, "You alone must decide this course, Son. Think deep before you do. Are the risks of potential victory overshadowed by the dangers of intentional defeat?"

While he mulled that over, his schedule grew busier than ever. Thankfully, Ailsa assigned her depressed student, Edan, to take over the daily rounds. So focused were the students on their preparations for the next battle, few seemed to even notice.

Connor felt a bit offended by that. Did his work all season with the rounds, with sacrificing so much blood to Catriona's wrath, with betting at the Rhidorroch and training Striders to shoot account for so little?

Through it all, he watched for signs of the broader struggle Evander had suggested they were waging. Searching for something before he knew what it was proved difficult, and added to his sense of growing frustration. The more he learned, the less he seemed to know.

To lighten his darkening mood, Connor announced an impromptu Strider shooting day during the next army training. He loved firing arrows at Lorcc and the other fast movers of his army, and it warmed his heart to see how eager they were for him to shoot at them.

He actually hit one young Strider. Everyone gathered around the sobbing student while Aifric tended to the arrow in his posterior. Connor felt bad, but the boy took so much grief from the other students for not dodging the arrow that he apologized to Connor for failing.

"It's all right," Connor assured him. "I'll shoot you again some other time, I promise."

The porphyry concealed in his suite was another constant distraction. He felt a surprisingly powerful urge to absorb some again, even though he knew that would be disastrous without Ilse around. Each day the urge grew a little stronger. He hadn't figured out yet how to reveal the secret without getting instantly buried by Evander. Nor had he figured out how to fake his death well enough to fool Shona and escape to Granadure.

He spent a lot of time imagining different ways to die and how to pull them off, though. One time Aifric noticed his faraway look during one of the captain meetings while Shona and Catriona were arguing.

When she asked him what he was thinking about he muttered, "Nothing. Just planning a fitting eulogy."

"We're not dead yet," she whispered, and the intensity of her gaze surprised him. She was more complex than she pretended, and he was glad she was on his team.

He drew confidence from the progress of his army. He'd pit his troops against any other army in a heartbeat, if only those troops didn't have so many Sentries. That was one of the strongest arguments for allying with Ivor and Padraigin.

He was proud of Declan. The pudgy little Sentry had improved dramatically. He could already raise a tower as strong as any other student, and he was walking the earth with so much confidence, he almost spoke with Sentry-worthy roundabout obscurity. It looked like all he'd needed was a taste of success.

As much as Declan was progressing, he could never hope to stand alone against the Sentries of the other armies. Maybe Connor could dress Ilse in a mask and battle leathers and sneak her into his army?

He nearly laughed at that idea. No doubt she'd find a way to usurp control from him and send the entire army pillaging through the school.

Of all his forces, Shona worried him the most. She treated him well, almost too well, during their meetings, and she followed orders without question when he posed as General Anxiety. She never mentioned Anika's visit to his suite, although Rory must have informed her of it.

Either she finally believed he was fully committed to her, or she felt the threat posed by Ilse and her little company was contained. So he lay awake late into the night considering plan after useless plan. He couldn't wait. He had to come up with some solution, or Shona would own him.

It was in that state that he stood at the head of his assembled army on a sunny but cool morning just over a week later, awaiting the details of the mock battle to be fought that day. Despite his best efforts, he had failed to ferret out any advance information about the upcoming conflict from Rory or Tomas or Cameron. They'd just smiled and said it wouldn't be fair to give him such an advantage.

When did they start worrying about being fair? Their timing was terrible.

When he'd tried asking Aonghus, the Firetongue had laughed and spat a ball of fire in his face. Camonica just looked furious.

Donald, the leader of Rory's Striders, skidded to a stop in front of Connor and handed over the official declaration of battle. Connor thanked him and unrolled the parchment with his captains hovering eagerly over his shoulders. His heart fell through his boots and for the first time he was grateful for the concealing shield of his leather mask.

Fearghas grunted. "Sounds pretty straight forward."

"Agreed," said Lorcc who bounced in place beside the Blade. "I've run that plateau. Can't hardly call those ruins a fort. Ruined outer walls, barely a building standing."

"The trick'll be getting in and out before the others," Heber said. "Even if they don't work together against us, this type of operation leaves us at a forty-three percent disadvantage." At the others' disapproving frowns he added, "Well, it would if we didn't have General Anxiety."

The only thing abundantly clear to Connor was that the battle would be anything but straight forward. The battle plan sounded like the entire school was being mobilized to assault the very hideout where Ilse had told him she was using.

How had Rory found out? Tomas and Cameron had never come to investigate his fight with Anika in Connor's suite, despite how much racket they made. Had they been tasked with tracking Anika instead?

If Ilse hadn't abandoned that location, they were in for a very bad day. He studied the rules of engagement, and a plan began to take shape in his mind. Perhaps he could leverage his conspiracy with Ivor and Padraigin in a way to give Ilse and her team a chance to escape.

"What's your plan?" Fearghas asked as they prepared to follow Padraigin's army east across the rolling plain toward a distant sally port.

"I'll let you know before we arrive."

The rules were fairly simple. They needed to race the other armies to the ruined fort in the center of the plateau and capture the standard flying there. They must subdue any defenders and turn them over to Rory's army, then retreat to their original starting position with the captured standard. Points would be awarded for completing each of the objectives.

More important than how Rory knew Ilse was camped on that plateau was why would Rory risk the lives of the students by sending them to take that fort? Ilse and her tiny band would fight to the death before allowing themselves to be taken. The students' ignorance could very easily kill them.

He learned the answer to that question when he reached the plateau and began leading his army toward the far northern edge. Rory's army already stood in battle formation on the plateau, barely a quarter mile from the dilapidated fortress on its low hill. At the first signs of resistance, they would swarm the hill and take Ilse.

Why hadn't they done it yet?

He glanced at Shona, and she smiled warmly. Did she have anything to do with the battle plan? Would she really risk his position in the Tir-raon to help arrange a test of his loyalties? He couldn't betray Ilse, but he couldn't afford to openly oppose Rory. He was grouted on both sides.

Connor arranged his army at the northern edge of the plateau, closest to the towering bulk of Mount Murdo, but farthest from the broken-down fort a full half mile away. Directly across from his position, Ivor held the southern edge where it fell away into near-vertical cliffs. His army was positioned closest to the fort at just over a quarter mile. Redmund held the eastern side above more steep terrain, while Padraigin held the west, closest to the school.

By the time Connor's army arrived at the fort, the standard would already be captured and Ilse's band would be discovered and subdued.

"It's hopeless," Heber said nearby. "I can't make the numbers work in our favor."

"What can we do, General?" Fearghas asked.

Connor grinned, embracing the one insane idea forming in his mind.

"We cheat, of course."

Chapter 52

It took only a moment for his disciplined troops to assemble as he commanded. He arranged the Boulders in a tight formation of four close-packed columns, with the Solas and his captains in front. The Striders waited in pairs twenty feet out from the Boulders. Declan stood at the rear, looking nervous but determined.

"The key will be reaching the fortress fast," Connor told the army. "Be prepared to improvise."

"You'll catch 'em by surprise again, General," Catriona shouted, eliciting a cheer.

"Let's hope. If this works, you'll all get the bash fight you've been wanting."

Another cheer.

"They'll still think they can overwhelm us, but we can win through, despite the odds."

Even Heber cheered, although only half-heartedly. Thankfully he kept his depressing statistics to himself.

Connor took his place at the head of the army, downed a vial of soapstone, and shoved a piece of marble into his mouth. If only he could know if Ilse was still in the fort or not.

Time to find out.

In that moment a bright starburst exploded above one of the Sentry towers at the forefront of Rory's company, signaling the start of the competition.

"Now!" Connor shouted.

The close-packed soldiers linked arms, forming a single, tight column. The ground rumbled, then shook, nearly knocking some students sprawling as it heaved upward into a steep hill. Connor tapped soapstone and pulled streamers of water from the nine water bladders his Boulders carried. He spread it under everyone's feet and hardened the bottom layers to ice, leaving the top fraction of an inch liquid to help make the slope slippery.

The entire column began sliding forward together down the steep slope. Before the front ranks could slam into the ground at the base of the hill, Declan rolled the hill forward through the ground, allowing them to slide onto the newly-raised earth.

Their slide accelerated rapidly over the smooth ice, driven by so much weight down the continuously shifting earth. Within seconds, they accelerated across the plain so fast on the moving hill the Striders in full fracked sprint could barely keep up.

As they began to slide, Connor whooped. It was working! The hot wind dragging tears from his eyes smelled of fresh-turned earth, and Connor shouted again. Fearghas took up the cry and it spread through the army until they roared across the plain at full volume, sounding like they had left their brains packed in boxes and waiting for their return.

If they were to have any chance at winning, they needed a little insanity. Neither Padraigin nor Redmund had shifted to attack him directly. The need to reach the fort and secure the standard overrode any other concerns.

As fast as Connor's army was moving, they still wouldn't beat Ivor to the fort. The clever champion had borrowed Connor's tactic from the last battle and laid down a pathway of ice over which all of his Striders pulled sleds bearing Boulders.

Copying was a sign of respect, right? Ivor would arrive first, but only with a fraction of his army. That was a calculated risk. If he could win the standard quickly enough and escape before the other armies arrived, the battle would end almost before it began.

If something slowed him down, he could end up a prisoner of war and lose spectacularly. It was clear he hadn't planned for Connor to speed across the plateau so fast with his entire army. Worse, there was no way he was ready for Ilse if she was indeed trapped in the fort.

Both Redmund and Padraigin must have realized they were hopelessly too slow. The only chance their armies could win the day was to change tactics, so they both turned south. If they moved fast, they could intercept Ivor as he attempted to return to his army with the standard. Their challenge was now to take him and the standard. If either of them could pull that off, they'd snatch victory away from Ivor at the last moment.

That was fine with Connor. The fewer people fighting in the ruins the better. He still hadn't decided what he would do if Ilse was really there, but the situation was looking just a bit more promising.

Then the ground just in front of Redmund's army collapsed in a cloud of dust. For a second, Connor wondered if Padraigin or one of Ivor's Sentries was trying to slow Redmund down. As the dust cleared he realized the truth with a new wave of dread. The ground had dropped into a narrow trench leading back toward the fort, as if a tunnel had collapsed.

Had Ilse dug that secret tunnel as her escape route? If she hadn't already passed through it, she was now trapped.

There was nothing Connor could do but assess the situation when he arrived. So he focused on making sure his army continued its rapid progress. Declan was grimacing with the strain, but he maintained the rapid pace, shifting enough earth to make any Sentry proud.

When they reached the north side of the low hill upon which the fort sat, Declan flattened their hill. That close to the fort, the curve of the hill concealed them from Ivor's army. With the other two armies already heading south to intercept Ivor's soon-to-be fleeing forces, Connor and his people were momentarily alone.

Connor split his forces and sent Shona and half the army around the east side of the hill, while Catriona led an identical party to the west, with Striders flanking them both. Their orders were simple. Cut off Ivor's smaller force and knock them all out of the battle.

"Declan, give them what cover you can," Connor ordered, then ran for the fort at the top of the hill. "Fearghas, on me."

Connor scrambled over the broken outer wall and paused to survey the area, hoping and fearing to find Ilse. The fort consisted of little more than a broken down keep, surrounded by piles of rubble that had been outbuildings. The back half of the keep had collapsed, but the front section still stood. It leaned so far over, it would have surely fallen years ago if not for a thick oak tree buttressing the front corner. Part of the roof remained, although huge holes gaped through.

Fearghas flanked him several yards to the left and signaled the all clear. Directly across from them, Ivor and Jok jumped the broken-down remains of the southern section of wall, about two hundred yards away.

He hoped Ivor was in a cooperating mood. Waving Fearghas to stay behind him, he trotted toward Ivor, hands raised in a sign of peace.

"What's the plan, General?" Fearghas whispered. "I can take Jok if you can subdue Ivor."

"The plan is a bit more complex than that. Just follow my lead."

Fearghas groaned. "Can't anything be straight-forward with you?"

"I wouldn't want to disappoint."

Ivor strolled toward Connor with water and fire flickering back and forth between his half-raised hands. "Another impressive trick, General. You realize, every general from now on is going to copy that tactic when they have to move an army at speed?"

"They can try," Connor said. "But will they have the flair to make it work?"

"I don't really have time to chat," Ivor said. "Are you offering a surrender?"

"I'm offering a deal. You take the standard. I find any defenders and deal with them."

Both Jok and Fearghas looked stunned, but Ivor laughed. "Are you expecting me to argue?"

Connor extended his hand. "Deal?"

Ivor took it, grinning. "Jok, find that standard and let's get out of here."

"Go help him," Connor told Fearghas. The Blade looked confused, but obeyed. Together, the two disappeared into the dilapidated fort, the only place where a standard could be concealed.

Connor had already tapped quartzite and scanned the area with enhanced hearing, but found nothing. If Ilse was still there, she was hiding. He doubted they'd jump out and attack the two students unless provoked.

"That was a little obvious, don't you think?" Ivor asked when they were alone.

"Not enough time for subtlety, I'm afraid," Connor replied. "I'll have to explain it somehow to Fearghas."

"I don't see any defenders," Ivor said. "Capturing some would guarantee second place. It was a good idea, as long as they haven't all left."

Connor would accept defeat if it meant Ilse was already gone.

Jok ran out of the Keep, holding the standard high and pumping his other fist in victory. Fearghas followed him, looking like he wanted to tackle Jok and steal the flag.

"See you later, General." Ivor saluted, then raced back to the ruined southern wall and clambered over with Jok in tow.

"Why did you let them go?" Fearghas demanded. "We could have taken them?"

"Ivor left most of his army behind," Connor reminded him. "Our forces will cut him off while Redmund and Padraigin engage the bulk of his army. Ivor will get bogged down dealing with all of that. We'll have time to find the defenders and subdue them."

Ilse's voice pulled him around. "I might have something to say about that."

She and her team stood in the doorway of the broken-down keep. They did not look friendly.

Chapter 53

earghas grabbed Connor's arm, "Quick, General. Let's take them!"

"Go," Connor ordered him. "Find Shona and tell her to rally the troops and get that standard. I'll deal with this group."

Connor was relieved when Fearghas didn't argue, but only said, "Hurry, General, or Captain Rory will steal the prize."

Connor followed Fearghas' pointing finger. Sure enough, Rory and his army were bearing down on the fortress, but the student armies were crashing together right in front of him, blocking his path.

The standard blew into the air on a Pathfinder-generated wind. Somehow Jok must have lost his grip on it, and the armies scrambled for it. Their organized ranks disintegrated into a chaotic bash fight as students scrambled to recover the precious flag.

"Go," Connor repeated and Fearghas sprinted away.

Ilse advanced on him, flanked by the scowling siblings.

"I'd hoped you had gotten away," he said.

"You shouldn't have brought an army to check," she growled.

"It wasn't me," he said quickly before Erich and Anika could close on him. "I don't know who discovered you, but we've only got seconds before Rory arrives to take you."

Erich cracked his knuckles and shared a fierce grin with Anika. "Many hurt, much break heads."

"You don't have time," Connor repeated. "The flag won't distract them for long."

They allowed him to prod them north around the keep, then they ran for the eastern edge of the compound, away from the fighting.

"Why the interest in the silly flag?" Ilse asked as they ran.

"It's part of the game."

"So if we get it, we win?" she asked.

The keep blocked Rory from view, but no doubt he was coming fast. "Rory won't let you win."

"What do you suggest?" Ilse asked, looking like she still wasn't convinced he wasn't part of the assault.

"Trust me and don't struggle too hard."

"If you betray us," Ilse said in a stone-cold voice. "I will be forced to follow my secondary objective."

"Just play along."

At her terse nod, he tapped marble and ignited the old keep. It caught fire like it had been waiting for a chance to burn for decades, and a thick column of dense smoke billowed out. He tapped quartzite and drew an eager wind down to blow the heavy smoke back over the battlefield. Hopefully that would help conceal what he was doing.

Then he wrapped each of the Grandurians in sheets of ice from neck to toe and began sliding those prisons of ice northeast along a flowing sheet of water. It took only seconds to clear the wall and descend the hill. On flat ground, he jumped onto the water next to the ice prisons and rode, increasing their pace until they slid across the ground as fast as a galloping horse. He dared to hope they might just reach safety.

A moment later, his hopes wilted as a pair of Striders raced around the hill, pulling Shona on a sled. Behind her came Rory and the bulk of his army.

"Must move faster," Ilse stated through chattering teeth. "Angle further to the east."

"There's sheer cliffs that way."

"Exactly."

Hoping Ilse's unorthodox brilliance could save them one more time, Connor did as he was told and increased their pace. Shona and her Strider pullers still caught up a moment later.

Bouncing across the ground next to him, Shona said, "Excuse me, General, but you're going the wrong way."

"I thought I ordered you to take the standard," he told her, not slowing.

"Don't play the fool with me, *General.* We need you to take the flag, and orders are to turn the prisoners over to Captain Rory."

"I keep the prisoners until we get the flag. This way there's no confusion who wins the points for the capture."

Shona jumped off the sled, joining Connor on the ice sheet. He was tempted to knock her off, but she grabbed the buckles of his armor. He couldn't spare the effort fighting her and still get Ilse free.

Shona ordered the Striders to keep pace out of earshot, then touched Connor's cheek with one cool hand. "Connor, I know this is hard for you, but you have to make a choice. Cast aside Ilse's manipulations and decide. Are you a Guardian or are you unworthy of my patronage?"

Connor slowed the movement of the waters. Patronage was a lie, but he wasn't ready to break with Shona. Too many lives still hung in the balance.

Ilse spoke, "What's it going to be, boy?"

Shona touched his cheek again. "Oh, Connor, they have you so confused, don't they?"

Before he could respond, Anika shattered her ice prison with a single, convulsive heave. Connor and Shona ducked the flying shards, but Anika tackled Shona off the sliding ice sheet to the ground, forcing Connor to halt.

The two women rolled, pummeling each other. Connor moved to help, although he couldn't say which of them he planned to stop, but Erich also shattered his ice prison and intercepted him.

"I don't want to hurt you," Connor started to say.

Erich laughed, a rich, hearty laugh, and slugged Connor so hard in the chest that even tapping granite, the blow sent him tumbling from his feet. By the time he shook off the blow and rose, Anika and Erich together had thrown Shona far back toward Rory's now-charging army. The Striders who had been pulling her raced to her aid, and the siblings broke the ice prisons of the rest of their small company.

"Last chance," Ilse said to Connor.

He couldn't leave, not like that.

Ilse read his expression and sighed. "You can't live in both worlds, Connor. Farewell."

Then she spun to the east and started to run, with the siblings close on her heels and Dietmar flanking them. Margrit began to give chase, but a small stone slung by one of the Striders with Shona clipped her in the back of the head and she fell, stunned.

Anika noticed the danger and ran back. The two Striders closed on Margrit, a net held between them, with Shona hurrying behind. Connor moved to intercept the Striders, but they easily avoided him and threw their net over Margrit, knocking her back to the ground, fully entangled.

Anika reached Margrit and ripped the net free. Ilse and Erich turned back, but Anika shouted something in Grandurian, hoisted Margrit over her shoulder, and gave chase. Ilse grabbed Erich, and the two of them resumed their run, with Dietmar falling back to help protect Anika from the Striders.

The ground just in front of Anika surged upward into a wall extending fifty feet in both directions, cutting her off from the rest of her party.

Rory and his army had arrived.

Anika crashed into the wall, shoulder tucked, in a desperate attempt to break through. The wall cracked, but held, and she stumbled back, looking surprised.

The captain and the Sentry class teacher flowed across the plain atop a tower of earth, flanked by Donald and half a dozen Striders. Anika faced them in a fighting crouch, a snarl of defiance on her lips.

Connor wanted to howl with frustration. He couldn't help Anika, not in the face of Rory and his army. She glanced at him, and he read the truth in her eyes.

Her fate was in her own hands.

Captain Rory leaped off the tower, hands high in a sign of peace. "Please surrender."

Margrit tapped the external powers of quartzite and a howling wind tore at Rory and sent nearby Striders skipping away like blue larks before a storm. Rory advanced through the wind, and Anika tackled him with a wild battle cry.

The two crashed to the ground and Anika beat at Rory with crazed abandon, but he ducked his head and held on, keeping her from standing. Tomas and Cameron arrived and secured her hands and feet with thick chains. Within seconds, she lay trussed and helpless. She arced her back in a final, futile act of resistance and her furious scream tore at Connor's heart.

Striders subdued Margrit, and soon dozens of soldiers ringed the prisoners. Connor stood to one side, helpless.

"Connor, come away," Shona said softly. He hadn't noticed her approach.

The earthen wall settled back into the ground and in the distance, Ilse and Erich were just disappearing over the outer lip of the plateau. He saw no sign of Dietmar. Either they had an escape route in mind, or they planned to slide down the near-vertical cliffs and hope their granite strength held out until they reached the bottom.

"Connor." Shona pulled his head around and took his face in both of her hands. "I wish there was some other way. I know they confused you, but it had to be done."

He didn't trust himself to speak. She drew him back toward the battle that still raged around the fortress. It felt like he had left it hours before, but in reality bare minutes had passed. "We need to capture the standard."

Connor couldn't stay and witness Anika carried away in chains. Instead, he focused all his frustrated rage on the battle and returned to the fight with a vengeance.

It didn't matter.

He had stayed away too long. Although he descended on the battling students in a rage of living fire and ice as cold as the dead place in his heart, alone he couldn't defeat everyone. The battle was a mess, with armies mixed in too tight and students fighting individual duels. In the chaos, Ivor escaped with the standard.

As Connor led his battered army back toward the Carraig, with Shona walking close beside him, Fearghas said, "Well at least you captured some of those defenders. We'll get second place for that."

"Who were they?" Declan asked.

"It doesn't matter," Connor said softly. "It was all part of the game."

And the stakes had just escalated to deadly levels.

Chapter 54

Connor had to attend the feast that night, although he just wanted to return to his own small room in the Sculpture House to think. The capture of Anika changed the stakes. Ilse would not leave without attempting to free her, and that would lead to deadly clashes with Rory and his soldiers. How many students might get caught in the fighting?

Worse, she probably considered him an enemy. Would she try to assassinate him first, or wait until they freed Anika? Either way, the next time he met Ilse, at least one of them was probably going to die.

Instead of dealing with those life-and-death matters, he was forced to join the feast along with his army and Ivor's. His soldiers seemed ecstatic about taking second place. In the overall standings, they still held the lead, which meant they also got to join the celebration feast. That angered Ivor's soldiers, and the two groups faced each other in uneasy celebration across the banquet tables. Connor sat at the high table at one end of the hall with Ivor and their captains.

"You played that perfectly," Ivor muttered as he took his seat.

"The next phase is going to be the tricky one." He wished he could share the truth with Ivor. He could use his help.

He considered the idea, but the students' grumblings drew his attention. Their concerns seemed so petty to Connor, he wanted to slap them all.

So he started a food fight.

He waited until Jok was delivering a much-embellished account of his exploits during the battle. He leaned over to Ivor and said, "Let's have a little fun."

And he threw a pastry, splattering jelly filling across Jok's face.

That was all the spark the room needed. Students leaped to their feet, shouting battle cries and pelting each other with anything they could get their hands on. The free-for-all was glorious, and escalated far better than Connor had hoped.

"You're insane!" Ivor laughed as he ducked a three layer cake. "I wish I'd thought of it."

"Stop copying my ideas," Connor shouted, flinging a whole fish at Jok's pig-eyed friend, knocking the boy off his seat.

Food and drink sprayed across the room. Hams and turkeys and eoin thighs knocked laughing students off their feet. It was a good thing they had all purged igneous powers prior to the feast. Ivor and Connor both ordered their tertiary affinity Petralists not to engage with elemental powers.

The Solas tried to blind opponents, but one of them got a turkey shoved over his head for his trouble, and the other was doused with wine that was accidentally set on fire. Since it was Connor's Solas, Ivor allowed him to snuff out the flames and send them dancing across the hall, the flashes of light highlighting the amazing confectionery battle.

The captains at the leadership table decided to lead by example. Jok gleefully rubbed mashed potatoes into Shona's hair, but she nearly drowned him in gravy. Catriona seized a pair of long fish fillets and laid about, using them like swords until they crumbled and someone knocked her over with a meat pie to the face.

Wrestling Ivor for a bowl of apples helped distract Connor from weightier matters. They settled on sharing them and pelted each other's armies with hard little missiles. Of course, that turned most of the assembled students against them and they were overwhelmed by tidal waves of thrown food.

Then the head cook arrived, and the fat woman's wrath was a sight to behold. She berated everyone with such shrill fury for desecrating her work that she sucked all the joy out of the assembly.

Connor finally eased her fury by insisting they had wasted all that delicious food as the most efficient way to work through the many courses and get to dessert. "We heard you prepared something truly fantastic," he promised. "And we just couldn't wait."

"General Anxiety is absolutely right," Ivor agreed.

"Actually, I've changed my name again," Connor said to a round of good-natured groaning. He stood tall, but it was hard to present an imposing figure while dripping eighteen flavors of food from his mask.

"As of tonight, my name is General Insanity, because, well, look around."

The crowd cheered and laughed, not realizing the name was more a warning than a joke. Insanity had claimed Connor, and no matter what choices he made, someone was going to die who shouldn't need to.

"I'll just call you insane," Ivor said.

The head cook seemed to think at least some of the cheering was directed to her. She blushed and waved her army of assistants to bring in the desserts. Dozens of cakes, pies, and pastries soon lorded over the trashed tables, and students eagerly dove in.

The food fight had settled everyone's anger, and laughter rang through the hall. That feeling of camaraderie seemed to encourage students to come ask him questions. Many of them asked about the prisoners. No one else seemed to understand that they were actual Grandurians. They thought Ilse's company was part of Rory's army, set there to provide some stiffer defense.

Connor deflected most of the interest and tried to carry on with the same carefree attitude he had crafted for his disguise, but it proved difficult. He needed to track down Rory and see if they could do anything about Anika. Until then, he needed to focus.

As the feast began winding down, Ivor rose to his feet and offered a boisterous toast. He had begun drinking heavily during dessert and became more talkative and friendly as the night wore on. After he sat down, he leaned across the table past Connor, his arm in Connor's plate.

"Shona, my girl, who do you think is going to win the Tir-raon now?"

Shona, who sat just left of Connor gave him a disgusted look. "I think you stink and you'll need even more help than normal to get undressed."

He winked. "You offering?"

She raised her glass in a mock toast. "You got lucky today, Ivor. Celebrate the win because it's the only one you're going to get."

Ivor growled, looking far more out of control than Connor had ever seen him. "Why can't you just admit it? When I win, you'll beg me to choose you just like all the other girls."

"Only in your wildest dreams."

Connor couldn't imagine what Ivor's game was, but he was starting to think the direction of the conversation was no accident.

"Like my uncle always says. A dream can't become real until it's turned into a goal."

"What are you talking about?" For the first time Shona looked nervous.

Ivor surged to his feet and bellowed, "I have an announcement!"

As the buzz of conversation faded to an expectant hush Shona hissed, "Don't you dare!"

With a triumphant smile and despite a slight sway in his stance he declared, "You are all witness. When I'm declared champion, I formally announce my choice for breeding rights."

That generated a ripple of excited murmurs, and not a few of the girls sat up straighter and tried to brush food out of their hair.

"I choose Shona!"

Many girls sagged with disappointment, but few looked surprised. They lived with the reality of breeding rights and arranged marriages. Only Connor was shocked to hear it spoken so callously.

Shona glanced at Connor, looking desperate. "Well, do something!"

When he didn't provide an immediate response, she left the table and marched from the room.

"She's something, isn't she?" Ivor leaned one arm companionably on Connor's shoulder. "But too proud."

"You're assuming you'll win." Connor wondered if Ivor was drunk enough to remember if he punched him in the face.

Ivor shrugged, and the drunken facade fell away. "Doesn't matter. I'm covered either way."

"That was all an act?"

"Do you think I'm stupid enough to get drunk in public?" Ivor asked. "I thought you knew me better, my friend."

"Why then?" Most of the students had returned to their

feast, or chattered about Ivor's announcement, and no one actually seemed to be watching them.

"You're no fool," Ivor said. "Today went flawlessly. No one even seemed to notice your ridiculous movement with the prisoners. The plan is working, but there's always a chance something will go wrong."

"So how does that equate to you making a claim for Shona's breeding rights?" Speaking those words was like the foulest of curses.

"Like I once told you, I calculate every advantage," Ivor said. "If I win, getting breeding rights from Shona links my new house to Dougal's, which only improves my position. I know she's planning to cement you to her family, and you're welcome to her. She's a strong one, so it'll be anything but a boring life."

"And if you lose?" Connor asked, trying to keep his tone conversational.

Ivor shrugged. "At least I showed my patron I tried. They'll still take me. They can't afford not to." He gave Connor a shrewd look. "You need to make similar plans, just in case."

"I have plans in place," Connor said. "But I don't like you making a move this early. I thought we were trying to break the game, not embrace the darkest aspects of it."

"We're surviving," Ivor grimaced. "If we can break it, all the better. If not, we still need to live in this world."

"We can do better than accepting the rules they define," Connor insisted.

"We can try," Ivor said. "But we still need patrons. Don't become a martyr."

He might not have a choice. Connor almost revealed the secret. The truth hovered on the tip of his tongue, crouched to spring, but he didn't dare. Not yet. He realized he would need to reveal it to Ivor, though. With his powerful friend on his side, they could make the other Guardians listen.

After a glance around to make sure they were still alone, Ivor added, "I'll make a suggestion since you're so new to the game. You really should announce that you're choosing Padraigin for first breeding."

Connor nearly choked on a mouthful of pie. "Why?"

"Think about it," Ivor said. "You've got Shona wrapped up, which links you to arguably the most powerful house in the nation. There's challenges there, but you're up to dealing with those.

Padraigin is a unique opportunity. She's of the royal house of Althing."

"Really?"

He nodded. "I thought maybe you didn't know. Gaining control over her first child would tie you close to the Arishat League. During these difficult times, that could be a huge leverage."

"I'll think about it," Connor said, feeling sick. He liked Ivor, but it rattled him to see his friend play the great game of houses with such cold logic. Breeding, and marriage, and controlling the lives of children was not something Connor could consider without emotion. If he ever reached that point, he feared the part of his heart that controlled his humanity would have to die first.

Connor excused himself from the feast a little while later, but Catriona fell into step beside him as he headed out the hall and down the dim corridor.

Once they were alone she spoke. "General, what did you think of Ivor's announcement?"

"I think he was drunk."

"And I think Shona reacted poorly."

"You do?"

"Of course. I know she likes to pretend she's above it all, but anyone will accept the champion. It has to be done."

"As you say."

He quickened his pace, but she didn't take the hint. After a moment, she asked in a hesitant voice, "Have you made your choice yet?"

Connor nearly stumbled. "No, not yet."

The princess touched his arm and drew him to a halt. "I know her father arranged for your sponsorship, so you're linked to her house, but remember you're free to make any choice you want."

"I'll keep that in mind," he said slowly.

She bit her lip then forced a smile and leaned closer. "I can promise a lot if you choose me, General."

He nearly laughed in her face. What would she say when she learned his true identity? She might have rescinded her blood oath to kill him, but would she really agree to breed with him?

Even if she did, he wasn't ready to consider such a union. To him, she was one of the least attractive girls in the school. Some of that feeling might be residual resentment from her beating him half to death on several occasions, but he couldn't imagine fathering a child through her.

"I'm sure you'll be a contender," he managed to say.

Grinning, she kissed the cheek of his leather mask and returned to the party. Connor stood in the hall for a moment, not quite believing how the evening had turned out. He'd thought Anika's capture was a big problem.

He couldn't have chosen a better name than insanity. Every noble born Petralist was well and truly insane. It felt like all the secret plotting and gealls were all coming to a head at the same time. He sensed a building storm, like prickles of energy against his skin.

What would he need to do to survive? Was it worth losing his humanity to save his life or the lives of his distant family?

The alternative included lots of blood on his hands.

Chapter 55

onnor decided to spend the night in his Dawnus suite. There was more room to pace there. As the Tir-raon raced toward the ultimate battles, his life as Connor was slipping away, replaced more and more by the false identity of the general.

It was late enough that Connor doubted even the spies were lingering. For once, Tomas and Cameron weren't on duty outside, but he waved at the hulking replacement, a man Connor knew only casually.

He paused on the way to his inner apartment to visit his training facility. The newly-completed maze feature loomed in the dim recesses of the huge space, and he couldn't wait to run his army through it. In fact, he might run it himself after changing out of his battle leathers.

Only a single lamp illuminated his apartment, and that suited his mood. The rooms were large enough that it was easy to avoid the furniture.

The twang of a bowstring being released sounded loud in the still apartment.

He spun at that familiar sound, already tapping granite, and the arrow aimed at the back of his head instead skipped along his scalp, tearing his ear.

Connor dove to the side, applying his granite curse to his entire body even as he tapped sandstone to ease the throbbing pain. His heart raced and his breathing quickened as his body reacted to the unexpected danger.

As he rolled back into a crouch, the shadows seemed to come alive and attack him.

The slender dagger driving for his eyes was no shadow.

Connor just barely blocked the strike. His attacker was dressed in black, nearly invisible, and they slashed across his leather mask, two amazingly fast strikes that shredded it and scraped the stone-hard skin of his face beneath.

As the mask flapped, Connor's initial surprise changed to anger. He didn't have any tertiary affinity stones ready, but the idea of a bash fight perfectly fit his mood.

"It's rude to introduce yourself with a knife," he growled, punching at the shadowy figure. They somehow slipped around his blow and struck again at his eyes. He only barely managed to duck his head enough for the blade to stab into his eyebrow instead.

The attacker was fast, faster even than Tomas and Cameron, so Connor crouched and spun, throwing his arms out wide like a horizontal windmill. The move surprised his attacker, who had closed to strike again. One open palm caught the person in the side and tumbled them into the nearby wall. They made a soft cry of pain from the impact.

It sounded like a woman.

Tough. He respected women until they tried to kill him. That tended to dampen his manners. Connor lunged, planning to slam the woman into the wall again. Somehow she managed to twist aside just enough that he only barely brushed her clothing.

Then the woman smacked him in the face. It wasn't a strong blow, but she was holding something that burst into a cloud of choking dust.

Connor lashed out with one leg, a tactic used by few Boulders, who almost universally fought with hammerlike fists. He caught her in the stomach and sent her flying into a distant couch. He moved to follow, but the powder coating his mouth and nose was suffocating him. He could barely breathe, and pawed at it.

Then his strength evaporated.

His granite curse faded like dew before a noonday sun and exhaustion dropped him to his knees. He groaned from the sudden weight of limbs that felt as heavy as iron bars. He could barely move.

The weakening powder.

It had to be, but why hadn't it knocked him unconscious like it had always done to Shona? Was the assassin Ilse, come to kill him after all?

His thoughts felt as fuzzy as moldy cheese, and it was hard to think, but this was not like anything Ilse had tried before. She had promised to make it quick, but he'd expected that meant she'd drop a mountain on his head or something.

A soft creak from the couch told him his assailant was rising. He was kneeling, helpless and barely able to move. She'd kill him soon. So he fell to the side, using the motion to make it easier to slip a hand to the pouch at his belt and paw for a piece of quartzite or marble. His fingers felt like frozen sausages, and he struggled to grip the little stones.

As his fingers slipped and fumbled, the black-clad attacker approached and stood over him, dagger glinting in the soft light. She reached a hand to the black hood shielding her face and pulled it free. "The Mhortair claim your life as bounty to justice."

"Aifric?"

With the hood gone, Connor could just make out her features, but might not have recognized her without hearing her voice. Her hair was pulled back in a tight pony tail, her expression was hard, and her eyes, usually so warm and friendly, held nothing but the promise of death.

She gasped and pulled away the loose flaps of his mask. "Connor?"

"Hi."

Aifric looked stunned. "But you're. . ."

"If you don't kill me for a minute, I can explain." Speaking was difficult, but he forced the words out. "Then maybe you can tell me what makes a Healer decide to commit murder."

Was he living a crazy nightmare? By the Tallan's dirty socks, the whole situation made no sense. Why would Aifric kill anyone? She was one of the nicest people he knew, or thought he knew.

Aifric helped him to the couch, then lit another lamp. Her hands trembled so hard, it took a few tries. Then she sank into a seat and stared at him.

"I know we didn't win," Connor said. "But don't you think this is a bit extreme?"

"Connor?" she repeated in a whisper, glancing at her dagger, then dropping it to the floor. "Why couldn't you have been anyone else?"

Something she said earlier finally registered. "You said Mhortair. That's what the Assassins call themselves."

"How could you possibly know that?"

"I know a lot of things. Like friends don't assassinate friends."

That one was a bit of a stretch. He had a number of friends who had promised to assassinate him if circumstances required it, but he decided not to split that seam until he had to.

"I wouldn't hurt you," she promised.

Connor laughed weakly. "Well if you ever decide to, it looks like you'd do a pretty good job. You nearly killed me about twenty times in five seconds."

"You were supposed to be General Insanity!"

"Everything about this situation is insane. Why would you want to kill him? Hasn't he been a good leader?"

"Too good," she said, leaning forward and regaining some of her composure. "Connor, my intelligence suggests that you are Blood of the Tallan."

"Do you always accuse people of being the devil incarnate right after you try to assassinate them?" He tried to keep his tone light, but Gisela's words rang in his mind. The Mhortair would kill him if they knew of his powers.

They knew.

"Don't dodge the question," Aifric said, her expression hardening. "Are you?"

"Not if it means you trying to kill me again."

"I'm not going to kill you," she said, sounding exasperated. She rose and paced away, rubbing at her face and muttering, "Nothing is ever easy around you, is it?"

"You weren't complaining when I gave you lots of practice healing broken bones."

She turned to face him. "My mission is clear, Connor. Identify the Blood of the Tallan and dispose of them before they become a threat."

"I'm glad you're willing to look beyond ridiculous orders when you have to."

She returned to her seat and sighed. "Oh, Connor. I know your heart. You're not the monster we feared."

"Is that why I kept running into you in those odd places? Have you been hunting me?"

She nodded. "I heard rumors, and I've spent lots of hours scouting all over the city. Your incursions into Hector's rooms were but one item I was investigating."

"How did you know about that?"

Instead of answering, she asked, "How long have you known the extent of your powers?"

She already knew, so keeping secrets wouldn't help. He shrugged. "Last summer."

"You were at Alasdair!" She frowned at him. "We could have avoided all this confusion if you'd told me more that time I asked in the hospital."

"In my defense, you never said you were planning to hunt me down and assassinate me," Connor retorted.

"Secrets are a burden we both share, I guess. Alasdair was when Shona discovered you and started planning to control you, wasn't it?"

"Something like that."

"This complicates things."

"Things got complicated when you tried to kill me," he pointed out.

She waved away his words. "That was a misunderstanding."

Connor barked a laugh. "Getting gruel instead of bread for breakfast is a misunderstanding."

"Just give me a minute to think," she snapped.

"Be my guest, but only if you tell me how you weakened me."

"It's a secret."

"You know my secret."

She pulled a little flask out of a pocket and handed it to him. "Take a single sip."

The liquid burned like living fire going down, and Connor coughed so hard, he wondered if he might get a lung to come up. When the coughing passed, he realized he felt a bit better. "Aonghus would love this."

"You'll have trouble establishing your primary affinities until morning," Aifric said. "So I recommend you don't try."

"How does it work?"

"Secret," she reminded him, looking exasperated. "Now be quiet."

"How can you be an Assassin and be here at the Carraig as a Petralist Healer?"

She shrugged. "High Lord Goban knows little of the family I arranged to get adopted into. They're distant relations of his, living out in the country on the border with Ravinder. He never asked any questions after confirming my healing affinity. Now please be quiet while I think."

"Sure."

He watched her as she sat quietly composed. Her face had softened a little now that she wasn't preparing to commit murder and she looked more like the Aifric he knew. He still scarce believed the bubbly, enthusiastic personality he knew concealed the secret assassin.

Even though her blade had nearly plunged into his brain, he was impressed. He had thought he'd done a good job as Kilian, but she'd duped everyone without the need of a mask. That was a brilliant performance.

"So who are you really? You're not Aifric the Healer."

"I am Aifric," she said, giving him her normal enthusiastic smile. "When I take an identity, I become that person completely."

"How many people are you?"

"Nineteen."

Connor blinked. "Doesn't it get crowded in there?"

"Not at the same time. That would be like max-tapping insanity."

"Oh, that's good," Connor grinned. "Especially with my new name. Do you mind if I use that some time?"

"Aren't you worried you'll irritate me enough that I might change my mind about killing you?"

"Not really. It's not your way."

"Oh, and you know my way?"

"Sure. I know Aifric. When you're her, you're one of the most kind-hearted people I know. When you're Mhortair-Mairi, you're deadly, but focused on your target. I'm not a target any more. I'm your friend."

Aifric laughed, looking more like herself every second. "You're right, Connor. I came here to eliminate a threat, but instead I've found a friend." She sat up taller and announced, "My name's not Mairi, but I'm going to help you."

"Good." He really didn't need another friend trying to murder him. "I need all the help I can get. Can you sew?"

"What?"

He pointed at the ripped mask. "I need a replacement."

He actually had several, but she didn't need to know that.

Aifric looked pained. "Ah, I'm really bad at sewing."

"You're a Healer," he protested. "You get to sew people up all the time."

She shook her head. "Not me. I seal wounds with my gift. I never touch a needle."

"Well, we'll think of something," he said, liking the idea of having a secret assassin on his side.

Aifric leaned closer. "You need to leave the Carraig, Connor."

"Working on it." If she only knew how much.

"No, you need to leave now. You can't remain until the completion of the Tir-raon. Shona, and more particularly her father, are far too dangerous."

"There are some complications."

"You don't understand. If they secure your allegiance, I will be forced to kill you."

She spoke it with such dramatic inflection, she probably thought the declaration would intimidate him. He shrugged. "I hope it doesn't come to that, but you need to be true to yourself."

"How can you accept what I just said so calmly?"

"You're not the first friend who's promised to kill me. I can handle it."

She tilted her head, considering him. "You're a very strange man."

"I live in strange times. I'm friends with a Healer who's really an Assassin." He paused, then asked, "So are you duty bound to try to save people after trying to kill them?"

"It depends on the situation," she admitted.

"And you say I'm weird."

"I'm serious. I care about you and I want to continue being friends, but I will kill you if I must."

"Fair enough." Connor rose and gestured toward the dining room. "Are you hungry? I wore more of the feast than I ate. I think we might have a lot to talk about."

Aifric rose slowly to follow him. "You're not anything like I pictured the Blood of the Tallan."

He grinned. "It's hard imagining the devil as so good looking."

She laughed. "Connor, I believe your return offers a glimmer of hope to salvage the nations of the Arishat League from the storm about to burst across the continent."

He paused. "I should try to work that into my next name."

She took his hand in hers. "Just be yourself, and you'll find a way to be successful."

"That's a little vague. Especially when you're waiting in the shadows to kill me if I make a wrong turn."

"I will be waiting in the shadows to protect you. Because I believe in you."

That simple statement struck him with surprising force. "Thank you." He helped her to a seat at the table that was piled with food, despite the late hour. "I have few true supporters. Most people just want to control my curse."

"You are blessed with great power," she said, her expression serious. "You will help shape the future. As such, there will always be those seeking to twist your powers to their gain."

"Is that what you'll do?"

She shook her head. "I will find those who seek to do so, and I will kill them all."

Aifric raised a glass of wine in a toast. "To friendship."

Chapter 56

Captain Rory reached the bottom of the fourth long set of stone stairs that led to the dungeon carved into the bedrock, deep below the central keep of the Carraig. Few knew it existed, and fewer still could pass its impressive security. With lantern held high to drive back the shadows that seemed reluctant to relinquish their usual hold over the empty corridors, he eventually reached a heavy, iron-banded oak door. It opened only after Tomas peered through the look-see port and verified his identity.

A single small table and four wooden chairs made up all the furnishings in the round guardroom. The cheery fire in the hearth was the only splash of color in the otherwise universal gray of the room, but couldn't drive out the pervasive chill. Cameron sat in one of the chairs near the fire, positioned to watch the single closed, steel door.

"How is she?" Rory asked.

Tomas shrugged. "The burn-through process is complete. She cursed us the entire time."

Cameron added, "Learned all sorts of fun new Grandurian curses. Wish I'd brought some paper to take notes."

"As if you could write," Tomas said.

"It's called short hand."

"Only if you can read it back later."

Rory refused to be drawn in by their banter. "You two, report upstairs and check on Connor. I'll watch the prisoner for the next hour and begin the interrogation."

"Is that wise, sir?" Tomas asked. "She's a fierce one."

"I can handle her."

"No doubt sir, but shouldn't you have back-up?"

"Not this time."

The two Fast Rollers saluted and left. Just before the heavy door closed behind them, Cameron's voice drifted back to Rory. "No, make it the number of scratches on his face."

"Done."

He blew out a breath after the door closed. He trusted those men with his life, but sometimes he wanted to throttle them.

The reinforced door to the cell held a small look-see port that he slid partially open to peer inside. Anika lay on a narrow steel cot attached to the wall on the far side of the room and appeared to be sleeping. Her breathing looked normal and her ghastly rust-colored hair spilled over the side and hung almost to the floor. He watched her for a few minutes as he tried to order his thoughts and prepare for what would undoubtedly be a difficult interrogation.

The longer he looked, the more distracted he became. Instead of finalizing the list of questions he needed answered, he began reviewing memories of every contact he'd had with the fiery, fantastic woman who was now his prisoner.

He recalled the thrill of the very first time he tasted her strength and tenacity, enjoyed her taunting, and took up her challenges. The woman's fighting powers and shapely figure had wormed under his skin and affected him like no other woman ever had.

If only she weren't Grandurian! He should hate her, should see her as a ruthless enemy to crush, but somehow everything got twisted out of every conceivable sense of normal around her. Even while he held her down for his men to capture her, he had to fight not to release her and throw her over the wall to help her escape.

As he closed the look-see port, he wondered what was happening to him.

With a shake of his head, he commanded discipline on his thoughts. He had worked hard for too many years to reach his current position to let that devious, sensuous woman unman him.

Rory unlocked the door, drew it open, and stepped inside, but paused in surprise. The cot was empty.

Anika launched herself onto his back from where she stood pressed against the wall to his left. He tapped granite even as he stumbled farther into the room under the unexpected assault, but she dug her feet into his battle leathers and tore at his eyes with her fingernails, shrieking in fury the whole time.

Rory grabbed at her hands, but she eluded his grasp and forced him to clench his eyes against her fierce attack. Even lacking granite strength, she knew how to target his few vulnerabilities.

"I just want to talk," he bellowed as the two of them spun through the center of the room together, locked in the fierce struggle.

"No talk!" Anika shouted, shoving a couple fingers up his nose and yanking hard.

She didn't let go fast enough and he grabbed her wrist and heaved, sending her tumbling off his back. She slid across the floor and struck the opposite wall with a thud, then lay still.

Rory cursed himself for a fool and hurried over to make sure he hadn't hurt her. She twisted like a cat and kicked his leading knee with both feet just as he was leaning forward, all his weight centered over it. The blow upset his balance just enough to topple him. Anika leaped on his back, grabbed his face with both hands, and started slamming his skull against the floor.

He let her. Although her strength surprised him, she couldn't really hurt him, and he enjoyed the feeling of her hands on his face.

No, he had to stop getting distracted. Rory surged to his feet, carrying her with him. Before she could slide off, he encircled her with his arms and held her close. Usually when they wrestled, her body shifted to the perfect lines of granite, and the softer feel of her straining muscles fascinated him far too much.

"Let go!" she bellowed.

"No. You settle down so we can talk."

With another shriek of fury, she redoubled her attack against his face, although she had to be bruising her hands. He was tempted to reduce his tap rate to lessen the damage, but that would make him vulnerable.

Fighting someone he cared about was proving extremely frustrating. So Rory grabbed her waist, lifted her into the air, and spun her around. She lacked the strength to resist, so he pulled her back against him and sat on the cot with her on his lap, his arms wrapped around her, holding her hands down.

For à time she struggled mightily against him, but he just sat back against the wall and held her. With her hands trapped by his, and his arms holding her on his lap, she lacked the ability to accomplish much. Rory let her vent as much frustration as she wanted to and found himself smiling as he held the wild woman.

Then she abruptly stopped and sagged against him, breathing hard. She leaned her head against his shoulder and for the first time he noticed that she smelled like clover and clean mountain passes.

"Let go," she said softly.

"Will you behave?"

He held her gently but firmly like that for another minute before she sighed, "Yes."

Rory didn't quite believe her but decided to take the chance and loosened his hold. She turned toward him and slid one hand down the side of his face. "Mine honor makes force I fight except you hold me down, mine capitain."

"Well, we can't have you fighting can we?"

She shifted until she sat across his lap and leaned against him. He cradled her against his chest like that for a moment, and it felt so fantastic that without really thinking about it he eased his tap rate and for a second they sat together, just a man and a woman, with no granite.

Anika pushed away and gave him a dazzling smile, but the glint in her eye betrayed her.

He tapped granite again just as she stiff-handed him in the throat. The blow still made him gag, and she slammed her forehead against his. She recoiled, eyes glazing from the impact, and rolled off his lap.

Rory lifted her and dumped her on the cot. "Serves you right. Now, sit still or I'm going to have to hurt you."

Anika recovered quickly, cocked her head to one side, and asked in that throaty voice that sent shivers down his spine, "No want hold me again?"

"I don't think that's a good idea."

Instead of attacking again, she blew him a kiss, then spat at his feet.

"Will you just stop?" He considered for the briefest moment attempting to use Cameron's flowered prose, but she was already trying to kill him and that would pretty much guarantee the interview ended in disaster.

"Am stop," she said with a glare, then leaned back against the wall.

"Good. Now I have to ask you some questions."

Anika bared her even, white teeth and hissed.

Rory sighed, "At least tell me why you didn't run."

"Tell why you cheat?" she snapped back.

"I never cheat."

"Ha! On battle, you no wrestle. No have help, no could beat."

"It was a battle, woman! Of course I used every resource."

Anika sniffed in disgust and turned away.

Rory rubbed his chin. "I know Ilse will try again, but if you tell me how to contact her, I'll send a message for you."

"Why do that?" She turned back.

"Tell her to leave, to abandon her mission. I don't want to have to kill her."

Anika shook her head, "No, mine capitain. Last mission. Make free or kill."

"They'll never free you."

"Is one make free. You try stop and you die," Anika said with quiet certainty. "I no can stop."

"Then I can't help you."

With a heavy heart, Rory turned toward the door.

"Mine capitain?"

He turned back and she leaned forward, her expression sad. "Am sorry have be enemy."

If only there was some way to reconcile. He'd never wanted a woman like he wanted Anika.

He sighed. "Me too."

Chapter 57

Jean entered the secret library with a sense of relief. Shona had been distracted enough by Ivor's surprise announcement that she'd only given Jean a series of vague orders. But then, she'd nearly walked into Jok passing through the inner-wall gate. He'd insisted on seeing her nearly every day, and she lacked the emotional energy to deal with his ardent affection.

The secret library was her calm sanctum. There she could relax and immerse herself in history and learning. The subjects she studied might be onerous, but she loved the pursuit of knowledge.

The hunt for answers to the questions of patronage, unclaimed, and Tallan only knew what else drove her. She'd felt rushed before, but with Anika captured, time was gone. Would Ilse try to kill Connor outright, or try to force him to help her in some desperate plan? Either way, Jean could easily see pitched battle at the Carraig.

She was starting to despair ever escaping any other way.

The secret library was small, unlike the inner library Ailsa had led her to so many weeks before. It felt more like an intimate study, with a single fireplace, two overstuffed chairs, and a small table. It contained only one bookshelf, which held the four tomes Evander let her read. She inhaled sharply as she scanned the shelf.

A new book had been added. *Treatise on the goals and underlying mission driving the foundation of the Carraig.*

With eager fingers, she picked up the tome and settled into one of the chairs by the fire to dive into it. The language was archaic, but its title suggested it might hold more of the deeper truths they needed so badly.

The last book had revealed much about Tallan, and she'd been surprised to learn that Donleavy was not the original capital of Obrion. She doubted many of the students understood that the Carraig was built atop the ruins of the original capital city, which had been destroyed in the Tallan Wars. She had found many references to the ancient Queen Dreokt, who had ruled for centuries, and who had been universally feared.

As she worked through the dense language of the new tome, her excitement grew. On the second page, she found the first nugget. As she studied the unfamiliar terminology, the door opened. Only Evander ever came there, so she rose to greet him with a curtsy.

The giant gave her a tiny bow in greeting and approached, towering over her as he glanced at her place in the book. She no longer feared his presence. She sensed no animosity, and as always, wanted to know more about the mysterious giant. His scent of leather and fresh-turned earth helped put her at ease, as did his gentle smile, but she longed to ask him about who he was really.

She suspected he didn't interact much with people, but behind the wall of his confusing Sentry-speak, she sensed that he enjoyed their visits. She hoped to find a way to get him to open up more and confide in her.

"Can a road taken in haste be thoroughly enjoyed?" he asked in his deep voice.

"I wish I could take more time," Jean admitted, "but I never get enough."

"History relinquishes its memories with a begrudging hand."

Jean pointed at the section she had just begun studying. "Do you know what this means?"

Evander hesitated and his black-eyed gaze bore down on her with somber weight. "A hunter may enter the den of a bear if his strength is sufficient to take the prize, but he risks much that would be avoided had he chosen a safer path."

She had held enough almost-conversations with him in recent weeks that she was getting the knack of interpreting them. "So crossing a threshold is a way to reach for a greater power, but there are dangers in attempting it?"

He gave her a little bow and turned to leave. "Tread with

care, young one. This knowledge may destroy the one you seek to set free."

"He'll take the chance if he must."

"Does the river choose to flow when the dam bursts?"

"Please, tell me more," she begged, taking a step after him.

He hesitated, and for the first time she caught a hint of doubt in those deep, dark eyes of his. "Among your allies the key to this knowledge already lies hid, but your search may yet uncover unknown gems."

After he left, she played the cryptic conversation over in her mind. He might have actually been trying to tell her something, but seemed nervous to speak openly. They were treading through ancient secrets, like traversing an underground crypt. Anything that made the mighty Evander nervous should terrify her. The problem was, she needed to understand before she could know, and by then it might be too late.

Chapter 58

Kilian burst into the workroom where Hamish was again testing the smash packer. He'd determined that he could squash an entire day's worth of food small enough to fit into a single pocket. Verena, who was studying crystals through the close view goggles, didn't seem impressed.

"We have a problem," Kilian announced, his expression grave.

"The kitchens denied my request for another pallet of sweetbreads?" Hamish asked. He needed that food for research.

"We have a real problem." Kilian never understood the deeper truths about food research and anti-hunger planning. He held up a tiny parchment. "We just received word from Ilse."

Verena rushed over, the close view goggles pushed up on her head. "What happened?"

"Someone found out her location. Anika and Margrit were taken by Rory."

"Oh no," Verena gasped.

"It's worse. Ilse says Connor might have had a hand in the betrayal."

"He wouldn't!" Hamish exclaimed.

"It's unlikely," Kilian said. "But Ilse says she's going to give Connor one more chance. He has to help them free Anika and leave with them, or she will treat him as an enemy."

"That's not fair," Hamish protested. "Bad things happen, but she can't make it his fault."

From what they had learned of the setup of the Carraig and the situation there, Connor was in a very difficult spot. They couldn't ask him to sacrifice himself to free Anika. He'd already given his life once.

"From Ilse's recent reports, the situation is deteriorating," Kilian said. "The intrigue is growing more complex and the opposition desperate. It is time to remove him."

"So if he doesn't agree to help her, she'll kill him?" Verena exclaimed, looking terrified, but furious. "I won't allow it. I already lost him once."

"We need to send her another letter," Hamish suggested.

Kilian shook his head. "Not possible. Ilse's gone to ground. Another bird might be tracked and give away her position. There's no communication until after the mission is complete."

"That's stupid! What are we going to do?"

"That is the question, isn't it?" Kilian asked.

"We all need to go, to help," Verena said. "Together, we can free Anika and rescue Connor."

Hamish nodded enthusiastically. They'd spent time in recent days fine-tuning their personal flying platforms. His suit was as ready as the Swift. Those noble born Petralists would be caught completely by surprise.

"I cannot go," Kilian said. "I was already preparing to leave for Merkland."

"You're going after Dougal?" Verena guessed.

He nodded. "Dougal is the key. I need to end his reign of terror before he unleashes any remaining rampagers or launches the full might of Obrion against us."

"But we can't leave Connor to die," Hamish protested. He'd been patient only because it had sounded like Connor was safe and ultimately preparing to escape with Ilse.

"No, we cannot," Kilian agreed. "Connor is critical to the future of our freedom."

"Then it falls to us," Verena declared. "Hamish and I must go."

Kilian crumpled the parchment in his hand and allowed a rare expression of frustration. "I hate to risk the two of you. This mission is extremely hazardous, and I need your expertise for the successful pursuit of the war."

"But we need Connor more," Verena said, facing him with that resolute expression Hamish had come to hate. It usually meant she was going to insist on something, despite his objections. This time, he applauded it. "I'm going, Kilian. I don't think even you could stop me."

He gave her that roguish smile that the ladies all seemed to love. "I expect nothing less." Then he glanced at Hamish. "If you allow anything to happen to Verena, I'll kill you myself."

"Hey, that's not fair! What if something happens to me?"

"Nothing worthwhile is ventured without a little risk," Kilian said with a straight face.

"Oh, that's so not fair," Hamish grumbled.

"You both realize I'm standing right here," Verena said, looking annoyed. "And I can shred you both with the weapons packed on the Swift."

"That's why we love you," Kilian said, then his expression turned grave. "You must leave immediately. Use extreme caution, but get him out of there. If you can, rescue Anika and Margrit."

"You would abandon them?" Hamish asked.

"Not willingly, but in war we must make difficult choices." Kilian looked suddenly tired. "Difficult, but necessary. You must save Connor. The others understand the risk. Bring them home if there is any way, but do not allow yourselves to be distracted."

"We won't," Verena promised.

She shared a glance with Hamish and he read in her eyes the same resolution he felt.

They'd level the entire Carraig before they left anyone behind.

Chapter 59

After lunch the next day, Connor found Ailsa, Gisela, and Jean all in the Sculpture House, and they piled into Ailsa's tiny office. He told them about Ivor's announcement, but did not mention that Aifric was a Mhortair Assassin. That was a secret too dangerous to share.

While they digested the news, Jean grimaced. "Now's probably an appropriate time to share with you all that on my last date with Jok, he proposed to me."

"What?" Connor exclaimed.

"Don't act so shocked," Jean retorted. A blush was spreading across her cheek, but she looked angry.

"I'm not shocked he wants you," Connor said. "A man would have to be blind and three weeks dead not to realize you're a better catch than any other woman at the Carraig."

Jean's anger softened, and Gisela smiled at him. "You are a good friend to having for compliments."

"I was just surprised he'd proposed." Connor tried to clarify.

"He didn't propose marriage," Jean said, her flush deepening. "He proposed I become his First Mistress, to be precise."

"They have a title for affairs?" Connor asked.

"Affairs are quite formal for the nobility," Ailsa said. "Are you all right, Jean?"

She nodded. "Even though I turned him down, he persists

in wanting to take me on dates. I haven't been able to completely break off from him."

"I'll see what I can do," Connor said. "Shona should be able to stop it."

"Don't," Jean said. "I can handle Jok, and Shona enjoys the potential threat he poses as leverage against you. Don't give her more."

"Have a care," Ailsa cautioned. "Nobles are not known for being patient with commoners, even ones they profess to care about."

Connor could attest to that.

"I sense a growing level of desperation among the high lord representatives," Ailsa said. "Time to act is growing short, Connor."

"I know. I can't delay until the game ends. I can't allow Anika and Margrit to die, and I'm sick of all the lies."

"If you were locked under patronage, the game would be making sense," Gisela said. "From inside the world they live, all is justifying."

"I don't have to live in their world though, do I?" Connor snapped, then sighed. "Sorry, I'm just frustrated."

Jean took his hand in hers. "We all are. The world has gone from crazy to insane. You picked the right name. There don't seem to be any limits any more."

"Sometimes I wish I'd tried to run the night we sensed the watchers back at your mansion," Connor grumbled.

"They never would have let you escape," Ailsa said. "Then your position would be far worse."

Connor barked a laugh, "How could anything be worse?"

"Many men would love to stand in your position, wielding mighty power, with one of the most desirable women in the kingdom begging your favor, and others clamoring for nothing more than the right to share your bed."

"If I don't do something," Connor said. "This game is going to kill me."

Ailsa regarded them each in turn, then nodded, as if reaching a decision. "You're right, Connor. We have assembled all the information we need. Now is the time to act."

"Be careful," Jean cautioned. "I mean, I agree, but there's still Evander's threat and Shona's promise of declaring our families daor."

"We'll find a way." Connor shared her dread, but he

couldn't submit to Shona, not until he exhausted every other possibility.

Ailsa rose, came around the desk and swung open a concealed panel embedded in one of the overloaded bookshelves. As she worked the lock on the steel safe set into the wall she said, "Before lifting the hammer, one needs three things: a clear vision of the intended outcome, knowledge sufficient to implement the plan, and the tools to do so."

The little door swung open on silent hinges and she extracted a small canvas sack. "Come with me."

She led them out of her office and down to the vault where the wealth of power stones were stored, then closed the door behind them, plunging them into darkness. Connor activated a bit of limestone and she nodded her thanks.

"Why did you lead us down here?" Jean asked.

"It is unlikely our conversations are ever listened to, and there is shielding built into the outer walls of the building, but for this conversation, we need the extra precaution."

She placed the sack on the worktable where they prepared the daily rounds. "Connor, you have the knowledge. I believe the vision of what must be done will become clear very soon." Opening the sack she continued softly, "Thus you need but the tools to succeed."

Connor leaned forward, intrigued as she extracted a beautifully carved statue, barely larger than the sandstone pendant he had only recently obtained from Ivor.

"Soapstone," she said solemnly as she placed onto the table a dull gray stone, carved into three interlocking, translucent cubes. When he leaned forward for a closer look, he noticed water bubbling in the heart of the stone.

Ailsa next revealed a polished blue stone, carved in the shape of a clenched fist under rippling flames. "Marble."

An exotic bird with wings extended came next. "Quartzite."

The final statue was shaped like a Sentry tower. "Slate."

Jean leaned closer. "They're beautiful."

"They be sculpted," Gisela whispered, her eyes as wide as lanterns.

Ailsa nodded. "They are indeed."

"But, you'll get in trouble, won't you?" Jean asked.

Aunt Ailsa's warm laugh helped dispel some of the tension from the vault room. "Oh, my dear. That is the least of our concerns."

Connor drew forth the sculpted sandstone pendant. It seemed wrong to keep it hidden. Ailsa smiled to see it, as she had when he had told her Ivor had returned it.

"My boy, you face dire times and you may well need the power these stones can offer."

He reached out to touch the slate tower and his finger tingled with the suppressed power concealed in the beautiful carving. Even though he stood in a steel clad vault, removed from the earth, he sensed the ground below and was confident that if he grasped that statue, he could make a connection from almost anywhere. It was thrilling, but the magnitude of power compacted into the stone reminded him more than a little of the explosive power of diorite coiled to destroy, and he pulled his finger away.

Ailsa watched him closely. "Don't attempt to use one of these except in a moment of ultimate need, for they open the way to a threshold that, once you ascend through, you can never come back."

Jean inhaled a sharp breath. "That's the connection!"

"What?" Connor asked.

"That term. Threshold. I saw it today in the book I'm studying. Evander warned me there are dangers, but I hadn't yet figured out how one even attempts to enter a threshold."

"The term is *ascend*," Ailsa said, and her cautioning glance took them all in. "The knowledge of thresholds is an even more closely guarded secret than the sculpted stones that allow powerful Petralists to access them. Evander was right to warn you. Few Petralists possess the strength of tertiary affinity to even approach a threshold, but those who do, if driven by a sculpted stone, can ascend to far greater powers."

Connor thought back to Camonica's obscure reference to thresholds and Aonghus's warning. They knew the secret, but had either of them ascended?

"What happens if one ascends through a threshold of power?"

"It is a major event," Ailsa said. "I have seen only one ascension. The Petralist is forever changed, and they are pushed to the uttermost limits of endurance. The one I witnessed nearly died, and was as weak as a kitten for days afterward."

"Doesn't sound like a good idea then," Connor said.

"On the contrary, when they recovered, not only had they unlocked abilities previously impossible for their elemental affinity, but their primary and secondary affinities were also far stronger than they had been."

"That makes it sound worth the risk."

"There are other dangers," Ailsa cautioned. "For today, know that a threshold offers the promise of great power, power that might mean the difference between life and death." She paused, and it was hard to draw his gaze away from the little statues. "Do not attempt a threshold lightly. The dangers are real."

"I won't," he promised, but he kept thinking about the potential gain. That indeed might be the key to victory. Connor surveyed the four statues on the table. "That's why sculpted stones are such a closely-guarded secret."

"Exactly. Few know the true reason, and you must all swear to keep the secret."

Jean and Gisela agreed immediately, and Connor shrugged. "I'm keeping so many secrets now, I'm going to need a few more personalities to keep them straight."

He took up the little statues, returned them to the sack, and hefted it. "Thank you, Aunt Ailsa. I hope I won't need them until we find a time to discuss the benefits and dangers in more detail, but I'll keep them just in case."

"A wise choice." She pulled from the very back of a shelf containing their few unprocessed granite rocks a little leather bag. She handed it to Connor, and inside he found bags of powdered granite and basalt.

"Those are enhanced," Ailsa explained. "Concentrated to triple their normal strength, an edge you may need."

"Thank you!" That was definitely a gift he could use.

"They will expire more quickly, and should you tap to exhaustion, the negative effects will also be multiplied."

"You must showing me secret of this trick," Gisela said.

"Perhaps one day." She placed hands on Connor's shoulders. "You have the knowledge and now the tools. You must craft your own destiny."

His excitement settled into resolve. "I'll find a way. I can't leave everyone in danger, and I have to deal with Shona's threat against our family."

"And Evander," Jean added.

He grimaced. "Yes, I'll figure out how to face him."

"Maybe he'll just let you leave," Jean suggested. "With so many gealls running their course and plots being revealed, perhaps those are the greater evils he suggested he was looking for."

"Perhaps," but somehow he doubted it.

Aunt Ailsa said, "Warn us when you decide what you are going to do, and we'll help in every way we can."

"I can tell you one thing," he said, the beginnings of a plan forming in his mind.

"I'm going to break some rules."

Chapter 60

Midnight passed with Connor still awake in his little room in the loft of the Sculpture House, waiting. Ilse could not afford to delay until Anika was tortured or even killed. He felt convinced she would make her move that very night, and it fit his mood perfectly.

It was past time to take control of the game, and he'd finally figured out what he needed to do. That knowledge gave him a sense of freedom he hadn't felt since the last time he died. He just needed Ilse to give him a chance to explain before really trying to kill him.

A soft step outside of his door sounded loud in the hush that had settled over the Sculpture House. He prepared to tap granite, which he had already absorbed.

"I'm awake," he spoke loudly. "So stop skulking."

The door swung open and Dietmar poked his head in. The wiry Wingrunner looked as grim as Conner expected. "Ilse waits."

Connor stood, already wearing his full Insanity battle gear, but without the mask in place yet. Powders and spare stones hung at his belt, and he'd prepared his tertiary stones, drinking a soapstone mixture, nestling a piece of slate into his boot, and tucking a bit of marble under his tongue. If Ilse had come for a fight, she wouldn't find him an easy target.

Dietmar, who was never afraid to run boldly through the

Carraig in daylight, looked nervous, glancing at every shadow as they crept through the building.

"Relax," Connor whispered as they ghosted through the main workroom. "You're as jumpy as a pedra rancher at milking time."

Dietmar frowned. "No milk pedra. Ride them."

That did sound like a lot of fun.

Ilse and Erich waited in the deep shadows of the formal gardens north of the dark mass of the Rhidorroch. Ilse had a poet's heart to stage their final meeting in the same place she had first revealed herself to him at the Carraig.

The little team looked grim. They had lost almost half their members and they were clearly ready to fight to the death if the night's incursion did not go well.

"About time," Connor said. "What took you so long?"

That gave her just the pause he hoped for. Erich still swelled with granite power and loomed over Connor. "Will come, or many fight?"

"We can't leave yet," Connor said, trying not to feel intimidated by the fuming Rumbler.

"It's beyond time for you to make up your mind," Ilse said.

"Well, I'm not leaving without rescuing Anika and Margrit," he said, hands on hips. "Shame on you for even considering it."

"This is no time for games." Ilse gave him a disgusted look and waved Erich back.

"No, it's time to make a break," Connor said. "We free the prisoners and get you out of here."

"Don't force my hand," Ilse warned.

"Just stop threatening long enough to listen," Connor said. "I can't arrange to leave while you're all lingering."

"What is your plan?" she asked with abundant distrust.

"I'm going to orchestrate a scene with Shona and really infuriate her," Connor said.

"Is good," Erich said with a smile.

"To what end?" Ilse asked.

"To get her to threaten to remove my patronage," Connor said. Ilse nodded in understanding, but he finished anyway. "Then

I turn unclaimed in front of lots of witnesses and run away to the mountains. Everyone, including Shona, will think I'm going to die as a ravening, mindless beast."

"Dougal knows the truth," Ilse said.

Connor grinned. "Doesn't matter. He's trapped himself in his own web of lies. He can't tell anyone without revealing the truth he's worked so many years to conceal. He'd lose all his Guardians."

"That's brilliant," Ilse said. "Was this Jean's idea?"

"She helped me figure it out," Connor admitted. "And of course, when I show up again somewhere as living proof of that lie, he'll lose all his Guardians anyway."

"Finally, we have a plan," Ilse said, looking relieved.

"We just need to get you and your team out of here," Connor said. "Come on."

As he led the way through the gardens at a jog, Ilse asked, "Do you know where they're keeping my girls?"

"I'm about to find out."

They exited the north side of the gardens and approached the cluster of buildings that housed Rory's army. When Ilse realized who he was going to visit, her tension returned like an avalanche.

"This is unwise," Ilse whispered as they crouched just outside the barracks where Rory's army slept.

"It's the only way," he replied in a normal voice.

Ilse started at the volume and cocked back a fist. He gave her a confident smile to hide his own worries. This would be the hard part.

"It'll be easy."

Despite a vigorous shake of her head, he marched toward the pool of light surrounding the entrance. Even if they argued the rest of the night away, Ilse wouldn't come up with a better idea.

Connor pushed open the door and entered the long barracks, lit only by a single oil lantern on a table, the wick turned almost all the way down. The feeble light seemed to flirt with the shadows more than drive them away.

"What do you want?" A Boulder in a wooden chair tipped back against the wall challenged him in a sleepy voice.

"I will speak with Captain Rory," he declared loudly enough to disturb some of the sleeping soldiers, who cursed the guard.

The Boulder recognized Connor's mask and he snapped a quick salute.

"General. . .what's your name today?"

"Pick one. Where's Rory."

He pointed down the barracks to a door on the far side.

"Thank you. Carry on."

Connor expected to have to awaken the captain, but was surprised to find Rory sitting in a hard-backed wooden chair next to a small desk, one uneven leg propped up on an old boot. Rory looked tired and sat with chin on fists.

"Hello, lad," Rory said with a heavy sigh. "I figured I'd see you tonight."

"Captain." He had figured Rory would see the only solution, at least to one part of the problem.

Rory gestured at a ceramic bottle on the desk. "Care for a drink?"

"Probably not the best time."

The captain grunted and leaned back. "It's so much easier when we can fight them before we know them."

"What would you say if I told you I could get her out?"

Rory shook his head. "She wouldn't leave. Not Ilse, not even then. Not until you go with them or they kill you."

"What if I could arrange that?"

That got his attention. "Lad, I don't like the position you're in, but Lady Shona needs you. Running would only make things worse for everyone."

"I didn't say I was running."

He frowned. "You already tried dying for a cause, lad. Didn't work out last time."

"I know. I've got a better idea this time."

Rory sighed. "Life gets complicated around you."

"I don't plan it. No one will leave me alone."

"No matter what you choose, no one ever will."

"They might after tonight."

Rory rose and clapped him on the shoulder. "It's a hard lot, but I hope you make the best of it."

"I don't want it."

"That's why I trust you."

"Then tell me where she's being held."

Rory sighed. "It's not going to end well, lad. That I can promise you."

"At least let me try."

Rory raised his glass. "That is one remarkable woman. If only. . ."

Then he downed the dregs out of his cup and told Connor how to find the dungeon.

As Connor tuned to go he warned, "Don't hurt my men."

He nodded. "They know how to get out of my way.

Chapter 61

n Connor's second knock, a panel slid open in the reinforced door blocking his entry to the dungeon guardroom. Tomas grinned and yanked open the door before he could begin his carefully rehearsed lies.

"Come on in, lad."

Cameron, who sat in a hard wooden chair that looked like it probably left splinters every time anyone used it, groaned and tossed Tomas a small pouch of jingling coins. The rest of the circular room was unadorned stone.

"I hope you have a plan once you get outside," Tomas said as he bounced the coins on his palm, then lay down on the floor. Cameron heaved himself out of his seat and lay down next to Tomas. "Because the Tallan's own fury will descend on you once word gets out."

He should have known they'd be even less fooled than Rory. Ever since he met the two Fast Rollers, they'd been able to see to the heart of things faster than anyone else. He felt bad forcing them to choose between a friend and duty a second time, but was relieved they chose friendship.

"I know. It's been good seeing you both again."

Then he tapped soapstone and drew water from a tank he had sensed in the prison complex. When water gushed through the look-see port, he encased them in ice thick enough that it would take time for them to break out.

Cameron laughed. "I'll take those coins back."

Tomas gave Connor a disgusted look. "I bet on your creativity, lad. You can't just go around using the same tricks every time."

"Sorry. Too many distractions."

When he opened the door to Anika's cell, she lunged out and pulled him into a crushing hug. Her hair had shifted from rust to more the color of muddy water and smelled like tree sap. "Mine very okay friend," Anika laughed and gave him a fierce kiss on the cheek.

"Ready to go?"

She only hesitated long enough to accept a bag of granite powder Erich had insisted on sending down with Connor before the two of them ran for the exit. On the way out, they freed Margrit, who also gave Connor a fierce hug.

When he pressed a little piece of quartzite into her hands, she squealed with excitement and kissed him on the lips.

"A pleasure to save you," he said, trying to conceal his astonishment.

"Am many sorry," Margrit said, blinking and squinting at him. "No see many well with no stone." She popped the quartzite into her mouth and her eyes began glowing softly with her Longseer power. She visibly relaxed.

Connor had never heard of a nearsighted Pathfinder before. It seemed somehow wrong.

He led the ladies out of the keep without issue. Outside, Erich laughed and embraced his sister with such enthusiasm he might have crushed her without the protection of granite.

While the others greeted Anika and Margrit, Ilse shook Connor's hand and gave him a warm smile. "Well done."

Connor led the small, happy party toward the outer gate of the Carraig complex. Dawn would arrive soon and already linn workers were beginning to stir. None of them would pay a group of Petralists any special heed. Still, it was past time to leave.

They exited the inner wall and Connor waved to the guard. Their course took them past Lord Nevan's palace, where Jean would join up with Ilse's team and escape.

Someone stepped out of the shadows between two of the huge granite columns fronting Lord Nevan's palace. It wasn't Jean.

"I'm sorry, lad, but I can't let them leave. Not yet."

"Captain Rory? What are you doing here?"

Anika rushed past, grinning like a schoolgirl about to take her first dance at the Sogail. Erich followed close, glowering so deep he could almost suck on his own eyebrows.

Anika leaped into Rory's arms and they embraced with a fierce passion. Giggling, she punched him in the jaw.

Setting her back on her feet, Rory said. "Before you go lass, I owe your brother a fight."

Anika nodded enthusiastically, her blue eyes glowing like she'd eaten a Solas. Erich only cracked his knuckles and shook out his shoulders. "Is good. Many break head."

Ilse planted herself between the two men. "We don't have time for this."

Anika and Erich both bombarded her with a flood of arguments in Grandurian. Smiling, Rory added, "If it helps convince you, I'll promise to call my army to surround you unless you let this happen."

Ilse threw up her hands in disgust. "Captain, your timing is terrible."

Rory shrugged, "Some things just have to be done."

She pointed a warning finger at him, then swung the same threatening gesture on Erich. "Very well. Fight for Anika's honor, but I forbid you from making too much noise."

They both agreed and she stepped aside, a hint of a smile softening her angry expression. Connor watched in disbelief as the entire party paused from their flight away from enemy territory to allow the two men to fight.

"Really?" He blurted out. "Can't we do this another time?"

"No," half a dozen voices spoke together.

They had no sense. They were ruining his plan.

The two men faced off and began circling each other. Anika blew Rory a kiss. "Many luck, mine capitain."

In response, both men swelled to massive size and lunged. They collided with a flurry of punches and kicks, beating on each other so brutally, Connor couldn't keep the individual blows straight. He had seen both men fight more than once, but never had he witnessed such a raw display of unbridled battle fury.

They began shouting war cries, and Ilse hissed, "Quiet!"

Even in the midst of their titanic battle they hushed, although nothing could dim the heavy pounding of rock-hard fists striking stone skin. The fight ranged across the road with neither man gaining advantage. They didn't seem interested in trying any tricky moves, but just max-tapped in a full-on bash fight to rival the stories of legend.

Anika circled the two combatants, clapping occasionally, grinning so wide Connor could have used her face as a fish net in the Lower Wick.

After a full minute, Connor began fearing one of them would run out of granite and die under the other's hands. He couldn't decide which of the two he wanted to win, but didn't want either of them hurt. The constant pounding of their fists and grunts of exertion so close to Lord Nevan's palace would surely alert someone. They didn't have time to waste.

"We have to stop this," he urged Ilse.

"Not yet," she said in a distracted tone, her eyes locked on the mighty struggle.

It seemed wrong for Ilse to respond to a situation as a woman instead of a captain. "You're completely ruining your image. You realize that, right?"

"Hush," she said. "In our country, such contests are important."

"As important as escaping?"

"In their own way, yes."

With no other course left open to him, Connor dipped a finger into the pouch of enhanced granite Aunt Ailsa had gifted to him. He could never stop those two with his normal strength, so it was time to put Ailsa's gift to the test.

He absorbed just a little of the precious powder. The special granite faded into his skin and his curse roared to life with such power Connor gasped with awe. It rippled up his arm and even though he didn't tap it, his muscles expanded and quivered with the need to smash something. His entire body thrummed with strength, but the intense itching faded to a cool numbness. He lifted one hand and stared. Unlike the normal ash color it usually took on when hardened by granite, his skin had faded to black that still somehow glowed in the dim light.

"I said don't interfere." Ilse glanced at him, then looked again, expression startled. "What have you done to yourself?"

Before he could answer, Rory ducked a heavy blow of Erich's and as the Grandurian spun halfway around from the unspent force of the blow, Rory curse-punched him in the ribs.

Erich tumbled away and rolled into the darkness between two of the huge pillars fronting Lord Nevan's house.

"Let's move away from there," Connor said, and everyone including himself started in surprise at the deep richness of his voice. He could get used to that.

Erich emerged from the shadows and grasped one of the columns.

"No!" Ilse shouted. Too late.

With a heave of his massive shoulders, Erich ripped the pillar out and stepped through an avalanche of falling stone facade.

Ilse threw her hands up into the air in disgust. "Really?"

"Many sorry," Erich said, looking chagrined. Then he hit Rory with the granite column. Connor lost sight of the captain as he flew away into the darkness like a Sogail contest ball.

Anika began scolding Erich loudly in Grandurian and his grin of victory faded under the tirade. He tried defending himself but Anika stormed off after Rory with a final shout, "Is cheat!"

Lights came on inside Lord Nevan's palace and voices shouted for explanations and call to arms.

"We need to leave," Ilse barked. "You two quarrel later."

"I think we're beyond that." Rory stepped out of the shadows beside another pillar and ripped it out with another thunderous avalanche of broken building. Connor couldn't imagine how he returned so fast, but those concerns paled with the need to scramble out of the way as the two men began sparring with thirty foot granite pillars.

The crashing din of their duel echoed like a thunderstorm that had swallowed diorite. With a final mighty crash, both pillars exploded, and the two men stumbled apart. The area looked like all the Cutters of Alasdair had gone insane and tried to pound the front of the palace like a huge stone in the blocking yard.

"Erich, enough! We must go!" Ilse shouted.

On a third floor balcony overlooking the street, Shona stepped to the rail and peered over. Connor ducked, hoping she wouldn't recognize him in the dim light, with his skin darkened. They had to leave, and fast, or Ilse's entire team would be captured.

Footsteps pounded inside the house and the outer doors were thrown open by ten Boulder guards. Captain Rory bellowed, his deep voice echoing into the night.

"Fast Rollers!"

Near the front of the building, Erich broke away from Rory, but his granite strength gave out and his muscles deflated. He sagged in post-powder withdrawal and fell to his knees. Anika rushed to his side and lifted him off the ground, her body strong with granite power. She paused to blow Rory a kiss before retreating.

The Boulders assembled at the bottom of the main steps in front of Captain Rory. Ilse took up a rear guard position facing them.

Connor hissed, "Go! Get out of here!"

Shona cried, "Connor? What are you waiting for? Take them!"

Ilse didn't hesitate, raising earthen barriers between her little team and the Boulders. She then erupted the earth under Connor's feat, tumbling him in the air.

He was relieved she recognized he couldn't leave yet, but his hopes for their escape faded. Lights from two Solas peeled away the darkness, revealing Rory's entire army standing at the ready across Ilse's path of retreat. All of the tertiary affinity teachers stood with them.

Connor landed hard and scrambled to his feet, filled with despair, but unable to help.

Ilse and her team skidded to a halt and tried to run the other way. The army gave chase, and Rory and the Boulders from Lord Nevan's palace intercepted them.

Anika dropped her brother and threw herself at Rory just as fire and water and earth enveloped Ilse in an elemental flood. Dietmar tried closing on the enemy, but a dozen Striders outflanked him and tangled him in nets.

Margrit tried helping Erich to his feet, and she glanced once at Connor, despair in her eyes.

The fight ended almost before it began. Ilse and her team were stripped of power stones and shackled together like cattle. Erich was the last. He staggered to his feet, barely able to stand, but growling threats to the soldiers preparing to chain him.

Rory, who had released granite and returned to normal size, waved the men back and punched Erich in the face, driving him to the ground, unconscious.

"I win." He staggered with exhaustion, but smiled over his fallen opponent until he glanced at Anika in chains. Then his smile faded, replaced by a look of regret.

Connor released granite with difficulty and his skin faded to normal as he drew closer, unable to leave, but filled with despair to see the mighty Grandurians captured. They'd been so close!

Ilse, her face blackened with soot, her uniform disheveled, but her expression calm, met his gaze. "You betrayed us."

Shona arrived before he could think of a way to convince her without also revealing to all the gathered soldiers that he was instead planning to betray their homeland.

"Connor, you outplayed them all!" Shona squealed, throwing herself into his arms and kissing him passionately. She wore only her night dress, and it did little to protect her modesty.

"You need to call me General," he reminded her softly and shuffled farther away from the others, most of whom were discreet enough not to stare at Shona.

Shona didn't seem to care. "You are amazing!" She gave him another passionate kiss and whispered into his ear, "This victory is exactly what we needed. No one can stop us now."

Connor wasn't sure how the capture of Ilse helped Shona directly, but that thought only added another layer of worry. Shona clung to him, and she was quite distracting. She might be planning to enslave him, but she was enthusiastic in her affection. . .when he did exactly what she liked. The thought of spending a life with Shona made him want to go beat Ilse again for pausing in their flight.

No, it wasn't Ilse's fault. It was Rory's. He'd played Connor like a fool, and that betrayal hurt more than anything he'd experienced so far.

Shona tried to kiss him again but he said, "Everyone's watching. And remember the mask? I'm your general."

Shona laughed and whispered into his ear, "I'll call you mine very soon."

He dropped her to the ground. She was just trying to be seductive or something, but she really could have chosen a better time to remind him of their very different standings. He didn't want to be owned. He wanted to be free, to be joined to a woman he loved through a mutual agreement, a partnership of equals.

That was a concept Shona just could not understand.

Jean wrapped Shona in a cloak, meeting Connor's eye behind Shona's back. She was pale with fear, but Connor wasn't sure how to comfort her. The night that had started so well had ended in disaster.

Shona led him back to face Ilse. "You should have run when you had the chance."

For once, he absolutely agreed with Shona.

"Some things are worth the risk." She glared at Connor, "You will regret this night, boy."

"Don't listen to her," Shona said as Connor tried to think of a way to convince Ilse he had acted in good faith. "You're a hero. That tongue of hers could convince the Tallan himself his cause was just."

"Indeed, I think I could," she said with a little smile.

How could she smile when chained and captive and probably soon to be tortured? Even for her, that was a little optimistic.

Rory barked the order to move out. Led by Tomas and Cameron, who gave Connor an apologetic salute, the company headed toward the main Carraig complex.

"Excellent work, Captain," Shona grinned at Rory.

"All part of the plan, my lady." His voice was rougher than usual, his expression stony.

"Keep the prison secure from now on."

"Of course."

Rory turned and followed his troops without even once looking at Connor.

Connor watched him go, fuming. Rory had known he'd try to rescue Anika and had staged the whole thing to draw in Ilse and the rest of the company. He had thought he was taking bold steps toward freedom, but all he accomplished was to cement his position to Shona more tightly than ever.

He was going to have to do something more creative, more unexpected if he wanted to escape the noose closing around him.

Shona gave him a last lingering kiss, then took his face in both of her hands. "You did so well, my Connor. I love you."

She skipped back into the palace, humming to herself.

Jean drew Connor away from the cluster of soldiers and linn workers gathering around the broken front of the palace. "Connor, what happened?"

When he explained, she groaned. "I can't believe Rory would do that to you."

"He got to fight for Anika," Connor said, feeling disgusted. "Just in time to condemn her to die."

"He has to care for her," Jean protested.

"Then he's going to hate himself."

Jean leaned against him. "Oh, Connor, what are we going to do?"

"I don't know, but even if we escape, we can't go to Granadure without Ilse."

"We have to do something."

"I did something tonight," he pointed out. "Didn't actually make things better."

After seeing her back to her room, Connor headed back to his own small room that felt more than ever like a prison cell. He didn't sleep, but spent the night working on the next steps he should take.

He came up with only one idea.

Chapter 62

The next morning, Connor was surprised to learn that a school-wide assembly was scheduled for that afternoon. No one knew exactly why, but talk of a major announcement set the students gossiping and added to his worries. Shona had suggested the capture of Ilse would change things in a big way. He needed to understand more.

And he needed to understand why a friend had betrayed him.

So he went to find Rory.

Just before the lunch hour, Connor tracked Captain Rory down in a private sparring court in one of Lord Dail's military supply buildings. Rory was sweating from exertion and Tomas, who was the only other person in the wood-lined, enclosed court looked on the verge of collapse.

When Rory spotted Connor he stepped away from Tomas. "Go get some lunch."

Tomas gave the captain a tired salute and hurried away. He muttered to Connor, "Hope you have a lot of granite. He's in a rare mood to kill today."

"So am I."

Tomas broke into a run.

Connor picked up the hammer Tomas had dropped and tapped some of the normal Alasdair White itching through his system.

Rory wiped sweat from his face and hefted his identical weapon. "Thought I'd see you today."

"We need to talk." Actually, he felt more like yelling.

"Words or hammers?"

"Both."

"Good."

The two of them attacked at the same time and came together with a resounding crash of hammers. Connor unleashed all of the pent-up frustration from the past weeks, all of his worry for Ilse and her company, and all of his anger at Rory's betrayal. He threw every ounce of it at Rory. He struck and struck again, raining blows on his bigger opponent.

Rory matched his every move.

The two of them shifted across the width of the stone-floored practice court and then back again. Sweat sprang out on Connor's face and he tasted the salt of it, felt the sting of it in his eyes, but didn't slow. Even strengthened by granite, his arms began to burn and his hands to ache under the constant heavy pounding, but he didn't relent. His breath came fast and the court smelled of broken stone and sweat and anger.

When he finally began to slow, unable to maintain the intense pace, Rory stepped back, lowered his hammer, and braced hands on knees, panting. "Took me twice as long to work through it all."

"I'll go again if you want." Connor felt empty, stripped of rage and left with only a slow-burning determination.

"That bout served its purpose," Rory said. "You actually fought like you know what you're doing for a change."

"Training is paying off." Connor threw down his hammer and paced away. It was good they had burned through his anger. He needed to think, to move carefully for a change.

"Captain, you lied to me last night."

"A little, but not as much as you lied to me."

He wanted to shout, to deny he'd misled anyone, but the simple words shattered his attempts at justification and scored deep. He had been planning to subvert everything Shona was doing at the Carraig, critically damage her position. The consequences to her could have been disastrous and lifelong. He paced away again to avoid punching Rory in the mouth. He didn't want the captain as an enemy, but there were a lot of things he didn't want and his opinion didn't seem to matter.

"I just wish you hadn't lied about letting her go."

Rory led him to a pair of benches and a bucket of water set against the wall near the door. After ladling a drink for himself he said, "Listen to me, lad. Truth is tough when you're dealing with high lords and politics. Shona sees things one way, but that's not the whole truth. Or the only truth, for that matter."

"And you're going to tell me the truth this time?"

"About last night, yes."

"Why would I believe you?"

"Because it's a truth that matters to me."

Connor drank a ladle full of water, dropped onto a bench, and motioned Rory to continue.

"I did what I did because I had to know."

"Know what?"

"If it was all a lie. Was Anika just playing me, manipulating me the way they like to do, or could she really. . ." He trailed off and shrugged.

"So now you know," Connor said softly. "And knowing cost her everything."

"It sounds worse when you say it like that."

"Doesn't really matter how you say it, does it?"

"Kind of makes pursuing a relationship difficult," Rory sighed.

Connor nearly laughed in Rory's face. How could he consider a relationship with Anika? Not only was she generally terrifying, but they were soldiers in opposing armies. Even if they could get over that, capturing her and locking her away in chains was something he couldn't help her forget by sending some flowers to her cell.

"Captain, let them go."

Rory leaned back against the wall and closed his eyes. "I can't."

"I'm here," Connor declared with resignation. "I am Shona's. She has everything she wants, so just let them go."

"I sincerely wish I could, lad, but you're not the only one trapped by your position." Pain shone in his eyes.

"What are we going to do?"

"I don't know." Rory rose and clapped him on the shoulder, his expression grave. "But don't give up. Life may not be what we want, but we can make the best of it. There's always hope."

So much for trying reason. It worked in Alasdair but there, in that isolated location, it was easier to think straight. With all the high nobles clustered around the castle, they muffled clear thinking like wool ear plugs muffled sound.

He'd have to pull the plugs out.

"Captain, I don't think people are going to like my idea of hope."

Rory nodded. "Probably not, but think before you act, lad. You won't get another chance." He retrieved the discarded hammers. "Best get your mask on. You'll be needed at the assembly."

"What's it all about?"

"I don't know everything. All I can say is it's Lady Shona's doing."

She had seen some kind of opportunity immediately and was already moving to secure her new position. Shona was nothing if not focused, and that boded poorly for Ilse and her team. He spent the time walking back to his suite considering various options for responding, but couldn't lay specific plans until he knew more.

When he entered his private rooms, he retrieved the mask and a fresh set of battle leathers. When he returned to the salon with them in hand, he stopped in his tracks.

"Hello, Connor," Ivor said. "I think we need to talk."

Chapter 63

hat are you doing here?" Connor asked, dropping his costume and stepping into the room. He still had a little granite, but all of his tertiary affinity stones were in the pouch on his belt. If Ivor had come to fight, he was in trouble.

Ivor looked more intrigued than angry. He nodded toward the costume. "I can't believe I didn't see it sooner."

"How did you learn?"

"Patience," Ivor said, dropping into one of the overstuffed chairs and selecting a fruit from a silver tray. "Sheigra overheard the entire ruckus over by Nevan's palace last night."

Connor sank onto the couch as his heart sank through his boots. He'd worked so hard to shield his conversations from Pathfinders, but just about everyone had let their guard down the night before. Shona had used his name, as had Jean. Others probably had too.

Ivor leaned forward. "I find it fascinating that you have contacts in Granadure. Were you really betraying them, or did you just botch an attempt to run?"

"It's complicated."

"No doubt," Ivor nodded. "But why run a geall like that when your army is doing so well and when the nation's on the brink of warfare?

"Don't you ever feel trapped?" Connor asked, gesturing around the room. "By all of this?"

Ivor shrugged. "All of this is pretty nice compared to what most get."

"It's still a cage," Connor retorted.

"Life is a cage sometimes," Ivor said. "Look at Shona. Look at the other nobles. They're stuck in cages no bigger than ours. At least we're given a chance to help fashion our futures. How many people get that?"

"It's not enough," Connor said, wishing Ivor could see.

"What else is there?" Ivor asked. "If you push too hard, you'll lose patronage. And even if escaping to Granadure somehow blocks Guardians from turning unclaimed, what then?" At Connor's surprised look, he added, "I told you, Connor. I study everything. I've considered Granadure and the Arishat League. But do you think they'll be any better? Think they'll let you live in peace?"

"Maybe."

Ivor laughed. "Don't be naive. Here, we get the chance to lead powerful houses and armies of Petralists. There, we'd be forced to fight with nothing but ungifted weaklings at our back. Sure, you might feel free for a few weeks or even months, but then you're dead."

"There may be another way," Connor argued, although Ivor had just voiced many of his own fears. Was there no way to find freedom and peace in the world?

"I haven't found it yet," Ivor said. "But if you have, why are you limiting yourself?"

"In what way am I limiting myself?"

Ivor laughed. "I hardly believed it, but all the little clues add up too perfectly." He saluted. "To think, I'm friends with the Blood of the Tallan."

"Who else knows?" Connor asked. "Has Sheigra told her father?"

"Not yet, but why not?" Ivor sounded honestly puzzled. "Why all the games? Why not reveal the truth? You could have won the contest with ease. Everyone would flock to you instead of trying to beat you down."

"That's part of the problem." Flocking hordes of people would act like living shackles, locking him to Obrion and preventing any chance of ever seeing Verena again.

"Shona wants to own you," Ivor admitted. "On the one hand, she's perhaps the most desirable woman in the kingdom. Her father is one of the most powerful. United to their house, confirmed as Blood of the Tallan, you could live like a king."

"A marauding king," Connor said. "If I embrace that life, they will require that I destroy Granadure and the other nations of the Arishat League and restore Obrioner rule everywhere."

Ivor shook his head. "You're still not seeing straight."

"I've looked at it from every angle." He felt like pounding a fist against the stone walls in frustration.

"Your problem is you don't think like a Petralist. You think like a linn." When Connor motioned him to continue he said, "You need to flip the geall on them."

"How?"

"Reveal your curse."

"Not going to work." He had been hoping Ivor would come up with something unique.

"If she's not good enough for you, get another patron," Ivor said. "Revealing your curse shifts control from her to you. If you reveal what you really are, you break the game more completely than we ever could with our little plots fiddling with the standings. You could define your terms, and if she doesn't like them, I guarantee another noble house will. She couldn't take the risk of not accepting your demands. She would lose everything."

"She's got my family," Connor admitted. "She'll enslave my entire village if I don't do what she wants."

"She's bluffing," Ivor said after a moment's pause, but his enthusiasm had faded. "She can't risk losing you."

"Want to bet the lives of my family on that?"

"You were willing to bet their lives last night," Ivor pointed out.

Connor paused to think about that. What if he did reveal his curse? That could generate more than enough confusion and strife between the high lord families as they fought over him to orchestrate turning unclaimed. He'd need to act before any of them formally offered patronage, or no one would believe it, but if he timed it right, he could still escape and everyone would accept it.

He still wasn't sure how to free Ilse and her team, but once he freed himself, he could sneak back into the Carraig and break them out. Or even return as a rampager and scatter their guards, releasing the Grandurians as a tragic accident.

He liked the idea of that.

"You're right," he said to Ivor. "I think it's time to flip the whole geall on Shona and turn the Tir-raon on its head."

"How?"

"Do you trust me?"

Ivor hesitated, and Connor wondered how he'd have answered that. Did their friendship trump their duties and responsibilities as Guardians and champions?

After a few long seconds that seemed to take an hour, Ivor finally laughed. "I'm as insane as you!"

"Good," Connor grinned, feeling immensely relieved. "We're going to need a bit of insanity to pull this off. I can't tell you exactly what I have in mind, but I will."

He swore that he'd find the right time to share the truth about unclaimed with Ivor. His friend deserved to know the truth.

"I'll hold you to that," Ivor said. "And in return, I'll make a scene during the assembly and we'll show the world who you really are."

"I appreciate your help," Connor said, and he meant it. "We're going to have some fun with this."

"To freedom," Ivor grinned.

"Geall on."

Chapter 64

As students poured into the huge assembly hall and formed ranks in their assigned armies, Connor climbed the stairs to the dais. Dressed in his mask and battle leathers, he scanned the long rows of people.

Lord Nevan stood near the low rail watching the growing crowds. Shona stood beside him, and instead of battle leathers she wore a blue and silver gown cut to accentuate her full figure. She looked regal, every inch a high lady and heir to a major house. Shona was not attending as a student but as a leader.

Shona gave him a dazzling smile and nodded to the back of the platform where a portable curtain walled off a small section. He stepped around it, and his heart sank.

Ilse and her company sat chained in a row and looking exhausted. They glared at Connor, and he frowned back. With the Fast Rollers keeping a close eye, he couldn't speak with them, couldn't try slipping any power stones to them. Shona had moved more boldly than he'd expected. It was like he was trying to braid rope while Shona was setting the strands on fire before handing them to him.

Shona beckoned and he joined her, grateful the mask helped conceal his expression. "I didn't expect to see them."

"We couldn't waste this opportunity," she said with controlled excitement. "With this victory, we can break out."

Interesting turn of phrase since he was planning to break out of her break-out.

Ivor gave Connor a nod of encouragement when he arrived with Padraigin and Redmund in tow. The other high lord representatives peeked behind the curtain as they arrived, then peppered Shona and Lord Nevan with questions. They promised that everything would become clear very soon.

"I don't like your games," Lord Kane muttered.

Shona gave him a happy smile. "That's because our games have advanced beyond chasing cats with sticks."

No, she wanted to chase entire nations, using Connor as the stick.

As soon as the other champions took their places on the platform, Lord Dail beckoned the hall to silence. "You are all gathered today to celebrate a great victory." He turned. "Lord Nevan will explain."

Connor wondered how much they had paid to get him to relinquish the podium so quickly.

Lord Nevan's Pathfinder not only magnified his voice, but somehow made it sound richer as it echoed across the vast chamber. "Our mock battles are designed to prepare you for the harsh realities of war," he declared. "In the very near future, many of you will depart for the front lines to lead the fight against Grandurian oppression."

That generated a wave of cheering.

"But war is not some future event in distant lands. The threat is at our doors! In fact, last night an attempted assassination of the Lady Shona was thwarted within the castle compound."

He ceded the speaking position to Shona, and everyone hung on her words. Shona took her time, clearly enjoying the attention.

"My friends, as Lord Nevan stated, our community was indeed invaded last night. And by a specially trained strike force of Grandurian assassins!"

While the crowd gasped or shouted angrily, Shona beckoned. Rory and his men prodded Ilse's company to their feet and to the front of the dais. They looked battered, but defiant.

"Kill them!" Students and teachers alike shouted, fists raised, expressions darkened with hatred, screaming for the blood of the hated Grandurians.

Connor was dumbfounded to see his own army, led by his captains, as enraged as anyone else. Little Declan looked ready to climb on the platform and challenge Ilse to single combat, and Fearghas kept clutching his shoulder, as if reaching for the sword that wasn't there. Their hatred was a living, ugly thing, shocking in its intensity.

Then he realized they had been conditioned since birth to fear and hate the Grandurians even more than common linn would. Those students would lead armies against Granadure, so they had been taught to react instantly and without remorse.

He suddenly felt far more afraid for Ilse and her team.

For her part, Ilse didn't seem to share his concern. She surveyed the angry crowd with her usual unflagging calm. Anika and Erich snarled at the students and looked ready to give battle to every taker.

Shona held up her hands for calm. "These assassins were captured just outside Lord Nevan's palace. Some of you may have seen the destruction they caused before being defeated by Captain Rory and our very own General Insanity!"

The crowd erupted into loud cheering and Shona drew Connor to her to wave. She wrapped one arm around his waist, thus reinforcing her claim on him before the entire school. Claiming the Grandurians had come as assassins was a brilliant lie since everyone would assume it, thus offer no awkward questions.

Shona continued, "With this great victory, new responsibilities will unfortunately tear me away from my duties here at the school. The general and I must leave at once to deliver the prisoners to my father for interrogation."

So that was her ultimate goal. Shona hoped to escape the school before the completion of the Tir-raon. She could avoid the irksome negotiations and leave with him in tow.

"I protest," Lord Kane shouted above the din, leading a chorus of similar exclamations from the other high lord representatives. "You are bound by the conditions of the Tir-raon and cannot leave."

"Matters of state trump those concerns," Shona started to argue, but he shouted right over her.

"We have the right to participate in the interrogation," Lady Una cried. "What if there are more assassins?"

Shona tried to reassure them, but she'd lost control of the conversation.

"What are you trying to hide from us?" Lord Kane finally bellowed.

Ivor's voice drowned out the others. "I can answer that." He moved to the front of the platform and raised his voice high. "Lady Shona is keeping secrets." He made an extravagant bow to her, and Connor loved the look of trepidation on her face.

Ivor pointed at Connor. "General Insanity is not who he claims to be."

"You've been smoking pedra dung again," Shona said dismissively, but her voice carried an edge of fear.

"I want to know why you're trying to conceal the nation's greatest hope, hiding him in plain sight under a mask. You can't hide any longer!"

Time to flip the geall on them all.

With growing eagerness, Connor reached up and removed his leather mask. "Today I share my real name with all of you! I am Connor!"

The high lord representatives looked at each other with confusion. None of them knew him. Lord Dail looked worried, and Lord Nevan flabbergasted.

Lord Kane looked disgusted. "All that pretense with the mask for this?"

Clamors of surprise rippled across the hall as students and professors recognized him.

Connor waved. "You should see your faces."

Shona grabbed Connor's shoulder. "What are you doing?"

He shrugged. "Ivor knows. Better to take the pedra by the jaws than let him control the news."

Many students looked like they couldn't decide whether to be angry, or to laugh at the joke. His army looked stunned, but Aifric raised her fist high and shouted, "Hurray for General Connor!"

That tipped the scales in his favor. Lorcc took up the cry, followed by Declan. Fearghas looked like he wanted to skin a raging torc, but raised his fist in salute. Princess Catriona looked like she'd been kicked in the face by a mule. Then she suddenly grinned and waved so hard, she almost knocked over the girl standing beside her.

Ivor shouted over the din of a new argument between the high lord representatives. "Know this! Connor is not Dawnus."

That got everyone's attention.

"We've seen his powers," Lord Kane argued.

Ivor shook his head. "Not all of them."

Shona took a threatening step toward Ivor, quivering with rage and hissed, "Shut your cursed mouth, linn, or I will see your patronage canceled."

Her towering rage was impressive, but Ivor laughed it off. He held the upper hand, and he knew it.

Ivor shouted to the attentive crowd. "Shona orders me to conceal the truth from all of you, the truth that could win the war and save thousands of lives. What say you?"

Students shifted their anger to Shona, screaming at her. Catriona shouted above the rest, "Ivor is a general. You're nothing, Shona! Tell us, Ivor!"

Students took up the chant of "Tell us Ivor!"

He grinned at Shona. "Still think you can keep the secret?"

"You will pay," she promised him.

"You first."

He raised his hands high and the crowd fell to into an expectant hush, allowing him to speak in a conversational tone. He pointed at Connor. "I'm thrilled to introduce you to the heir of Obrion's greatest glory. Welcome Connor, Blood of the Tallan!"

Shocked silence dropped over the crowd. Shona shed her ineffectual anger and, grinning with pride, took Connor's hand and declared triumphantly. "For once Ivor is correct. Connor is Blood of the Tallan!"

She could shift plans faster than Jean's grandmother could shove a tonic down a person's throat.

"Can it be possible?" Lady Una asked, her voice cracking.

Connor took a step forward and most of the assembled high nobles shuffled back. That was so much fun, he took another step and most of them retreated again.

Lord Kane did not. With fists on hips he glared from Shona to Connor. "Your theatrics are impressive, but we'll need more proof than your word to believe such a ridiculous claim."

Shona shrugged. "Show them, Connor."

Chapter 65

If Connor was going to stand unmasked before the world, he would show them what it meant to be Blood of the Tallan. He had already downed soapstone before leaving his Kilian apartments and slate wafers rested in both boots. So he popped a piece of marble into his mouth and wedged it under his tongue, then slipped a piece of quartzite into his cheek.

Padraigin drew closer, her expression filled with wonder. "Can you really use both of those?"

"Anyone can pop a few stones in their mouth," Lord Kane said.

Connor ignored him and tapped slate. For a moment he worried he was too far removed from the earth, standing as he was on that raised wooden platform in the huge assembly hall with Tallan only knew how many levels of building between them and the earth. With what he knew of the warren of the undercity, it was challenging to find a solid connection to earth anywhere in the inner city.

He actually felt a vague, distant sense that something might be out there, like peering through a heavy fog while standing on Lookout Rock above Alasdair. There had to be a way. He could not imagine generations of lords standing on that stage, cut off from their most powerful battle stone.

Pulsing out his earth senses in every direction, he felt Redmund and Padraigin, like torches shining bright in a moonless night. At the gentle touch of his will on hers, Padraigin started, eyes wide with wonder. Redmund just scowled, looking like he took that touch as a personal insult.

Then Connor found the secret he'd hoped for. Slender strips of granite ran between the wooden planks of the platform. They were colored the same as the wood and were so well blended he hadn't noticed them before.

Gregor the Sentry had explained that one could not walk their earth senses through stone unless it was an igneous power stone and the Sentry possessed that affinity and was tapping it. Connor had absorbed a little granite prior to leaving his suite, so he tapped it, just a little, relishing that familiar itch of his lifelong curse.

Immediately, his earth senses slid across the platform along the inlaid granite, then connected to concealed pillars of granite that plunged through the floor and the basements below, all the way down to the earth.

The granite was old. It triggered the faint but sharp taste of very aged cheese. The ground far below felt tired, as if exhausted by generations of half-trained Petralists walking through it. Even so, the indomitable strength of the earth flowed up through the connection, reviving him and enlivening his mind.

"Well?" Lord Kane asked, even though only a few seconds had passed.

Connor gave him a confident smile. "Just building suspense."

One more secret of the Carraig had opened to him, like a delicate petal of an immense rose whose heart could never truly be revealed. He decided what he needed to do.

The crowd was pressing closer, some looking on with expectant wonder, others with contemptuous doubt. Connor seized the earth far below and drove it up through hollow tubes that drilled down through the walls of the undercity, no doubt expressly for that purpose. The platform began to vibrate, then Connor grasped the main supports with fingers of earth, tearing them free and lifting the entire platform on columns of earth.

Many of the high lord representatives cried out in surprise, but Connor kept the platform level, rising at a stately pace a dozen feet above the awestruck crowd. Then he drew more earth over the top of the platform, flowing toward him like thick-bodied serpents. Even as the platform continued rising, Connor rose high above it on a Sentry tower, complete with little crenellations.

The crowd began cheering and shouting his name, recognizing that the use of slate proved he was more than Dawnus. Connor laughed, then lifted his arms to draw their attention.

He wasn't finished yet.

Holding firm in his mind the image of slate as a sunken pit, lined with stone, he added the two gateways of soapstone and marble like doors on opposite sides of the pit, facing outward, and reached for those powers.

In his private training, he'd managed to work with all three elements only a little. He could not afford failure. So he started with marble, sucking on the little stone under his tongue until his mouth burned and the fierceness of elemental fire tinged his slate strength with a wild flavor.

Flames crept up his tower, spiraling around in multi-hued colors. While the flames grew, he embraced soapstone. Water was his strongest element, and it answered his call, despite the distraction of the other elements. Water erupted from a tank behind the platform, and Connor added spirals of bubbling liquid to the tower, intermingling it with the existing flames.

The clapping grew louder. Riding the wave of exultation pouring from the crowd, Connor tapped quartzite and extended fingers of thought into the air, imagining the gateway like a stained-glass roof over the others.

The air seemed to like the idea of lording over the others and did not immediately rebel. Connor planned to form a gentle breeze, but the stale air in the assembly hall didn't seem to want to move. So he reached farther and found a strong breeze slipping along the outer wall. He grabbed it by the horns and pulled.

A window high up the wall burst open and a howling wind tore into the room. Connor drew it close, encircling the tower with a whirlwind that absorbed the flames and water, whipping the other elements around him in a beautiful, multi-colored spiral.

"Blood of the Tallan!" Lord Nevan shouted, triggering a round of applause.

Connor glanced down, peering through the elemental display at Shona, whose initial triumphant smile was fading to a worried frown.

He shouted with joy, his cry merging in with the thunderous applause from the hall. He was really doing it! He was controlling all four elements.

Then quartzite seemed to realize it was actually playing nice with the others, and it bucked against his control. The whirlwind became wilder, threatening to spray the other elements across the room. Connor tried to hold on, but riding multiple elements required a loose touch, and at his reflexive tightening of control, the other elements began fighting him too.

His tower swayed, with fire and water spraying high into the air. The applause faded as the crowd realized he was losing control.

Then Ivor seized the flames. Connor gratefully relinquished control to him, and the fires coalesced into the form of a giant bird that glided gracefully across the hall and out that open window before exploding into glittering bits of light.

Padraigin connected a second later, her will reinforcing his over the winds. Connor released them to her, and the whirlwind faded away in a loud fanfare of invisible trumpets, followed by a triumphant marching beat from heavy drums.

Connor settled the tower back to the platform and returned the stage to the assembly floor. Ivor and Padraigin waited for him there, and he gripped their shoulders.

"Thanks."

"Couldn't let you have all the fun," Ivor said.

Padraigin gave him an enthusiastic hug, squealing like a little girl. "I can't believe it. You're really real!"

Connor turned to the gaping high lord representatives. "So, was that more or less what you were expecting?"

Lord Kane threw his head back and laughed. The big man crossed the distance between them and gripped Connor's hands. "It really is true! The Blood of the Tallan is returned!"

That opened the floodgates, and the other assembled representatives gathered around Connor in an excited mass, touching him as if proving to themselves that he really existed, chattering excitedly. The crowds of students in the hall pressed toward the stage, hands raised to Connor, cheering. His army shouted the loudest.

Redmund's voice boomed above the din. "Accolades built upon sandy foundations are but dross dipped in glitter."

"Think bigger, man," The pudgy Lady Una cried. "This is more than being a mud-wind or a flaming-wet Dawnus. We've waited for the return of this gift for centuries." She grabbed Connor's arm. "You're not officially tied to any house yet, are you?"

He could have kissed her.

"Uh, no. I. . ."

"Well, we can offer immediate adoption," she cried.

Lord Runda and Lord Kane spoke over each other, declaring they'd give him anything he wanted. The others piled on offers as fast as they could speak, pressing in around Connor with feverish intensity. If he wasn't planning to turn unclaimed, his worst fears would be realized. Those men and women seemed almost desperate enough to tear him apart and claim a limb.

Shona looked like she wanted to throw them all out that distant window.

Lord Nevan tried to regain control. "Ladies and gentlemen, Connor is sponsored by High Lord Dougal's house."

"But he has no official tie yet," Lady Una shouted. She seemed desperate to find a way to claim Connor, even though she was already sponsoring Padraigin.

"He will," Shona declared angrily. "As soon as he wins the Tir-raon, his choice will cement connection to my house."

"Is this true?" Lord Kane asked.

Redmund shouted, "He hasn't won yet!"

"But he's Blood of the Tallan," Lady Una protested.

"Rain falls upon the noble and the base alike," Redmund declared. "Only the skilled hands craft a shelter from the storm."

"You really think you have a chance to beat him?" Padraigin asked.

"I claim the right to fight him again." Redmund actually spoke clearly.

Connor caught Ivor's eye, and his friend looked like he wanted to punch Redmund in the head. He was flipping their flipped geall.

"Oh, just admit he's going to win." Ivor tried to rescue the plan. "The Tir-raon is all a shambles this year."

"Besides," Shona said. "Like I said earlier, Connor and I need to take the prisoners to my father. The game's over."

Was she really helping Ivor demolish the Tir-raon? Did she realize how much power she'd be ceding to the champions?

The other representatives argued so heatedly that Lord Dail ordered a cessation of the discussion until the assembly could be dismissed. Everyone on the dais clearly realized that if Shona left with Connor and the prisoners, they'd lose all possibility of ever controlling either.

The crowds wouldn't disperse until Connor descended the stage and mingled with them. They pressed in from all sides, desperate to touch him. They might have crushed him if he hadn't tapped a little granite.

Tomas and Cameron led some armored Boulders to restore a semblance of order and forced the crowd to make enough room for Connor to walk through. If only he could figure a way to help Ilse escape while the number of guards was reduced.

Many women wept, and the men fought for a chance to grip his hand. The outpouring of emotion was overwhelming. It enveloped Connor, filling him with wonder, and with a hint of guilt. How would those students react when they learned he'd abandoned them?

"You'll all get a chance to meet with the general again," Lord Dail finally promised, and with the help of Rory's army, managed to clear the hall.

When Connor returned to the stage and negotiations resumed, Lord Nevan proposed a compromise. "It appears to me that all objections can be resolved by allowing a final battle between the established armies to declare this year's winner."

"With control of the prisoners the prize," Lord Kane declared.

"And Connor must choose his house and pairings immediately," Lady Una added.

Lord Nevan tried to protest the additional conditions, but the others shouted him down. Connor was tempted to tap slate and break apart the platform. Ilse's company might just make a break for freedom, and he might knock some sense into the fools. Running another battle was a terrible idea.

Shona said, "I cannot surrender Ilse, the captain of the Grandurians, for she has other information that my father requires for the invasion. However, let's make the game more interesting by placing the remaining prisoners into the battlefield. The general who wins through to them can kill them or interrogate them first."

The representatives who didn't have champion contenders argued against that idea, but had little standing to defy it. The others eventually forced an agreement that if the winning general killed the sacrificial Grandurians they would win the right to first interrogation of Ilse, who would later be surrendered back to Shona.

Connor listened to the negotiations with growing desperation. The attempt to subvert the game had flipped completely. Not only would he have to fight again, but he needed to win through to the prisoners. He had no idea how he'd help them escape, or even if they would allow him to do so rather than just attacking and forcing him to kill them.

If they died, Granadure would consider him an enemy, and he'd lose Verena forever. Unless he fled into Althing, he'd be forced to lead the invasion of Granadure and perhaps kill more people he cared about.

The world was well and truly insane.

Even if he won, would choosing any other house be a better form of slavery than the one Shona offered? The freedom to choose his course might grant him the leverage to accept Shona on his own terms.

All he had to do was kill the Grandurians who had risked so much to save him. Before they murdered him first.

He really wished for simpler friends.

"Hold on," Connor interrupted the ongoing heated discussion. "The Tir-raon's not about murdering unarmed opponents. That runs contrary to the oaths we all took at the beginning of the games." He was actually very proud of that argument.

"He's right," Ivor added.

"And are you really willing to risk the lives of your students against that highly-trained strike force?" Padraigin added.

That made them think, and for a second, Connor dared to hope they'd escape the insanity of the battle idea.

Then Lord Kane said, "We are a nation on the brink of war. Our students will face Grandurians in a matter of weeks. What better test than to fight them now?"

"And we can have Captain Rory's forces ready to assist," Lady Una added.

"We won't need him," Lord Runda said. "Any of our champions will easily defeat those Grandurians."

Connor tried arguing more, but Lord Kane waved away his concerns. "We'll give them a little powder so they can fight for their lives. No one can ask for more than that. We're giving them a chance."

The others liked the idea, but Connor tried again. "Think about what you're planning!"

Anika interrupted, speaking from where the prisoners stood nearby, having listened to the arguments about their fates in silence the entire time. "Is okay. We take many with die."

"Settled," Lord Nevan declared. "The final battle of this term will be held tomorrow morning!"

Connor glanced at the Grandurians, and they all faced him with resolute determination. They really preferred dying in battle to imprisonment and probable torture. On one hand, he could understand their position, but it made trying to help them so much harder.

The representatives and Shona left in a group, still haggling about details. Shona glanced back once, but he couldn't tell what she was trying to communicate. Connor watched, feeling more chained to a fate he abhorred than ever. If he lost, Ivor or the other champions would kill the Grandurians without hesitation.

If he won, he'd face Ilse's company in the long-dreaded battle to the death, but with the entire school looking on.

Rory ordered his men to lead the prisoners away. As they started to clank off in their heavy chains, Ilse caught Connor's eye and spoke with calm intensity. "We will kill you."

Redmund paused nearby, his expression downright murderous. "I'll kill you first."

"You're taking things a bit too personally," Connor said.

The powerful Dawnus shook his head. "You insult everything I stand for, and I will not lose my honor to you."

"You've already lost it," Padraigin snapped.

The other champions left, leaving Rory and Connor alone in the huge assembly hall. The captain said, "That was unexpected."

Connor barked a laugh. "It's a total mess. You still think it was a good idea to take them prisoner?"

"You're the reason they're here. You should have made them leave a long time ago."

"You know I can't control them."

"Perhaps not," Rory said with a slow nod. Then he added in a deadly whisper.

"This you do control. If she dies, I will kill you."

Chapter 66

ean rose from her padded chair in the secret library and stretched. Exhaustion tugged against her resolve and urged her with increasing force to curl up near the fire to sleep, if only for a few minutes. She paced away from the huge tome that she had pored through all night, driven by worry for Connor.

She hated seeing the weight he was forced to bear, and his plan to try using the rampager powder terrified her. If he lost control, he could kill someone or get killed in turn. The shackles were tightening around him, so she did the only thing she could that might help.

She studied.

The book proved a treasure of information, but much of it she barely understood. It reminded her of those days when she first began diagnosing patients with her grandmother. She tried so hard, but lacked the foundational knowledge to see clearly sometimes. The only way to gain that knowledge was through long experience, stubborn persistence, and the guidance of one who knew the path she sought to tread.

Her studies of the ancient text were so much more difficult because she lacked that final resource, and most of her questions went unanswered.

Jean dropped back into her chair and massaged her temples. She vowed to keep studying, even though the clinical part of her mind recognized the symptoms of deep fatigue and suggested rest would prove more productive.

"Sleep is a relentless enemy whose advance may be slowed but never truly halted."

Jean yelped and started up out of her chair. How long had she sat there, more asleep than awake?

Evander stood nearby, looking down with his black-eyed gaze. The giant, mysterious man made a tiny bow. "The nuall, though master of the forest, cannot run the night through."

"I am pretty tired," she admitted and brushed fingers through her hair. "I'm sorry I don't look fit for company."

He smiled, a surprisingly warm gesture. "Nay, fair one. To gaze upon your face took my thoughts by the hand back to the days when I walked with the earth as a young man."

She blushed. "I hope you have a lot of happy memories."

His smile faded and his eyes sagged. "Nay, fair one. The pleasant spring of my youth was scorched in the fires of tragedy."

Deep in those sad eyes, a tiny flicker of fierce anger burned, and Jean found herself drawn to him, moved by his grief and simmering anger at some ancient tragedy. She placed a hand on his arm and pulled him down until she could kiss his cheek. "Remember only the good times, and know they can come again."

Evander's smile returned, but it held a heavy sadness. He patted her hand. "The joy of a new spring rises only after the storms of winter. We will walk new roads of grief before that happy morning."

The fire in his eyes intensified, belying the calm tone of his voice and Jean shivered. "I'm worried those roads are already here. That's why I've been studying all night. There's so much to learn, but I don't understand!"

"Only through drops of time and diligence may the well of knowledge fill."

"I don't have that much time. At least answer one question for me."

When he didn't deny her request, she flipped back through the book to a page she had marked with the ribbon from her hair.

"Tell me what this means." She pointed at the page and Evander leaned forward to read.

Belay the choice to allow any to cross the first threshold not driven by strength or speed. The burden of trust must weigh heavily upon them, for they alone may push the ascendant to their will.

Evander rose to his full height and sighed, the sound like wind whispering along the tops of the mountain. "The unspoiled finger of youth may touch with innocence the depths of sorrow and the ultimate root of the downfall of my brother and the death of most of my friends."

"Tell me about them," Jean urged, moved by the depth of emotion she sensed in him, and eager to learn more than the tantalizing suggestions of his tragic past.

Evander settled into the chair she had just vacated, bringing his head closer to her level. The chair creaked ominously, but held, and Jean settled on the padded arm beside him. So close, she noted the ink stains on his fingers and enjoyed his unique scent of clean earth and oiled leather.

He considered her for a moment, his deep, black eyes mysterious and penetrating at the same time. "Trouble of ages, like the arc of days, overshadows the world. Commotion abounds when the protection of rage alone prevents the loss of control."

"But rage leads to loss of control," Jean protested, confused.

Evander shook his head. "Memories bearing the weight of sorrow wear a path in the valleys of the mind as surely as do those soaring with happy light."

Jean wasn't sure how to respond to that. Evander was old, but she wanted to slap him and make him explain those memories and reveal the truths he held so close. A thousand questions bubbled through her mind and she struggled to formulate the right words.

"You spoke of danger," she said. "What should Connor fear the most?"

"Dougal."

That one word, spoken with solemn surety, terrified her. If Connor failed to escape, Dougal would own him through Shona. She gripped Evander's arm. "You mentioned protection. Is that what you were talking about when you said rage could protect somehow?"

"The monster within alone may withstand the monster without."

"He's already planning to turn unclaimed to escape the trap," Jean said, still nervous about Connor attempting such a risky road. "Is there more to it than that?"

Evander opened his mouth to respond, but paused and cocked his head to one side as if listening. Then he rose and strode across the room, placed a hand upon one of the ornate pillars and bowed his head in concentration. His shoulders hunched and his form shifted into lines of tension. The shift was minute, but Jean was used to spotting the telltale signs of patients in distress and the change screamed at her that something was very wrong.

"What is it?" She placed one hand lightly on his arm and could feel the corded muscles under his leather jacket ripple with energy.

Evander straightened and took her hand. "The dawn of a day of trial is upon us. Be strong, young one, and hold true the course of your heart."

Then he strode rapidly from the room.

Jean abandoned the library. The final battle of the Tir-raon was scheduled to begin after breakfast and she needed to find Connor and share what she had learned, or thought she'd learned from Evander.

A whisper of doubt lingered in her mind. Evander was running the deepest geall of all. She wanted to believe he really had urged Connor to use porphyry. Was that suggestion instead the most elegant way for Evander to silence those who had learned too much?

Chapter 67

onnor awaited his army on the practice field just outside the walled compound of the Rhidorroch after breakfast, acutely aware that he wore no face mask. The sun blazed bright in a deep blue sky and already warmed the chill morning air. He decided to take that as a good omen, and slipped his hand into the small leather bag of powder stores strapped to his belt. It also held his enhanced powders and his sculpted stones. He had decided to bring them all, even the last of his porphyry.

He might need them. There could be no finishing second place. For him, there would be no returning from this battlefield. He must free the Grandurians, then turn unclaimed. He could not leave any of the treasures behind.

His troops began arriving in large groups and hurried into position as if afraid to miss anything. Most of them regarded him with open curiosity and saluted with enthusiasm. When he saw no open hostility, he relaxed. The tight bond he had enjoyed with his army as their general was one thing he dearly wished not to sacrifice, and he welcomed the chance to drop the facade and just be himself.

Declan was the first of his captains to approach. The chubby Sentry walked with a wide smile and more confidence in his step than Connor had ever seen. He saluted smartly, then grasped Connor's hand.

"It's such an honor, sir!"

"You don't care that I'm a commoner?"

He shrugged. "You're not the first Guardian at the Carraig.

Like my teacher says, the fruit is honored not by its origins but only for being eaten when ripe."

"Thanks. You spoke that like a true Sentry."

Declan grinned. "It'll be great having another Sentry to help today."

"We're going to need all the help we can get," Connor agreed.

Fearghas arrived then, with Heber trailing behind. They saluted and Connor greeted them with a smile.

"Finally makes sense," Fearghas said.

"What does?"

"You. Never sat right that you ignored my original threats. Course, being Blood of the Tallan, you're a Blade too. Pretty clever, but must've been hard to conceal."

"Sure was." He needed to get some obsidian from them. It was the one primary affinity he still lacked.

"Well I still want first crack at taking one of those Grandurians," Fearghas added with an excited gleam in his eye.

"We'll see." He hated having to keep more secrets, but had no choice.

Ivor and Padraigin had met with him secretly the night before. They would support him, but Redmund seemed obsessed with winning. He seemed to think that if he could best the Blood of the Tallan in battle, he'd win the honor he so desperately sought.

"Heber, I'm glad you're here," Connor told the other Blade. "Stay close because I'll probably need you to run some numbers once we get to see the battlefield."

"Aye, General," Heber said with another salute. "I'm happy to calculate any statistical probabilities, although I suspect you run your own calculations on troop placements and affinity balancing."

"Uh, sure."

Shona joined the group and without preamble gave Connor a lingering kiss, her body leaned close against his. Some of the male students whistled or catcalled, but most of the girls glared at her.

Connor gently pushed Shona back into line. She seemed anxious to solidify her hold over him, but he wished she wouldn't do it when he was trying to organize the army. She was doing more harm than good.

He walked between the columns of his assembled forces, shaking hands and greeting each of the students individually and answering their questions.

Papil asked, "What's it like creating a hurricane, sir? Air and water together could level cities."

"Let's hope it's enough to level the playing field today," he answered with a smile, generating a ripple of laughter. Her idea was a good one, but it got him thinking about ways they could combine elemental powers between different Petralists. Usually the different tertiary affinities worked strictly separate, but why not a Spitter and a Pathfinder working together to produce a hurricane?

"How are you feeling today?" Aifric asked, touching his forehead with one warm hand.

"Ask me in an hour."

She leaned close and added in a fierce whisper. "I'll be watching your back today."

When he reached Catriona, she blushed. "Thank you, General!"

"For what?"

"For choosing me as your sparring partner, of course."

"I thought you were still mad about that."

She made less and less sense. She had even left her hat behind and wore her hair tied back to maximize visibility of the bald spot he'd cut out of her hair. It was starting to grow back in, but was still terribly ugly.

Catriona grinned. "I finally realized what you were doing. I'm so sorry I misunderstood your purpose."

"I'm glad you figured it out." He had no idea what she was talking about.

"Me too! To think, the Blood of the Tallan chose me, and then singled me out for personal instruction. You honor my house and I look forward to the chance to repay you for it."

"For now just fight hard."

"Aye, sir!"

Lorcc arrived with his scouts, escorting Donald with the official battlefield orders. Donald explained that the battle would take place on the rolling plain again, but that a small island had been added to the lake. It would hold the four sacrificial Grandurians.

"Ground's different, sir," Lorcc added. "Still rolling hills all around, but there's now an eight-foot wall circling the entire lake, about a quarter mile out. Smooth ground inside, straight shot to the bridges."

"Bridges?"

"Aye," Donald took up the explanation again. "Each army will be positioned before a gate in the wall on each primary compass point around the island. Straight shot to the lake, with narrow bridges leading to the island and the enemy."

"That seems too easy," Fearghas said. "No one'll need to fight. Just a race to the island."

Donald shook his head. "Not so fast. Only the generals and three supporting troops can enter the gates, and only their assigned gates."

"Still stupid," Fearghas muttered.

"Not when you know the assigned gate is the one directly across from each army's starting position."

"That does complicate things," Heber said.

So they would need to circle the lake to reach the gate on the far side. Only then could Connor pass through and approach the island where most of Ilse's team waited to kill him. Rory had stationed troops at each of the walkways to prevent the Grandurians from trying to escape, but he needn't have worried. They wouldn't run. All the fighting they wanted was about to come to them.

"This complicates things," Declan said. "The other armies will hit us from both sides. If they can drive us back far enough, Redmund can slip past and into the gate."

"That would be his plan," Connor said. "But I've thought of it first."

"What do you mean?" Shona asked.

"One other thing," Donald interrupted. "No fighting inside the wall other than against the prisoners, and no use of any tertiary affinities."

Connor concealed a frown. He'd been thinking of pretending to drown them in the lake. It would offer great cover for them to escape through the secret ruins under the plain.

"What were you saying earlier?" Shona asked.

"Don't worry about the other armies. They'll be helping us."

"Why would you think that?" Fearghas asked.

Padraigin rushed up with fracked speed and skidded to a stop in front of them. "Because we told him so, of course."

"You what?" Shona exclaimed.

"We all fight for the Blood of the Tallan," Padraigin said.

The other captains cheered, but Shona looked troubled. Connor saluted Padraigin, filled with gratitude that she and Ivor were supporting him, even though he hadn't explained his full plan.

"You know the layout?" Connor asked.

Padraigin nodded. "Just finished scouting it. Ivor and I are in position. We'll block Redmund and open a corridor for you to get through."

"Perfect."

"Redmund has sworn to defeat you, to prove he's mightier, despite your advantages."

"I love it when they're optimistic."

Redmund had grown intensely hostile since the truth about Connor's curse had been revealed, and seemed more determined than ever to win. Padraigin raced away with another salute and a fanfare of invisible trumpets.

Lorcc whistled softly. "You know, if I didn't hate that woman so much, I could fall in love with her."

Shona smacked him on the side of the head. "Keep your focus."

As the others began organizing their forces, Shona pulled Connor aside. "What did you promise Padraigin in order to win her support?"

"She was a little vague," Connor said with a shrug. "Said she'd think of something."

"You can't make agreements like that," Shona exclaimed. "She could come up with anything."

"I've decided to trust her."

He loved how that boiled in her mind. She grew so mad, she couldn't come up with a good reply. Mingled with the anger was a flicker of fear. Perhaps she was realizing that she needed to approach him more carefully. The balance of power in their relationship was shifting. It had to be driving her insane.

Perfect.

Chapter 68

onnor stood at the head of his army on the west side of the walled lake, the side closest to the Sculpture House. Padraigin held the south and Ivor the north, while Redmund faced Connor across the lake.

It was a strange twist to face the final battle with Redmund his primary opponent. Everyone had assumed he and Ivor would face a desperate final confrontation, but everything had changed.

He hoped he could change it further, or people were going to die.

"Do you think they'll really keep their promise?" Shona asked close beside him. It wasn't her assigned position, but she had moved to stand with him after everyone settled into ranks, and he couldn't spare the energy to argue about it. She was a familiar presence, like a boil on the skin. Thinking about it just made it itch more and he couldn't exactly poke her with a knife to make her go away.

"We have to trust them."

"Either one of them could turn against us. They could let Redmund slip right through."

"It's not their style."

"Well, they could be plotting together to betray all of us and win through to the island first."

"I know."

"And you're still going to let them?" She looked genuinely confused.

"Look Shona, if I refused to trust anyone, I would've cracked a long time ago. If either or both of them betray us, I'd rather know about it right away. And either way, at least some of us will be clear to secure our gate."

Shona slipped an arm through his, a soft smile on her face. "I love your attitude."

He disengaged his arm. "I'm supposed to be a general, remember? People will start doubting me if it looks like you have to hold me up."

The other captains joined them. "All forces ready," Fearghas reported. "No fancy tactics today, General?"

"Didn't have time to build anything. Besides, Frazier warned me he'd cut off my thumbs if anyone borrowed any more of his equipment without asking first."

"You should have asked him right then."

"I did. He said no."

Lorcc ran up with the scouting report. "Sir, looks like Padraigin was right. Both her army and Ivor's are oriented against Redmund, with no apparent rear guard. Redmund looked pretty upset. Not sure if he's going to commit to one direction, or split his forces.

"Let's hope he splits them," Shona said. "He'd get crushed."

"He'll keep them together," Connor predicted. "Probably attack through Padraigin's army. He is a bit stronger in earth than she is, so he'll try to overwhelm her."

"Double strength that way," Heber said. "Increases his shock and awe coefficient by forty eight percent."

"And their stench factor by five hundred," Shona added to general laughter.

"We can work with it," Connor said. "When he attacks, Catriona will lead our Boulders to join them, with Declan in support. The rest of us will join Ivor and move against the far gate."

"Who's in your final attack squad?" Fearghas asked. The Blade kept glancing across the lake toward the island. The Grandurians waited there, and the last time Connor had tapped quartzite, they'd actually looking bored. He could have sworn he'd heard Erich snoring.

"I still think a rear guard is a good idea," Catriona said.

"No," Connor said. "We strike hard. If something goes wrong, we'll still have the advantage in the race to the gate."

A ball of fire streaked across the lake, signaling that the battle was about to begin.

"Join your squads," Connor told them. "Whatever happens, know that I'm honored to lead you."

Connor stood at the crest of that low hill alone as his captains returned to their ranks and he scanned the area one more time. All of his worries drained away, leaving him feeling surprisingly calm. Somehow he'd convince the stubborn Grandurians to cooperate one last time, although he still didn't know how he was going to rescue Ilse.

The only thing he really needed to focus on was the battle.

A thrill of excitement grew in his heart. He finally faced an open, honest competition, no mask, just himself. He was ready, and would show them what a common linn could really do.

Just as a gout of fire erupted over the battlefield, signaling the start of the contest, the ground shook so hard, many students stumbled and fell. A bellowing roar so vast and deep it sounded like a living avalanche shattered the air. Connor turned with everyone toward the distant heights of Mount Murdo, scanning for the source of the disturbance.

It wasn't hard to find. The ground beyond the northern arc of the great outer wall, beyond Ivor's army, erupted upward like the back of a giant charging torc. That rolling wave of earth, which cast a boiling cloud of dust into the air above it, crashed into the wall and consumed a hundred feet of it.

A monstrous being so vast it strained Connor's ability to believe it erupted out of the ground at the point of impact. It landed on eight gigantic legs, and Connor felt the tremors through his boots.

It wasn't a dream.

It charged right at Ivor's army.

Fearghas, who stood close by Connor muttered, "Oh, we're grouted."

Chapter 69

The nightmare monster looked a lot like a gigantic scorpion made of earth and stone, but with the enormous, flat head of some kind of angry fish. Its sinuous, rectangular torso extended about two hundred feet in an unbroken mass, propelled by eight thick legs. The deadly claws on all of its three-toed feet looked longer than Connor. Spikes sprang out from the rim of its rounded torso, the knees of every leg, and all over its head. It flicked its forward-arcing tail over its back, whipping the tip and cracking it all the way above its head.

As cries of alarm echoed through all four armies, Connor applied quartzite to his voice. "Ivor! Get out of there!"

Padraigin was busy urging Redmund's army to join hers. None of the soldiers needed much encouragement. They fled around the walled lake, making for the dubious safety of the other army lines.

"Boulders to the front," Connor shouted. "Striders get out on the plain. Pick up stragglers. Everyone else, brace to take in Ivor's people and meet that monster!"

As his captains barked orders and soldiers scrambled to redeploy, Connor tapped quartzite to his eyes, and his vision swooped in on the beast, that was closing the distance to the lake with alarming speed.

As their armies merged, Ivor joined Connor atop the low hill.

"What were you thinking?" Ivor cried.

"What? You don't want to join forces against that monster?"

"Didn't you summon it?"

Connor could barely summon a squirrel.

"Call me crazy, but I don't think anyone could summon something like that."

"I will not," Ivor snapped.

"Not what?"

"Not call you anything else." He looked frustrated. "Your name is Connor. Accept it, and stop changing it."

"It's just an expression," Connor exclaimed.

"You can't use that expression, not with how often you change your name."

The monster paused at the far tip of the wall circling the lake and shifted its head back and forth like a bloodhound sniffing the air. Only, this dog had three narrow, vertical nostrils. It opened its huge mouth to reveal four rows of jagged teeth that looked like stalactites, and roared so loud it sounded like the mountain of Alasdair blew up again right in their faces.

Shona rushed up to them and grabbed Connor's arm, her eyes wide with fear and her skin far paler than granite gray. "It's an elfonnel!"

"Impossible," Ivor breathed.

"You've got to be kidding," Connor exclaimed. The stories Jean had told him about the elements raging to life and laying waste to entire towns chilled him. "You can't call *that* an elfonnel. The name doesn't fit."

Shona gave him an incredulous look. "Seriously?"

"I think you're right," he clarified. "It can't be anything else, but now that I see it, I realized that elfonnel sounds too happy. It doesn't convey the proper sense of terror."

Ivor said, "You've lost it, haven't you?"

The monster took a pounding step forward and rotated its massive head to better focus on them. It sported two huge silver eyes on both sides of its head, and it looked like it was trying to decide which side of the lake to trample.

Connor silently urged it to chase Redmund.

"Call it what you want," Shona said. "That think is an element incarnate."

"They're not supposed to be real," Ivor protested.

"It doesn't get much more real than that," Shona said. "Bonded to earth."

She was right. The stone-like shape of its armored hide and the earth tone of its head made the element clear. Connor tapped slate and extended feelers of thought toward the monster, but stopped after little more than a hundred yards. In the distance he could feel a vast presence throbbing through the ground, as if it held the beating of the earth's very heart. He shied away from approaching any closer and that brief contact terrified him more than anything he'd seen.

"We have to get everyone out of here," Shona said. "If it attacks--"

The elfonnel bellowed again, louder than ever, and lunged toward them.

"Make that *when* it attacks," Connor shouted.

"What do we do?" Shona cried.

"Run!" He and Ivor shouted for their armies to retreat.

Their forces fled back toward the Sculpture House, but Connor could already see running would not help. The monster could step right over the inner Carraig wall and trash the entire complex. There was nowhere to hide.

The constant thunder of the elfonnel's approach drowned out his words as he tried to organize a rear guard, and students began to panic. He tried to think back on what Jean had told him about elfonnel's, but all he remembered was that they laid waste everywhere they appeared, and fighting them had always proved futile.

Of course, that's exactly what he had to do. He might not be able to kill it, but there had to be a way to slow it down.

The elfonnel closed with terrifying speed and the sight made him want to absorb basalt and run right over his own troops to get away. He forced down the urge and grabbed Shona's arm.

"Organize the rear guard!"

"Don't do anything stupid," she shouted back, looking terrified but in control.

He gave her a reassuring smile. "Trust me."

Strange enough, that didn't seem to ease her worries, but for once she rushed to do his bidding.

Connor found Ivor marshaling his tertiary Petralists. "Come on! We have to slow it down."

"You're crazy!"

"What other emotion has any hope of helping?"

Ivor blinked. "Good point."

As he pushed through the last of the retreating army, fighting against the flow, he tried to calm his mind and come up with some kind of plan. How could he stop a raging element come to life?

He needed Jean, but didn't have time to find her. The monster rounded the corner of the wall around the lake, clearing its path straight to Connor and the fleeing armies. Connor reached for his elemental powers. He had to make some kind of a stand.

He was not the first one to realize that.

Pudgy Declan stood alone behind the retreating armies, turned to face the onrushing monster. He lifted hands high and a fist of earth erupted out of the ground in front of the elfonnel and slugged it in the jaw.

It didn't even slow.

The fist of earth shattered and sprayed dirt back all the way over Declan.

"Run you fool!" Connor screamed, and broke into a run.

Instead of retreating, Declan rose into the air on the best Sentry tower he'd ever raised. At twenty feet high, he barely reached the monster's lower jaw, his shoulders bowed with strain, hands embedded in the rails of his pitiful fortification.

Connor connected with soapstone and reached for the waters of the underground lake. It took a moment to work his elemental senses past the ever-present shielding, but he finally seized them and heaved with all his might.

The elfonnel had nearly reached Declan, who drew out thirty spears of earth from the ground. They struck under the monster's legs and in front of its face, impaling it simultaneously in dozens of places.

It crashed off its feet, its momentum driving it forward like a plow with wakes of earth erupting away from it as it scoured a deep gouge across ground. It groaned to a halt right in front of the Sentry.

Connor struck as it opened that gigantic mouth wide. Water erupted out of the ground on both sides of Declan's tower and blasted the elfonnel's face like twin tidal waves. The impact threw up a wall of water so thick that Connor lost sight of both the elfonnel and Declan. He could still feel it through his water senses, though. It reeled back from his onslaught, then lunged straight forward.

The monster burst through the water like a breaching whale and its gaping mouth swallowed Declan and his tower in a single gulp.

Connor stared, horrified at the sudden disaster, not quite believing it.

"He's gone," Ivor breathed beside Connor, his expression shocked.

The elfonnel lifted its head and roared, louder than ever. The blast of air from its mouth smelled like deep earth, with a hint of smoke and the scent of recently shattered rock. That strangely pleasant breath knocked Connor back a couple of steps even though he stood more than a hundred yards away.

The monster sniffed the air again and its head tilted down toward Connor. It opened its deadly maw and charged.

Rage burned away the horror in Connor's heart and he embraced it and sucked deep from marble until the spicy insanity of fire burned in his eyes and living flames sprayed out his open mouth.

"Tell me you have a plan?" Ivor asked.

"See if it bleeds." Connor charged.

Chapter 70

As the elfonnel thundered down upon Connor, seven long, snakelike tongues whipped out of its mouth and snapped at the air in anticipation of eating him just like it had Declan.

He hoped it liked its meals hot.

Connor sucked everything out of the small stone in his mouth until it cracked to dust under his tongue. Driven by marble insanity, he charged the monstrosity and, with less than a hundred yards separating him from abrupt death, he unleashed it all.

White-hot fire blasted out of him in a ten-foot sheet of destruction. His scream of vengeful rage for Declan's sacrifice melded with the roar of the fire as it slammed into the open maw of the giant. The impact snapped the monster's head back and launched its front legs off the ground.

Its shriek of pain dug at Connor's ears and echoed back from the distant castle in a satisfying wave. It sounded like someone had kicked every man in the kingdom between the legs at the same time.

His fire burned out in a sudden rush that left him feeling hollow. The post-marble burnout settled over his heart and nearly pulled him to the ground. Burning through marble that abruptly often left Firetongues depressed or even suicidal. Although he was prepared for it, he still sagged under the emotional drain.

The elfonnel returned to all eight feet with a thud that shook the ground. Its wide head was blackened and its tongues lolled listlessly from its charred mouth. But if anything, the damage only looked to have enraged it.

"You've got to be kidding me," Connor muttered as he fished in his pouch for another piece of marble. He paused with it halfway to his mouth. Aonghus had warned him not to walk with fire while suffering burnout effects, or the flames could rebound against him. So instead he tapped quartzite and with his next breath connected with the air.

The elfonnel lunged, moving incredibly fast. Sheets of water whipped past Connor and enveloped its head, hardening to ice and interrupting its charge.

Connor glanced back at Ivor and waved his thanks. Ivor gestured mightily for him to run, but why waste a near-death encounter with a giant monster? Seizing the turbulent currents of air that still churned from the super heating of his recent flames, Connor drove himself off the ground with a blast of wind.

The monster bashed its head to the ground, shattering the ice and clearing its silver eyes. It caught sight of him and leaped, pulling its front half right off the ground and snapping at him as he soared out of control past its head. Jaws that could swallow small buildings narrowly missed. Had its tongues not just been charred, they might have caught him. One came close and he punched it in the beak before rising out of range.

He cleared the head and got a close-up look at the elfonnel's full, terrifying length. Its huge, segmented back was armored and large enough to hold all four armies. Fear again undercut his courage. His fire had barely slowed it. How could they fight such a monster?

Connor glanced toward the Sculpture House and cringed to see the armies had gathered there and formed ranks. His captains stood at the front. When he tapped a little quartzite to sharpen his sight and hearing, he found them encouraging the troops to follow the general's lead and stand strong.

The fools. They were going to get killed.

He found Papil in the press, standing close to Fearghas and when she met his gaze he said, "Tell them to retreat and form up at the Carraig."

She saluted.

And the monster whipped him right out of the air with its long tail. The brutal blow knocked the wind out of him as the world spun crazily. He'd been knocked out of the air often enough to know what was coming next, and max-tapped granite just before crashing into the top of a nearby hill. Earth exploded out in every direction, and the shock of the landing rattled him, despite the protection of granite.

Connor shook dirt from his face and decided he needed a new name for the monster. Elfonnel failed to convey the proper sense of elemental terror it inspired. Maybe better to call it "My Army Is Doomed". Then again, Maid was kind of pessimistic and didn't quite fit the nightmare that had crashed what had been a pretty straight-forward battle.

He staggered to his feet and checked to make sure his body was numb due to granite and not because the monster had broken him into pieces. He tasted dirt and snorted out a clump of dried grass that had lodged up his nose when he plowed into the hilltop. Even with it gone, everything smelled like weeds.

None of that mattered when he looked up and found that the elfonnel had turned after him. It snapped its jaws repeatedly, and the sound was like the smashing of boulders. He half expected to see it spit out broken chunks of teeth.

It was coming for him. Looked like the monster held grudges.

"You still don't know how to pick your battles, lad."

Connor turned to find Captain Rory approaching at a run from the far side of the hill, flanked by Ivor, Tomas, and Cameron. A pair of Striders trailed him, as did Redmund.

"Glad you're here, Captain."

Tomas turned to Cameron. "I told you. He does want to kill us."

"Earth bound," Rory said, his eyes locked on the fast-turning giant. "Wish I'd studied harder in school."

"Didn't know you could read, sir," Cameron said.

"Nah," Tomas responded. "Just the pictures for him."

"Fire barely slowed it," Connor said, "And Declan. . ."

Rory nodded. "I saw it, lad. Brave young man, but you can't stop an earth-bound with slate."

"Gotta bash their heads in," Tomas said.

"I'll throw you up there," Cameron offered, "and you tell us how well that goes."

"We don't have much time," Ivor noted, encircling the monster's head with white-hot flames. That distracted it a moment as it bashed its head against the ground to scatter the flames. The impact reverberated up through Connor's shoes. "Let's decide what to do quick."

"It looks like it wants to chase me. I'll keep it distracted," Connor said. "Rally the troops and figure out how to hurt it."

Rory clasped hands with him, and Ivor grinned. "I hope you've got some clever ideas today, Connor. We're going to need them."

"Working on it," he said, turning back to the fast-approaching elfonnel. "So far I've just decided I can't call it a Maid."

"What are you talking about?"

"Tell you later."

The others retreated down the southwest side of the hill to circle the monster. All of the other armies were assembled together. Against any other enemy, that much concentrated Petralist power would have seemed unstoppable.

Facing the elfonnel, they looked like close-packed ranks of snack foods.

Connor waited atop the hill another moment until the monster focused those dead eyes on him again. Sure enough, it wanted to stomp him first. He purged granite and switched to basalt. The invigorating freedom of the stone helped buttress his courage.

He still had no idea how to stop it, but he needed to buy his army some time. So Connor popped another piece of marble into his mouth as he raced off the north side of the slope just before the monster arrived.

Ringing himself with crimson flames, he crossed its path and shouted, "Come on, slate-face! See if you can catch me!"

It growled, sounding like an avalanche, and altered course after him, accelerating with remarkable speed. Its eight gigantic legs propelled it forward in an odd, rolling gallop that consumed the distance. Connor drew deeper from basalt and fracked. That hurt, but not as much as getting trampled would.

He flew across the open plain, slowly leaving the angry monster behind. It moved remarkably fast, but no earthbound elfonnel was going to catch him in a fully fracked sprint. It seemed to realize that face and bellowed with rage.

The plan was working! Grinning, Connor looked back to tease the monster again, but gaped. Ripples of earth were pulsing in front of it, rolling across the ground after him and closing the distance fast.

It was an elemental monster, but he hadn't expected it to actually use the elements against him. That seemed unfair. Connor turned hard, but the pulsing feelers of its earth influence turned to follow him.

His confidence cracked under renewed fear. It was smarter than he'd hoped. No matter how fast he ran, its earth powers could move faster. He didn't bother tapping slate. He was running too fast, and that little glimpse he'd gotten into the magnitude of its earth powers made it clear he'd never stand a chance fighting for control of the ground.

As the ground buckled around him, Connor tapped marble and shot himself into the air on a gout of flame. The earth directly below him collapsed into a trench, with cresting waves on either side that smashed together with terrifying force.

Connor landed already fracked and ran in shifting arcs, trying to stay ahead of the monster, but not make himself too easy a target. His mind raced as he grasped for any ideas how to stop the thing. Fighting it would just get him eaten like Declan, but he couldn't keep running from it either.

The ground in front of him exploded upward, and Connor leaped, tapping quartzite and using air to boost himself farther. The wind tumbled him wildly, but he'd clear the wall.

Or maybe not. It morphed into grasping fingers of earth to catch him. Shouting with fear and frustration, Connor tapped soapstone, forming a spinning sphere of water that severed the earthen fingers.

"Can't you kill me like a normal monster, you Tallan-cursed mud-for-brain?" Connor shouted back at the charging elfonnel. In response, the ground erupted around him as he landed, forming impassable walls blocking his escape.

"Such a cheater," Connor muttered. The walls didn't smash him flat, which meant the monster wanted to finish him personally.

That thing was really starting to make him mad.

It also terrified him more than anything he'd ever seen. Connor tapped marble and erupted off the ground, hoping to soar out of danger, but slender spears or rock-hard earth shot out of the surrounding walls, forming a latticed cage. He crashed into it and rebounded.

He stood and faced the monster as the cage melted back into the ground. He needed an idea, some way to delay it and escape, but fear chilled his thoughts like frozen soup as the monster bore down on him, mere seconds away.

He was alone on the plain, and he could not stop it.

Chapter 71

erena soared toward the stunning castle and pulled off her flying goggles for a better look. She had heard about the magnificent Carraig, but the tales didn't do the glittering, basalt-sheathed towers justice. She angled her approach in that direction for a better look.

"Elfonnel!" Hamish cried, flying close beside her and pointing to the east, to a wide plain with a lake in the center.

Verena hadn't noticed much beyond the castle complex. She followed Hamish's pointing finger and noticed for the first time the massed troops, and gasped at the sight of the huge monster charging across the distant plain.

"I didn't think anyone at the Carraig could raise an elfonnel," she breathed, feeling a shiver of fear. She affixed her long view goggles and focused on the distant monster. At first she wondered why it was leaving the soldiers alone, but an explosion of earth in front of it drew her gaze.

"Someone clearly can," Hamish said, pulling a biscuit out of a satchel strapped to his stomach and shoving it under his face mask for a big bite.

He offered to share, but she waved it away. They needed to know what was going on, but then she saw a figure explode through an earthen wall in a glittering globe of fast-spinning water. Her heart raced as she focused on the figure, who landed and raced away from the monster.

"That's Connor!" she shouted, pivoting the Swift in his direction.

"He's got that thing pretty angry," Hamish said, sounding concerned. "But look at that."

She glanced to the right at the little lake, surrounded by a wall, with a small island in the center. Four figures stood there, while soldiers were advancing across one of the bridges.

"That's Ilse's team," Hamish exclaimed. "Looks like they're surrounded."

"But where's Ilse?" She hoped the wily captain hadn't fallen in battle, and the thought only made her more worried. The conflict had escalated far beyond what they'd expected. She couldn't accept that they had arrived too late.

"Hamish," she said, making a decision. "Get down there and help them on the island. I'm going for Connor."

"He's my best friend," Hamish objected.

He was right, but no force on earth could turn her from helping Connor in the face of an elfonnel. The monster looked to be earthbound, and its staggering size terrified her.

"I have to help him," she said, facing Hamish, who hovered nearby. "Besides, you've always wanted to test that suit against Petralists."

"You owe me," Hamish grunted, then rolled away and dove toward the island.

"Good luck," she said, then accelerated over the plain after Connor.

He was running wild arcs, dodging explosions of earth and grasping, deadly fingers that erupted out of the ground. He'd never outrun an earthbound elfonnel. Verena wasn't sure what they'd do to stop it, but first she had to get Connor out of there.

Even though she poured on every bit of available speed, she was still long seconds away when walls of earth rose around Connor, hemming in the way. She cried out in terror when his attempt at escape on a fiery column was blocked. The monster would devour him before she could arrive.

"Tallan grant him a way to escape," she breathed, hating to watch that giant monster bearing down on him, but unable to look away. She'd traveled too far only to witness him die only seconds before she could rescue him.

As the elfonnel closed on Connor, its freakish silver gaze locked on him, its pounding gait shaking the ground underfoot, Connor purged basalt and absorbed some enhanced granite. The magnified curse poured through him, filling him with unmatched strength and stretching his muscles, even though he hadn't tapped it yet. His skin darkened to ebony and hardened like living stone.

He still couldn't fight that monstrosity, but he wouldn't just let it eat him. He prepared to unleash all of his elemental powers in one explosive strike. Maybe that would create an opportunity to escape again. Escape would be short lived unless he found a place to hide, but he couldn't think of anywhere it couldn't find him or a shield strong enough to even give him a chance.

Then he did.

As the monster filled his vision and leaped the last hundred feet, giant maw gaping wide to swallow him and half an acre of ground in one bite, Connor tapped slate and opened a hole directly under his feet. He pulled the ground aside like a blanket and fell a dozen feet. Tapping granite, Connor curse-punched the thick, stone block that formed that part of the hidden roof of the secret underground ruin.

Connor's arm swelled so big, it nearly burst the flexible plates of his battle leathers, and his enhanced fist punched through the stone. He burst through the false ground just as the elfonnel crashed into the earth above, two of its snakelike tongues snapping down the hole after him.

Connor blasted fire back up the hole, crisping the tongues and searing the inside of the elfonnel's gaping mouth as its stalactite-like teeth gouged eight feet into the earth. Then he plunged into darkness of the ruined city.

Ringing his limbs with flames, he glimpsed row after row of benches on every side, encircling an open, oval field of dead grass. The benches rose all the way up to merge with the false ceiling, the remnants of a gigantic arena of centuries ago.

Connor crashed into the ground in the center of the arena. Fine earth erupted around him, the fine powder triggering an enormous sneeze that Hamish would have been proud of.

Protected by enhanced granite, he shook off the impact and rose to stare up at the hole he'd just made.

The elfonnel's angry bellow echoed down from above. He'd escaped for a moment, but it wouldn't take the monster long to follow. So he ran across the soft earth of the arena, imagining how it must have looked centuries ago with all those benches filled with shouting spectators.

They'd never witnessed a death battle against an elfonnel. Lucky them.

Taking shelter in a tunnel-like exit, he tried to calm his breathing. With an effort, he connected with slate, but made sure not to extend his earth senses beyond his own feet. Even then, he felt the elfonnel's influence pounding against the ground in every direction, like a storm surge.

Then the earth around the little hole he'd made erupted up and away, flowing aside like an inverted waterfall. Light spilled through the hole for the first time in who knew how many decades, illuminating the ruins.

Then something immense blotted out the light.

The elfonnel was coming down after him.

Verena screamed in despair as the elfonnel leaped a hundred feet and crashed to the ground over Connor, ripping up tons of earth in a gigantic bite. It chomped a hole nearly ten feet deep in the ground and swallowed it in a bobbing, gulping move.

It just swallowed Connor.

With tears streaming down her face, Verena descended lower, barely able to control the Swift through her grief. It was impossible. He couldn't have died, not when she was so close.

Instead of turning in triumph away from its latest kill, the elfonnel dug at the ground with its front legs and bellowed again. It sounded angry, howling the kind of rage that only Connor could generate.

She soared two hundred feet over its head and spotted a hole in the ground. It looked like some kind of cave. Hope ignited in her heart, driving back the crippling despair, but the ground flowed up and away, forming a much wider hole.

Connor had somehow escaped the monster, but that didn't mean he was safe yet. It looked like the elfonnel was preparing to follow him into the cave.

"You're not getting him that easily," she growled, pivoting the Swift and taking aim at two of the monster's great, silver eyes.

The speedslings spun up in record time, and Verena opened fire. Thousands of hornets ripped the air between her and the cursed monster that dared attack her Connor. One in ten of the hardened little hornets burned with angry, crimson flames, tracing the route the projectiles took and helping her fine-tune the aim.

She guided the deadly little hornets into the monster's eyes, and they tore into the soft targets with wonderful savagery. The granite plunged deep, and one out of every dozen exploded with embedded diorite.

The elfonnel reared back, its cry of pain shaking the air and upsetting Verena's aim. Grimly determined, she reset and fired on the second eye. It too exploded in a wave of silver liquid and the monster shuddered from the pain.

Verena shouted defiance at the monstrosity as she fired. Her speedslings wouldn't last long, and couldn't kill it, but she'd distract the monster as long as possible.

The monster turned to face her, and she slid sideways in the air to track with it.

That's all that saved her life.

Spears of earth erupted from the ground, shooting into the air like they were driven by marble thrusters. The first wave missed by a few feet, hissing as they passed close by her. Verena threw the Swift into a sideways roll, avoiding a dozen more earthen missiles.

When she gained some altitude and turned back toward the elfonnel, she cursed to see its eyes already healed. It was a being of pure element. Superficial damage couldn't hurt it for long.

The elfonnel opened its huge, crag-toothed maw and bellowed at her, creating a gale-force wind that rocked the Swift. Its breath smelled of fresh-turned earth and windswept mountains.

"Eat this," Verena shouted, aiming the Swift at the monster's mouth and triggering her latest invention, inspired after witnessing Kilian's elfonnel lose control.

A slender, quartzite-powered missile strapped under the Swift erupted from its mount. Its flight stabilized by little fins set along its length, it leaped the distance between her and the elfonnel and plunged into that open mouth. The chunk of diorite mounted inside the steel cone at the front of the missile exploded, shredding the monster's mouth with steel and fire.

Gigantic teeth burst asunder and rained out of the elfonnel's maw, along with five of the serpentlike tongues. The entire elfonnel rocked back from the impact, and for a moment she looked down into the hole it had created. Impossibly, she caught sight of rows of stone bleachers. They looked old, as if an ancient stadium had been buried under the plain. How had Connor known about that?

The elfonnel planted its eight thick legs and crouched. Instead of jumping at her, the ground all around it erupted into the air in sheets of earth she couldn't hope to avoid.

With a cry of fear, Verena maxed the thrusters and opened wide the Puking Dooms, rocketing the Swift higher. The earth struck, tossing her higher still and spinning the Swift wildly away.

By the time she recovered and turned back to face the monster, it had disappeared into the cave after Connor.

Chapter 72

"Anika! Erich!"

Hamish swooped down toward the island where the sibling Petralists were facing a large group of approaching soldiers, led by leather-clad Fast Rollers. Dietmar and Margrit stood behind the siblings, and they looked ready for battle.

Hamish grinned. Who better to test his suit against than the very best of Dougal's fighters? He landed in front of Erich, surprising the huge Rumbler so much, he nearly punched Hamish before recognizing him.

Anika gripped Hamish's hand. "Good Builder boy, mine friend. Come in time for many big fight to death."

"I've been taking lessons," he responded in Grandurian, grateful he'd been studying the language. He didn't think he could endure trying to piece together what was going on from their broken Obrioner.

"Good," Erich said, clapping him on the shoulder. "I like the suit."

Hamish grinned, but glanced at the Fast Rollers, who had paused about thirty feet away when he landed. "What's going on here?"

"We're supposed to be waiting for Connor so we can kill him," Anika said.

"The coward hasn't shown," Erich growled. "Sent those soldiers instead."

"He's busy playing tag with an elfonnel," Hamish explained, realizing they might not have seen the monster yet.

Erich frowned. "Is many great fool play game with such monster."

Hamish couldn't argue with that. He yearned to race after Verena and help Connor, but had to do something about those soldiers first.

"No killing Connor," Hamish ordered. "Not until we figure this out."

Erich grinned. "You've grown strong in recent months, Builder, but are you ready to give me orders?"

"I'm here to help. Just follow my lead." Hamish turned to face the Fast Rollers, who were advancing again.

The two in the front, who he vaguely remembered from Alasdair, stopped ten feet away. "You're Connor's friend," one of them said when Hamish removed his goggles. "The Builder from Alasdair, right?"

"You planning to collect the bounty?" Hamish asked, preparing to unleash his arsenal if the soldiers drew any closer.

The man's brutish companion grinned. "Maybe later. Right now we've got orders to bring this lot to Captain Rory. You should probably come along too."

Erich growled. "Fight Rory. Is good first die."

"Duel's off for now," the first man said. Hamish recalled that his name was Tomas. "A giant monster just crashed into the Carraig. We're all joining forces to fight it. Your Captain Ilse is with Rory and they've reached a peace accord for now. So either join us, or we beat you into submission right now."

Erich looked ready to take up the challenge, but Anika placed a restraining hand on his arm. "If Machtig Riesen is come, is many best fight."

"What did you call it?" Hamish asked.

"Machtig Riesen," she repeated. "Is elfonnel."

"I hope you know how to beat that thing," Tomas said.

"Have ideas," Erich said.

"You can't punch an elfonnel to death," Hamish said. "I've seen them before."

"Then you're the expert," Tomas said. "Come on. Rory will want to speak with you."

As the groups merged in uneasy truce, Hamish fell into step beside Tomas. The Fast Roller said, "You've got to tell me about that suit, Builder."

"It's kind of a secret weapon."

Tomas grunted. "Well, I hope you've got a lot more secret weapons. I think we're going to need them."

Chapter 73

It sounded like someone was fighting the elfonnel. Connor hoped none of his friends did anything exceptionally stupid, but he couldn't help them if he was dead. The extra seconds helped him formulate a plan of escape.

He was concealed pretty well in the little tunnel exit, but the elfonnel would find him immediately once it focused on him again. He needed to buy a little more time.

So he tapped slate and formed a shield around his feet. Ilse had said that the best shields embodied what was not there, a weight with no weight, so he tried to imagine himself no more than a shadow in the darkness.

His little shield wouldn't survive active searching from the beast, but it might conceal him if the monster was too busy looking elsewhere. Concentrating on the summoning technique that Ilse had taught him, Connor formed an image in his mind, filling it with the power of elemental earth, then melding that concentrated power into a shell of granite.

The ground at his feet glowed with rainbow light, which coalesced in a miniature crack of thunder, and his summoning abruptly appeared.

Connor grinned down at a little squirrel with enormous feet.

Usually Connor liked squirrels, but he had to admit this one was remarkably ugly, with feet as big as a wick-rabbit. The little beast blinked up at him, and he could almost hear it grumbling at what he'd done to its feet.

The light from the opening in the roof extinguished as the gigantic elfonnel wormed through and stepped into the arena. It was too tall to fit in the cave, but it was made from the elements, so it changed size, shortening its legs and shrinking its torso enough to fit underground.

That gave Connor an idea. Luckily it wasn't a very complicated idea because some of his attention was consumed by controlling the little squirrel, and the rest barely held onto the little shield.

Before the elfonnel could shatter his shield and locate him, Connor sent the little squirrel scampering away, out the exit, and around the outside of the stadium toward another pile of rubble. As soon as it began moving, the elfonnel rotated in its direction and opened that hideous mouth. Its serpentlike tongues snapped the air, as if in anticipation, and it lunged.

It didn't bother with the exit tunnel, which was good since Connor still crouched there. Instead, it plowed right through the stadium after the little squirrel. Connor managed to get the squirrel around the next ruined building before the elfonnel caught sight of it, and the elfonnel gave chase, flattening everything in its path.

After it left, Connor began tiptoeing carefully away in the opposite direction, which he thought would lead him to areas of the ruin he had explored before and the distant tunnel back to the Carraig undercity. If he could lead the elfonnel around in useless circles for a while with the squirrel, he hoped to return to his friends and make a plan for dealing with it.

The squirrel wasn't quite as fast as a Strider, but it moved far faster than a natural animal could, scampering over rubble and through tiny openings the elfonnel couldn't follow. For its part, the elfonnel burst through ruined buildings and shrank its torso further when the ceiling grew too short. Nothing really slowed it down, and the squirrel barely kept ahead. Connor hoped to find a really tiny tunnel. If he could make the elfonnel small enough, maybe he could actually fight it.

The little squirrel possessed remarkably good senses, which surprised him. He'd summoned it, and his mind controlled it, so why wasn't it limited to what he could see or hear or smell?

He was just glad it was working.

As he moved at a slow jog down darkened streets that he didn't dare illuminate, he tapped quartzite. The light pouring into the stadium reached into the darkness enough to help his enhanced sight. He also applied quartzite to his nose and found he could smell the stone of the surrounding ruins, which helped him avoid running into any buildings.

Then he rounded a corner and entered a huge, flat-paved plaza with a gigantic fountain. Its many-tiered levels included fantastic animals and mighty warriors and melded right into the ceiling. The sight gave him hope. This was one of the streets he had explored.

Connor turned left and purged granite, then absorbed basalt. He would dare tapping a little speed to escape the darkness and the deadly elfonnel still shaking the ruins as it chased his little summoning.

Then his squirrel rounded another corner and the sight drew him up short, grabbing his full attention. The squirrel was looking at that same fountain he'd just passed. With a sinking feeling of dread, he turned its gaze a bit farther and spotted his own shape in the distance.

He was so grouted.

Somehow he'd gotten turned around and led the enraged elfonnel right back to himself. He wished he had time to play with the squirrel. From its perspective, he looked really imposing. The squirrel faltered as he tried to pick another direction to send it scurrying away.

Too late. The elfonnel burst right through the nearby building, spraying stone and dust across the plaza, and stomped the little squirrel flat.

That part of his mind recoiled back and sent Connor stumbling. The feeling of that little squirrel getting stomped was really unpleasant, as if part of his mind had been made of bread dough that got poked while it was still rising.

The elfonnel turned toward Connor and growled, the ominous sound echoing down the dark tunnels of the ruined city.

Connor ran.

All thought at shielding and pretense gone, he fracked and sprinted away as fast as if Anika had said she wanted to wrestle him instead of Rory. The elfonnel gave chase, and it barreled through the darkened corridors like a horizontal avalanche. The sound struck like a constant wave, pushing him faster. The ground shook with the promise of impending doom, and he felt the elfonnel grab the earth beneath his fast-moving feet.

Usually Connor couldn't establish much connection with earth while running with Strider speed, but impending death was a great motivator. He threw his will into blocking the elfonnel's control.

He delayed it for a fraction of a second, racing out of the danger just before the ground erupted up to the ceiling in a wave that would have crushed him flat. The elfonnel's overwhelming elemental influence shattered his earth senses a second later, and Connor felt the slate crumble in his left boot. He stumbled, but regained his footing before falling.

Leaning almost horizontal, he tore around a corner, sending streamers of marble along the ruined street ahead to make sure the path was clear. He was out of time, and out of ideas.

As the elfonnel barreled around the corner behind him, smashing a ruined palace flat to make the turn, Connor's flames illuminated something new.

Evander.

The giant Sentry was racing toward Connor on that incredible, half-reclined earthen craft he loved to ride. It was like a narrow, padded seat, with spokes for his legs, and branches extending forward for his hands. The ground behind him rippled upward into a solid wall, blocking the way.

Connor skidded to a stop, all hope gone. As Evander slowed to meet him, he shouted, "You realize you're trapping us down here with that thing, don't you?"

"Tranquil beats the heart in a home undefiled, but anger rules when intruders break through and destroy."

"I can't believe the last thing I'm going to hear before I die is another indecipherable riddle," Connor exclaimed.

The elfonnel rounded the last corner and spotted them a hundred feet away. A rolling wave of earth boiled out from it toward them. Solid walls of rubble hemmed them in, blocking any escape.

Connor snatched for another piece of slate, knowing he'd never get it into his boot in time, but refusing to just wait for death. He also purged basalt, but would never have time to absorb more granite.

Ten feet away from them, the earthen wave halted, as if frozen solid. Then it settled back, restoring the ruined street the way it had been.

Connor glanced at Evander, who was frowning at the elfonnel. The big man glanced at him. "The studious mind grasps every moment of learning, when the fool thinks of naught beyond terror."

"I hate you," Connor mumbled.

Evander winked, then his earth-craft leaped forward, bearing him toward the elfonnel with the speed of a Strider. Connor gaped, but could do nothing more than stare after Evander as he made his suicide charge.

The elfonnel seemed surprised for a single heartbeat, then bellowed and charged to meet Evander. The two crashed together in a mighty explosion of earth that swept back up the passage in a suffocating wave that blasted Connor off his feet.

He somersaulted in slow motion, his movements hampered by the earth filling the hall. His movements slowed, then stopped, leaving him suspended in soft earth, not knowing which way was up. He couldn't move, couldn't breathe. He was surrounded by impenetrable darkness, completely trapped.

Connor realized he'd actually prefer dying a quick death while battling the elfonnel over a lingering expiration due to suffocation. It was even worse than the time he'd been hanged.

Fighting panic, and unable to wiggle his hand to his belt pouch to absorb granite, Connor tapped quartzite and screamed. That was all the air available to him, but it was enough. He seized it with quartzite senses and used it to batter the earth away, forming a little sphere of clear space.

Pushing the earth back freed him enough so he could fall on his head. At least he knew which way was up again. Connor gasped for breath, but there wasn't much. It tasted thin, as if all the earth had beaten it into submission. So he absorbed enhanced granite and max-tapped his enhanced curse, swelling his body to impossible size.

In any other situation, the thrill of such awesome power would have made him laugh. Buried in earth, he just grinned and leaped upward, ripping at the ceiling of his little prison with fingers strong enough to rend the toughest stone.

In a frenzy, he tore through the loose earth and climbed eight feet before bursting free. The passage was mostly filled, but a two-foot space near the ceiling remained clear, and Connor greedily breathed in the rich-smelling air.

The sounds of titanic struggle drew his gaze and he crawled back up the tunnel. After twenty feet, he reached the edge of a huge underground cavern that must have been created when the two monsters crashed together and began to fight.

Two monsters?

Connor hadn't thought anything else could surprise him, but he was wrong. Evander was nowhere in sight. In his place reared a mighty, man-shaped giant that stood at least sixty feet tall. It sported four massive arms and a muscled torso that made Connor's enhanced bulk seem pitiful. Formed of earth and stone like the elfonnel, its head looked vaguely like Evander. It was fighting the elfonnel, pounding on the beast with fists the size of wagons.

Connor stared in awe, the lone witness as the two monsters struggled in the huge cavern they'd formed, crashing into each other again and again. Evander's giant grabbed the elfonnel by the head and swung it, nearly smashing Connor flat.

They probably wouldn't even notice if they squashed him. That was a bit insulting, given how much effort the elfonnel had expended tracking him down.

Then the giant drove the elfonnel upward with elemental strength. It burst through the ceiling, and light flooded the hidden battleground as the plain overhead collapsed inward.

Not waiting to see if the monsters would seal the hole again, Connor tapped marble and blasted himself up through the hole, soaring high into the air. He laughed, drinking in the fresh air and savoring the cool breeze across his dirt-coated skin.

A nimble little flying craft that looked like an armored chair, zipped up next to him, matching his speed perfectly, rumbling with the power of quartzite thrusters.

Verena was piloting it.

She was wearing thick furs, a helmet, and strange goggles that couldn't conceal her blue eyes that glittered with joy. She gave him a dazzling smile.

"Need a ride, stranger?"

Chapter 74

onnor and Verena landed on a low hill where the leadership team was gathered. The armies were assembled nearby, facing the plain. Ailsa was overseeing a team near the Sculpture House. Led by Jok, the Boulders there were setting up long tables with supplies of power stones to resupply troops.

Rory waited for him in the center, with Anika close at his side and Ilse and Erich flanking them. Aonghus stood near them with Camonica, who was scowling at the Grandurians. Teachers, school administrators, high lord representatives, the other champions, and their captains made up the rest of the leadership team.

Hamish, who was wearing a unique armored suit, with leaves of stone for the breastplate, broke away from Jean, who had been standing beside him, holding his hand and grinning with radiant joy.

Seeing Hamish again was like returning home. Laughing, Connor rushed to meet him. They collided and gripped each other's arms, laughing even more. It was so good to see Hamish again, all his worries faded away under renewed optimism. Somehow, everything would be all right.

"What are you wearing?" Connor asked, stepping back to examine Hamish's suit.

"It's a long story," Hamish grinned, pulling a breadstick from a pouch at his belt and offering half of it to Connor. For once, he accepted without hesitation.

Hamish was taller than Connor remembered, and far more muscular, although that effect might be due to the suit. "But what about you? What have you done to your skin?"

His skin was still ebony from the enhanced granite, and his muscles quivered with power, even though he wasn't tapping it. "It'll pass." He couldn't explain what Ailsa had done to the powder in front of everyone.

Jean rushed over and gave him a hug, eyes glittering with joy. "Oh, Connor, we were so worried. They said the monster had trapped you."

"It did for a minute, but I'm all right."

She retreated to stand with Hamish again and took his hand. It looked like she didn't plan to ever let go, and Hamish couldn't look happier. Connor's heart sang to see them so happy together. For years he'd plotted against Hamish and Stuart to win Jean, but now it felt absolutely right that she had chosen Hamish.

Verena joined him and slipped under the crook of his arm. She had shed her bulky flying furs and helmet and felt perfect there beside him. He really wanted to kiss those minty lips of hers, but another thunderous clash from the battling monsters on the plain drew him around.

"Glad you're safe, lad," Rory said.

"It was pretty close," Connor admitted. "That things smart, and it's got amazing elemental mastery."

Rory nodded. "Redmund and Padraigin have organized every Sentry we've got to shield this hill, but I doubt they'll hold if that thing gets a chance to focus on us."

"Let's hope it doesn't," Connor said, tapping quartzite to study the distant battle.

Evander's giant and the elfonnel were fighting with undiminished savagery across the plain. Huge areas had collapsed in on the sunken ruin, and Connor cringed to think of that ancient secret destroyed after remaining preserved for so long. He wished he'd gotten a chance to explore it more.

Connor turned to Ilse and extended a hand. "Are we okay?"

"We've reached an accord. All other concerns are on hold until the current threat is resolved."

Shona joined them, glaring at Verena. "Then there will be consequences."

Connor met her angry gaze. "Right now, you will respect the peace."

Her eyes widened and she stood taller. "You forget your place, Connor."

"You're wrong." He scanned the gathered men and women. "We cannot face that monster divided. I've fought it and seen what it can do, and I believe my place is at the head of this united army. Either accept that, or challenge me here and now."

The high lord representatives clamored objections, but Lord Dail silenced them. "We are no longer playing a game. Today war has descended upon our school and we face the very real threat of death and destruction. This is a military matter, and we will accept the decision of our military commander. Captain Rory, what say you?"

All eyes turned to Rory, who considered Connor for a moment before giving him a wry smile. "You've come a long way from the scared boy I met by the river, lad. You're right, though. We need the Blood of the Tallan to lead this fight. I will support you."

Aonghus laughed and pumped his fist in the air. Camonica, who could have argued that she should assume command, gripped Connor's hands in both of hers, her expression adoring. "You are Blood of the Tallan, Connor. You're our nation's one and brightest hope. I'll follow you to the gates of Tallan's Fury."

That was more than a little unnerving, but he patted her hand. "Thanks for your support."

Ilse gave him a tiny nod. "Until the Machtig Riesen is destroyed."

"That's a great name," Connor said. It was so much better than Maid.

"I am not calling the elfonnel some Grandurian gibberish," Shona snapped. She still glared at Verena, but looked torn about what to think about his usurping command of the armies. On one level, it strengthened her position, but it also gave him far greater independence from her. As each of the others added their support, she didn't dare oppose him though.

"I was thinking of calling it the Doom," Connor said. "It really is the Daddy of All Other Monsters."

Verena frowned. "You know, that doesn't really spell--"

"Work with me," Connor said. "New names aren't as easy as I make it look."

"But what if it's a girl?" Cameron asked as he and Tomas joined their captain.

"Depends on who raised it," Verena said.

"I know who raised it." Aifric drew closer. "Somehow, High Lord Dougal is responsible."

"My father can't raise an elfonnel," Shona scoffed. "Go heal that broken mind of yours."

"He may not be able to raise it, but he may be the only man alive who might be able to control one after it forms."

"She might be right," Verena said. "I've heard it's possible, and he's clever enough to do it. But where did he get one?"

"Why would he want to control a monster like that anyway?" Shona demanded.

"To gain power over the Blood of the Tallan," Aifric said

Connor was amazed she would risk saying so much, revealing things that no Healer would know. If her true identity was revealed, she'd be executed.

"I don't care who raised it or who's controlling it," Connor said. "We have to destroy it. Then we'll find out who's responsible and they can pay for the mess they caused."

He turned to Ivor, Padraigin, and Redmund. "What do you say, my friends? Will you follow my lead in this?"

Padraigin grinned and made a graceful curtsy. "I'd say the Tir-raon is pretty well broken at this point so yes, I will join with you."

Ivor shook his head slowly, but smiled. "I said I hoped you had some good ideas, but this wasn't exactly what I had in mind."

"It's a start," Connor said, extending his hand.

Ivor took it, his grip firm. "Then I'm interested in seeing where we go next."

Redmund scowled at the others. "The head uncovered to the elements takes the brunt of the storm."

"But the socks least-washed gain a strength unmatched by any other," Connor responded.

Redmund frowned, and Jean said, "That's disgusting, Connor."

"And it doesn't make any sense at all," Verena added.

At least she didn't punch him in the face.

Hamish leaned close to Connor and whispered, "You've stolen an entire army! I love it."

"Now that the chain of command is secure," Rory said, his tone crisp. "Can someone tell me how by the Tallan's twisted memory we're going to destroy that thing?"

"Our best chance is if Evander destroys it," Verena said.

"I can't see how he summoned that giant," Ivor said.

"It's not a summoning," Hamish said. "Evander's raised his own elfonnel, although I'm surprised they can both unleash the earth at the same time in the same place."

"That's perhaps the greatest risk," Verena said. "We've been studying elfonnel, and we have first-hand experience, but if one of those monsters gains the upper hand, they may be able to absorb the elemental power of the other."

"Are you suggesting if the elfonnel defeats Evander, it'll grow stronger?" Connor asked.

"It's possible," Verena said.

Jean spoke up. "But from my research, the living elements can really only be defeated by other living elements."

"Let's hope Evander wins," Connor said. "But let's plan in case he doesn't. What can we do against it?"

"Sometimes dropping a mountain on them helps," Verena said, glancing up that the towering heights of Mount Murdo. "Although against earth, it may not be such a good idea."

"Not to mention such a catastrophe would destroy the entire Carraig," Lord Dail exclaimed.

Connor said, "Lord Dail, I want you and the other representatives to return to the inner city and organize a full evacuation."

Lord Dail paled. "Do you have any idea how complex an undertaking that is?"

"Would you prefer everyone dying if those monsters decide to fight closer to the castle?"

As the group scurried off, Connor said, "Let's get everyone resupplied, especially the tertiary affinities. If we unite all of our elemental powers, we might be able to tip the battle in Evander's favor."

"I'll inform Ailsa," Jean said, breaking reluctantly from Hamish and trotting away toward the Sculpture House.

They began discussing the best way to mobilize their troops against the elfonnel, but Padraigin exclaimed, "Look!"

Connor tapped quartzite and saw that the elfonnel was sinking into the earth. Evander's giant was beating it with thunderous blows from all four arms, smashing it so fast and so hard that its armored hide was cracking.

"I think he's winning," Rory said, looking relieved.

Within seconds, the elfonnel faded from sight and the giant stood tall, staring down at the spot where it disappeared.

"He did it!" Shona shouted, and a cheer rippled through the army.

Then the giant spun and started lumbering toward them at a terrifying run.

"What's he doing?" Shona asked, sidling next to Connor, opposite Verena.

"It looks like he's coming for us," Ivor said, sounding nervous.

"Evander wouldn't attack us," Connor said.

"Unless he's lost control," Verena said, eyes wide with worry. "It can happen."

"Tallan take it," Connor muttered. "That's replacing one monster with a worse one."

"We need to prepare," Ilse urged as the giant closed to within half a mile, still charging full speed.

"Boulders form ranks," Connor ordered. "Striders take to the field. All tertiary Petralists prepare to repel the giant."

Captains scurried to relay commands, and soldiers formed ranks, fear replacing joy as they faced the onrushing monster. Connor felt terrified to think of Evander losing control. It was his army under attack, his soldiers about to die in the face of that monster, and the thought filled him with towering anger.

"Verena, get in the air," he urged. "I've got to stop him."

"You can't," she said, gripping his hand. "I can't lose you."

Oh, he wanted to kiss her so bad, but instead released her hand. "I can't let him destroy my army. I can at least slow him down."

Besides, Evander might not be coming for everyone. He might only be coming to exact revenge upon Connor for breaking the secret, ruined city. Dying again was not really something Connor wanted to do, but he couldn't let hundreds of other people die just because they happened to be standing between him and Evander.

He sucked on marble, preparing to launch himself over his troops and charge Evander's giant. There had to be a way to remind Evander who he was, to reason with him.

If not, he'd make Evander choke on him.

Evander's giant bellowed, "Beware!"

"He can talk!" Hamish exclaimed.

The ground behind them shook, and Connor spun toward the Sculpture House. Boulders were scattering as the ground under the long tables of power stone shook.

Then the elfonnel exploded out of the earth, gaping maw snapping up the entire cache of power stones and half a dozen Boulders too slow to escape. Its entire immense bulk erupted out of the ground like a breaching whale, and it crashed back to the earth, looking as healthy as it ever had.

It trumpeted, a sound like the exploding mountain above Alasdair, and pivoted toward the people fleeing in disarray, focusing on a pair of women, running toward Connor, but hopelessly too far away.

Aunt Ailsa and Jean.

Chapter 75

ean!" Hamish shouted, and quartzite thrusters erupted under his feet and hands, shooting him into the sky. Connor blinked. That was fantastic!

Verena leaped aboard her Swift and took off a fraction of a second behind Hamish. Connor longed to rush after them, but he had taken command and he had to organize his army. They were about to get caught right between renewed fighting.

But he couldn't just watch Ailsa and Jean die.

"Striders, get over there and pick up stragglers!" he shouted.

Padraigin was already running, her long, graceful legs fracking as she tore down the hill, with Lorcc matching her pace and a dozen Striders giving chase. They'd reach the fleeing women in seconds.

They didn't have that much time.

The elfonnel lunged, snapping down at Ailsa and Jean, the sight burning into Connor's mind with searing terror.

Jok reached them half a heartbeat faster. Grabbing the ladies, he threw them into the air with a mighty heave of his max-tapped granite arms. They just barely cleared the snapping beaks of the elfonnel's many tongues.

So it gobbled up Jok instead, its huge jaws ripping a six-foot trench in the ground.

Relief for Jean's and Ailsa's survival mingled with renewed horror at Jok's abrupt end. Connor took a step toward them, but Shona gripped his arm.

"Let others save them. You have to save the army."

Hamish crossed the distance with amazing speed, catching Jean right out of the air before she could crash back to the ground. Verena arrived half a second later and caught Ailsa.

As she banked away, the elfonnel charged after her, and the ground beneath her exploded, striking the Swift a brutal blow that threw it into a wild spin. Verena hadn't taken the time to strap herself in, and both she and Ailsa tumbled off the flying craft.

Padraigin and Lorcc caught Ailsa as she fell, then raced back toward the army lines with her held between them.

Verena tumbled the other way, toward the monster.

Three of its beaked tongues snatched at her, and she made a pitiful display of defiance by punching at them. Amazingly, the first two beaks somehow missed her, sliding just past her torso.

The third one clamped onto her shoulder and her scream echoed across the plain, striking Connor's ears like daggers. With quartzite-enhanced vision, he clearly saw the panic on her face as the elfonnel's tongue yanked her into its open mouth.

Chapter 76

he sound of the elfonnel's enormous jaws slamming shut on Verena rang through Connor's soul like the Tallan's own laughter. He stood rooted in place while the echoes of it screamed all the way down to the deepest recesses of his mind.

Verena was gone.

"No!"

Connor screamed so loud something tore in his throat. Fear burned his guts, so deep, so tangible it was like claws ripping his innards. It was swept away by an all-consuming rage so vast it made the insanity of marble seem laughable. That rage boiled up through him and drove all fear aside.

"Oh, what a tragedy," Shona said, actually looking shocked, but not quite sad.

He. Would. Not. Allow it.

Connor leaped into the air and tapped quartzite, forming a howling cyclone that echoed his cry with its mighty roar. Driven by that implacable rage and carried aloft like a living tornado, he soared toward that maw that was already opening in search of its next victim.

Hamish arrived first. Flying even faster than Connor, every thruster opened wide and roaring with power, he clapped his arms together, pointed at the monster.

Two slender javelins shot from his arms, propelled by white-hot flames. The burning missiles raced into the monster's mouth and exploded.

The blast of air tumbled Hamish away, but Connor ripped the air apart and tore through the center of it. He seized some of the flames and wrapping himself in them as he flashed past rows of blasted teeth and the charred stumps of snakelike tongues.

The elfonnel roared with pain, but Connor drove through the torrent of its breath and matched its cry with a defiant howl he could not recognize as his own. The valve of its throat was like a cart-sized stone. Before it closed behind its breath, Connor flew through.

The hollow tube of its throat was dark and empty, scoured clean like a storm drain. Half running, half flying down its length, he raised a piece of limestone high and commanded it to come alive. Light blazed forth like a miniature sun, illuminating the stygian darkness, but revealing no trace of Verena's body. When he reached the far end, a second valve whisked open and he plunged into the torso of the beast.

The tunnel there narrowed to seven feet, blocked by a curtain waterfall of some viscous material. He punched through with his fiery whirlwind. On the far side, the tunnel opened wide, like a low-ceilinged underground cavern at least sixty feet long, and more than half full of that sludgy black ooze. The entire chamber rocked with the monster's ponderous stride, and it smelled like old vinegar and rotten eggs.

He had reached the beast's belly, and nothing floated above the black ooze.

A trickle of the filth worked through the barrier of his fiery whirlwind, and Connor touched it with his left index finger. It burned like icy fire and the tip of his finger faded from the shiny black of enhanced granite to normal flesh, even though he continued to tap the power stone. His hand throbbed with a deep ache that beat against his power for several heartbeats before expiring.

His finger didn't fade to black again, but remained simple, vulnerable flesh. That meant the monster consumed Petralist powers somehow. That's why it went after Ailsa's stone supply. It was feeding, replenishing its strength.

What did that vile stuff do to Verena's unprotected skin?

The disgusting efficiency of it renewed his towering rage and he max-tapped marble to intensify his protective fires, then dove into the inky sludge. At first, the disgusting ooze resisted the fire, but then began to smolder and after three long heartbeats, it lit with an explosive whoosh.

In seconds, the entire stomach transformed from a filthy pit of black acid eating through hapless Petralists into a firestorm as the top layer of ooze burned like kerosene. Connor let the stomach burn, hoping the sludge would dissipate, but he controlled the flames immediately around him.

Burning back the sludge, Connor dove deeper into the belly of the beast, hunting for Verena. Boiling her in monster acid was not much better than leaving her to dissolve alone in the monster's belly, but he could think of no other way to dig through to her without dying too. As he groped blindly through the burning sludge, his hand grasped a human ankle. With a surge of hope and a mighty heave, he yanked the person out of the boiling acid. The sludge melted away to reveal the face, but it wasn't Verena.

It was Jok.

Connor gagged, nearly vomiting at the sight. Jok had been brutally smashed by the monster's teeth, and the sludge had eaten into his torn flesh. He looked partially dissolved, barely recognizable as human.

So Connor did the only thing he could. Enshrouding Jok's body with purifying fire, he cremated him on the spot. At least the monster wouldn't consume his remains.

The smell of charred flesh, mingled with the stench of the burning sludge was making Connor sick. He felt light-headed from the smoky air. He wouldn't last much longer.

Terrified by what he might find, he nevertheless dove back into the sludge. Almost immediately, he found another body.

It was Declan.

Seeing Jok's corpse had shaken Connor, but looking down at Declan's broken little body struck him like a curse-punch to the stomach. He dropped to his knees beside the brave young Sentry, whose expression was locked into a mask of determination. Tears flowed as Connor touched Declan's head.

"I'm so sorry," he whispered.

He twisted the sorrow into renewed rage at the monster, leaped to his feet, and screamed fury, his cry echoing through the stomach chamber. He would destroy this monster. Somehow, he would avenge the useless death.

He cremated Declan, holding to that resolve like a shield against the horror of the day and with grim determination, dug back into the black sludge. He found the next body in seconds. It was a Boulder Connor barely knew. The boy looked intact, if not exactly alive.

Connor couldn't bear to cremate another student, not one who only looked to be sleeping. He had to try something to help. So he shoved a blast of air down the boy's mouth. Black slime gushed out and his chest heaved. The boy coughed and vomited all over Connor's boots.

He didn't care, but laughed with joy to see a life spared. Even though the boy remained unconscious, he explored deeper with renewed hope, leaving the boy on the cleared area behind him. In the next frantic minute, he pulled another five men and two women out of the ooze, all unresponsive, all stripped of their powers, their skin burned. Some of them were savaged like Jok and Declan had been, but with the others, he shoved blasts of air down their mouths to clear their airways. Three of them responded, coughing and vomiting, but none of them awoke.

The others he cremated. It was the only honor he could offer.

Burdened by grief and by guilt that he'd let those soldiers die when they depended on him to protect them, he continued digging. He held onto hope he could save more, and was desperate to find Verena, but terrified to think that the best he could do for her might be to cremate her remains like the others.

The monster began thrashing more violently, and Connor spotted open holes in the ceiling of the stomach where fresh ooze began pouring in to replenish the acid he had burned away. He plugged each of those with hardened air to help staunch the flow, but he needed to find Verena fast and figure out how to break out before his powers ran out and the monster's stomach defeated him too.

His marble began to run low, so Connor concentrated on managing the fires raging in the cavernous stomach, directing those flames with more precise control. He tried to calm his labored breathing, but smoke hung thick in the low-ceilinged room. Despite his efforts with quartzite to keep that smoke at bay, breathing was becoming difficult. He'd run out of air even sooner than running out of fire. So he focused on using the flames from the burning ooze as his shovel to dig through the semi-liquid acid, determined to find Verena, alive or dead.

Then something reflected the flames within the ooze directly in front of him and he risked using more fire to illuminate the object.

Verena.

Unbelievably, she lay in the midst of the acidic slime, completely whole.

A gentle thrumming vibrated through his marble senses as the flames rebounded off an invisible barrier just larger than Verena's curled figure, and he understood. She had used a shieldstone like the ones she had employed against Rory to such effect outside of Lord Gavin's manor house.

Her face, which had been white with terror, lit up like the rising of the sun when she saw him, and she launched herself out of the ooze.

Connor caught her and carried her back to the others. She clung to him and wept into his shoulder, her body wracked with sobs of relief and terror. "I was so scared," she whispered.

"Me too."

Despite the danger they still faced, hope lit his soul like a max-tapped Solas. He tried to say more, but his voice was constricted by emotion, and he blinked back tears of joy.

The other rescued Petralists still had not stirred, and their breathing remained dangerously shallow. He burned away encroaching slime and sat on the stone-like floor of the monster's stomach, cradling Verena.

"It was eating right through my shield."

"If you hadn't thought of that. . ." He couldn't finish the thought, could not admit again how nearly he had lost her forever.

Verena lifted a gauntleted hand and examined the glove. "This should have lasted longer. I don't understand."

"What is it?" He was happy to think about something other than the desperate situation they were stuck in.

"I lined it with blind coal, a new power stone I've been studying."

"So there are other power stones!"

She nodded. "This should have deflected that last beak, or allowed me to break out of the stomach, but it's all gone."

"I'm glad you're not."

Connor hugged Verena tighter and she winced, holding her left arm at an awkward angle. He took it gently and tapped the warmth of sandstone from the pendant at his neck. He found the forearm broken and the muscles badly ripped, and began binding the hurt and easing the pain, despite the fact that if they didn't figure out a way to escape in the next moments, they would die together in the belly of the beast.

Verena let out a sigh of relief. "I hadn't planned our reunion to go quite like this."

Her big blue eyes seemed to swallow his vision, and he touched her cheek, savoring the feel of her skin, despite everything. "I missed you."

He wanted to kiss her so badly, but hesitated. Did she really want him? Could he really kiss her there, in the belly of the Doom?

Verena leaned forward and pressed her lips to his, moving with a bit of hesitation, as if she shared his fears. That only made him want to kiss her more, and his heart sang as their lips touched, then pressed together. He pulled her tight against him, drinking in the feel of her, the minty taste of her lips, and the feel of her arms around his neck.

When she released him, his heart sang with joy. She really did care, had crossed the length of Obrion to come to him.

Then the entire room rolled, as if the elfonnel was tumbling aside. Connor wrapped Verena in protective arms, tapping granite. At the same time, she activated her shieldstone. They bounced off the walls twice before the elfonnel settled back to normal, but it began bucking and pitching wildly.

The fight had resumed.

Connor drew the unconscious Petralists close to them with air and increased the protective flames around the group to hold back the spraying sludge.

"How do we get out of here?" Verena exclaimed.

"Maybe back up the throat?"

They looked up the sloping floor toward the hinged valve that blocked the exit. Even if they could climb back up there while the elfonnel bucked and spun under them, he doubted it would open easily for them, and he couldn't leave the others behind to be consumed anew by the black sludge.

Verena reached the same conclusion and kissed his cheek gently. She tried to smile, but terror shone in her eyes.

"We're trapped, aren't we?"

"Yes."

Chapter 77

amish, with Jean in his arms, landed hard near Rory, fighting back tears. Connor's scream of heartfelt rage still echoed across the battlefield and hung over the plain like a shroud. Or maybe those were the echoes of that awesome explosion?

Everyone in the army stared at the elfonnel in shocked disbelief. Jean sobbed into his shoulder. "Not Connor too!"

"He's not dead yet," Hamish declared. "I have to help."

"Be careful."

He set her down, but Rory grabbed his arm. The captain looked more enraged than Hamish had ever seen, and for a second, he worried the man was going to crush him.

"Give me a lift," Rory growled, gesturing toward Evander's giant, who was drawing dangerously close. "I need to talk with that thing."

Hamish wanted to rush back to attack the elfonnel, but what could he do against it? His diorite javelins should have broken its jaw, but had done little more than clear a path for Connor to plunge inside. The damage was already gone. That monster healed faster than they could permanently damage it.

So he gripped the captain by the back of his battle leathers and opened wide the release rate on his thrusters, lifting the two of them into the air. At that moment, the ground under the army rippled, and the top layer moved, splitting the army and carrying everyone out of the giant's path.

"Did our people do that?" Hamish asked.

Rory nodded. "Not sure what that thing's planning, but I don't want it trampling my army."

As the giant raced through the open corridor, Hamish flew up to its head level.

"You kill that thing!" Rory shouted, pointing a finger at it. "And don't let it get away this time. We'll do everything we can to help."

It glanced at them and its enormous head bobbed slightly. Hamish took that for a yes. Then it raced past, lowered its shoulder, and plowed into the elfonnel, sending it tumbling.

Hamish returned Rory, who began barking orders before they even reached the ground. "Boulders retreat to the inner wall! Mobilize there and assist in evacuating the city. Striders, clear all the palaces. All tertiary Petralists on me!"

Ivor met them, looking grim. "What do you have in mind?"

"Hit it with everything we can," Rory growled. "Support Evander's efforts and tear that thing apart." He glanced at Hamish. "Don't you have something to do?"

"Aye!"

That captain was one formidable man. Hamish leaped back into the air and surveyed the renewed duel. Evander's giant and the elfonnel were clashing like titans, and the ground all around them bucked and heaved, as if they fought for control of the elements too.

Hamish chose to believe Connor was still alive inside that thing. If he was, he had to get out fast or the fighting would kill him. He must be already rattled by the pitching and tumbling. As tertiaries began pounding the elfonnel with fire and ice, aimed primarily at the eyes and at its joints, Hamish soared above the beast and studied it. What was Connor doing, and how could he help?

Smoke began seeping out its nostril holes. It bellowed again, but sounded more pained than angry, and it seemed distracted. Evander's giant pounded it off its feet, but it rolled before the giant could pile-drive it with all four elbows in the stomach.

Connor was definitely alive, but cooking the monster from the inside would probably charbroil him too. Hamish needed to reach him, but hesitated to fly down the monster's throat. His battle suit was holding up amazingly well, but there were limits.

Maybe the nostrils?

He zipped over the monster's head as it thrashed back and forth in apparent agony. Evander's giant seized it by the head with two arms and beat on it with the other two. The Petralists continued to hit it, but didn't seem to be accomplishing much.

He was surprised to see Shona and Rory leading a squad of Boulders that included Erich and Anika to attack the elfonnel's rear legs while the giant held it pinned. Shona attacked bravely, but although she cut a fabulous figure in those battle leathers, Hamish hated her for holding Connor prisoner.

Connor wouldn't be in the nostrils. They'd be in the belly if they still lived. Hamish needed to get them out. He flew back to the monster's broad top side, but the thick plates of stone-like armor coating its torso mocked his hope. He could never break through that, even with the Ashlar's hammer. He'd used his two diorite javelins. They'd worked better than he'd hoped, but all he had left was a handful of diorite chunks. The only way he could think to use those would likely kill him.

His eyes fell on Erich, who was tumbling away from one of the elfonnel's stomping feet. He smiled. The crazy Grandurian was exactly who he needed.

He swooped down to Erich, who was grinning, even though his right shoulder sagged and his right arm hung at his side. Blood caked the side of his face, but he was grinning despite obvious pain.

"I nearly caught that leg," Erich laughed in Grandurian.

"Yeah. Nice work, but that's not nearly insane enough to stop that thing."

"You have a better idea?"

"Oh, yeah. We'll probably get killed."

Erich's grin widened. "I'm in."

Hamish had Erich climb onto his back, then flew up to the monster that was straining against the giant, but for once couldn't seem to break out. The Petralists had concentrated all their attacks against its whiplike tail and rear legs. Its rate of healing seemed to be slowing, and a dozen cracks lingered in its armored hide.

The smoke curling from its nostrils had increased tenfold. Connor was definitely taking his revenge against the monster's innards, but he needed to get out before he died in there.

"We fight eye?" Erich slipped into Obrioner.

"No. We're going to sucker punch it."

"Is good." Erich glanced down at his useless right arm. "But no much punch."

"Just speak Grandurian, please." He couldn't take Erich seriously when he talked like that. "I don't need you to punch it."

As he swept in between two of the middle legs and hovered under the creature's long, gray belly, he noted with rising optimism that the armor plating did look thinner, just like on any other animal he had studied before it showed up on the dinner table. "How's your throwing arm?"

"Not strong enough to penetrate that skin."

Hamish pulled from the special, padded compartment built into the side of his waist satchel the bag of diorite and thrust his hand into the deadly stone chips. Despite the shiver of fear that raised the hair along his arms with crackling energy, he threw wide open the destructive power of the diorite.

He handed it up to Erich. "Don't drop it. If anything can hurt this beast, it's this."

"What is it?"

"Diorite." At Erich's puzzled look, Hamish said, "Remember the big explosions Dierk triggered with the thump driver outside of Alasdair?"

"Yes! Those were great."

"He used less than one tenth of the diorite you're holding to do that." Of course, with that much diorite, they might blow Connor up with the monster, but he didn't have enough to risk using too little. Connor could heal if they could only get him out of there, but he'd die for sure if they hesitated.

Erich regarded the little pouch with new respect and laughed. "Perfect."

"Just don't miss."

Erich gave him an incredulous look. "How could I miss that thing?"

Above them, the stomach lurched downward and for a second Hamish feared the monster somehow understood the threat they posed and planned to crush them. Thankfully, it stabilized again, but the message was clear. Time to go.

Erich tapped granite and became significantly heavier. As Hamish increased the release rate of his thrusters to compensate, the Petralist heaved the tiny sack high in a powerful throw with his left hand.

Hamish didn't wait to watch. As soon as the bag left Erich's hand, he fled with every ounce of power he could draw from the suit's thrusters and shot out from between its legs.

He barely reached one stony knee when a vast explosion tore through the creature's midsection and blew the middle two legs right off both sides. The blast of air tumbled Hamish away, and one of the severed limbs clipped him and sent him lurching sideways with a gut-wrenching twist. Hamish didn't even see the ground before crashing into it with enough force to crack several of the outer leaves of his armor. He tumbled and rolled a long way, and even after his body stopped moving, the ground kept spinning.

When he finally did leverage himself to a sitting position, he checked his body and was amazed to find no broken bones. His suit was incredible!

He did hurt all over, and tapped sandstone wafers set against his skin. They couldn't heal as fast as a real Healer, but they generated a gentle warmth that helped ease his hurts. Given enough time, they would do the job.

The monster lay on its side, half its legs ripped off, the center of its torso shattered, with a long gash blasted right through what was hopefully its stomach. The Boulders who had been attacking it had retreated from the fury of the explosion.

Stony flesh and black sludge, some of it still burning, covered the ground under the blast radius. A stench like burned, rotten eggs hung like a pall in the air.

Then he noticed the bodies.

Lying scattered in the midst of the disaster were the bodies of many people, some covered in black slime, others lying as if asleep. None of them moved.

Actually, one thing moved. His eyes were drawn to a figure walking out of the mess, surrounded by a fading cyclone and with fire burning the ground in front of them into a singed carpet. They held another, smaller figure cradled in their arms.

Connor. And Verena.

Chapter 78

onnor exulted. He was alive, free of the elfonnel, with Verena in his arms. Despite the death and terror that surrounded them, in that second he felt happy.

Verena kissed his cheek, then turned his face toward her. "I don't know how we got out of there, but I'm happy we did."

Her big blue eyes seemed to swallow his soul, and he leaned in to kiss her. Her eyes widened farther and she tipped her head back so fast he missed her lips and kissed her chin instead. Turning, he followed her astonished gaze.

Evander's giant stood nearby, and it was heaving the half-broken elfonnel into the air.

"Get out of there!" Hamish yelled, waving them toward him. Erich lay nearby, looking dazed.

Connor had granite, not basalt, but he ran as fast as he could anyway as dripping gobs of monster rained down around them. Striders, led by Ivor and Padraigin, tempted the dangerous ground, rushing in to snatch up the prone bodies and carrying them to safety.

Hamish pounded Connor so hard on the back when they reached him that he almost dropped Verena. "I can't believe you survived that!"

"What happened?"

"Diorite."

"You could have blown us up," Verena said. As he protested, she pulled him close, kissing his cheek. "I'm glad you took the chance. We wouldn't have lasted long in there."

Then Verena popped right out of Connor's arms with a squawk of surprise. Shona held her high and dropped her on her backside, glaring.

"You not only lack the decency to die an honorable death, but you endangered Connor too," Shona said.

Verena scrambled to her feet to face Shona. "And you endanger yourself by breaking the peace agreement."

Shona laughed. "The day you can hurt me hasn't arrived, wench."

Connor pushed them apart before they could attack each other. "Both of you calm down."

"Looks like the elfonnel's nearly done for," Shona said, pointing at the monster struggling in the giant's grasp.

It did look weaker, but then it twisted and chomped down on the giant's shoulder, shearing most of the top, left arm off.

"You had to say it, didn't you?" Hamish frowned at Shona. "Just invite bad luck when we least need it."

The two monsters tumbled to the ground with a crash and began rolling over each other. As they did so, they both healed.

"Tallan take it!" Connor shouted. "What do we have to do to kill that thing?"

Captain Rory rushed up with Anika and Ilse. "Glad to see you survived that thing, lad," Rory said. "Any way to kill it from inside?"

Connor shook his head. "We were lucky to survive. I think some of the people it swallowed will survive, but some of them. . ."

Rory gripped his shoulder. "It's an ugly thing, war."

"I did what I could for them," Connor said, his voice thick with emotion.

"Now let's do something about that elfonnel," Ilse said.

"I'm open to ideas," Connor said.

"Elemental attacks barely slowed it," Ivor reported. "We hit it with everything while the giant was beating on it. We're running low on power stones already."

"Then get everyone back," Connor said. "Regroup at the inner wall. We'll focus on evacuating everyone to safety while we figure out how to help Evander."

"Where's safe?" Rory asked.

"Granadure," Connor said.

"If only I could reach Kilian," Verena said, sounding frustrated. "He'd know what to do."

"Don't bring that criminal here," Shona snapped.

"He's not here," Connor interrupted before they could start arguing again. "Let's focus on what we can do. We regroup at the Carraig. Move out."

While the monsters continued shaking the plain with their contest, they jogged for the main gate of the inner wall. Connor searched for Aunt Ailsa. He needed to speak with her. The only item in their arsenal they hadn't attempted yet was the sculpted stones she'd given him. She'd warned him not to use them except for a moment of ultimate need.

That moment had arrived.

He located her with Jean and Hamish. She looked tired and worried, but smiled to see him and Verena approach.

"Aunt Ailsa, do you or Jean remember anything about how long an elfonnel rampage usually lasts?" he asked.

Jean shook her head. "The accounts varied, and I got the sense that they sometimes lingered for hours."

He grimaced. "That's too long."

"I wish there was more we could do," Ailsa said.

"There may be," he said. "It's time I used those gifts of yours."

She didn't speak for a moment, but continued jogging, her expression serious.

"What gifts?" Hamish asked. "Did you bake something?"

"Don't you ever think of anything besides food?" Jean and Verena both asked at the same time, then laughed.

It felt good to see everyone smile, even though the elfonnel threatened to destroy everyone. Connor loved having his friends together, and that sense of family reinforced his decision. He had to do whatever he could to protect them.

"I'm going to use it," he told Ailsa. "Unless you have a compelling reason why I shouldn't."

She shook her head. "Nothing compelling, Son. You may be right, but I still worry it's a huge risk."

He gestured behind them at the battling monsters. "Not dealing with that thing is a bigger one."

"What are you talking about?" Verena asked, placing a hand on his arm.

He glanced around, but most of the army was focused on moving as far away from the monsters as possible. Shona was distracted talking with Camonica. He wouldn't find a better chance.

"Ailsa sculpted some stones for me," he said, untying the bag at his hip and handing it to her.

She accepted it with reverence. Those stones could buy him a place in the ranks of the nobility, although Shona would probably try confiscating them when she learned about them, claiming that as his patron, they belonged to her. Verena peered inside, then slipped a hand into the pouch. Her eyes widened a moment later and she glanced at Ailsa.

"These are magnificent!"

"Thank you, dear." Ailsa smiled with an artist's pride.

"As soon as the army is set up in defensive formations, I'll use one."

"Which one?" Verena asked.

"I'm not sure yet." He considered that as they ran.

Probably not slate, since both of the monsters commanded such mastery over that element. Quartzite was out too. It was just too unstable. Fire would be a good choice, but he wasn't sure it would damage a being made out of earth. Besides, he hesitated to embrace the insanity of fire that deeply. Aonghus might call it a purifying fire, but he'd only get one chance.

That left soapstone. Water was his strongest element anyway, and he felt confident with the power of a sculpted stone, he could hurt that beast.

When they reached the Carraig inner wall, Connor set his captains and leaders organizing the evacuation and setting up defensive positions. Ivor, Padraigin, and Redmund each led similar groups of tertiary Petralists, while Rory and Camonica commanded the primaries. Ilse and her band remained a mostly-independent group that hovered around Rory and Anika, who refused to be parted.

"How are everyone's power stores?" Connor asked.

"Not good," Rory reported. "Most of the army's about spent. Even the tertiaries are guarding the last of their stones. We might get one final assault, but that's it."

"I'm nearly out too," Hamish said.

Verena scowled. "If I could find the Swift, I could resupply."

"No time for that," Connor said.

Out on the plain, the elfonnel toppled Evander's giant, but instead of leaping on it, the beast instead raced away and smashed down the Sculpture House, tearing through the rubble. It was probably hunting for more power stone.

The Sculpture House had been his home, and the sight of the casual destruction sparked a fresh anger. He couldn't wait any longer.

Heber joined them. "General, power stores are down seventy-six percent and battle-ready forces are at one third nominal. If that monster eats the rest of the power stores, we won't have more than an eight percent chance of surviving the day."

"Thanks for summing up the situation," Rory growled.

"You do realize that all that basalt sheathing around those palaces is all power grade stone?" Hamish asked.

Everyone turned to face him, and Connor shared their astonishment. "Say that again."

He shrugged. "I licked one of the walls. It's good quality stuff."

"Impossible," Rory breathed as they all craned their necks up to stare at the unfathomable wealth gleaming in the afternoon sun. Connor couldn't imagine how such a staggering amount of treasure could be used as building material.

"One more mystery of the Carraig," Jean muttered, jotting a note on a little notebook she pulled from a deep pocket of her skirt.

"Send some Boulders to crush some of that sheathing," Connor ordered. "If it's power-grade stone, we'll use it."

Then he turned to Heber. Before he attempted the sculpted stone, he needed one last thing. "Give me some obsidian."

"Of course, General."

He didn't have a lot left, but Connor took the little pouch eagerly and gazed at the powdered volcanic glass. With eager anticipation, he shoved two fingers inside. Even powdered to dust, the sharp edges tugged at his skin. He drew in a deep breath and concentrated. Obsidian was the only igneous stone he hadn't established affinity with and he felt the stares of every set of eyes watching him, acutely aware of how much depended on him making it work.

After three breathless heartbeats, he felt something trickle into his fingers. Unlike the skittering itch of granite or the boundless energy of basalt, obsidian pulsed like unspoken words flowing up his arm. Connor focused on the strange, almost understood beat, and as it crept into his chest and touched his heart it suddenly burst into full clarity.

It sounded like Verena's laughter.

As that sound echoed through his torso and into his mind, his exhaustion faded and he stood taller. Her laughter filled him with hope and his mind lit up like a glorious sunrise after a long night. Concepts that had always seemed confusing suddenly seemed simple under the light of obsidian power.

Connor laughed with the wonder of it. Why did he ever wait so long to try obsidian?

"Careful, General," Heber said. The Blade was watching him closely. "Obsidian takes a little getting used to."

"What's there to get used to? This is incredible!"

"That's precisely the danger, sir. It can easily become an addiction, but used too much it loses its strength until it does nothing for you."

"I'll take that risk today."

Fearghas clapped him on the shoulder. "When this is over, we'll spar together. That's obsidian at it's best."

"You're on." That would be a lot of fun, but he hoped to gain more than just a faster sword.

"Give me some room."

Everyone backed up except for Ailsa. "Connor, remember the danger."

"One danger at a time."

Ivor approached. "I want to go face it with you, Connor. Together, we stand a better chance."

He shook his head, gripping Ivor's shoulder. "Not this time, my friend. I've got sculpted soapstone, and I can't have anyone else fighting me for control."

Ivor gasped. "How?"

Connor winked and hefted the little sculpted statue of interlocking soapstone cubes. "It's all in knowing the right people. You and the other champions, work with Rory and oversee the evacuation. If I fail, it'll be up to you."

Then he clamped his jaws over the stone. Ailsa had explained that with the sculpture, he didn't need to swallow it, but just suck on it like he did with quartzite. His body jerked from the jolt of power that exploded through him , and his water senses spread through the entire Carraig like a lightning bolt. He felt every ounce of water, sensed every living being, could track the pulsing of their blood. He even sensed the elfonnel and the giant, like shadows across his mind, tramping the shattered Sculpture House in their battle.

The concentrated force of the soapstone rattled his limbs, and every bit of water within a hundred yards rushed in, as if eager to do his bidding. With a flicker of thought, he drew the waters beneath him into a six-foot wide pedestal.

The monsters were tumbling over each other again, and their fierce struggle rolled them right over the dark wall of the almost-completed Rhidorroch.

Frazier shouted in fury and turned to Connor.

"Wasn't my fault this time."

"Will you kill that thing already?"

Connor saluted, then waved to Verena. She was standing near Shona, and both of the girls waved back. Dealing with Shona and somehow extracting himself from her service without triggering the full weight of her wrath scared him more than facing the elfonnel.

He pivoted and flowed over the broken remnants of the formal garden to face the distant elfonnel. Evander's giant tackled it and the two monsters resumed fighting, but that didn't seem to accomplish anything but destruction.

"What's the plan?" Hamish asked, hovering nearby.

"If the fight goes badly, get Jean and Verena out."

Hamish looked like he wanted to argue, but he'd already admitted he lacked the power stores to fight much more. So he sighed, nodded, and pulled from a pocket on his battle suit a tiny, pale colored cube that looked like a squashed cookie.

"What's this?" Connor asked, accepting the dense little item.

"That, my friend, is an entire cake," Hamish declared. "Packaged by the smash packer for travel. You'll need your strength."

"Thanks." As Hamish headed back to the others, Connor grinned and tucked the little pastry into his belt pouch. He never accepted anything from Hamish's pocket, but he might actually eat that one.

His hand closed on the little bag of porphyry in his belt pouch. He'd forgotten all about it during the fighting. He couldn't imagine a time when he might actually want to use it, but he was glad it hadn't gotten lost.

Connor focused on the elfonnel and fingered the pouch of sculpted stones Ailsa had given him.

Suddenly, all the clues came together into a simple truth.

"I know what to do."

Chapter 79

As Connor flowed over the broken lands on his platform of water toward the towering monsters, he passed the shattered Rhidorroch. One more bit of senseless destruction the elfonnel was about to pay for.

As his water senses flowed over the area, he connected with the huge underground storage tank under the Rhidorroch. He'd used those waters during his nomination trial to form the wondrous dome, shattering the entire obstacle course in the process.

The tank was full.

Connor seized upon the waters and they responded to his touch with remarkable enthusiasm. He suspected it was a product of the sculpted stone, and he was happy the waters seemed eager to respond to his need.

So he gave them something to do.

Fifty thousand gallons exploded out of the Rhidorroch and blasted the elfonnel in the side, just as it knocked Evander's giant off again. The wave knocked it rolling, skittering in slippery mud. Connor wanted to drive it farther across the plain, but it was just too big. So he reached farther and seized the waters of the lake and drew them to him in a tidal wave.

The elfonnel found its footing, and its eight legs locked onto the earth, somehow holding it fast against the crashing waters. Even as the initial wave faded, it trumpeted a deep-throated challenge and plowed through the waters at him.

Connor wrapped its head in water and drained the heat away, forming a solid casing of ice.

It paused and started bashing its head against the ground, cracking the ice, but Connor kept shoring the prison back up. Evander's giant took advantage of the elfonnel's distraction to seize it and lift it high.

While the monsters struggled, Connor targeted the elfonnel's front right shoulder. Maybe he could disable it, keep it from moving so fast? That would give him time to figure out how to take it apart. Water, like an extension of his will, flowed around the joint, filling the entire area and hardening to ice.

Water always expands as ice, and packed in so tight, the expanding ice cracked the armored plating around the joint. It sounded like the splitting thunderclap of lightning strikes nearby. He took it as a good sign, poured in more water, and repeated the process.

The monster convulsed and beat its head so hard against the giant holding it aloft that the ice shattered. How could it hit itself so hard and not give itself a concussion?

The giant stumbled back and the elfonnel slithered back to the ground, casting a silver-eyed glare at Connor. It opened wide that gigantic maw, its serpentlike tongues snapping in Connor's direction.

So he filled its shoulder joint with water for the third time and hardened it again. The joint popped, and with a final concentrated spear of rushing water, Connor severed the limb entirely.

"Yes!" he shouted as the elfonnel roared in pain, its leg falling to the ground like a giant tree.

Then it dropped, its entire torso plunging into the ground. Earth rippled away, forming a towering wave that struck Connor and tossed him into the air. The rippling effect continued into the Carraig. Buildings shook, towers cracked, and at least two palaces toppled, unable to handle the unexpected shaking of their roots. The thunder of the collapsing structures echoed across the plain like the monster's laughter.

When the elfonnel stood again, its leg was reattached.

So much for plucking it like a stone chicken. Connor could never defeat it unless he separated it from its element. That's what Evander's giant had been trying unsuccessfully to accomplish.

He needed to do something fundamentally different. So he drew deeper from the soapstone, biting down on the stone in his mouth and embracing the element with his entire will. Like the day he'd formed the great dome over the Rhidorroch, he stepped into the element, becoming one with it until the waters were but extensions of his limbs.

The unconquerable strength of water rushed through him like the tides, and as his control became complete, he sensed the threshold. It really was like an invisible door just above him. On the far side, he sensed even greater powers, like hints of a coming dawn. But with that feeling came a tremor, an aftertaste of unease. Through that threshold lay power, perhaps enough to defeat the monster, but there also lurked the dangers Ailsa had alluded to.

With a bellowing challenge that shook the plain, the elfonnel charged past the grasping hands of the giant and bore down on Connor.

That danger was all too real, and far more pressing than the imagined risks of the threshold. He needed those powers or everyone who depended upon him was going to die. Connor drew deeper from the soapstone and in his mind, he leaped.

He touched the threshold, but felt an intangible resistance pressing him back down. He tore at the barrier, trying to force his way through, but it withstood his efforts.

So Connor tapped obsidian again, and his thoughts accelerated, as if they'd been nearly sleeping before. With a flash of insight he understood. Grasping the full might of the sculpted soapstone, Connor released it all in a single, overwhelming rush, driving his mind upward into the threshold as if carried upon an invisible tide.

Every drop of free-floating water within a quarter mile rushed in toward him with a roar and crashed together at his feet in a spectacular series of cresting waves that built upon each other, lifting him high into the air on a watery spire until he could look down upon the towering turrets of the Carraig far below.

The power of the sculpted stone mimicked the physical waters, and he ascended upon that torrent. The invisible restraint of the threshold weakened under that rush of elemental power, and Connor's mind burst through.

It felt like he was plunging into the mysterious depths of the untamed ocean, as if all his life, he'd only ever dipped a single toe into the waters. Now he dove deep, plunging into the heart of the great waters.

It was his heart. The pulsing of his blood moved in time with the great tides, flowing together with the mighty rivers. He no longer walked with the element of water. He was the water. It felt as if the very nature of his body had shifted just a fraction, but that fraction made all the difference. In a moment of radiant glory, his senses exploded outward in every direction, as if he was rising high over the land until the entire nation stretched below his gaze.

Everywhere he looked, water glowed like liquid amber in his mind. He could touch any of it, snap his senses to that spot, and see or hear everything happening there.

It was too much to comprehend, and for a terrifying second, it felt like his soul was on the brink of dissipating into those many waters. Then his mind snapped back to the present, and again he stood upon a bubbling tower of rippling water, staring down at the elfonnel on the plain below.

Connor grinned and his voice sounded like the crashing of waves in a storm.

"Now I will kill you."

Chapter 80

As Connor gathered the many waters to strike at the elfonnel crouched at the base of his tall, watery spire, the monster suddenly pitched to the side. It staggered to and fro, like a drunken man on the deck of a ship in a storm. Then it stopped, all eight legs splayed and rigid, threw its massive head back, and bellowed, a deep-throated cry of hatred that shook Connor high atop his watery perch.

He had no idea what was happening to the monster, but hopefully the strange behavior was a sign that it was finally weakening. Evander's giant circled it cautiously, as if expecting some kind of trick.

Without warning, Connor's vibrant strength evaporated, and his intimate connection with elemental water sundered. It was as if he'd been riding the crest of an enormous wave that unexpectedly crashed to the shore. His ethereal senses snapped, severing contact with the element, and releasing the waters of his towering spire into an abrupt thunderous waterfall.

As he plunged down with the water, Connor tried to reestablish connection, but his thoughts turned sluggish and he felt an overwhelming weariness, as if all the waters of the great deep piled upon his shoulders. In desperation, he tapped obsidian, which helped spin his thoughts up to speed again.

That's when he realized what was happening. He'd been warned, but had forgotten the danger. Ascending through that threshold spent his strength and stretched him, mind and body, beyond his natural capacity. Just like burning igneous stones to exhaustion triggered a post-exhaustion reaction, ascending did the same thing.

It couldn't happen now, though! He had to destroy the monster, not collapse at its feet in his moment of victory.

His body didn't care, and he crashed to the ground, saved from breaking bones by the churning flood that was churning away in every direction. He plunged deep, striking the ground, then tumbled about in the wild currents until the waters dispersed, leaving him gasping in several inches of soupy mud.

Connor tried to rise, to stand and face the elfonnel and reestablish his contact with water, but his muscles refused to obey. A coughing fit doubled him over, and the tiny piece of soapstone, all that remained of the incredible sculpted creation, slipped out of his mouth into the mud.

A voice spoke into his mind. It was a strong voice, cultured and deep, and filled with exultant joy.

"You belong to me!"

"You're one of my imaginary friends," Connor retorted. "So that means you belong to me."

"You will usher in the day of my ultimate glory," the voice continued.

"Will you be quiet?" Connor said. "My mind, remember? So my glory when I win freedom to craft my own future."

The voice chuckled. "The freedom you seek is but a shadow of hope."

"Leave me alone," Connor exclaimed. It was getting difficult to convince himself the voice wasn't some deranged part of himself that snapped free during that last tumble into the waters. The alternative was as scary as anything he'd dealt with all day.

The voice did not leave, but spoke with growing strength. "All that has happened to you, every challenge that has formed you, has driven you to this moment, serving as the push required to achieve this moment of destiny."

Like Connor's mother was fond of saying, such claims were like rising dough. They were impressive to look at until one poked them and they collapsed, having been filled with nothing but hot air.

"What do you want?"

"You will destroy my enemies and lay waste to every land that opposes my will."

"Get in line," Connor retorted. It seemed every nation

wanted to win his loyalty and use his curse to solve their military problems. "And get out of my head."

"You are my slave until I release you or death claims you."

"Not much incentive for me to agree," Connor said, trying to crawl away from the elfonnel that had just rammed Evander's giant off its feet. It seemed consumed by a vast rage, driven beyond its normal strength. Earth erupted all around Evander's giant, burying it. More earth rushed in, swept off the plain like a rug yanked across a room. It piled on top of the giant, forming a small mountain and leaving the false ceiling of the ancient, ruined city bare.

All Connor managed to do was flop onto his face in the slippery mud. "Who are you?"

"Dougal," came the ringing reply. "Your master."

Connor cringed from the strength of that voice. How was he speaking right into Connor's head? He'd heard of people hearing voices in their head, but never someone else's real voice. Had he swallowed a speakstone he didn't know about?

"You're late," he said. All his life, he had wanted nothing more than to serve High Lord Dougal as Guardian, but now he was grateful events had prevented him from swearing allegiance to Shona's father. At least she sometimes pretended she wanted him as a partner.

"The choice is no longer yours to make," Dougal said, and an invisible force seized Connor's mind, shackling his will with icy chains.

Connor tried to fight, but didn't even know what was going on. How could he fight an invisible enemy? If patronage was a lie, how was Dougal in his head? He struggled to focus, to drive the insistent voice out of his head, but his thoughts began to grow dim, and a dark confusion settled over his mind. He couldn't even remember what he was fighting.

Glancing through the haze that had descended over his vision, Connor noticed the elfonnel stop its wild stomping around the prison it had constructed for Evander's giant and turn toward him with terrifying intent. The monster lowered its head, trumpeted its rage, and charged.

It was hard to think, but the sight of that galloping mountain of monster sparked a single clear thought.

He was so grouted.

Chapter 81

e's down!" Hamish shouted, pushing up his long vision goggles. "He's just lying there. I think he's hurt."

"How?" Verena exclaimed.

"Of course he'd fall right when it looked like he was doing so well," Cameron grumbled.

"You'd think he'd wrap it up," Tomas agreed, gesturing at the devastated landscape. "He's just about broken everything."

Then the elfonnel trumpeted a challenge and charged Connor.

"We have to help him!" half a dozen voices cried in unison.

As one, every Petralist still standing broke into a charge. Most of the army had gathered into a single body to witness Connor's lone assault against the monster, and Hamish had been impressed by the outpouring of support. They might be mostly high born nobles, but Connor had somehow won the hearts of those mighty warriors.

As he broke into a run with the hundreds of angry Petralists, he decided there were few better ways to face death by monster. He only wished he'd had a better breakfast.

Then a hand grabbed his shoulder and pulled him to a stop. It was that Healer, Aifric.

"What are you doing?" Hamish asked. "Haven't you ever wanted to be part of a suicide charge?"

"No one has to die today," Aifric said. "And if you really want to help Connor, you'll carry me up onto the mountain."

"You're cracked. He needs help over there."

"You saw him fall. He's now vulnerable to the real enemy."

"What enemy? The monster's right there!" He gestured to the charging elfonnel that was still bearing down on Connor, even though Striders were already ringing it, slinging stones and trying to distract it.

"The real monster is the one controlling the elfonnel."

"Wait, what?"

"It's more than raging, uncontrolled elements," she said, and the conviction in her voice made it hard to doubt her.

"How does a Healer know all this?"

She leaned closer, her expression hardening. "Are you going to help me save him or not?"

He glanced from her to the horde of Petralists closing on the elfonnel. He really wanted to join that crowd, but what if she was right? He wished he hadn't lost sight of Jean in the press. She'd be able to see the truth of what Aifric was saying.

"Why do you think the monster focuses so much on Connor?" she asked.

Hamish shrugged. "He's got the most stones. It's hungry."

She rapped a knuckle on his helmet. "Think deeper, Hamish. It's been targeting him for another reason. It would take too long to explain, but you have to trust me. I can stop the person who right now is attempting to destroy Connor's mind. If he succeeds, he'll turn Connor into a far deadlier monster than the elfonnel ever could be." She held his gaze with her fierce eyes. "Do you want to have to kill your best friend?"

Kilian had turned elfonnel and lost control. Could Connor somehow unleash a similar disaster? He didn't know how Aifric knew that truth, but Kilian had also suggested Dougal might somehow manage to seize control over Connor's mind. He didn't dare ignore her warning.

"Fine, but if you're lying, I'll kill you myself."

"If I'm lying, I'll kill myself first," she retorted.

"That's mental."

She leaped upon his back. "How about, 'I'm glad to see you're such a loyal friend'."

"That works better."

"Let's go."

Not entirely sure it was wise to take to the skies with the crazy woman on his back, and not confident that enough quartzite power remained to take them up the mountain and back, Hamish activated the thrusters and leaped into the air.

Chapter 82

The haze of confusion over Connor's thoughts lifted a little and he blinked against the mud and water covering his face. The elfonnel had drawn dangerously close, despite being harried by Striders. Bolts of fire and ice rained across its face, and when Connor painfully turned his head the other way, he was shocked to see the entire massed army of the Carraig charging in his direction, led by Rory and Verena.

They dared rush the elfonnel, for him? They were idiots, but he was moved by their willingness to sacrifice. It was hard to think, but that much seemed clear.

He glanced back at the elfonnel looming over him and tried to gather his thoughts. He tapped obsidian. Like a bucket of ice water splashed over his face, his thoughts sharpened, and he felt the connection to Dougal's mind like an invisible shackle.

Dougal's thoughts echoed down that conduit as his control over Connor solidified, becoming complete. Connor's sense of his own body faded, and for a moment, he was Dougal.

Being an old, crazy guy was really unpleasant.

Dougal really was controlling the elfonnel, although Connor still didn't see how it was possible. Dougal had released the mind of the Petralist lost within the monster to grab at Connor's, but was attempting to reestablish his dominance over the beast. It was clear that Dougal had expected the elfonnel to rampage away through the school or return to fighting Evander's giant while he cemented his hold over Connor.

Dougal had made one little mistake. He had pushed the elfonnel to focus on Connor so exclusively that it was the one thought that drove it. It wanted to eat Connor above all else. He shivered to feel the intensity of that hunger, which radiated up from Dougal's connection with the monster and back to him.

If it could fight him, so could Connor.

He needed to think, but tapping obsidian had only seemed to give Dougal a stronger hold over his mind, so Connor released it. For a moment, obsidian wouldn't turn off, as if Dougal was somehow maintaining the connection. But Dougal needed to focus almost entirely on the monster as it drew within striking distance. His efforts paid off enough to turn it for a moment to chase a Strider.

In that moment, his control over Connor slipped and Connor shackled obsidian. Although his thoughts immediately plunged back into the murk, it wasn't as thick as before. Connor fought to regain control over his body, but all he managed was to twitch his left hand.

Lorcc and Padraigin skidded to a stop beside him.

"General!" Lorcc cried. "Are you all right?"

He couldn't answer, couldn't form a single word, couldn't even shake his head.

Padraigin pressed a hand to his head, and he felt healing warmth flow into him. That contact helped drive Dougal's presence back a bit and Connor's mind awakened.

"What?" Padraigin exclaimed, frowning over him.

"He's in my mind," Connor croaked. "Get me out of here."

Padraigin's eyes widened with fear. "This is terrible. Take him to the Healers. I must find Aifric."

Lorcc hefted Connor and ran back to the main bulk of the army. His friends surrounded him in a protective barrier as Lorcc lowered him.

"What's wrong?" Verena exclaimed, dropping to her knees beside him.

"Are you hurt?" Shona asked, crouching on the other side.

Without the active healing power helping, Connor couldn't form the words to explain.

"He said something about someone in his mind," Lorcc said.

"What does that mean?" Verena asked.

The Strider shrugged. "Padraigin seemed to understand, and raced off to find Aifric."

Connor stopped listening. It was too hard to do that and try to move. Fighting Dougal's control was like wrestling a torc with his bare hands. How had the elfonnel fought him?

It was out of control, raging mad, hungry for vengeance. It was a creature of elements and raw, simple emotion, which had been stoked to a boil.

Like a rampager.

Oh, he was so slagged. Connor needed to move his hand.

Just then, Shona took his left hand in hers, and Verena grabbed his right, drawing it to her lips. He struggled to move them, wanting to howl at the girls for interrupting his moment of epiphany. He only managed to twitch each hand, not even enough to pull them free.

Shona soothed him. "Don't try to move. Hold on, and we'll get you help."

Verena leaned over him and he managed to roll his eyes to his side.

"What?" She leaned closer, intently watching.

He rolled them again and twitched his hand.

"Do you need another sculpted stone?" she whispered so Shona couldn't hear.

Connor rolled his eyes side to side, then twitched his hand again. Hesitantly, Verena pulled his hand down toward his side. He blinked his eyes in thanks and twitched his hand again. It touched the pouch at his belt.

Verena caught on and pulled out the only other stone available to him. Her breath caught in her throat when she saw it.

"No, Connor. This is a really bad idea."

Connor twitched his hand toward the bag again.

"Are you sure?" she looked terrified that she might be misunderstanding.

He blinked his eyes closed.

"What are you doing?" Shona asked. "What is that?"

"Perhaps his one hope," Verena retorted, shoving his hand into the bag.

Shona snatched for the bag, but Verena pushed her hand away. "Leave it. We'll know in a minute."

Connor focused all his will on absorbing porphyry.

He felt nothing. Dougal was somehow blocking his affinities.

Chapter 83

"So where is this enemy?" Hamish shouted. He was hovering five hundred feet above the first row of hills surrounding the Carraig. The vast bulk of Mount Murdo reared before them, and if Aifric wanted to climb that, she'd have to do it alone. His thrusters were almost spent.

"Working on it," she said, leaning her face close to his, her arms and legs wrapped around his back. It made flying a bit tricky, but he had enough practice that he'd managed all right.

"You don't know?"

"Of course not. It's the secret hiding place of a concealed enemy. They don't put up signs. Don't worry, I can find it."

"How?"

She hesitated. "I have really good hearing."

"Are you serious?"

"It has to be somewhere close. I'll hear something."

They didn't have time to hunt around the mountain for a mystery enemy. He glanced back toward the Carraig. The Striders were still playing catch-the-devil with the elfonnel, and the army had swallowed up Connor, but they wouldn't last.

"Just start flying," Aifric ordered. "We have to start somewhere."

"I have a better idea." Hamish activated his long view goggles and scanned the mountainside. There was so much to see, he couldn't study any one area in detail, but just swooped his vision across the hills and valleys below them as he slowly hovered toward the east, hoping to spot something, anything.

His swooping gaze caught sight of a familiar object and he paused to focus on it. Verena's Swift. It had floated away from the battlefield and gotten tangled in the branches of a tall pine tree. The supply box behind the seat contained all the stones he needed to resupply.

"I've got to stop for a minute," he said, aiming for the Swift, his optimism buoyed by the prospect of a fully functional suit.

"We don't have time," Aifric cried. "Every second counts."

"And if we crash, we'll definitely be late."

Despite her arguments, he needed to land. His thrusters were down to the last breath of power, and he could resupply in a matter of minutes.

Then he saw what Aifric was hunting.

"There!" He pointed at a squat Sentry tower, almost concealed within a copse of trees.

"Go!" Aifric cried.

Hating to leave the promised security of the Swift, Hamish decided he could drop Aifric and maybe return before losing all power. He moved toward the Sentry tower, not daring to open the thrusters wide for fear they'd crumble to dust under that much strain. As they neared the spot, he picked out the form of the giant, Gregor.

"That's got to be it," Aifric said, her voice excited. "It makes sense that Dougal would bring Gregor on this mission."

"When this is over, you'd better explain how you know all this."

"If I tell you, I'll have to kill you."

She didn't sound like she was joking, and he wasn't sure how to respond to that. They floated high over a concealed clearing behind the Sentry tower. Gregor had not seemed to notice them creeping closer so high overhead. Aifric pointed past his ear and whispered, "There. That little house. He'll be in there."

"You realize that once we land, Gregor will just swallow us up in the earth?"

"Can you stop him?"

"If you had let me stop to replenish, I could have," Hamish said. "I've got almost nothing left."

"Do you have enough to buy me a few seconds?"

"I hope you know what you're doing," Hamish grumbled.

"Trust me."

He hated when people said that, but patted her arm and said, "Be careful."

Hamish had seen what Gregor could do, and even with his stones at full power, and all his weapons at capacity, he would have hesitated to face him. But if Aifric was right, this was the only way to save Connor.

So Hamish dove.

He slowed as he passed over the little, round, earthen house in the clearing, and Aifric leaped right off his back. She lacked Kilian's impressive fire to slow her fall and improve her presentation, but she landed on the roof and rolled with the impact, landing on her feet in the entrance. Almost before she touched down, she slipped through the curtain door.

If they lived through the day, Hamish would tempt her threat and find out who that Healer really was.

Of course, he had to live through the day first.

As soon as Aifric touched down, Gregor rotated. He didn't turn like anyone else would, but the entire top of his tower rotated to face the unexpected threat.

Hamish dove for his face.

The huge Sentry actually showed surprise.

So Hamish shot him in the face with five hundred hornets. The little projectiles rained down over the huge Sentry, a quarter of them exploding with fantastic enthusiasm. The unexpected barrage knocked Gregor right over backward, but he didn't even have the decency to fall off his tower. Instead, it flowed horizontal with him, wrapping him in a protective cocoon that insulated him from Hamish's hornets.

With the little speedsling empty, Hamish holstered it and pried the last piece of soapstone out of his suit. The little rock was the one holding the inner layer of the defenses in his battle jacket in place. When he extracted it, the water that had been swirling in a constant, slow circle under the hardened granite leaves of his jacket stopped moving. It began leaking out the seam of the bladder that he'd sewn into the jacket.

Hamish sighed. People were going to think he peed himself.

He threw wide the little stone's power and dropped it at the base of Gregor's tower. Just then, spears of earth shot out of the tower at him, and he activated the full power of his quartzite thrusters to escape. They gave him a single roaring thrust, just enough to dodge above the first volley. Then the thrusters crumbled to dust, their powers spent.

For a second, Hamish glided over the trees in glorious silence, but for the wind in his face. He glanced back in time to see water gushing out of the ground at the base of Gregor's tower. That would interrupt the Sentry's hold over the earth for a moment.

Hopefully that was enough time for Aifric.

Hamish's grin faded as he began the long fall toward the ground. At the last minute, he activated all the remaining marble in his jacket. Gushing flame charred the ground but provided enough lift to slow his fall so that he didn't shatter on impact.

Groaning from the abuse, Hamish climbed to his feet and oriented on a nearby towering pine tree. As he started to run, he activated a small speakstone, the partner to the one he'd attached to Aifric's sleeve when he patted her arm.

He had agreed to help Aifric, but that didn't mean he trusted her.

Immediately he heard a cry of pain from a man's deep voice.

Then Aifric spoke, her voice cold and without mercy.

"Hello Lord Dougal. It's time to die."

Chapter 84

The mental binds holding Connor prisoner evaporated. He gasped and shot upright in a convulsive move as all his muscles responded at once.

"He's back!" Shona cried, hugging him.

Verena embraced him on the other side, and the two recoiled from touching each other. Connor didn't have time to deal with them because as soon as his mind broke free of Dougal's restraint, the porphyry began eating into his hand.

Connor threw his head back and screamed, his voice changing into the wild howl of a rampager. Everyone recoiled from him, shocked faces forgetting about the elfonnel for a moment.

Connor was the new horror, and he was already in their midst.

He lunged to his feet as his limbs swelled and his hands and feet transformed into terrifying claws. Strength boiled through him and he embraced the rage of porphyry. It was his best defense against the enemy attacking his mind.

That enemy tried to regain dominion over him, but the force of that will, which had been like iron bands before, now felt like whispers of smoke.

Dougal's voice echoed as if from a great distance. "How?"

Connor roared and drove the hated man away. As the transformation concluded and he took a deep breath, he sensed fear and smelled fresh meat all around. He was surrounded by mortals, their pulsing blood triggering a desperate hunger. He growled, and many of them screamed.

Then one of them stepped right in front of him.

Verena.

The sight of her was like purifying fire and it burned away the ravening hunger, redirecting his rage against the monster that threatened her life. He glanced to the side where Shona's familiar rosewater scent was mingled with rank fear, and she recoiled away from him, looking more shocked than he'd ever seen her.

He turned back to Verena and crouched a bit lower, extending one mighty claw toward her. She swallowed, but stepped closer and pressed the back of his hand against her smooth cheek.

"Come back to me when this is over," she said, and her hands shook against his paw.

He sniffed her scent, drawing the smell of her hair, high mountain winds, and a hint of mint deep into his lungs and holding it as a shield against the rage. Then, with a howling challenge, Connor leaped the ranks of shocked troops and tore across the plain toward the elfonnel. The monster had turned from pursuing Striders a quarter mile away and bellowed an answering challenge. It was a thousand times larger than Connor, imbued with elemental powers and nearly invincible.

He didn't care.

Driven by burning rage, he sped for the monster faster than a fully fracked Strider, covering dozens of yards with every mighty leap. As the elfonnel lunged at him, its massive maw wide open to snap him into its gullet, he coiled and leaped like a living spring.

Connor soared over its mouth and landed on its left nostril. Barely pausing to tear great gashes in that tender target, he leaped again, crossing the monster's head in a flash. He swarmed over the left side of its face, targeting the two massive silver eyes there.

Those soft targets exploded with satisfying gore, drenching him with silver liquid that burned his tongue and only enraged him further. He wanted to rip the cursed monster apart one inch at a time, but first he had to disable it.

As the elfonnel reared, shaking its head in agony, Connor dug his claws into its hardened armor and leaped, heading for the eyes on the other side.

Chapter 85

amish nearly collided with a tree as he ran, so absorbed was he in listening to the speakstone pressed against the side of his helmet. Aifric really had attacked High Lord Dougal and injured him in his secret hideout.

Were Healers allowed to do that?

"You've made a terrible mistake." Dougal's voice sounded far too calm.

"The only mistake I made was in not reaching your heart with that stroke." Aifric spoke calmly, like one who was comfortable with killing. It wasn't the voice of a Healer.

Then Gregor's voice boomed across the stone, sounding distant. He was probably still outside the little house. "Are you all right?"

Hamish cringed, imagining the huge Sentry preparing to break through the door and tear Aifric apart. He ran harder, entering a tiny clearing and finally catching sight of the Swift, still hovering twenty feet into the air. If he had any thrusters left, he could reach it in a second.

Instead, he started to climb the tree, moving as fast as he could, but knowing he'd never replenish his suit in time to help Aifric.

Dougal's voice called out, but instead of ordering Gregor to murder Aifric, he ordered, "Return to your duty."

"There is one inside with you," Gregor said, his customary Sentry-speak suppressed, his voice concerned.

"She is a spy, and I need her presence. This is the critical moment, my friend. Shield this house from any and all contact. Even you must not risk your earth senses within."

Hamish paused halfway up the tree, gaping. Had Aifric lied to him? Had he somehow helped Dougal further his plot against Connor? He wasn't sure what to believe. He'd heard Dougal cry out, heard Aifric promise to kill him. Had that been a lie?

Dougal spoke again. "We have worked for this moment too long."

Hamish frowned at the speakstone. That sounded more like Aifric than Dougal, but it was Dougal's voice.

"The kite knows not whence the wind blows, nor wither it goes, but rises upon the currents, confident only in the string."

Then Hamish heard only silence, so he scrambled up the tree, grateful the pine had lots of branches. Just as he hauled himself into the seat on the Swift and activated the quartzite thrusters to maneuver it to the ground, Dougal spoke again.

"You are of the Mhortair, and you command the sounds with serpentinite." His voice sounded tight, as if he was in a lot of pain.

"I was told you might know of the Assassins," Aifric said, her voice confident. "Few Obrioners do."

"I know more than you think."

Hamish stared at the stone, digesting the news. Aifric was an Assassin? Serpentinite sounded like another unknown power stone. There were even more secrets buried behind Aifric's deceptive smile than he'd imagined.

He needed to get back there and learn the truth. As soon as the Swift settled to the ground, he leaped out and flung open the supply box. Wedging the speakstone into his helmet he began pulling fresh stones from the supply box and fastening them into his suit.

"You made the mistake we counted on, although not in the way we expected," Aifric said. "I had assumed destroying you would define my career. Now you'll be nothing but a footnote as I move on to deal with the return of the Blood of the Tallan."

That didn't sound good. What was she planning for Connor?

"An event which you so rudely interrupted just now," Dougal said. "You impress me, girl. By your dress, you've managed to infiltrate the Carraig as a Healer. It is a shame you choose to interrupt the day I foster the return of the Blood of the Tallan."

"We have different ideas about what form his return should take."

"Indeed. I'm afraid I lack the time to debate the advantages of my vision of the future."

"As if you could sway me." She actually snorted and sounded confident, but Hamish worried she was overplaying her hand. The key to succeeding in a surprise attack was to get it over with quickly, but she was dragging it out too long.

Dougal spoke again, sounding far more confident than a wounded man facing a deadly Assassin. "Now, if you will hand me my sword, I will prepare to meet you properly."

"If that's how you want to die."

Hamish picked up sounds of a sword being drawn. Was she actually giving him a weapon? Was she cracked?

He completed replacing the thrusters and the most important stones in his suit and grabbed up a handful of small diorite bombs from a special compartment. He was out of time, and Aifric was in more danger than she realized.

Aifric said, "You will tell me how you controlled that monster and what you hoped to achieve by unleashing it on the school."

"I think first I will teach you some manners."

"This is going to hurt," she warned, and the sound of swords clashing echoed across the speakstone.

Then he heard nothing but a strange crackling sound, followed by silence.

Was the fight over? Had Aifric killed Dougal, or had he somehow flipped the surprise back on her?

Hamish leaped into the air, engaging his thrusters and tearing into the sky, wishing he'd returned to help Aifric sooner. Worry of what he'd find when he reached her drove him on.

As he powered through the air toward where Gregor's tower had been, Aifric's voice spoke, so soft he barely heard it above the rushing of wind.

"Hamish, help me."

He soared over the tiny clearing, bombs poised to throw, but paused and settled into a hover, not sure what to make of the sight. Aifric lay on the ground in the center of the clearing, face down, her hair disheveled. There was no sign of the little building she'd entered, no sign of Gregor or his tower, and no sign of High Lord Dougal.

Hamish studied the clearing for a moment, searching for a trap, but finding no evidence that anyone else had ever been there.

Aifric rolled over slowly, as if in pain, caught sight of him, and motioned him closer.

Wary of a trap, Hamish settled to the ground beside Aifric. No one emerged to challenge him, the earth did not attack, driven by a Sentry's will. He and Aifric were completely alone.

"Hamish?" she asked, her expression confused.

"Aifric, what happened?" he asked, dropping to one knee beside her.

She shook her head slowly. "I. . .I don't remember."

"But where did Dougal go?"

Aifric frowned, thinking for several seconds. "I'm not sure. Everything is hazy."

"We need to get you to a Healer."

She chuckled. "I am a Healer."

"Are you?"

"Sure. I'm Aifric." She sat up with his help and said. "Get me back to the Carraig. I need to help Connor."

"I thought that's what we were doing."

"Not any more. Let's go."

As Hamish lifted into the air, cradling Aifric in his arms, he wondered what had happened. Dougal had been there, but where did he go? What had he done to her?

He stared when he caught sight of the plain, stripped of earth, and the new mountain in the center. Then he noticed the elfonnel fighting a rampager, and that drove worries about Dougal from his mind. He activated another speakstone in his helmet.

"Verena, what's going on?"

"Where did you go?" she exclaimed. "Hamish, Connor absorbed porphyry."

"Did you tell him what happened with Kilian?"

"No. I haven't had time to tell him anything. Get back here."

Hamish had been considering returning for the Swift and flying it back to Verena, but they'd have to go get it later. Holding Aifric tight, he headed for the Carraig as fast as he could fly.

Chapter 86

onnor raged across the elfonnel, tearing and ripping, a whirlwind of destruction, leaving a bloody trail in his wake.

The monster healed as quickly as he injured it.

He had already ripped out both sets of eyes four times, but couldn't hurt it enough to make a difference. The Petralists hammered it with their elemental powers, but it shook off the attacks and only seemed to grow angrier.

So did Connor.

He paused on the center of the elfonnel's forehead to throw his head back and howl with frustrated rage.

The newly-created mountain nearby erupted in a geyser of earth, and Evander's giant leaped from the crest, sliding down the flank of the mountain like he was on a sledding board over ice.

The elfonnel didn't wait for it, but lurched forward, its motion different than it had been for the last few minutes. It scattered the Striders who had been annoying it, and closed on the ranks of the Boulders, who had hung back from the fight. The monster's target became clear as the little humans scattered in every direction.

Verena.

Lacking her Swift and her power stones, she was just a girl who couldn't run fast in the mud. The elfonnel ignored closer targets and focused on her. Ivor noticed the danger and scooped her into his arms, racing out onto the plain with Strider speed, leading the elfonnel away from the others. He leaped off the boundary where the false ground ended, plunging twenty feet to the false ceiling of the hidden city, and raced away on the long stones that formed it.

The monster followed, but it crashed through the false ground, smashing a ruined palace underneath. Instead of lunging after Ivor, the ground underneath it surged upward into a rolling wave that burst through the false ceiling over the ruin and flowed after the Dawnus.

Shattered stone from the false ceiling rained down all around Ivor, who ran with nimble speed, dodging and weaving. Verena snatched one large chunk of stone out of the air and clutched it close.

It was targeting Verena. That truth blazed through Connor's mind like a forest fire. He tore at the monster's head, but accomplished nothing. While transformed into a rampager, every emotion was raw and powerful, and the love he felt for Verena eclipsed everything else.

He needed to try something different.

Thinking rationally was excruciating in his monster form but, driven by his concern for Verena, he managed one idea and seized upon it.

He jumped from the elfonnel's head.

It didn't even seem to notice him depart. That only angered him more. Didn't he deserve some kind of acknowledgment for all the pain he'd inflicted upon it?

Connor sped back toward the dispersed ranks of the army, vaulting out of the sunken ruin to solid ground. Humans scattered away from him like herds of eoin from a nuall. He caught a familiar scent and bounded over to Ailsa. To his rampager sight, she looked frail and vulnerable, but her heartbeat was even and she regarded him with a calm, if guarded expression.

She was holding the tiny bit of soapstone that was all that remained of the beautiful sculpture she had given him.

"Oh, Son," she said, her expression sad. "What have they done to you?"

Speaking was a waste of time, so he crouched over her and reached out a clawed hand for the soapstone.

"Are you sure?" she asked, but dropped it into his paw. "I've never heard of. . ." Her voice trailed off. "I've never heard of anything to do with unclaimed that wasn't terrifying. Perhaps you do need to do it this way."

Connor crushed the soapstone in his paw and flung the powder into his maw. It stuck to his long tongue and he growled. That's why he usually drank it in a mixture.

Water splashed into his mouth and he gulped the powder before it could wash out. He spun to find Ivor and Verena nearby. He glanced back at the plain where the elfonnel was battling Evander's giant again, wrecking more of the sunken ruin.

Ivor grinned. "It was distracted, so we came back around." He took a slow step forward, his expression amazed. "It really is you, isn't it?"

He tried to say, "Thanks for the water." All that came out was a growl that sounded like, "Thuffer wawa."

Ivor saluted. "Any time."

Then Verena stepped in front of him and her scent filled his nostrils. He smelled no fear on her.

She looked heartbroken, but still reached out and actually touched his hard purple hide. "I love you, Connor. Remember to come back to me."

"Imp mix," he growled, frustrated it didn't sound anything like "I promise."

She seemed to understand, tears in her eyes, and she drew his maw down to her shoulder, kissing his purplish cheek. That simple touch shivered through him and ignited a new fire in his heart.

Another familiar scent drew Connor's gaze to the right. Shona had approached, but she retreated from him and grimaced. "I'll kiss you when you change back."

"I hope you know what you're doing," Ivor said. "Because our powers are all just about spent."

He retreated, but Verena remained close, in his shadow, and squeezed his paw. "Will you kill this thing already?"

Connor leaped away from her to meet the giant monster. With Verena's kiss still warming his cheek, he penetrated the red haze of raw emotion and embraced the pulsing rush of soapstone coursing through him. For a second it resisted, but his need overwhelmed the hesitation and the waters surged in response. The unbreakable strength of water fused with his rampager fury, tempering it and reinforcing it at the same time.

Waters rushed in from every direction, sucked out of the earth and the secret lakes concealed under the plain. They frothed around Connor, forming a maelstrom that spun in time with his pounding pulse.

The elfonnel actually paused at the sight, but it was too close to escape and too dumb to know death had arrived. Evander's giant seized the distracted creature and threw it into the air with a mighty heave.

With a flicker of thought, the whirling waters exploded forward, throwing Connor onto the monster's head. He gripped with his claws and held on as a tidal wave tumbled the elfonnel over, forming a giant sphere and rolling them out onto the shattered, sunken ruin. Howling with the need to kill, Connor kept them rolling, preventing the elfonnel from connecting with the earth, its source of power.

The beast thrashed and Connor sensed its panic. As it rolled, he rushed down its long torso. As he reached each of its legs, he paused and concentrated. After ascending through the threshold, he was one with the water, even in his rampager state, and it obeyed with fierce loyalty. Drawing upon it with all his will, he drove spears of ice into each shoulder blade, severing them and casting them out of the whirling sphere so the monster could not hope to reattach them.

After removing all its legs, leaving it little more than a howling log, Connor clawed his way back to its neck. The joint was so thick, he failed to drive enough water into it to break it. So he packed water all around it, forming a collar of ice, then drove half of the waters at his command down its gullet and froze them in the long tube of its throat.

Then he leaped straight up, using a pulse of water to throw himself two hundred feet into the air. Using streamers of water, he yanked himself back the other way. Hard. He descended like a living meteor, and with every ounce of strength, he drove into the ice ringing the monster's neck, becoming a living chisel striking the stone.

The stone shattered. So did his hands and his arms.

Ice and armored flesh erupted in every direction, shredding his watery sphere and spraying water half a mile across the plain. Connor flew from the monster's back, too stunned to even try to catch himself as he tumbled wildly through the ebbing tide.

So great was the shock that it burned through the last of his porphyry, and his body transformed back to human. The pain and disorientation shuddering through him severed his control over the waters.

Connor lay in a puddle, gasping. The transformation had reset his bones, but he ached all over, consumed by exhaustion so deep, he could barely blink his eyes open to look at the results of what he'd done.

For a moment, he felt a flash of panic. He was no longer unclaimed. Dougal could strike at his mind again. He didn't know how Dougal had managed it the first time, and his only known defense was exhausted.

When Dougal did not strike again, he forced himself to relax. He was too tired to panic over something he couldn't control.

The elfonnel lay in the distance, its head detached from the body, staring into the sky, mouth locked open in its final, ultimate surprise. The silver glow faded from its eyes, and its gigantic torso cracked and imploded, melting into the earth.

The head didn't melt away, and for a second, Connor worried it would somehow again regenerate.

Evander's giant didn't give it the chance. It leaped over the decomposing corpse and smashed all four mighty arms into the head with all its strength. This time the head imploded.

Instead of melting away like the body had, the head burst into a strange cloud of dust that rose into the air, obscuring both it and Evander's giant from view. Connor frowned. It was hard to think, but with the waters blanketing the area, that kind of dust should have been impossible.

He refused to believe the monster was again somehow regenerating. If it did, it deserved to kill them all. Such an indomitable will could not be quenched.

The elfonnel did not rise again. The dust settled slowly, and it was gone, as was Evander's giant. In their place stood a pyramid-shaped mound of hardened earth eighteen feet tall. On the narrow peak rose a rectangular cairn of perfectly round stones.

Connor just wanted to sleep for a year, but the sight filled him with a strange sense of awe, and he had to know what it meant. So with a groan, he staggered to his feet and stumbled toward the pyramid.

Chapter 87

Thankfully, Connor found stairs cut into the side of the pyramid. He didn't have the strength to climb it otherwise. Every step felt like an act of will, but he needed to know.

Halfway up, a powerful hand gripped his arm.

He blinked in surprise. Evander stood beside him.

"You look terrible," Connor said.

Evander looked like he'd tried stopping an avalanche with his face. His dark skin was bruised, his eyes drooped, and his shoulders sagged. Strength still radiated from his hand on Connor's arm, but he looked completely spent.

The giant Sentry offered a weary smile. "Even the ship that glides upon the waves is battered by the tempest."

"You can say that again."

As they neared the top of the strange pyramid, Connor looked out over the shattered plain. His army was approaching, and although he couldn't see their faces yet, he knew his friends would all be there. It was a comforting thought.

"Thanks for your help," he told the big man as they completed the climb. "Someday, you'll have to explain to me exactly what you did to raise that giant."

Evander said nothing, but stepped to the top of the pyramid. The round stones that he had thought a solid cairn, actually formed a box about seven feet long and four feet wide, filled with fine sand. The scene filled Connor with an odd sense of reverence.

Just as they approached, the sand began to shake. Connor retreated a step, unsure if it represented danger, but not quite believing it did. Evander stood his ground. The body of a middle-aged man with salt-and-pepper hair and scraggly beard shivered up through the sand until it lay unmoving on top.

"At last you find peace, my old friend."

Connor glanced from the corpse to Evander, who dropped to his knees beside the cairn and took the dead man's hand.

"Who is it?" Connor asked, his voice a hushed whisper. He'd seen far too much of bodies and death. That one showed no visible marks, and seemed sad.

"One who fell to an ancient evil long before you released his soul from torment."

"So he was responsible for raising the elfonnel?" It looked like Verena was right, and the elements needed a Petralist to allow them to rise to trample through the world.

"Reason is rarely anchored in the harbor of madness."

"But you know him?"

Evander nodded. "The storms of time obscure and conceal more than the snows of a winter tempest, and the days subsequent to war are turbulent and full of chaos."

Thinking hurt too much, but Connor considered Evander's words. "How can you lose track of a monster like that, even if you're distracted?"

Evander shrugged, "The wind that one day will rise into the mighty tempest is but a gentle breeze until that fateful day."

Connor wanted to shake him and scream at him to speak plainly, but Evander might just throw him off the pyramid and he didn't have the strength to handle another fall. Evander remained bowed over the dead man, but Connor turned away. That short conversation hinted at truths he needed to know, but he was too tired to figure them out.

To the west, his army had drawn close enough for Connor to recognize them. Rory and Anika walked in the front ranks, close together, hands clasped. Hamish walked hand in hand with Jean, and Verena trotted beside them.

When he turned, she rushed forward, shouting his name, her expression one of exultant joy. The rest of the crowd took up the cry. As the group stopped at the base of the pyramid, still cheering, Shona and Verena moved to the front, standing together, beaming. They'd probably start fighting any second, but he'd take one happy moment. Connor raised his fist in a silent tribute and everyone responded in kind.

That seemed to appease their worry and everyone began congratulating one another. Some soldiers laughed while others cried. Healers passed through the ranks and also descended on a number of unmoving forms at the base of the pyramid he had not noticed before. Aifric directed their work, but didn't leap into the healing process like she normally would. She looked exhausted and worn.

Connor couldn't make it down the stairs again, but didn't want to remain close to the fallen man who might have been insane, might have been the one responsible for so much destruction. So he slid down the back side of the pyramid, away from the crowds. He wanted to join the party, but in a minute. He just needed a quiet moment to enjoy being alive.

Ivor rushed around the pyramid and dropped to one knee beside him. Shona and Verena followed, but he leaned close before they arrived, his expression intent. "Connor, why did you turn unclaimed? How did you control it? How did you return?"

Connor gestured Ivor close and whispered the secret. "Patronage is a lie. The monster you saw is powered by another stone."

Ivor leaned back, looking stunned, slowly shaking his head.

"Believe it," Connor said, gripping his wrist. "But share it with no one. That secret will get you killed. Trust me."

Then Verena dropped to the ground beside him and embraced him with jubilant enthusiasm. He tried to hug her back, but he had taxed himself beyond the limits of his strength. Despite his best effort, darkness settled over his eyes and dragged him into unconsciousness.

Chapter 88

Connor awakened slowly and enjoyed the feeling of soft comfort while the memories of that terrible day of struggle faded like shadows of a nightmare. He'd never be free of them, but for the moment they no longer held sway over him. He sighed and opened his eyes. He lay in Shona's own oversized bed in her apartment in Lord Nevan's palace.

That startled him fully awake and he jolted upright. Leave it to Shona to arrange such a not-so-subtle reminder of her plans for him. He glanced to his left and nearly leaped right out of bed.

Evander sat in a chair beside the bed, watching him with the long patience only Sentries could master. Well, other than gigantic vultures, but that was an unsettling thought.

Connor leaned back against the pillows. "Please don't ever do that again. I'm surprised you're not still sleeping after what you did today."

Evander raised an eyebrow, and Connor sensed a sudden tension to him. Evander seemed to loom over the bed, even though he was still seated, and Connor felt a trickle of icy fear. "Are the deeper secrets so easily laid bare to your mind, young one?"

Connor took a moment to consider his words. He sensed that if he said the wrong thing, Evander would rip his arms off. After all he'd done, the thought was infuriating, but still terrifying.

"I already told you, I have no idea how you managed to raise that giant." He wanted to ask about elfonnel and how they were formed, but didn't dare. That seemed to be another of those secrets Evander was willing to kill to protect.

Evander relaxed just a bit and Connor allowed himself to breathe again. Without any power stones, Evander could break him like a twig. Even if Connor had power stones to help, he might only live a few seconds longer.

"The circle of history repeats," Evander said softly, "and yet there is time to prevent the full reckoning."

"Did you get hit too many times? Today's reckoning seemed pretty complete to me."

Evander leaned forward. "When a monster is born to lay waste to the world, when best would you slay it?"

Connor thought of the deadly nuall that ranged the Maclachlan Mountains. "Well if you knew it was a monster when it was born, why not kill it before it grew strong?"

Evander nodded and his huge fists curled around the knobs of the chair's arms. His voice was still soft, but carried an edge of threat. "And yet I waited until you awoke."

Those spine-chilling rushes of fear were getting really old. He hated to think his life might be in more danger lying in that soft bed than it had been during any time on the battlefield. He glanced toward the door, but escape was impossible.

He licked suddenly dry lips. "Why did you wait?"

"When will the potential become the choice? That is the question that toppled kingdoms of old and holds in thrall the balance of lives even now."

"I don't understand."

"The greatest threat of your condition is thus spoken by your own lips."

"What is my condition?" Connor asked, although he wasn't sure he wanted to know yet another hidden truth that might kill him. "Teach me how to not become a monster."

"A brick may build or destroy, but the hand that throws it chooses to make it a missile."

"I don't understand."

Evander cracked a smile. "Of this truth, one cannot argue."

"Well, if you'd share your knowledge instead of spoon-feeding bits and pieces to Jean, maybe I'd understand enough to be wiser."

"The raindrop, though tiny, may flood the greatest castle, when united with sufficient brethren." He paused, then added, "As the child grows, its meals increase, and thus the spoon may become a ladle."

Connor took that as a hopeful sign. Either Evander was promising to share more freely what he knew, or it was just about dinner time. He'd welcome either event.

The giant man rose from his seat, towering over Connor. "The time of my choice is at hand and the world will bear witness if I chose folly or wisdom."

He turned and walked to the door, but turned again. "The time of your choice will come. Do not force me to change my course."

"I won't."

What else could he say?

Evander bowed his head and muttered, "But of the other, what confusion clouds that choice and when will we know?"

Then he left.

Connor lay back in the bed and blew out a relieved sigh. What was that all about? Even for a Sentry, that man was confusing. He needed to find Jean. She'd spoken with Evander more. Maybe she could act as a translator.

He needed to get out of Shona's apartment and find Verena. Was she all right? Had the truce held, or had she fled with Hamish and Ilse's company? He shuddered to think that after fighting so bravely together against the elfonnel that his army would have turned immediately upon Ilse's band. He refused to believe they'd been killed, but that left him with the problem of finding them and figuring out how to plan his exit again. He could have picked a better time to faint.

Instead of his battle leathers, he found a fine pair of dark gray, linen slacks, a snowy, white shirt, and a black leather vest. With nothing else to wear, he donned the outfit and exited Shona's apartments. He was as hungry as Hamish after a six-hour fast.

Before he could find the kitchen, Lord Nevan appeared and actually bowed. That was almost as unnerving as waking in Shona's room with Evander hulking over him.

Lord Nevan took his arm and led him down the grand staircase toward the main entrance. "Come, master Connor. Everyone's been waiting for you."

"Why?"

Lord Nevan chuckled. "Your modesty is charming. You defeated the elfonnel and somehow returned from the terrible fate of the unclaimed. You are declared champion. Given the situation, the declaration is to be held forthwith, along with your choosing."

Connor was still trying to argue for more time when Lord Nevan dragged him out the main double doors into the late afternoon sunlight. A huge crowd waited for him in the street. Most were student soldiers, but some were linn workers or school administrators. As soon as he appeared, they cheered. Papil shouted, her voice enhanced by quartzite and booming across the Carraig grounds.

"He has awakened! Come celebrate the victory of the Blood of the Tallan!"

People rushed forward in a flood, fighting to shake his hand or hug him. Many of the girls grabbed his face and planted passionate kisses.

Connor tried to appreciate their enthusiasm, but his heart felt like a lump of ice. They adored him, thanked him for saving their lives, and even swore allegiance to him. With every well-meaning word, they tightened the bands of his captivity. More crowds came running, adding to the wild, festive atmosphere and pushing for their turn to touch him.

Finally, Lord Nevan restored a semblance of calm and the entire procession moved toward the main gate in the inner wall. Many of the towering palaces had been damaged, and the streets were covered with rubble and shattered basalt sheathing. Instead of risking the ruined inner grounds, a makeshift stage had been constructed right across the inner gate. There they would officially declare him champion, there they would expect his choice.

He still didn't see Verena, Hamish, or any of the Grandurians. He hoped that meant they'd escaped. He couldn't imagine how he was going to follow. He was out of porphyry, and turning unclaimed had been his one trump card. Even if he did find some, now that he'd turned and returned, would that even work to break his hold on Shona?

As they walked in a huge, jubilant throng, Princess Catriona pushed through to his side. She had changed out of her battle leathers and wore a fine gown that she did not seem to care was being dirtied by the press.

"General, so glad to see you feeling better."

"Thank you. You fought well today."

"If you really think so, may I ask a boon?"

Really? She was asking a boon of him? The world had gone crazy.

"Sure."

She blushed and leaned closer so others could not easily overhear. "I know you're tied to Shona's house and she has to be your choice for first breeding rights."

It still amazed him that they could speak of such things without any hesitation, as if discussing what course to choose for dinner.

She rushed on. "But the boon I ask is that you choose me for second breeding rights."

That surprised him enough that he stopped in his tracks and was nearly trampled by the crowd pushing from behind. "What are you talking about?"

Catriona looked startled. "I'm sorry. Of course you wouldn't know."

"Know what?" He was seriously considering beating her over the head with her own spiky shoes.

"The listener post was not damaged in the elfonnel's attack, so word has already reached Donleavy of the battle here and of your heroics."

"Thanks," he managed. Great, now the king knew about his curse. The feeling of a noose tightening around his neck grew more pronounced.

Shona slipped past Nevan to Connor's side and slid a possessive arm around his waist. She wore a form-fitting, crimson blouse and royal blue skirt. She looked stunning. Worse, she seemed completely confident and at ease beside him, despite having good reason to worry he'd moved beyond her direct control after taking command of the Carraig's armies. Had something happened while he slept?

Shona gave Catriona a dirty look. "Connor, I was going to tell you that good news after the ceremony."

"Were you going to wait to tell him the rest?" Catriona asked.

"What rest?"

If Shona didn't know, Connor really didn't want to.

"Given Connor's unique gifts, the king has granted preliminary approval for sharing that gift with the bloodlines of all of the major houses." She beamed with excitement.

"What?" Connor and Shona exclaimed together.

"It makes sense," Catriona rushed on. "You can't expect to hoard him all for yourself, can you?"

Shona might have been the one trying to manipulate him from nearly the first day she realized the potential for his curse, but she looked disgusted by the idea of sharing him with every noble house.

"We'll see," she said curtly.

They reached the platform and Shona led Connor up the steps.

"Remember your boon," Catriona called.

Connor ascended the stairs in a daze. Could she really be telling the truth? Would the king really order such a thing?

Chapter 89

vander waited on the platform, towering over the assembled high lord representatives, school administrators, and professors. On the opposite side of the platform stood the other champions. Padraigin waved enthusiastically, and even Redmund looked content. He'd probably convinced himself that since they'd worked together during the fighting that they all shared equally the victory.

Ivor looked thoughtful.

All of the others cheered and took turns congratulating him as enthusiastically as the larger crowd had. Unlike the honest cheers of the others, as each of the high lord representatives passed, they all whispered promises of wealth and power if he but chose their family. More than a few sought the same boon Catriona did if they failed to secure first breed rights.

They sickened him.

He seriously considered puking all over them, but his stomach was already empty. He gratefully turned away from them when Evander strode to the podium that was laughably short for him. Expectant silence settled over the crowd as Evander motioned Lord Dail forward. He looked like an infant beside the towering giant, but launched into a long-winded monologue about the honor of the occasion and the glory won by those wounded or fallen on the battlefield.

As he droned on, Shona nudged Connor and gestured to the far side of the stage with a smug little smile on her lips. When he turned in that direction, someone lowered a thin divider he had not even noticed before. Captain Rory stood there beside Verena, whose hands and feet were shackled with heavy chains, her face bloody, and her nose clearly broken.

She met his gaze with tears in her eyes. Her shoulders were slumped in defeat, her expression dejected. The sight of her struck him like a curse-punch from a max-tapped Boulder, and it took all his self-control not to stagger under the shock. It was replaced a heartbeat later with a towering fury. He would shatter those chains and heal her wounds and rip to shreds whoever had dared hurt her.

Shona caught his arm and hissed in his ear, "Connor, control yourself or you'll only make it worse."

He growled between clenched teeth, "Let. Go."

Instead her grip tightened with the strength of granite. "You are bereft of all stones while I am not. You will do my will or she dies, that I promise you."

Every instinct howled for him to lunge against her greater strength or strike out against her, to do anything to fight to Verena's side, but her words shackled him as securely as the chains bound Verena.

Connor glanced at Verena again, and she shook her head in silent plea, as if asking his forgiveness for falling into Shona's hands.

He had been a fool to go anywhere without first demanding access to powder. He still felt weak, despite the rest. He wouldn't be able to fight his way past a toddler, let alone beat a determined Shona, plus Rory and perhaps most of the other Petralists on the stage.

"I thought you agreed to a truce," he whispered through clenched teeth.

"Oh, I did," Shona said with maddening smugness. "I promised not to hurt her until the monster died, and I didn't."

"Let her go." He hated her for forcing him to beg.

At the podium, Lord Dail was winding down his exultant monologue. He gestured toward Connor. "And so with the utmost pride and pleasure, I pronounce Guardian Connor champion of the Tir-raon!"

Amid the thunderous applause, Connor hated the irony that only now did they finally proclaim him Guardian. Now he stood chained to Shona, about to be passed around like a stud horse to the high lord families.

Never before had the title felt so empty. Had he really fought so hard to embrace slavery? He considered exacting revenge upon Shona by choosing a different house, or choosing a different partner for first breed rights. He scanned the crowd, noting the eager faces. Any house would claim him in a heartbeat, and any of the girls would take him just as readily.

Choosing any of them would only guarantee Verena's death. He joined Lord Dail and waved at the crowd while his soul screamed in futile rage.

He made his choice, and glanced up at Evander who was watching him with an unreadable expression. Had Evander been speaking of this when he talked of choices? Why couldn't he have just told Connor the simple truth that he was about to sell his soul into slavery?

Shona joined him, eliciting a disapproving frown from Lord Dail and a ripple of angry muttering from the high lord representatives. Connor pulled her aside, ignoring even more grumbling.

"Let her go and I'll do it, Shona."

She had the decency not to visibly gloat. She only nodded once. "Very well, announce your choice and then I'll release her."

"No. She goes free first."

"Impossible."

"Fine then I'll choose Catriona."

"You wouldn't dare!"

"Why not? I wouldn't have anything to lose, so it wouldn't matter who I choose would it?"

Lord Dail approached. "It's time to make your choice of family allegiance and first breed rights, young man."

"Well?" he asked Shona.

She tilted her chin up. "Fine. I agree."

Although Lord Dail glowered at the interruption, Connor backed farther away from the podium and turned. Shona beckoned Rory forward. He led Verena onto the center of the platform. She was heavily shackled, and the chains prevented her from standing erect, so she shuffled forward like an invalid. She looked miserable, but anger burned in the look she cast at Shona.

"Connor, choose freedom," she urged him in a trembling voice, trying unsuccessfully to raise hands toward him.

"I have. The only freedom that matters."

At Shona's direction, Rory unlocked the shackles. Verena rushed to embrace Connor, but Shona intercepted her and pushed her back. "I agreed to release you but nothing more. Now begone before I change my mind."

"Don't do this, Connor," Verena begged, tears in her eyes.

"I need a piece of quartzite," Connor announced.

Rory produced a fist-sized stone, clearly knowing in advance what Connor would choose. He handed it to Verena, his face set in an expressionless mask, but his sorrow still leaked through. Of everyone in the assembly, Rory perhaps understood the depth of anguish Connor felt in that moment.

Verena took the stone but held Connor with her gaze for another moment and communicated all of her love, all of her heartfelt grief in that long look.

Then she stood tall and faced Shona. Despite her broken nose, her bloody face, and her disheveled hair, in that moment she looked as regal as a queen. In a voice as hard as steel, she declared, "I hate you."

"You lose," Shona said simply. "Next time I see you, I will kill you."

With a final grieving look at Connor, Verena hugged the quartzite to her chest and launched off the platform in a rush of air. He watched her until she disappeared into the afternoon sun. Why she would fly west instead of north made no sense, but at least she was free.

Shona took his arm, and her dominant expression changed to one of regret. She half-raised her other hand toward his face, but then let it fall to her side with a soft sigh. "Oh, Connor. At every step, we're pitted against each other."

"This time, I don't think you can blame anyone but you."

She shook her head. "Somehow Verena has twisted your heart, my Connor, but she's not the only one who loves you. You'll see. We'll get through this and you'll realize we're perfect together."

He just stared. She was cracked mental.

She gave him an encouraging smile. "We'll make history, Connor. We'll change the world and bring peace to every nation."

Connor couldn't think how to explain to her how insane her idea of peace was. As she turned him back to the expectant crowd, she gripped his arm one last time. "You made the right choice."

"It's what a Guardian does."

In a voice far stronger than seemed possible, he spoke to the crowd. "I hereby announce my allegiance to House Dougal and first breed rights with Lady Shona."

As everyone cheered wildly, his heart turned to ice. He didn't even flinch when Shona kissed him on the lips and graciously waved her appreciation to the crowd.

Chapter 90

onnor stepped onto the rooftop veranda of Lord Nevan's palace and approached Shona as the last vestiges of twilight stained the western sky. She stood facing north, toward the deeper shadow of the shattered castle.

Despite vowing to serve her, Connor's hands shook with nervousness. Everyone else was celebrating a great feast in his honor. As much as he did not want to attend the event, he would have preferred that over obeying her summons to meet her atop the palace roof.

Shona turned and smiled, radiating genuine pleasure. Connor made a little bow and wished he understood better what drove Shona. Their relationship had always been so complicated, but how could she have used Verena against him like that? She had manipulated and blackmailed him into an intimate, lifelong relationship. How could she imagine that could ever work?

The cruelest irony, one that he doubted she'd ever understand, was that if she had only been honest with him, had truly loved him with open sincerity, she would have won his heart long before Verena had managed to worm her way into his affection.

Part of him wished she had. At least he could have looked forward to their relationship, even though he would have still abhorred the plan of conquest and destruction she seemed eager to embark upon.

She wore a simple, thin dress of midnight blue silk that accentuated her pale skin and blond hair. Its low collar complimented her graceful neck and fine features. It was too bad her heart did not match her external beauty.

She took his hand and drew him into a gentle embrace. Her smile turned wistful and she sighed. "You know Connor, we're formally promised now. I should be announcing our engagement in Donleavy tomorrow."

"Is that why you arranged for me to return?" Verena's voice startled Connor from the darkness behind them.

He spun, his heart singing to see her standing near the edge of the roof, dressed in her tan flying leathers, her face and hair recently cleaned, and her broken nose repaired. She had never looked more beautiful.

"Wait? You arranged to meet up here?" Connor looked from one to the other, more confused than he'd ever been. The two girls were staring at each other, neither concealing their hatred.

Verena took a careful step forward, her right hand poised over a satchel hung over her shoulder, which no doubt carried her arsenal of stones. "At first, I thought the message a trap and I came here to kill you."

"Why didn't you try?" Shona asked, not looking intimidated.

"You're actually alone." Verena took another step forward. "I could have ripped you apart a dozen times before you could even attempt to tap granite, but I'm curious what you intend."

Connor knew what Shona intended. He prepared to tap granite, which he had made sure to acquire before answering her summons, and spun to restrain her. Instead of leaping at Verena to rip her apart with granite-hardened hands, Shona paced away and leaned against the outer rail above the long drop down to the ground below.

Verena approached and slipped a hand into Connor's. He shared an incredulous look with her, then Shona turned to face them.

"I'd kill her now, despite what you'd think of me, Connor."

The fact that she phrased the threat that way gave him a tiny flicker of hope. "Why aren't you going to?"

She returned to him, and Verena stepped to the side, hand slipping into her satchel. Shona ignored her and cupped Connor's cheeks with both of her hands. "I want you for myself, and I will not share you with that chattel in the other houses. Catriona and the rest cannot have you!" She spoke fiercely, but sorrow filled her eyes with unshed tears.

Was she serious? He had no idea.

Then she kissed him lightly on the lips and leaned against him. He glanced at Verena, who stood with her hand still inside her satchel, her expression dumbfounded.

Shona sighed. "We could have been so perfect together." She held his gaze. "Our lives are complex, dear Connor, but never doubt I was truly looking forward to spending my life with you."

Connor didn't trust himself to speak. His emotions were in turmoil. He hated her for what she'd done to Verena, but he was awestruck that she would consider releasing him to Verena over sharing him with all the other noble houses. That suggested a level of concern he hadn't thought she possessed.

Shona retreated a step. "As much as I hate the thought of Verena having you, I will not share you with Catriona and all those other weaklings."

"What are you talking about?" Verena asked.

"The king wants to breed me with all the noble families," Connor explained with a grimace.

Verena gasped. "You people are disgusting."

Shona hesitated. "Why do you think you're here?" She stroked Connor's cheek. "Go before I realize what a fool I'm being."

Her sudden change of heart shocked him to the core. He had convinced himself she was an uncaring monster, driven only by self-preservation and ambition, but she actually cared? Before the warmth of that genuine love, his hatred wilted.

He took her hands in his. "Shona, I never wanted to hurt you. All I ever wanted was to serve you."

"I know." She gave him a sad smile. "But you were never mine to own, were you?"

She threw her arms around him and kissed him with desperate passion.

Verena stalked forward, but Shona broke off the kiss to snarl, "Give us a minute! You've already stolen him from me. Do not deny me this."

Verena frowned, but sighed and released the stone she'd held clenched in her fist. "I'll wait over there."

Shona turned back to Connor and he took her hands in his. He didn't understand this conniving daughter of a terrifying high lord, but he could appreciate this kindness. "Thank you."

She kissed him, and he tried kissing her back. Shona took her time and kissed him thoroughly, a long, sensual kiss filled with real passion and honest regret. It left him breathless and shaken.

Verena was going to punch him eighteen times for that one.

"The next time I see you, I expect another one of those," she said with a mischievous smile.

"Don't bet on it!" Verena shouted from the far side of the veranda.

"Will you be all right?" he asked. How could he properly thank her? What would happen to her? He hadn't told her what her father had attempted to do to him. Did she know? Was it all part of her plan? If so, then in releasing him, she was taking a terrible risk of angering him.

"I'm fine knowing you asked."

She pushed him gently away and he was not about to refuse the chance at freedom. He rushed across to Verena and swept her into his arms.

She gripped his collar, her face scant inches from his, her expression fierce. "If you ever kiss that woman again, I'll rip your lips off."

He tensed for a blow, but instead she pulled his face forward and kissed him soundly. Her kiss was far simpler, but he'd never felt the depth of emotion from Shona that poured from Verena. His pulse pounded, and his own passion responded to hers, like living fires intertwining with them.

That kiss left him grinning like an idiot, savoring the fading minty taste of her lips.

"Get out of here before I kill her," Shona shouted.

Verena led him to the edge and untied a rope looped around one of the veranda rail posts. She used it to draw the Swift up out of the shadows. Its thrusters were humming softly, barely generating enough air to keep it aloft.

Verena settled into the seat and Connor stepped into the stirrups on the back. As she pivoted away and increased the power to lift them into the sky, Connor glanced back. Shona stood in the center of the Veranda, one hand raised in farewell, tears glittering in the light of a single lantern.

Only when he could no longer see her without quartzite assistance did he allow himself to believe it was not all just another trap. He really was free!

Connor laughed as the weights and cares of the day fell away. He placed a hand on Verena's shoulder to convince himself she was really there and not about to disappear as part of a crazy dream.

As they soared off into the deepening night, Connor could not help but marvel at Shona's unexpected change of mind.

He really hadn't known her at all.

Chapter 91

Shona stood on the rooftop veranda looking up into the air long after Connor disappeared into the darkness, taking with him all of her hopes and dreams. His laugh echoed softly from the sky, mocking her grief. His leaving filled her with bittersweet sorrow and buckets full of lingering doubts.

Could she have played her hand any differently, somehow arranged events better?

A soft footstep turned her around.

Her father stepped out of the shadows, dressed in sturdy outdoor clothing so unlike his normal fine suits. He walked with the help of a cane, and winced with each step.

"What happened?" Shona cried, rushing to him.

"I'm fine, my dear," he said, but his voice sounded distant and strained.

Shona wiped uselessly at her tear-streaked face, but couldn't contain her sorrow. Her father wrapped her in his arms and held her as she sobbed into his chest. Only after the storm of emotion eased did he tip her chin up to look her in the eye.

He gave her an approving smile. "Well done, my dear. That was brilliant."

Shona sniffled away the last of her tears and wiped her face dry with the sleeve of her silk dress. She squared her shoulders and returned his smile.

"Thank you, father. I only ever want to please you."

Petralist Stones

Three for the masses
Two for the many
Four for the privileged few

Igneous

Basalt
Speed, agility
Tapped: Powder through
the skin
Obrion: Strider
Granadure: Wingrunner

Granite
Strength, summoning
Tapped: Powder through
the skin
Obrion: Boulder or
Fast Roller
Granadure: Wingrunner

Obsidian
Magnifies innate abilities
Tapped: Powder through the skin
Obrion: Blade
Granadure: Allcarver

Sedimentary

Limestone
Light
Tapped: Held or worn
Obrion: Solas
Granadure: Solas

Sandstone
Healing
Tapped: Held or worn
Obrion: Healer
Granadure: Healer

Metamorphic

Marble
Fire
Tapped: Under the Tongue
Obrion: Firetongue
Granadure: Flameweaver

Quartzite
Air, Senses
Tapped: Placed in Mouth
Obrion: Pathfinder
Granadure: Longseer

Slate
Earth
Tapped: Soles of feet
Obrion: Sentry
Granadure: Sapper

Soapstone
Water
Tapped: Powder swallowed
with water
Obrion: Spitter
Granadure: Water Moccasin

New Stones!

Diorite
Igneous Stone
Explosive Power
Tapped: Powder through
the skin
Obrion: Unknown
Granadure: Unknown

Porphyry
Igneous Stone
Rage Monster
Tapped: Powder through
the skin
Obrion: Unclaimed
Granadure: Rampager

Anthracite (Blind Coal)
Sedimentary Stone
Aggressive Slipperiness
Tapped: Held or worn
Obrion: Unknown
Granadure: Unknown

Serpentinite
Metamorphic Stone
Sound
Tapped: Unknown
Obrion: Unknown
Granadure: Unknown

Author's Note

If you enjoyed this book, I'm hoping you'll do me a huge favor and consider posting an honest review on your favorite sites. Amazon reviews help the most, and Goodreads reviews are very valuable, but don't feel limited. Blog about the book, tell all your friends, buy copies for everyone who lives in your city - whatever you feel is enough to share how much fun you had reading this book.

I had a ton of fun writing it.

Reviews help more than you know. They directly help the book become more visible, which is the best way you can support me, one of your favorite authors besides going out and buying all of my other books, of course.

Thank you!

Support from you, my readers, is the only way I can succeed as a writer. You're awesome for finishing the novel and actually taking time to read the boring Author's Note.

Thank you!

Really, I mean it. I hope you return to my imaginary worlds often.

No Stone Unturned was a major project, and it's the best chapter of the Petralist series so far. I'd feel sad that it's over, except now I can get to work on book four of the series - and that one's going to be even more amazing! I am really really thrilled to get that next draft completed and get it into your hands. If you thought the adventures Connor and his friends have had so far have been awesome, strap in for a wild ride as this story prepares to really take off!

Also, please check out my website for updates. I'll be adding some deleted scenes as well as a glossary of terms very soon.

About the Author

Frank Morin loves good stories in every form. When not writing or trying to keep up with his active family, he's often found hiking, camping, Scuba diving, or enjoying other outdoor activities.

Frank writes all types of fantasy, from his exciting *Facetakers* alternate history fantasy series, to these popular *Petralist* novels, and more. Check his website for updates and to sign up for his newsletter to receive the latest on all his releases, scheduled events, and insider information: www.frankmorin.org.

Or you can follow him on Twitter:
@MorinWrites
Or like his Author Facebook page:
www.facebook.com/authorfrankmorin

Frank lives in Oregon with his family, who are both his most rabid fans and his most brutal critics. In their home, storytelling is a cherished family tradition that keeps magic alive.

Frank is also part of the Fictorians, a group blog by writers for writers and fans of great writing. Check out their web site at www.fictorians.com.